The Sceptical Chymist

Robert Boyle

Contents

THE SCEPTICAL CHYMIST

BY

Robert Boyle

A PRAEFACE
INTRODUCTORY

To the following Treatise.

To give the Reader an account, Why the following Treatise is suffer'd to pass abroad so maim'd and imperfect, I must inform him that 'tis now long since, that to gratify an ingenious Gentleman, I set down some of the Reasons that kept me from fully acquiescing either in the Peripatetical, or in the Chymical Doctrine, of the Material Principles of mixt Bodies. This Discourse some years after falling into the hands of some Learned men, had the good luck to be so favourably receiv'd, and advantageously spoken of by them, that having had more then ordinary Invitations given me to make it publick, I thought fit to review it, that I might retrench some things that seem'd not so fit to be shewn to every Reader, And substitute some of those other things that occurr'd to me of the trials and observations I had since made. What became of my papers, I elsewhere mention in a Preface where I complain of it: But since I writ That, I found many sheets that belong'd to the subjects I am now about to discourse of. Wherefore seeing that I had then in my hands as much of the first Dialogue as was requisite to state the Case, and serve for an Introduction as well to the conference betwixt Carneades *and* Eleutherius, *as to some other Dialogues, which for certain reasons are not now herewith publish'd, I resolv'd to supply, as well as I could, the Contents of a Paper belonging to the second of the following Discourses, which I could not possibly retrive, though it were the chief of them all. And having once more try'd the Opinion of Friends, but not of the same, about this imperfect work, I found it such, that I was content in complyance with their Desires;*

that not only it should be publish'd, but that it should be publish'd as soon as conveniently might be. I had indeed all along the Dialogues spoken of my self, as of a third Person; For, they containing Discourses which were among the first Treatises that I ventur'd long ago to write of matters Philosophical, I had reason to desire, with the Painter, to latere pone tabulam, *and hear what men would say of them, before I own'd my self to be their Author. But besides that now I find, 'tis not unknown to many who it is that writ them, I am made to believe that 'tis not inexpedient, they should be known to come from a Person not altogether a stranger to Chymical Affairs. And I made the lesse scruple to let them come abroad uncompleated, partly, because my affairs and Prae-ingagements to publish divers other Treatises allow'd me small hopes of being able in a great while to compleat these Dialogues. And partly, because I am not unapt to think, that they may come abroad seasonably enough, though not for the Authors reputation, yet for other purposes. For I observe, that of late Chymistry begins, as indeed it deserves, to be cultivated by Learned Men who before despis'd it; and to be pretended to by many who never cultivated it, that they may be thought not to ignore it: Whence it is come to passe, that divers Chymical Notions about Matters Philosophical are taken for granted and employ'd, and so adopted by very eminent Writers both Naturalists and Physitians. Now this I fear may prove somewhat prejudicial to the Advancement of solid Philosophy: For though I am a great Lover of Chymical Experiments, and though I have no mean esteem of divers Chymical Remedies, yet I distinguish these from their Notions about the causes of things, and their manner of Generation. And for ought I can hitherto discern, there are a thousand* Phaenomena *in Nature, besides a Multitude of Accidents relating to the humane Body, which will scarcely be clearly & satisfactorily made out by them that confine themselves to deduce things from Salt, Sulphur and Mercury, and the other Notions peculiar to the Chymists, without taking much more Notice than they are wont to do, of the Motions and Figures, of the small Parts of Matter, and the other more Catholick and Fruitful affections of Bodies. Wherefore it will not perhaps be now unseasonable to let our* Carneades *warne Men, not to subscribe to the grand Doctrine of the Chymists touching their three Hypostatical Principles, till they have a little examin'd it, and consider'd, how they can clear it from his Objections, divers of which 'tis like they may never have thought on; since a Chymist scarce would, and none but a Chymist could propose them. I hope also it will not be unacceptable to several Ingenious Persons, who are unwilling to determine of any important Contro-versie, without a previous consideration of what may be said on both sides, and yet have greater desires to understand Chymical Matters, than Opportunities of learning them, to find here together, besides several Experiments of my own purposely made to Illustrate the Doctrine of the Elements, divers others scarce to be met with, otherwise then Scatter'd among many Chymical Books. And to Find these Associated Experiments so Deliver'd as that an Ordinary Reader, if he be but Acquainted with the usuall Chymical Termes, may easily enough Under-stand Them; and even a wary One may safely rely on Them. These Things I add, because a Person any Thing vers'd in the Writings of Chymists cannot but Dis-cern by their obscure, Ambiguous, and almost AEnigmatical Way of expressing what they pretend to Teach, that they have no Mind, to be understood at all, but by* the Sons of Art (as they call them) nor to be Understood even by these without Difficulty And Hazardous Tryalls. Insomuch that some of Them Scarce ever speak so candidly, as when they make use of that known Chymical Sentence; ***Ubi palam locuti fumus, ibi nihil diximus.*** And as the obscurity of what some Writers deliver makes it very difficult to be understood; so the Unfaithfulness of too many others makes it unfit to be reli'd on. For though unwillingly, Yet I must for the truths sake, and the Readers, warne him not to be forward to believe Chymical Experi-ments when they are set down only by way of Prescriptions, and not of Relations; that is, unless he that delivers them mentions his doing it upon his own particular knowledge, or upon the Relation of some credible person, avowing it upon his own experience. For I am troubled, I must complain, that even Eminent Writers, both Physitians and Philosophers, whom I can easily name, if it be requir'd, have of late suffer'd themselves to be so far impos'd upon, as to Publish and Build upon Chymi-cal Experiments, which questionless they never try'd; for if they had, they would, as well as I, have found them not to be true. And indeed it were to be wish'd, that now that those begin to quote Chymical Experiments that are not themselves Acquainted with Chymical Operations, men would Leave off that Indefinite Way of Vouching the Chymists say this, or the Chymists affirme that, and would rather for each Experiment they alledge name the Author or Authors, upon whose credit they relate it; For, by this means they would secure themselves from the suspition of falshood (to which the other Practice Exposes them) and they would Leave the Reader to Judge of what is fit for him to Believe of what is Deliver'd, whilst they employ not their own great names to Countenance doubtfull Relations; and they will also do Justice to the Inventors or Publishers of true Experiments, as well as upon the Obtruders of false ones. Whereas by that general Way of quoting the Chymists, the candid Writer is Defrauded of the particular Praise, and the Impostor escapes the Personal Disgrace that is due to him.

The remaining Part of this Praeface must be imploy'd in saying something for Carneades, *and something for my Self.*

And first, Carneades *hopes that he will be thought to have disputed civilly and Modestly enough for one that was to play the Antagonist and the Sceptick. And if he any where seem to sleight his Adversaries Tenents and Arguments, he is willing to have it look'd upon as what he was induc'd to, not so much by his Opinion of them, as the Examples of* Themistius *and* Philoponus, *and the custom of such kind of Disputes.*

Next, In case that some of his Arguments shall not be thought of the most Cogent sort that may be, he hopes it will be consider'd that it ought not to be Expected, that they should be So. For, his Part being chiefly but to propose Doubts and Scruples, he does enough, if he shews that his Adversaries Arguments are not strongly Concluding, though his own be not so neither. And if there should appear any disagreement betwixt the things he delivers in divers passages, he hopes it will be consider'd, that it is not necessary that all the things a Sceptick Proposes, should be consonant; since it being his work to Suggest doubts against the Opinion he questions, it is allowable for him to propose two or more severall Hypotheses *about the same thing: And to say that it may be accounted for this way, or that way, or the other Way, though these wayes be perhaps inconsistent among Themselves. Because it is enough for him, if either of the proposed* Hypotheses *be but as probable as that he calls a question. And if he proposes many that are Each of them probable, he does the more satisfie his doubts, by making it appear the more difficult to be sure, that that which they alwayes differ from is the true. And our* Carneades *by holding the Negative, he has this Advantage, that if among all the Instances he brings to invalidate all the Vulgar Doctrine of those he Disputes with, any one be Irrefragable, that alone is sufficient to overthrow a Doctrine which Universally asserts what he opposes. For, it cannot be true, that all Bodies whatsoever that are reckon'd among the Perfectly mixt Ones, are Compounded of such a Determinate Number of such or such Ingredients, in case any one such Body can be produc'd, that is not so compounded; and he hopes too, that Accurateness will be the less expected from him, because his undertaking obliges him to maintain such Opinions in Chymistry, and that chiefly by Chymical Arguments, as are Contrary to the very Principles of the Chymists; From whose writings it is not Therefore like he should receive any intentionall Assistance, except from some Passages of the Bold and Ingenious* Helmont, with whom he yet disagrees in many things (which reduce him to explicate Divers Chymical **Phaenomena,** according to other Notions;) And of whose Ratiocinations, not only some seem very Extravagant, but even the Rest are not wont to be as considerable as his Experiments. And though it be True indeed, that some *Aristotelians* have occasionally written against the Chymical Doctrine he Oppugnes, yet since they have done it according to their Principles, And since our **Carneades** must as well oppose their **Hypothesis** as that of the Spagyrist, he was fain to fight his Adversaries with their own Weapons, Those of the Peripatetick being Improper, if not hurtfull for a Person of his Tenents; besides that those *Aristotelians,* (at Least, those he met with,) that have written against the Chymists, seem to have had so little Experimental Knowledge in Chymical Matters, that by their frequent Mistakes and unskilfull Way of Oppugning, they have too often expos'd Themselves to the Derision of their Adversaries, for writing so Confidently against what they appear so little to understand.

And Lastly, Carneades *hopes, he shall doe the Ingenious this Piece of service, that by having Thus drawn the Chymists Doctrine out of their Dark and*

Smoakie Laboratories, and both brought it into the open light, and shewn the weakness of their Proofs, that have hitherto been wont to be brought for it, either Judicious Men shall henceforth be allowed calmly and after due information to disbelieve it, or those abler Chymists, that are zealous for the reputation of it, will be oblig'd to speak plainer then hitherto has been done, and maintain it by better Experiments and Arguments then Those Carneades *hath examin'd: so That he hopes, the Curious will one Way or other Derive either satisfaction or instruction from his endeavours. And as he is ready to make good the profession he makes in the close of his Discourse, he being ready to be better inform'd, so he expects either to be indeed inform'd, or to be let alone. For Though if any Truly knowing Chymists shall Think fit in a civil and rational way to shew him any truth touching the matter in Dispute That he yet discernes not,* Carneades *will not refuse either to admit, or to own a Conviction: yet if any impertinent Person shall, either to get Himself a Name, or for what other end soever, wilfully or carelesly mistake the State of the Controversie, or the sence of his Arguments, or shall rail instead of arguing, as hath been done of Late in Print by divers Chymists;*[1] *or lastly, shall write against them in a canting way; I mean, shall express himself in ambiguous or obscure termes, or argue from experiments not intelligibly enough Deliver'd,* Carneades *professes, That he values his time so much, as not to think the answering such Trifles worth the loss of it.*

[1: G. and F. and H. and others, in their books against one another.]

And now having said thus much for Carneades, *I hope the Reader will give me leave to say something too for my self.*

And first, if some morose Readers shall find fault with my having made the Interlocutors upon occasion complement with one another, and that I have almost all along written these Dialogues in a stile more Fashionable then That of meer scholars is wont to be, I hope I shall be excus'd by them that shall consider, that to keep a due decorum *in the Discourses, it was fit that in a book written by a Gentleman, and wherein only Gentlemen are introduc'd as speakers, the Language should be more smooth, and the Expressions more civil than is usual in the more Scholastick way of writing. And indeed, I am not sorry to have this Oppor-*

tunity of giving an example how to manage even Disputes with Civility; whence perhaps some Readers will be assisted to discern a Difference betwixt Bluntness of speech and Strength of reason, and find that a man may be a Champion for Truth, without being an Enemy to Civility; and may confute an Opinion without railing at Them that hold it; To whom he that desires to convince and not to provoke them, must make some amends by his Civility to their Persons, for his severity to their mistakes; and must say as little else as he can, to displease them, when he says that they are in an error.

But perhaps other Readers will be less apt to find fault with the Civility of my Disputants, than the Chymists will be, upon the reading of some Passages of the following Dialogue, to accuse Carneades *of Asperity. But if I have made my Sceptick sometimes speak sleightingly of the Opinions he opposes, I hope it will not be found that I have done any more, than became the Part he was to act of an Opponent: Especially, if what I have made him say be compar'd with what the Prince of the Romane Orators himself makes both great Persons and Friends say of one anothers Opinions, in his excellent Dialogues,* De Natura Deorum: And I shall scarce be suspected of Partiality, in the case, by them that take Notice that there is full as much (if not far more) liberty of sleighting their Adversaries Tenents to be met with in the Discourses of those with whom **Carneades** disputes. Nor needed I make the Interlocutors speak otherwise then freely in a Dialogue, wherein it was sufficiently intimated, that I meant not to declare my own Opinion of the Arguments propos'd, much lesse of the whole Controversy it self otherwise than as it may by an attentive Reader be guess'd at by some Passages of **Carneades:** (I say, some Passages, because I make not all that he says, especially in the heat of Disputation, mine,) partly in this Discourse, and partly in some other Dialogues betwixt the same speakers (though they treat not immediately of the Elements) which have long layn by me, and expect the Entertainment that these present Discourses will meet with. And indeed they will much mistake me, that shall conclude from what I now publish, that I am at Defyance with Chymistry, or would make my Readers so. I hope the **Specimina** I have lately publish'd of an attempt to shew the usefulness of Chymical Experiments to Contemplative Philosophers, will give those that shall read them other thoughts of me: & I had a design (but wanted opportunity) to publish with these Papers an Essay I have lying by me, the greater part of which is Apologetical for one sort of Chymists. And at least, as for those that know me, I hope the pain I have taken in the fire will both convince them, that I am far from being an Enemy to the Chymists Art, (though I am no friend to many that disgrace it by professing it,) and perswade them to believe me when I declare that I distinguish betwixt those Chymists that are either Cheats, or but Laborants, and the true *Adepti;* By whom, could I enjoy their Conversation, I would both willingly and thankfully be instructed; especially concerning the Nature and Generation of Metals: And possibly, those that know how little I have remitted of my former addictedness to make Chymical Experiments, will easily believe, that one of the chief Designes of this Sceptical Discourse was, not so much to discredit Chymistry, as to give an occasion and a kind of necessity to the more knowing Artists to lay aside a little of their over-great Reservedness, & either explicate or prove the Chymical Theory better than ordinary Chymists have done, or by enriching us with some of their nobler secrets to evince that Their art is able to make amends even for the deficiencies of their Theory: And thus much I shall here make bold to add, that we shall much undervalue Chymistry, if we imagine, that it cannot teach us things farr more useful, not only to Physick but to Philosophy, than those that are hitherto known to vulgar Chymists. And yet as for inferiour Spagyrists themselves, they have by their labours deserv'd so well of the Common-wealth of Learning, that methinks 'tis Pity they should ever misse the Truth which they have so industriously sought. And though I be no Admirer of the Theorical Part of their Art, yet my conjectures will much deceive me, if the Practical Part be not much more cultivated than hitherto it has been, and do not both employ Philosophy and Philosophers, and help to make men such. Nor would I that have been diverted by other Studies as well as affairs, be thought to pretend being a profound Spagyrist, by finding so many faults in the Doctrine wherein the Generality of Chymists scruples not to Acquiesce: For besides that 'tis most commonly far easier to frame Objections against any propos'd *Hypothesis,* than to propose an *Hypothesis* not lyable to Objections (besides this I say) 'tis no such great matter, if whereas Beginners in Chymistry are commonly at once imbu'd with the Theory and Operations of their profession, I who had the good Fortune to Learn the Operations from illiterate Persons, upon whose credit I was not Tempted to take up any opinion about them, should consider things with lesse prejudice, and consequently with other Eyes than the Generality of Learners; And should be more dispos'd to accommodate the **Phaenomena** that occur'd to me to other Notions than to those of the Spagyrists. And having at first entertain'd a suspition That the Vulgar Principles were lesse General and comprehensive, or lesse considerately Deduc'd from Chymical Operations, than was believ'd; it was not uneasie for me both to Take notice of divers **Phaenomena,** overlook'd by prepossest Persons, that seem'd not to suite so well with the **Hermetical** Doctrine; and, to devise some Experiments likely to furnish me with Objections against it, not known to many, that having practis'd Chymistry longer perchance then I have yet liv'd, may have far more Experience, Than I, of particular processes.

To conclude, whether the Notions I have propos'd, and the Experiments I have communicated, be considerable, or not, I willingly leave others to Judge; and This only I shall say for my Self, That I have endeavour'd to deliver matters of Fact, so faithfully, that I may as well assist the lesse skilful Readers to examine the Chymical Hypothesis, *as provoke the Spagyrical Philosophers to illustrate it: which if they do, and that either the Chymical opinion, or the Peripatetick, or any other Theory of the Elements differing from that I am most inclin'd to, shall be intelligibly explicated, and duly prov'd to me; what I have hitherto discours'd will not hinder it from making a Proselyte of a Person that Loves Fluctuation of Judgment little enough to be willing to be eas'd of it by any thing but Error.*

PHYSIOLOGICAL
CONSIDERATIONS

Touching

The experiments wont to be employed to evince either the IV Peripatetick Elements, or the III Chymical Principles of Mixt Bodies.

Part of the First Dialogue.

I Perceive that divers of my Friends have thought it very strange to hear me speak so irresolvedly, as I have been wont to do, concerning those things which some take to be the Elements, and others to be the Principles of all mixt Bodies. But I blush not to acknowledge that I much lesse scruple to confess that I Doubt, when I do so, then to profess that I Know what I do not: And I should have much stronger Expectations then I dare yet entertain, to see Philosophy solidly establish't, if men would more carefully distinguish those things that they know, from those that they ignore or do but think, and then explicate clearly the things they conceive they understand, acknowledge ingenuously what it is they ignore, and profess so candidly their Doubts, that the industry of intelligent persons might be set on work to make further enquiries, and the easiness of less discerning Men might not be impos'd on. But because a more particular accompt will probably be expected of my unsatisfyedness not only with the Peripatetick, but with the Chymical Doctrine of the Primitive Ingredients of Bodies: It may possibly serve to satisfy others of the excusableness of my disatisfaction to peruse the ensuing Relation of what passed a while since at a meeting of persons of several opinions, in a place that need not here be named; where the subject whereof we have been speaking, was amply and variously discours'd of.

It was on one of the fairest dayes of this Summer that the inquisitive *Eleutheri-*

us came to invite me to make a visit with him to his friend *Carneades*. I readily consented to this motion, telling him that if he would but permit me to go first and make an excuse at a place not far off, where I had at that hour appointed to meet, but not about a business either of moment, or that could not well admit of a delay, I would presently wait on him, because of my knowing *Carneades* to be so conversant with nature and with Furnaces, and so unconfin'd to vulgar Opinions, that he would probably by some ingenious Paradox or other, give our mindes at least a pleasing Exercise, and perhaps enrich them with some solid instruction. *Eleutherius* then first going with me to the place where my Apology was to be made, I accompanied him to the lodging of *Carneades*, where when we were come, we were told by the Servants, that he was retired with a couple of Friends (whose names they also told us) to one of the Arbours in his Garden, to enjoy under its coole shades a delightful protection from the yet troublesome heat of the Sun.

Eleutherius being perfectly acquainted with that Garden immediately led me to the Arbour, and relying on the intimate familiarity that had been long cherish'd betwixt him and *Carneades*; in spight of my Reluctancy to what might look like an intrusion upon his privacy, drawing me by the hand, he abruptly entered the Arbour, where we found *Carneades*, *Philoponus*, and *Themistius*, sitting close about a little round Table, on which besides paper, pen, and inke, there lay two or three open Books; *Carneades* appeared not at all troubled at this surprise, but rising from the Table, received his Friend with open looks and armes, and welcoming me also with his wonted freedom and civility, invited us to rest our selves by him, which, as soon as we had exchanged with his two Friends (who were ours also) the civilities accustomed on such occasions, we did. And he presently after we had seated our selves, shutting the Books that lay open, and turning to us with a smiling countenance seemed ready to begin some such unconcerning discourse as is wont to pass or rather waste the time in promiscuous companies.

But *Eleutherius* guessing at what he meant to do, prevented him by telling him, I perceive *Carneades* by the books that you have been now shutting, and much more by the posture wherein I found Persons qualifi'd [Errata: so qualify'd] to discourse of serious matters; and so accustom'd to do it, that you three were before our coming, engag'd in some Philosophical conference, which I hope you will either prosecute, and allow us to be partakers of, in recompence of the freedome we have us'd in presuming to surprise you, or else give us leave to repair the injury we should otherwise do you, by leaving you to the freedom we have interrupted, and punishing our selves for our boldness by depriving our selves of the happiness of your company. With these last words he and I rose up, as if we meant to be gone, But **Carneades** suddenly laying hold on his arme, and stopping him by it, smile-ingly told him, We are not so forward to lose good company as you seem to imagine; especially since you are pleas'd to desire to be present at what we shall say, about such a Subject as that You found us considering. For that, being the number of the Elements, Principles, or Materiall Ingredients of Bodies, is an enquiry whose truth is of that Importance, and of that Difficulty, that it may as well deserve as require to be searched into by such skilfull Indagators of Nature as your selves. And therefore we sent to invite the bold and acute **Leucippus** to lend us some light by his Atomi-cal Paradox, upon which we expected such pregnant hints, that 'twas not without a great deal of trouble that we had lately word brought us that he was not to be found; and we had likewise begg'd the Assistance of your presence and thoughts, had not the messenger we employ'd to **Leucippus** inform'd us, that as he was go-ing, he saw you both pass by towards another part of the Town; And this frustrated expectation of **Leucippus** his company, who told me but last night that he would be ready to give me a meeting where I pleas'd to day, having very long suspended our conference about the freshly mention'd Subject, it was so newly begun when you came in, that we shall scarce need to repeat any thing to acquaint you with what has pass'd betwixt us before your arrival, so that I cannot but look upon it as a fortunate Accident that you should come so seasonably, to be not hearers alone, but we hope Interlocutors at our conference. For we shall not only allow of your presence at it, but desire your Assistance in it; which I adde both for other reasons, and because though these learned Gentlemen (sayes he, turning to his two friends) need not fear to discourse before any Auditory, provided it be intelligent enough to understand them, yet for my part (continues he with a new smile,) I shall not dare to vent my unpremeditated thoughts before two such Criticks, unless by promis-ing to take your turnes of speaking, You will allow me mine of quarrelling, with what has been said. He and his friends added divers things to convince us that they were both desirous that we should hear them, and resolved against our doing so, unless we allowed them sometimes to hear us. ***Elutherius*** [Transcriber's Note: Eleutherius] after having a while fruitlesly endeavoured to obtain leave to be silent promis'd he would not be so alwayes, provided that he were permitted according to the freedom of his Genious and Principles to side with one of them in the managing of one Argument, and, if he saw cause, with his Antagonist, in the Prosecution of another, without being confin'd to stick to any one party or Opinion, which was after some debate accorded him. But I conscious to my own Disability's told them resolutely that *I* was as much more willing as more fit to be a hearer then a speaker, among such knowing Persons, and on so abstruse a Subject. And that therefore I beseeched them without necessitating me to proclaim my weaknesses, to allow me to lessen them by being a silent Auditor of their Discourses: to suffer me to be at which I could present them no motive, save that their instructions would make them in me a more intelligent Admirer. I added, that I desir'd not to be idle whilst they were imploy'd, but would if they pleas'd, by writing down in short hand what should be delivered, preserve Discourses that I knew would merit to be lasting. At first ***Carneades*** and his two friends utterly rejected this motion; and all that my Resoluteness to make use of my ears, not tongue, at their debates, could do, was to make them acquiesce in the Proposition of ***Eleutherius***, who thinking himself concern'd, because he brought me thither, to afford me some faint assistance, was content that I should register their Arguments, that I might be the better able after the conclusion of their conference to give them my sence upon the Subject of it, (The number of Elements or Principles:) which he promis'd I should do at the end of the present Debates, if time would permit, or else at our next meeting. And this being by him undertaken in my name, though without my consent, the company would by no means receive my Protestation against it, but casting, all at once, their eyes on ***Carneades***, they did by that and their unanimous silence, invite him to begin; which (after a short pause, during which he turn'd himself to ***Eleutherius*** and me) he did in this manner.

Notwithstanding the subtile reasonings I have met with in the books of the Peripateticks, and the pretty experiments that have been shew'd me in the Laboratories of Chymists, I am of so diffident, or dull a Nature, as to think that if neither of them can bring more cogent arguments to evince the truth of their assertion then are wont to be brought; a Man may rationally enough retain some doubts concerning the very number of those materiall Ingredients of mixt bodies, which some would have us call Elements, and others principles. Indeed when I considered that the Tenents concerning the Elements are as considerable amongst the Doctrines of natural Philosophy as the Elements themselves are among the bodies of the Universe, I expected to find those Opinions solidly establish'd, upon which so many others are superstructed. But when I took the pains impartially to examine the bodies themselves that are said to result from the blended Elements, and to torture them into a confession of their constituent Principles, I was quickly induc'd to think that the number of the Elements has been contended about by Philosophers with more earnestness then success. This unsatisfiedness of mine has been much wonder'd at, by these two Gentlemen (at which words he pointed at *Themistius* and *Philoponus*) who though they differ almost as much betwixt themselves about the question we are to consider, as I do from either of them, yet they both agree very well in this, that there is a determinate number of such ingredients as I was just now speaking of, and that what that number is, I say not, may be, (for what may not such as they perswade?) but is wont to be clearly enough demonstrated both by Reason and Experience. This has occasion'd our present Conference. For our Discourse this afternoon, having fallen from one subject to another, and at length setl'd on this, they proffer'd to demonstrate to me, each of them the truth of his opinion, out of both the Topicks that I have freshly nam'd. But on the former (that of Reason strictly so taken) we declin'd insisting at the present, lest we should not have time enough before supper to go thorough the Reasons and Experiments too. The latter of which we unanimously thought the most requisite to be seriously examin'd. I must desire you then to take notice Gentlemen (continued *Carneades*) that my present business doth not oblige me so to declare my own opinion on the Subject in question, as to assert or deny the truth either of the Peripatetick, or the Chymical Doctrine concerning the number of the Elements, but only to shew you that neither of these Doctrines hath been satisfactorily proved by the arguments commonly alledged on its behalfe. So that if I really discern (as perhaps I think I do) that there may be a more rational account then ordinary, given of one of these opinions, I am left free to declare my self of it, notwithstanding my present engagement, it being obvious to all your observation, that a solid truth may be generally maintained by no other, then incompetent Arguments. And to this Declaration I hope it will be needless to add, that my task obliges me not to answer the Arguments that may be drawn either for *Themistius* or *Philoponus's* Opinion from the Topick of reason, as opposed to experiments; since 'tis these only that I am to examine and not all these neither, but such of them alone as either of them shall think fit to insist on, and as have hitherto been wont to be brought either to prove that 'tis the four Peripatetick Elements, or that 'tis the three Chymical Principles that all compounded bodies consist of. These things (adds *Carneades*) I thought my self obliged to premise, partly lest you should do these Gentlemen (pointing at *Themistius* and *Philoponus*, and smiling on them) the injury of measuring their parts by the arguments they are ready to propose, the lawes of our Conference confining them to make use of those that the vulgar of Philosophers (for even of them there is a vulgar) has drawn up to their hands; and partly, that you should not condemn me of presumption for disputing against persons over whom I can hope for no advantage, that *I* must not derive from the nature, or rules of our controversy, wherein I have but a negative to defend, and wherein too I am like on several occasions to have the Assistance of one of my disagreeing adversaries against the other.

Philoponus and *Themistius* soon returned this complement with civilities of the like nature, in which *Eleutherius* perceiving them engaged, to prevent the further loss of that time of which they were not like to have very much to spare, he minded them that their present businesse was not to exchange complements, but Arguments: and then addressing his speech to *Carneades*, I esteem it no small happinesse (saies he) that I am come here so luckily this Evening. For I have been long disquieted with Doubts concerning this very subject which you are now ready to debate. And since a Question of this importance is to be now discussed by persons that maintain such variety of opinions concerning it, and are both so able to enquire after truth, and so ready to embrace it by whomsoever and on what occasion soever it is presented them; I cannot but promise my self that I shall before we part either lose my Doubts or the hopes of ever finding them resolved; *Eleutherius* paused not here; but to prevent their answer, added almost in the same breath; and I am not a little pleased to find that you are resolved on this occasion to insist rather on Experiments then Syllogismes. For I, and no doubt You, have long observed, that those Dialectical subtleties, that the Schoolmen too often employ about Physiological Mysteries, are wont much more to declare the wit of him that uses them, then increase the knowledge or remove the doubts of sober lovers of truth. And such captious subtleties do indeed often puzzle and sometimes silence men, but rarely satisfy them. Being like the tricks of Jugglers, whereby men doubt not but they are cheated, though oftentimes they cannot declare by what slights they are imposed on. And therefore I think you have done very wisely to make it your businesse to consider the **Phaenomena** relating to the present Question, which have been afforded by experiments, especially since it might seem injurious to our senses, by whose mediation we acquire so much of the knowledge we have of things corporal, to have recourse to far-fetched and abstracted Ratiocination [Errata: Ratiocinations], to know what are the sensible ingredients of those sensible things that we daily see and handle, and are supposed to have the liberty to untwist (if I may so speak) into the primitive bodies they consist of. He annexed that he wished therefore they would no longer delay his expected satisfaction, if they had not, as he feared they had, forgotten something preparatory to their debate; and that was to lay down what should be all along understood by the word Principle or Element. **Carneades** thank'd him for his admonition, but told him that they had not been unmindful of so requisite a thing. But that being Gentlemen and very far from the litigious humour of loving to wrangle about words or terms or notions as empty; they had before his coming in, readily agreed promiscuously to use when they pleased, Elements and Principles as terms equivalent: and to understand both by the one and the other, those primitive and simple Bodies of which the mixt ones are said to be composed, and into which they are ultimately resolved. And upon the same account (he added) we agreed to discourse of the opinions to be debated, as we have found them maintained by the Generality of the assertors of the four Elements of the one party, and of those that receive the three Principles on the other, without tying our selves to enquire scrupulously what notion either **Aristotle** or **Paracelsus**, or this or that Interpreter, or follower of either of those great persons, framed of Elements or Principles; our design being to examine, not what these or those writers thought or taught, but what we find to be the obvious and most general opinion of those, who are willing to be accounted Favourers of the Peripatetick or Chymical Doctrine, concerning this subject.

I see not (saies **Eleutherius**) why you might not immediately begin to argue, if you were but agreed which of your two friendly Adversaries shall be first heard.

And it being quickly resolv'd on that *Themistius* should first propose the Proofs for his Opinion, because it was the antienter, and the more general, he made not the company expect long before he thus addressed himself to *Eleutherius*, as to the Person least interested in the dispute.

If you have taken sufficient notice of the late Confession which was made by *Carneades*, and which (though his Civility dressed it up in complementall Expressions) was exacted of him by his Justice, I suppose You will be easily made sensible, that I engage in this Controversie with great and peculiar Disadvantages, besides those which his Parts and my Personal Disabilities would bring to any other cause to be maintained by me against him. For he justly apprehending the force of truth, though speaking by no better a tongue then mine, has made it the chief condition of our Duell, that I should lay aside the best Weapons I have, and those I can best handle; Whereas if I were allowed the freedom, in pleading for the four Elements, to employ the Arguments suggested to me by Reason to demonstrate them, I should almost as little doubt of making You a Proselyte to those unsever'd Teachers, Truth and *Aristotle*, as I do of your Candour and your Judgment. And I hope you will however consider, that that great Favorite and Interpreter of Nature, *Aristotle*, who was (as his *Organum* witnesses) the greatest Master of Logick that ever liv'd, disclaim'd the course taken by other petty Philosophers (Antient and Modern) who not attending the Coherence and Consequences of their Opinions, are more sollicitous to make each particular Opinion plausible independently upon the the [Transcriber's Note: extra "the" in original] rest, then to frame them all so, as not only to be consistent together, but to support each other. For that great Man in his vast and comprehensive Intellect, so fram'd each of his Notions, that being curiously adapted into one Systeme, they need not each of them any other defence then that which their mutuall Coherence gives them: As 'tis in an Arch, where each single stone, which if sever'd from the rest would be perhaps defenceless, is sufficiently secur'd by the solidity and entireness of the whole Fabrick of which it is a part. How justly this may be apply'd to the present case, I could easily shew You, if I were permitted to declare to You, how harmonious *Aristotles* Doctrine of the Elements is with his other Principles of Philosophy; and how rationally he has deduc'd their number from that of the combinations of the four first Qualities from the kinds of simple Motion belonging to simple bodies, and from I know not how many other Principles and **Phaenomena** of Nature, which so conspire with his Doctrine of the Elements, that they mutually strengthen and support each other. But since 'tis forbidden me to insist on Reflections of this kind, I must proceed to tell You, that though the Assertors of the four Elements value Reason so highly, and are furnish'd with Arguments enough drawn from thence, to be satisfi'd that there must be four Elements, though no Man had ever yet made any sensible tryal to discover their Number, yet they are not destitute of Experience to satisfie others that are wont to be more sway'd by their senses then their Reason. And I shall proceed to consider the testimony of Experience, when I shall have first advertis'd You, that if Men were as perfectly rational as 'tis to be wish'd they were, this sensible way of Probation would be as needless as 'tis wont to be imperfect. For it is much more high and Philosophical to discover things **a priore**, then **a posteriore**. And therefore the Peripateticks have not been very sollicitous to gather Experiments to prove their Doctrines, contenting themselves with a few only, to satisfie those that are not capable of a Nobler Conviction. And indeed they employ Experiments rather to illustrate then to demonstrate their Doctrines, as Astronomers use Sphaeres of pastboard, to descend to the capacities of such as must be taught by their senses, for want of being arriv'd to a clear apprehension of purely Mathematical Notions and Truths. I speak thus **Eleutherius** (adds **Themistius**) only to do right to Reason, and not out of Diffidence of the Experimental proof I am to alledge. For though I shall name but one, yet it is such a one as will make all other appear as needless as it self will be found Satisfactory. For if You but consider a piece of green-Wood burning in a Chimney, You will readily discern in the disbanded parts of it the four Elements, of which we teach It and other mixt bodies to be compos'd. The fire discovers it self in the flame by its own light; the smoke by ascending to the top of the chimney, and there readily vanishing into air, like a River losing it self in the Sea, sufficiently manifests to what Element it belongs and gladly returnes. The water in its own form boyling and hissing at the ends of the burning Wood betrayes it self to more then one of our senses; and the ashes by their weight, their firiness, and their dryness, put it past doubt that they belong to the Element of Earth. If I spoke (continues **Themistius**) to less knowing Persons, I would perhaps make some Excuse for building upon such an obvious and easie **Analysis**, but 'twould be, I fear, injurious, not to think such an Apology needless to You, who are too judicious either to think it necessary that Experiments to prove obvious truths should be farr fetch'd, or to wonder that among so many mixt Bodies that are compounded of the four Elements, some of them should upon a slight *Analysis* manifestly exhibit the Ingredients they consist of. Especially since it is very agreeable to the Goodness of Nature, to disclose, even in some of the most obvious Experiments that Men make, a Truth so important, and so requisite to be taken notice of by them. Besides that our *Analysis* by how much the more obvious we make it, by so much the more suittable it will be to the Nature of that Doctrine which 'tis alledged to prove, which being as clear and intelligible to the Understanding as obvious to the sense, tis no marvail the learned part of Mankind should so long and so generally imbrace it. For this Doctrine is very different from the whimseys of *Chymists* and other Modern Innovators, of whose *Hypotheses* we may observe, as Naturalists do of less perfect Animals, that as they are hastily form'd, so they are commonly short liv'd. For so these, as they are often fram'd in one week, are perhaps thought fit to be laughed at the next; and being built perchance but upon two or three Experiments are destroyed by a third or fourth, whereas the doctrine of the four Elements was fram'd by *Aristotle* after he had leasurely considered those Theories of former Philosophers, which are now with great applause revived, as discovered by these latter ages; And had so judiciously detected and supplyed the Errors and defects of former *Hypotheses* concerning the Elements, that his Doctrine of them has been ever since deservedly embraced by the letter'd part of Mankind: All the Philosophers that preceded him having in their several ages contributed to the compleatness of this Doctrine, as those of succeeding times have acquiesc'd in it. Nor has an *Hypothesis* so deliberately and maturely established been called in Question till in the last Century *Paracelsus* and some few other sooty Empiricks, rather then (as they are fain to call themselves) Philosophers, having their eyes darken'd, and their Brains troubl'd with the smoke of their own Furnaces, began to rail at the Peripatetick Doctrine, which they were too illiterate to understand, and to tell the credulous World, that they could see but three Ingredients in mixt Bodies; which to gain themselves the repute of Inventors, they endeavoured to disguise by calling them, instead of Earth, and Fire, and Vapour, Salt, Sulphur, and Mercury; to which they gave the canting title of Hypostatical Principles: but when they came to describe

them, they shewed how little they understood what they meant by them, by disagreeing as much from one another, as from the truth they agreed in opposing: For
they deliver their *Hypotheses* as darkly as their Processes; and 'tis almost as impossible for any sober Man to find their meaning, as 'tis for them to find their Elixir.
And indeed nothing has spread their Philosophy, but their great Brags and under-
takings; notwithstanding all which, (sayes *Themistius* smiling) I scarce know any
thing they have performed worth wondering at, save that they have been able to
draw *Philoponus* to their Party, and to engage him to the Defence of an unintelli-
gible *Hypothesis*, who knowes so well as he does, that Principles ought to be like
Diamonds, as well very clear, as perfectly solid.

　　Themistius having after these last words declared by his silence, that he had
finished his Discourse, *Carneades* addressing himself, as his Adversary had done,
to *Eleutherius*, returned this Answer to it, I hop'd for [Errata: for a] Demonstration, but I perceive *Themistius* hopes to put me off with a Harangue, wherein he
cannot have given me a greater Opinion of his Parts, then he has given me Distrust
for his *Hypothesis*, since for it even a Man of such Learning can bring no better
Arguments. The Rhetorical part of his Discourse, though it make not the least part
of it, I shall say nothing to, designing to examine only the Argumentative part,
and leaving it to *Philoponus* to answer those passages wherein either *Paracelsus*
or *Chymists* are concern'd: I shall observe to You, that in what he has said besides,
he makes it his Business to do these two things. The one to propose and make out
an Experiment to demonstrate the common Opinion about the four Elements; And
the other, to insinuate divers things which he thinks may repair the weakness of
his Argument, from Experience, and upon other Accounts bring some credit to the
otherwise defenceless Doctrine he maintains.

　　To begin then with his Experiment of the burning Wood, it seems to me to be
obnoxious to not a few considerable Exceptions.

　　And first, if I would now deal rigidly with my Adversary, I might here make a
great Question of the very way of Probation which he and others employ, without
the least scruple, to evince, that the Bodies commonly call'd mixt, are made up of
Earth, Air, Water, and Fire, which they are pleas'd also to call Elements; namely
that upon the suppos'd *Analysis* made by the fire, of the former sort of *Concretes*,

there are wont to emerge Bodies resembling those which they take for the Elements. For not to Anticipate here what I foresee I shall have occasion to insist on, when I come to discourse with *Philoponus* concerning the right that fire has to pass for the proper and Universal Instrument of Analysing mixt Bodies, not to Anticipate that, I say, if I were dispos'd to wrangle, I might alledge, that by *Themistius* his Experiment it would appear rather that those he calls Elements, are made of those he calls mixt Bodies, then mix'd Bodies of the Elements. For in *Themistius's* Analyz'd Wood, and in other Bodies dissipated and alter'd by the fire, it appears, and he confesses, that which he takes for Elementary Fire and Water, are made out of the Concrete; but it appears not that the Concrete was made up of Fire and Water. Nor has either He, or any Man, for ought I know, of his perswasion, yet prov'd that nothing can be obtained from a Body by the fire that was not *Pre-existent* in it.

At this unexpected objection, not only *Themistius*, but the rest of the company appear'd not a little surpriz'd; but after a while *Philoponus* conceiving his opinion, as well as that of *Aristotle*, concern'd in that Objection, You cannot sure (sayes he to *Carneades*) propose this Difficulty; not to call it Cavill, otherwise then as an Exercise of wit, and not as laying any weight upon it. For how can that be separated from a thing that was not existent in it. When, for instance, a Refiner mingles Gold and Lead, and exposing this Mixture upon a Cuppell to the violence of the fire, thereby separates it into pure and refulgent Gold and Lead (which driven off together with the Dross of the Gold is thence call'd *Lithargyrium Auri*) can any man doubt that sees these two so differing substances separated from the Mass, that they were existent in it before it was committed to the fire.

I should (replies *Carneades*) allow your Argument to prove something, if, as Men see the Refiners commonly take before hand both Lead and Gold to make the Mass you speak of, so we did see Nature pull down a parcell of the Element of Fire, that is fancy'd to be plac'd I know not how many thousand Leagues off, contiguous to the Orb of the Moon, and to blend it with a quantity of each of the three other Elements, to compose every mixt Body, upon whose Resolution the Fire presents us with Fire, and Earth, and the rest. And let me add, *Philoponus*, that to make your Reasoning cogent, it must be first prov'd, that the fire do's only take the Elementary Ingredients asunder, without otherwise altering them. For else 'tis obvious, that

Bodies may afford substances which were not pre-existent in them; as Flesh too long kept produces Magots, and old Cheese Mites, which I suppose you will not affirm to be Ingredients of those Bodies. Now that fire do's not alwayes barely separate the Elementary parts, but sometimes at least alter also the Ingredients of Bodies, if I did not expect ere long a better occasion to prove it, I might make probable out of your very Instance, wherein there is nothing Elementary separated by the great violence of the Refiners fire: the Gold and Lead which are the two Ingredients separated upon the *Analysis* being confessedly yet perfectly mixt Bodies, and the Litharge being Lead indeed; but such Lead as is differing in consistence and other Qualities from what it was before. To which I must add that I have sometimes seen, and so questionlesse have you much oftener, some parcells of Glasse adhering to the Test or Cuppel, and this Glass though Emergent as well as the Gold or Litharge upon your Analysis, you will not I hope allow to have been a third Ingredient of the Mass out of which the fire produc'd it.

Both *Philoponus* and *Themistius* were about to reply, when *Eleutherius* apprehending that the Prosecution of this Dispute would take up time, which might be better employ'd, thought fit to prevent them by saying to *Carneades*: You made at least half a Promise, when you first propos'd this Objection, that you would not (now at least) insist on it, nor indeed does it seem to be of absolute necessity to your cause, that you should. For though you should grant that there are Elements, it would not follow that there must be precisely four. And therefore I hope you will proceed to acquaint us with your other and more considerable Objections against *Themistius's* Opinion, especially since there is so great a Disproportion in Bulke betwixt the Earth, Water and Air, on the one part, and those little parcells of resembling substances, that the fire separates from *Concretes* on the other part, that I can scarce think that you are serious, when to lose no advantage against your Adversary, you seem to deny it to be rational, to conclude these great simple Bodies to be the Elements, and not the Products of compounded ones.

What you alledge (replies *Carneades*) of the Vastness of the Earth and Water, has long since made me willing to allow them to be the greatest and chief Masses of Matter to be met with here below: But I think I could shew You, if You would give me leave, that this will prove only that the Elements, as You call them, are the chief Bodies that make up the neighbouring part of the World, but not that they are such Ingredients as every mixt Body must consist of. But since You challenge me of something of a Promise, though it be not an entire one, Yet I shall willingly perform it. And indeed I intended not when I first mention'd this Objection, to insist on it at present against *Themistius*, (as I plainly intimated in my way of proposing it:) being only desirous to let you see, that though I discern'd my Advantages, yet I was willing to forego some of them, rather then appear a rigid Adversary of a Cause so weak, that it may with safety be favourably dealt with. But I must here profess, and desire You to take Notice of it, that though I pass on to another Argument, it is not because I think this first invalid. For You will find in the Progress of our Dispute, that I had some reason to question the very way of Probation imploy'd both by Peripateticks and Chymists, to evince the being and number of the Elements. For that there are such, and that they are wont to be separated by the Analysis made by Fire, is indeed taken for granted by both Parties, but has not (for ought I know) been so much as plausibly attempted to be proved by either. Hoping then that when we come to that part of our Debate, wherein Considerations relating to this Matter are to be treated of, you will remember what I have now said, and that I do rather for a while suppose, then absolutely grant the truth of what I have question'd, I will proceed to another Objection.

And hereupon *Eleutherius* having promis'd him not to be unmindfull, when time should serve, of what he had declar'd.

I consider then (sayes *Carneades*) in the next place, that there are divers Bodies out of which *Themistius* will not prove in haste, that there can be so many Elements as four extracted by the Fire. And I should perchance trouble him if I should ask him what Peripatetick can shew us, (I say not, all the four Elements, for that would be too rigid a Question, but) any one of them extracted out of Gold by any degree of Fire whatsoever. Nor is Gold the only Bodie in Nature that would puzzle an *Aristotelian*, that is no more [Errata: (that is no more)] to analyze by the Fire into Elementary Bodies, since, for ought I have yet observ'd, both Silver and calcin'd *Venetian* Talck, and some other Concretes, not necessary here to be nam'd, are so fixt, that to reduce any of them into four Heterogeneous Substances has hitherto prov'd a Task much too hard, not only for the Disciples of *Aristotle*, but those of *Vulcan*, at least, whilst the latter have employ'd only Fire to make the *Analysis*.

The next Argument (continues *Carneades*) that I shall urge against *Them-*

istius's Opinion shall be this, That as there are divers Bodies whose **Analysis** by Fire cannot reduce them into so many Heterogeneous Substances or Ingregredients [Transcriber's Note: Ingredients] as four, so there are others which may be reduc'd into more, as the Blood (and divers other parts) of Men and other Animals, which yield when analyz'd five distinct Substances, Phlegme, Spirit, Oyle, Salt and Earth, as Experience has shewn us in distilling Mans Blood, Harts-Horns, and divers other Bodies that belonging to the Animal-Kingdom abound with not uneasily sequestrable Salt.

The First Part.

I am (sayes ***Carneades***) so unwilling to deny ***Eleutherius*** any thing, that though, before the rest of the Company I am resolv'd to make good the part I have undertaken of a Sceptick; yet I shall readily, since you will have it so, lay aside for a while the Person of an Adversary to the Peripateticks and Chymists; and before I acquaint you with my Objections against their Opinions, acknowledge to you what may be (whether truly or not) tollerably enough added, in favour of a certain number of Principles of mixt Bodies, to that grand and known Argument from the ***Analysis*** of compound Bodies, which I may possibly hereafter be able to confute.

And that you may the more easily Examine, and the better Judge of what I have to say, I shall cast it into a pretty number of distinct Propositions, to which I shall not premise any thing; because I take it for granted, that you need not be advertis'd, that much of what I am to deliver, whether for or against a determinate number of Ingredients of mix'd Bodies, may be indifferently apply'd to the four Peripatetick Elements, and the three Chymical Principles, though divers of my Objections will more peculiarly belong to these last nam'd, because the Chymical ***Hypothesis*** seeming to be much more countenanc'd by Experience then the other, it will be expedient to insist chiefly upon the disproving of that; especially since most of the Arguments that are imploy'd against it, may, by a little variation, be made to conclude, at least as strongly against the less plausible, ***Aristotelian*** Doctrine.

To proceed then to my Propositions, I shall begin with this. That
[Propos. I.]

It seems not absurd to conceive that at the first Production of mixt Bodies, the Universal Matter whereof they among other Parts of the Universe consisted,

was actually divided into little Particles of several sizes and shapes variously mov'd.

This (sayes **Carneades**) I suppose you will easily enough allow. For besides that which happens in the Generation, Corruption, Nutrition, and wasting of Bodies, that which we discover partly by our **Microscopes** of the extream littlenesse of even the scarce sensible parts of Concretes; and partly by the Chymical Resolutions of mixt Bodies, and by divers other Operations of Spagyrical Fires upon them, seems sufficiently to manifest their consisting of parts very minute and of differing Figures. And that there does also intervene a various local Motion of such small Bodies, will scarce be denied; whether we chuse to grant the Origine of Concretions assign'd by **Epicurus**, or that related by **Moses**. For the first, as you well know, supposes not only all mixt Bodies, but all others to be produc'd by the various and casual occursions of Atomes, moving themselves to and fro by an internal Principle in the Immense or rather Infinite **Vacuum**. And as for the inspir'd Historian, He, informing us that the great and Wise Author of Things did not immediately create Plants, Beasts, Birds, &c. but produc'd them out of those portions of the pre-existent, though created, Matter, that he calls Water and Earth, allows us to conceive, that the constituent Particles whereof these new Concretes were to consist, were variously moved in order to their being connected into the Bodies they were, by their various Coalitions and Textures, to compose.

But (continues **Carneades**) presuming that the first Proposition needs not be longer insisted on, I will pass on to the second, and tell you that

[Propos. II.]

Neither is it impossible that of these minute Particles divers of the smallest and neighbouring ones were here and there associated into minute Masses or Clusters, and did by their Coalitions constitute great store of such little primary Concretions or Masses as were not easily dissipable into such Particles as compos'd them.

To what may be deduc'd, in favour of this Assertion, from the Nature of the Thing it self, I will add something out of Experience, which though I have not known it used to such a purpose, seems to me more fairly to make out that there May be Elementary Bodies, then the more questionable Experiments of Peripateticks and Chymists prove that there Are such. I consider then that Gold will mix and be colliquated not only with Silver, Copper, Tin and Lead, but with Antimony, *Regulus Martis* and many other Minerals, with which it will compose Bodies very differing both from Gold, and the other Ingredients of the resulting Concretes. And the same Gold will also by common *Aqua Regis*, and (I speak it knowingly) by divers other *Menstruums* be reduc'd into a seeming Liquor, in so much that the Corpuscles of Gold will, with those of the *Menstruum*, pass through Cap-Paper, and with them also coagulate into a Crystalline Salt. And I have further try'd, that with a small quantity of a certain Saline Substance I prepar'd, I can easily enough sublime Gold into the form of red Crystalls of a considerable length; and many other wayes may Gold be disguis'd, and help to constitute Bodies of very differing Natures both from It and from one another, and neverthelesse be afterward reduc'd to the self-same Numerical, Yellow, Fixt, Ponderous and Malleable Gold it was before its commixture. Nor is it only the fixedst of Metals, but the most fugitive, that I may employ in favour of our Proposition: for Quicksilver will with divers Metals compose an *Amalgam*, with divers *Menstruums* it seems to be turn'd into a Liquor, with *Aqua fortis* will be brought into either a red or white Powder or precipitate, with Oyl of Vitriol into a pale Yellow one, with Sulphur it will compose a blood-red and volatile Cinaber, with some Saline Bodies it will ascend in form of a Salt which will be dissoluble in water; with *Regulus* of Antimony and Silver I have seen it sublim'd into a kinde of Crystals, with another Mixture I reduc'd it into a malleable Body, into a hard and brittle Substance by another: And some there are who affirm, that by proper Additaments they can reduce Quicksilver into Oyl, nay into Glass, to mention no more. And yet out of all these exotick Compounds, we may recover the very same running Mercury that was the main Ingredient of them, and was so disguis'd in them. Now the Reason (proceeds *Carneades*) that I have represented these things concerning Gold and Quicksilver, is, That it may not appear absurd to conceive, that such little primary Masses or Clusters, as our Proposition mentions, may remain undissipated, notwithstanding their entring into the composition of various Concretions, since the Corpuscle of Gold and Mercury, though they be not primary Concretions of the most minute Particles or matter, but confessedly mixt Bodies, are able to concurre plentifully to the composition of several very differing Bodies, without losing their own Nature or Texture, or having their cohaesion violated by the divorce of their associated parts or Ingredients.

Give me leave to add (sayes *Eleutherius*) on this occasion, to what you now observ'd, that as confidently as some Chymists, and other modern Innovators in Philosophy are wont to object against the Peripateticks, That from the mixture of their four Elements there could arise but an inconsiderable variety of compound Bodies; yet if the *Aristotelians* were but half as well vers'd in the works of Nature as they are in the Writings of their Master, the propos'd Objection would not so calmly triumph, as for want of Experiments they are fain to suffer it to do. For if we assign to the Corpuscles, whereof each Element consists, a peculiar size and shape, it may easily enough be manifested, That such differingly figur'd Corpuscles may be mingled in such various Proportions, and may be connected so many several wayes, that an almost incredible number of variously qualified Concretes may be compos'd of them. Especially since the Corpuscles of one Element may barely, by being associated among themselves, make up little Masses of differing size and figure from their constituent parts: and since also to the strict union of such minute Bodies there seems oftentimes nothing requisite, besides the bare Contact of a great part of their Surfaces. And how great a variety of *Phaenomena* the same matter, without the addition of any other, and only several ways dispos'd or contexed, is able to exhibit, may partly appear by the multitude of differing Engins which by the contrivances of skilful Mechanitians, and the dexterity of expert Workmen, may be made of Iron alone. But in our present case being allow'd to deduce compound Bodies from four very differently qualified sorts of matter, he who shall but consider what you freshly took notice of concerning the new Concretes resulting from the mixture of incorporated Minerals, will scarce doubt but that the four Elements mannag'd by Natures Skill may afford a multitude of differing Compounds.

I am thus far of your minde (sayes *Carneades*) that the *Aristotelians* might with probability deduce a much greater number of compound Bodies from the mixture of their four Elements, than according to their present *Hypothesis* they can, if instead of vainly attempting to deduce the variety and properties of all mixt Bodies from the Combinations and Temperaments of the four Elements, as they are (among them) endowd with the four first Qualities, they had endeavoured to do it by the Bulk and Figure of the smallest parts of those supposed Elements. For from these more Catholick and Fruitfull Accidents of the Elementary matter may spring a great variety of Textures, upon whose Account a multitude of compound Bodies may very much differ from one another. And what I now observe touching the four Peripatetick Elements, may be also applyed, ***mutatis mutandis***, (as they speak) to the Chymical Principles. But (to take notice of that by the by) both the one and the other, must, I fear, call in to their assistance something that is not Elementary, to excite or regulate the motion of the parts of the matter, and dispose them after the manner requisite to the Constitution of particular Concretes. For that otherwise they are like to give us but a very imperfect account of the Origine of very many mixt Bodies, It would, I think, be no hard matter to perswade you, if it would not spend time, and were no Digression, to examine, what they are wont to alledge of the Origine of the Textures and Qualities of mixt Bodies, from a certain substantial Form, whose Origination they leave more obscure than what it is assum'd to explicate.

But to proceed to a new Proposition.

[Propos. III.]

I shall not peremptorily deny, that from most of such mixt Bodies as partake either of Animal or Vegetable Nature, there may by the Help of the Fire, be actually obtain'd a determinate number (whether Three, Four or Five, or fewer or more) of Substances, worthy of differing Denominations.

Of the Experiments that induce me to make this Concession, I am like to have occasion enough to mention several in the prosecution of my Discourse. And therefore, that I may not hereafter be oblig'd to trouble You and my self with needless Repetitions, I shall now only desire you to take notice of such Experiments, when they shall be mention'd, and in your thoughts referre them hither.

To these three Concessions I have but this Fourth to add, That

[Propos. IV.]

It may likewise be granted, that those distinct Substances, which Concretes generally either afford or are made up of, may without very much Inconvenience be call'd the Elements or Principles of them.

When I said, ***without very much Inconvenience***, I had in my Thoughts that sober Admonition of ***Galen***, ***Cum de re constat, de verbis non est Litigandum***. And therefore also I scruple not to say ***Elements*** or ***Principles***, partly because the

Chymists are wont to call the Ingredients of mixt Bodies, *Principles*, as the *Aristotelians* name them *Elements*; I would here exclude neither. And, partly, because it seems doubtfull whether the same Ingredients may not be call'd *Principles*? as not being compounded of any more primary Bodies: and *Elements*, in regard that all mix'd Bodies are compounded of them. But I thought it requisite to limit my Concession by premising the words, *very much*, to the word *Inconvenience*, because that though the Inconvenience of calling the distinct Substances, mention'd in the Proposition *Elements* or *Principles*, be not very great, yet that it is an Impropriety of Speech, and consequently in a matter of this moment not to be altogether overlook'd, You will perhaps think, as well as I, by that time you shall have heard the following part of my Discourse, by which you will best discern what Construction to put upon the former Propositions, and how far they may be look'd upon, as things that I concede as true, and how far as things I only represent as specious enough to be fit to be consider'd.

And now *Eleutherius* (continues *Carneades*) I must resume the person of a Sceptick, and as such, propose some part of what may be either dislik't, or at least doubted of in the common *Hypothesis* of the Chymists: which if I examine with a little the more freedom, I hope I need not desire you (a Person to whom I have the Happinesse of being so well known) to look upon it as something more suitable to the Employment whereto the Company has, for this Meeting, doom'd me; then either to my Humour or my Custom.

Now though I might present you many things against the Vulgar Chymical Opinion of the three Principles, and the Experiments wont to be alledg'd as Demonstrations of it, yet those I shall at present offer you may be conveniently enough comprehended in four Capital Considerations; touching all which I shall only premise this in general, That since it is not my present Task so much to assert an *Hypothesis* of my own, as to give an Account wherefore I suspect the Truth of that of the Chymists, it ought not to be expected that all my Objections should be of the most cogent sort, since it is reason enough to Doubt of a propos'd Opinion, that there appears no cogent Reason for it.

To come then to the Objections themselves; I consider in the first place, That notwithstanding what common Chymists have prov'd or taught, it may reasonably enough be Doubted, how far, and in what sence, Fire ought to be esteem'd the genuine and universal Instrument of analyzing mixt Bodies.

This Doubt, you may remember, was formerly mention'd, but so transiently discours'd of, that it will now be fit to insist upon it; And manifest that it was not so inconsiderately propos'd as our Adversaries then imagin'd.

But, before I enter any farther into this Disquisition, I cannot but here take notice, that it were to be wish'd, our Chymists had clearly inform'd us what kinde of Division of Bodies by Fire must determine the number of the Elements: For it is nothing near so easy as many seem to think, to determine distinctly the Effects of Heat, as I could easily manifest, if I had leasure to shew you how much the Operations of Fire may be diversify'd by Circumstances. But not wholly to pass by a matter of this Importance, I will first take notice to you, that *Guajacum* (for Instance) burnt with an open Fire in a Chimney, is sequestred into Ashes and Soot, whereas the same Wood distill'd in a Retort does yield far other Heterogeneities, (to use the *Helmontian* expression) and is resolv'd into Oyl, Spirit, Vinager, Water and Charcoal; the last of which to be reduc'd into Ashes, requires the being farther calcin'd then it can be in a close Vessel: Besides having kindled Amber, and held a clean Silver Spoon, or some other Concave and smooth Vessel over the Smoak of its Flame, I observ'd the Soot into which that Fume condens'd, to be very differing from any thing that I had observ'd to proceed from the steam of Amber purposely (for that is not usual) distilled *per se* in close Vessels. Thus having, for Tryals sake, kindled Camphire, and catcht the Smoak that copiously ascended out of the Flame, it condens'd into a Black and unctuous Soot, which would not have been guess'd by the Smell or other Properties to have proceeded from Camphire: whereas having (as I shall otherwhere more fully declare) expos'd a quantity of that Fugitive Concrete to a gentle heat in a close Glass-Vessel, it sublim'd up without seeming to have lost any thing of its whiteness, or its Nature, both which it retain'd, though afterwards I so encreased the Fire as to bring it to Fusion. And, besides Camphire, there are divers other Bodies (that I elsewhere name) in which the heat in close Vessels is not wont to make any separation of Heterogeneities, but only a comminution of Parts, those that rise first being Homogeneal with the others, though subdivided into smaller Particles: whence Sublimations have been stiled, *The Pestles of the Chymists*. But not here to mention what I elsewhere take notice of, concerning common Brimstone once or twice sublim'd, that expos'd to a moderate Fire in Subliming-Pots, it rises all into dry, and almost tastless, Flowers; Whereas being expos'd to a naked Fire it affords store of a Saline and Fretting Liquor: Not to mention this, I say, I will further observe to you, that as it is considerable in the *Analysis* of mixt Bodies, whether the Fire act on them when they are expos'd to the open Air, or shut up in close Vessels, so is the degree of Fire by which the *Analysis* is attempted of no small moment. For a milde *Balneum* will sever unfermented Blood (for Instance) but into Phlegme and *Caput mortuum*, the later whereof (which I have sometimes had) hard, brittle, and of divers Colours, (transparent almost like Tortoise-shell) press'd by a good Fire in a Retort yields a Spirit, an Oyl or two, and a volatile Salt, besides a [Errata: another] *Caput mortuum*. It may be also pertinent to our present Designe, to take notice of what happens in the making and distilling of Sope; for by one degree of Fire the Salt, the Water and the Oyl or Grease, whereof that factitious Concrete is made up, being boyl'd up together are easily brought to mingle and in-corporate into one Mass; but by another and further degree of Heat the same Mass may be again divided into an oleagenous, an aqueous, a Saline, and an Earthy part. And so we may observe that impure Silver and Lead being expos'd together to a moderate Fire, will thereby be colliquated into one Mass, and mingle *per minima*, as they speak, whereas a much vehementer Fire will drive or carry off the baser Metals (I mean the Lead, and the Copper or other Alloy) from the Silver, though not, for ought appears, separate them from one another. Besides, when a Vegetable abounding in fixt Salt is analyz'd by a naked Fire, as one degree of Heat will reduce it into Ashes, (as the Chymists themselves teach us) so, by only a further degree of Fire, those Ashes may be vitrified and turn'd into Glass. I will not stay to examine how far a meere Chymist might on this occasion demand, If it be lawful for an *Aristotelian* to make Ashes, (which he mistakes for meere Earth) pass for an Element, because by one degree of Fire it may be produc'd, why a Chymist may not upon the like Principle argue, that Glass is one of the Elements of many Bodies, because that also may be obtain'd from them, barely by the Fire? I will not, I say, lose time to ex-amine this, but observe, that by a Method of applying the Fire, such similar Bodies may be obtain'd from a Concrete, as Chymists have not been able to separate; either by barely burning it in an open Fire, or by barely distilling it in close Vessels. For to me it seems very considerable, and I wonder that men have taken so little notice of it, that I have not by any of the common wayes of Distillation in close Vessels, seen any separation made of such a volatile Salt as is afforded us by Wood, when that is first by an open Fire divided into Ashes and Soot, and that Soot is afterwards plac'd in a strong Retort, and compell'd by an urgent Fire to part with its Spirit, Oyl and Salt; for though I dare not peremptorily deny, that in the Liquors of *Guajacum* and other Woods distill'd in Retorts after the common manner, there may be Saline parts, which by reason of the Analogy may pretend to the name of some kinde of volatile Salts; yet questionless there is a great disparity betwixt such Salts and that which we have sometimes obtain'd upon the first Distillation of Soot (though for the most part it has not been separated from the first or second Rectification, and sometimes not till the third) For we could never yet see separated from Woods analyz'd only the vulgar way in close vessels any volatile Salt in a dry and Saline form, as that of Soot, which we have often had very Crystalline and Geometrically figur'd. And then, whereas the Saline parts of the Spirits of *Guajacum*, &c. appear upon distillation sluggish enough, the Salt of Soot seems to be one of the most volatile Bodies in all Nature; and if it be well made will readily ascend with the milde heat of a Furnace, warm'd only by the single Wieck of a Lamp, to the top of the highest Glass Vessels that are commonly made use of for Distillation: and besides all this, the taste and smell of the Salt of Soot are exceeding differing from those of the Spirits of *Guajacum*, &c. and the former not only smells and tastes much less like a vegetable Salt, than like that of Harts-horn, and other Animal Concretes; but in divers other Properties seems more of Kinne to the Family of Animals, than to that of vegetable Salts, as I may elsewhere (God permitting) have an occasion more particularly to declare. I might likewise by some other Examples manifest, That the Chymists, to have dealt clearly, ought to have more explicitly and particularly declar'd by what Degree of Fire, and in what manner of Application of it, they would have us Judge a Division made by the Fire to be a true *Analysis* into their Principles, and the Productions of it to deserve the name of Elementary Bodies. But it is time that I proceed to mention the particular Reasons that incline me to Doubt, whether the Fire be the true and universal Analyzer of mixt Bodies; of which Reasons what has been already objected may pass for one.

In the next place I observe, That there are some mixt Bodies from which it has not been yet made appear, that any degree of Fire can separate either Salt or Sulphur or Mercury, much less all the Three. The most obvious Instance of this Truth is Gold, which is a Body so fix'd, and wherein the Elementary Ingredients (if it have any) are so firmly united to each other, that we finde not in the operations wherein Gold is expos'd to the Fire, how violent soever, that it does discernably so much as lose of its fixednesse or weight, so far is it from being dissipated into those Principles, whereof one at least is acknowledged to be Fugitive enough; and so justly did the Spagyricall Poet somewhere exclaim,

Cuncta adeo miris illic compagibus harent.

And I must not omit on this occasion to mention to you, *Eleutherius*, the memorable Experiment that I remember I met with in *Gasto Claveus*,[2] who, though a Lawyer by Profession, seems to have had no small Curiosity and Experience in Chymical affairs: He relates then, that having put into one small Earthen Vessel an Ounce of the most pure Gold, and into another the like weight of pure Silver, he plac'd them both in that part of a Glass-house Furnace wherein the Workmen keep their Metal, (as our English Artificers call their Liquid Glass) continually melted, and that having there kept both the Gold and the Silver in constant Fusion for two Moneths together, he afterwards took them out of the Furnace and the Vessels, and weighing both of them again, found that the Silver had not lost above a 12th part of its weight, but the Gold had not of his lost any thing at all. And though our Author endeavours to give us of this a Scholastick Reason, which I suppose you would be as little satisfied with, as I was when I read it; yet for the matter of Fact, which will serve our present turne, he assures us, that though it be strange, yet Experience it self taught it him to be most true.

[2: *Gasto Claveus* Apolog. Argur. & Chrysopera.]

And though there be not perhaps any other Body to be found so perfectly fix'd as Gold, yet there are divers others so fix'd or compos'd, at least of so strictly united parts, that I have not yet observ'd the Fire to separate from them any one of the Chymists Principles. I need not tell you what Complaints the more Candid and Judicious of the Chymists themselves are wont to make of those Boasters that confidently pretend, that they have extracted the Salt or Sulphur of Quicksilver, when they have disguis'd it by Additaments, wherewith it resembles the Concretes whose Names are given it; whereas by a skilful and rigid *Examen*, it may be easily enough stript of its Disguises, and made to appear again in the pristine form of running Mercury. The pretended Salts and Sulphurs being so far from being Elementary parts extracted out of the Bodie of Mercurie, that they are rather (to borrow a terme of the Grammarians) De-compound Bodies, made up of the whole Metal and the *Menstruum* or other Additaments imploy'd to disguise it. And as for Silver, I never could see any degree of Fire make it part with any of its three Principles. And though the Experiment lately mentioned from *Claveus* may beget a Suspition that Silver may be dissipated by Fire, provided it be extreamly violent and very lasting: yet it will not necessarily follow, that because the Fire was able at length to make the Silver lose a little of its weight, it was therefore able to dissipate it into its Principles. For first I might alledge that I have observ'd little Grains of Silver to lie hid in the small Cavities (perhaps glas'd over by a vitrifying heat) in Crucibles, wherein Silver has been long kept in Fusion, whence some Goldsmiths of my Acquaintance make a Benefit by grinding such Crucibles to powder, to recover out of them the latent particles of Silver. And hence I might argue, that perhaps *Claveus* was mistaken, and imagin'd that Silver to have been driven away by the Fire, that indeed lay in minute parts hid in his Crucible, in whose pores so small a quantity as he mist of so ponderous a Bodie might very well lie conceal'd.

But Secondly, admitting that some parts of the Silver were driven away by the violence of the Fire, what proof is there that it was either the Salt, the Sulphur, or the Mercury of the Metal, and not rather a part of it homogeneous to what remain'd? For besides, that the Silver that was left seem'd not sensibly alter'd, which probably would have appear'd, had so much of any one of its Principles been separated from it: We finde in other Mineral Bodies of a less permanent nature than Silver, that the Fire may divide them into such minute parts, as to be able to carry them away with its self, without at all destroying their Nature. Thus we see that in the refining of Silver, the Lead that is mix'd with it (to carry away the Copper or other ignoble Mineral that embases the Silver) will, if it be let alone, in time evaporate away upon the Test; but if (as is most usual amongst those that refine great quantities of Metals together) the Lead be blown off from the Silver by Bellowes, that which would else have gone away in the Form of unheeded steams, will in great part be collected not far from the Silver, in the Form of a darkish Powder or Calx, which, because it is blown off from Silver, they call Litharge of Silver. And thus *Agricola*[3] in divers places informs us, when Copper, or the Oare of it is colliquated by the violence of the Fire with *Cadmia*, the Sparks that in great multitudes do fly upwards do, some of them, stick to the vaulted Roofs of the Furnaces, in the form of little and (for the most part) White Bubbles, which therefore the Greeks, and, in Imitation of them, our Drugsters call *Pompholix*: and others more heavy partly adhere to the sides of the Furnace, and partly (especially if the Covers be not kept upon the Pots) fall to the Ground, and by reason of their Ashy Colour as well as Weight were called by the same Greeks [Greek: spodos], which, I need not tell you, in their Language signifies Ashes. I might add, that I have not found that from Venetian Talck (I say Venetian, because I have found other kinds of that Mineral more open) from the *Lapis Ossifragus*, (which the Shops call *Ostiocolla*) from *Muscovia* Glass, from pure and Fusible Sand, to mention now no other Concretes; those of my Acquaintance that have try'd have been able by the Fire to separate any one of the Hypostatical Principles, which you will the less scruple to believe, if you consider that Glass may be made by the bare Colliquation of the Salt and Earth remaining in the Ashes of a burnt Plant, and that yet common Glass, once made, does so far resist the violence of the Fire, that most Chymists think it a Body more undestroyable then Gold it self. For if the Artificer can so firmly unite such comparative gross Particles as those of Earth and Salt that make up common Ashes, into a Body indissoluble by Fire; why may not Nature associate in divers Bodies the more minute Elementary Corpuscles she has at hand too firmly to let them be separable by the Fire? And on this Occasion, *Eleutherius*, give me leave to mention to you two or three sleight Experiments, which will, I hope, be found more pertinent to our present Discourse, than at first perhaps they will appear. The first is, that, having (for Tryals sake) put a quantity of that Fugitive Concrete, Camphire, into a Glass Vessel, and plac'd it in a gentle Heat, I found it (not leaving behinde, according to my Estimate, not so much as one Grain) to sublime to the Top of the Vessel into Flowers: which in Whiteness, Smell, &c. seem'd not to differ from the Camphire it self. Another Experiment is that of *Helmont*, who in several places affirms, That a Coal kept in a Glass exactly clos'd will never be calcin'd to Ashes, though kept never so long in a strong Fire. To countenance which I shall tell you this Tryal of my own, That having sometimes distilled some Woods, as particularly Box, whilst our *Caput mortuum* remain'd in the Retort, it continued black like Charcoal, though the Retort were Earthen, and kept red-hot in a vehement Fire; but as soon as ever it was brought out of the candent Vessel into the open Air, the burning Coals did hastily degenerate or fall asunder, without the

Assistance of any new Calcination, into pure white Ashes. And to these two I shall add but this obvious and known Observation, that common Sulphur (if it be pure and freed from its Vinager) being leasurely sublim'd in close Vessels, rises into dry Flowers, which may be presently melted into a Bodie of the same Nature with that which afforded them. Though if Brimstone be burnt in the open Air it gives, you know, a penetrating Fume, which being caught in a Glass-Bell condenses into that acid Liquor called Oyl of Sulphur *per Campanam*. The use I would make of these Experiments collated with what I lately told you out of *Agricola* is this, That even among the Bodies that are not fixt, there are divers of such a Texture, that it will be hard to make it appear, how the Fire, as Chymists are wont to imploy it, can resolve them into Elementary Substances. For some Bodies being of such a Texture that the Fire can drive them into the cooler and less hot part of the Vessels wherein they are included, and if need be, remove them from place to place to fly the greatest heat, more easily than it can divorce their Elements (especially without the Assistance of the Air) we see that our Chymists cannot Analyze them in close Vessels, and of other compound Bodies the open Fire can as little separate the Elements. For what can a naked Fire do to Analyze a mixt Bodie, if its component Principles be so minute, and so strictly united, that the Corpuscles of it need less heat to carry them up, than is requisite to divide them into their Principles. So that of some Bodies the Fire cannot in close Vessels make any *Analysis* at all, and others will in the open Air fly away in the Forms of Flowers or Liquors, before the Heat can prove able to divide them into their Principles. And this may hold, whether the various similar parts of a Concrete be combin'd by Nature or by Art; For in factitious *Sal Armoniack* we finde the common and the Urinous Salts so well mingled, that both in the open Fire, and in subliming Vessels they rise together as one Salt, which seems in such Vessels irresoluble by Fire alone. For I can shew you *Sal Armoniack* which after the ninth Sublimation does still retain its compounded Nature. And indeed I scarce know any one Mineral, from which by Fire alone Chymists are wont to sever any Substance simple enough to deserve the name of an Element or Principle. For though out of native Cinnaber they distill Quicksilver, and though from many of those Stones that the Ancients called *Pyrites* they sublime Brimstone, yet both that Quicksilver and this Sulphur being very often the same with the common Minerals that are sold in the Shops under those names, are themselves too much compounded Bodies to pass for the Elements of such. And thus much, ***Eleutherius***, for the Second Argument that belongs to my First Consideration; the others I shall the lesse insist on, because I have dwelt so long upon this.

[3: ***Agricola*** de Natura Fossil. Lib. 9. Cap. 11. & 12.]

Proceed we then in the next place to consider, That there are divers Separations to be made by other means, which either cannot at all, or else cannot so well be made by the Fire alone. When Gold and Silver are melted into one Mass, it would lay a great Obligation upon Refiners and Goldsmiths to teach them the Art of separating them by the Fire, without the trouble and charge they are fain to be at to sever them. Whereas they may be very easily parted by the Affusion of Spirit of Nitre or ***Aqua fortis*** (which the French therefore call ***Eau de Depart***:) so likewise the Metalline part of Vitriol will not be so easily and conveniently separated from the Saline part even by a violent Fire, as by the Affusion of certain Alkalizate Salts in a liquid Form upon the Solution of Vitriol made in common water. For thereby the acid Salt of the Vitriol, leaving the Copper it had corroded to joyn with the added Salts, the Metalline part will be precipitated to the bottom almost like Mud. And that I may not give Instances only in De-compound Bodies, I will add a not useless one of another kinde. Not only Chymists have not been able (for ought is vulgarly known) by Fire alone to separate true Sulphur from Antimony; but though you may finde in their Books many plausible Processes of Extracting it, yet he that shall make as many fruitlesse Tryals as I have done to obtain it by, most of them will, I suppose, be easily perswaded, that the Productions of such Processes are Antimonial Sulphurs rather in Name than Nature. But though Antimony sublim'd by its self is reduc'd but to a volatile Powder, or Antimonial Flowers, of a compounded Nature like the Mineral that affords them: yet I remember that some years ago I sublim'd out of Antimony a Sulphur, and that in greater plenty then ever I saw obtain'd from that Mineral, by a Method which I shall therefore acquaint you with, because Chymists seem not to have taken notice of what Importance such Experiments may be in the Indagation of the Nature, and especially of the Number of the Elements. Having then purposely for Tryals sake digested eight Ounces of good and well powder'd Antimony with twelve Ounces of Oyl of Vitriol in a well stopt Glas-Vessel for about six or seven Weeks; and having caus'd the Mass (grown hard and brittle) to be distill'd in a Retort plac'd in Sand, with a strong Fire; we found the

Antimony to be so opened, or alter'd by the **Menstruum** wherewith it had been digested, That whereas crude Antimony, forc'd up by the Fire, arises only in Flowers, our Antimony thus handled afforded us partly in the Receiver, and partly in the Neck and at the Top of the Retort, about an Ounce of Sulphur, yellow and brittle like common Brimstone, and of so Sulphureous a smell, that upon the unluting the Vessels it infected the Room with a scarce supportable stink. And this Sulphur, besides the Colour and Smell, had the perfect Inflamability of common Brimstone, and would immediately kindle (at the Flame of a Candle) and burn blew like it. And though it seem'd that the long digestion wherein our Antimony and **Menstruum** were detain'd, did conduce to the better unlocking of the Mineral, yet if you have not the leasure to make so long a Digestion, you may by incorporating with powder'd Antimony a convenient Quantity of Oyl of Vitriol, and committing them immediately to Distillation, obtain a little Sulphur like unto the common one, and more combustible than perhaps you will at first take notice of. For I have observ'd, that though (after its being first kindled) the Flame would sometimes go out too soon of its self, if the same Lump of Sulphur were held again to the Flame of a Candle, it would be rekindled and burn a pretty while, not only after the second, but after the third or fourth accension. You, to whom I think I shewed my way of discovering something of Sulphureous in Oyl of Vitriol, may perchance suspect, **Eleutherius**, either that this Substance was some Venereal Sulphur that lay hid in that Liquor, and was by this operation only reduc'd into a manifest Body; or else that it was a compound of the unctuous parts of the Antimony, and the Saline ones of the Vitriol, in regard that (as **Gunther**[4] informs us) divers learned men would have Sulphur to be nothing but a mixture made in the Bowels of the Earth of Vitriolate Spirits and a certain combustible Substance. But the Quantity of Sulphur we obtain'd by Digestion was much too great to have been latent in the Oyl of Vitriol. And that Vitriolate Spirits are not necessary to the Constitution of such a Sulphur as ours, I could easily manifest, if I would acquaint you with the several wayes by which I have obtain'd, though not in such plenty, a Sulphur of Antimony, colour'd and combustible like common Brimstone. And though I am not now minded to discover them, yet I shall tell you, that to satisfie some Ingenious Men, that distill'd Vitriolate Spirits are not necessary to the obtaining of such a Sulphur as we have been considering, I did by the bare distillation of only Spirit of Nitre, from its weight of crude Antimony separate, in a short time, a yellow and very inflamable Sulphur, which, for ought I know, deserves as much the name of an Element, as any thing that Chymists are wont to separate from any Mineral by the Fire. I could perhaps tell you of other Operations upon Antimony, whereby That may be extracted from it, which cannot be forc'd out of it by the Fire; but I shall reserve them for a fitter Opportunity, and only annex at present this sleight, but not impertinent Experiment. That whereas I lately observed to you, that the Urinous and common Salts whereof *Sal Armoniack* consists, remain'd unsever'd by the Fire in many successive Sublimations, they may be easily separated, and partly without any Fire at all, by pouring upon the Concrete finely powder'd, a Solution of Salt of Tartar, or of the Salt of Wood-Ashes; for upon your diligently mixing of these you will finde your Nose invaded with a very strong smell of Urine, and perhaps too your Eyes forc'd to water by the same subtle and piercing Body that produces the stink; both these effects proceeding from hence, that by the Alcalizate Salt, the Sea Salt that enter'd the composition of the *Sal Armoniack* is mortify'd and made more fixt, and thereby a divorce is made between it and the volatile Urinous Salt, which being at once set at liberty, and put into motion, begins presently to fly away, and to offend the Nostrils and Eyes it meets with by the way. And if the operation of these Salts be in convenient Glasses promoted by warmth, though but by that of a Bath, the ascending Steams may easily be caught and reduc'd into a penetrant Spirit, abounding with a Salt, which I have sometimes found to be separable in a Crystalline Form. I might add to these Instances, that whereas Sublimate, consisting, as you know, of Salts & Quicksilver combin'd and carried up together by Heat, may be Sublim'd, I know not how often, by a like degree of Fire, without suffering any divorce of the component Bodies, the Mercury may be easily sever'd from the adhering Salts, if the Sublimate be distill'd from Salt of Tartar, Quick Lime, or such Alcalizate Bodies. But I will rather observe to you, *Eleutherius*, what divers ingenious men have thought somewhat strange; that by such an Additament that seems but only to promote the Separation, there may be easily obtain'd from a Concrete that by the Fire alone is easily divisible into all the Elements that Vegetables are suppos'd to consist of, such a similar Substance as differs in many respects from them all, and consequently has by many of the most Intelligent Chymists been denied to be contain'd in the mixt Body. For I know a way, and have practis'd it, whereby common Tartar, without the addition of any thing that is not perfectly a Mineral except Salt-petre, may by one Distillation in an Earthen Retort be made to afford good store of real Salt, readily dissoluble in water, which I found to be neither acid, nor of the smell of Tartar, and to be almost as volatile as Spirit of Wine it self, and to be indeed of so differing a Nature from all that is wont to be separated by Fire from Tartar, that divers Learned Men, with whom I discours'd of it, could hardly be brought to beleeve, that so fugitive a Salt could be afforded by Tartar, till I assur'd it them upon my own Knowledge. And if I did not think you apt to suspect me to be rather too backward than too forward to credit or affirm unlikely things, I could convince you by what I have yet lying by me of that anomalous Salt.

[4: Lib. 1. Observat. Cap. 6.]

The Fourth thing that I shall alledge to countenance my first Consideration is, That the Fire even when it divides a Body into Substances of divers Consistences, does not most commonly analyze it into Hypostatical Principles, but only disposes its parts into new Textures, and thereby produces Concretes of a new indeed, but yet of a compound Nature. This Argument it will be requisite for me to prosecute so fully hereafter, that I hope you will then confess that 'tis not for want of good Proofs that I desire leave to suspend my Proofs till the *Series* of my Discourse shall make it more proper and seasonable to propose them.

It may be further alledg'd on the behalf of my First Consideration, That some such distinct Substances may be obtain'd from some Concretes without Fire, as deserve no less the name of Elementary, than many that Chymists extort by the Violence of the Fire.

We see that the Inflamable Spirit, or as the Chymists esteem it, the Sulphur of Wine, may not only be separated from it by the gentle heat of a Bath, but may be distill'd either by the help of the Sun-Beams, or even of a Dunghill, being indeed of so Fugitive a Nature, that it is not easy to keep it from flying away, even without the Application of external heat. I have likewise observ'd that a Vessel full of Urine being plac'd in a Dunghill, the Putrefaction is wont after some weeks so to open the Body, that the parts disbanding the Saline Spirit, will within no very long time, if the Vessel be not stopt, fly away of it self; Insomuch that from such Urine I have been able to distill little or nothing else than a nauseous Phlegme, instead of the active and piercing Salt and Spirit that it would have afforded, when first expos'd to the Fire, if the Vessel had been carefully stopt.

And this leads me to consider in the Fifth place, That it will be very hard to prove, that there can no other Body or way be given which will as well as the Fire divide Concretes into several homogeneous Substances, which may consequently be call'd their Elements or Principles, as well as those separated or produc'd by the Fire. For since we have lately seen, that Nature can successefully employ other Instruments than the Fire to separate distinct Substances from mixt Bodies, how know we, but that Nature has made, or Art may make, some such Substance as may be a fit Instrument to Analyze mixt Bodies, or that some such Method may be found by Humane Industry or Luck, by whose means compound Bodies may be resolv'd into other Substances, than such as they are wont to be divided into by the Fire. And why the Products of such an *Analysis* may not as justly be call'd the component Principles of the Bodies that afford them, it will not be easy to shew, especially since I shall hereafter make it evident, that the Substances which Chymists are wont to call the Salts, and Sulphurs, and Mercuries of Bodies, are not so pure and Elementary as they presume, and as their *Hypothesis* requires. And this may therefore be the more freely press'd upon the Chymists, because neither the *Paracelsians*, nor the *Helmontians* can reject it without apparent Injury to their respective Masters. For *Helmont* do's more than once Inform his Readers, that both *Paracelsus* and Himself were Possessors of the famous Liquor, *Alkahest*, which for its great power in resolving Bodies irresoluble by Vulgar Fires, he somewhere seems to call *Ignis Gehennae*. To this Liquor he ascribes, (and that in great part upon his own Experience) such wonders, that if we suppose them all true, I am so much the more a Friend to Knowledge than to Wealth, that I should think the *Alkahest* a nobler and more desireable Secret than the Philosophers Stone it self. Of this Universal Dissolvent he relates, That having digested with it for a competent time a piece of Oaken Charcoal, it was thereby reduc'd into a couple of new and distinct Liquors, discriminated from each other by their Colour and Situation, and that the whole body of the Coal was reduc'd into those Liquors, both of them separable from his Immortal *Menstruum*, which remain'd as fit for such Operations as before. And he moreover tells us in divers places of his Writings, that by this powerful, and unwearied Agent, he could dissolve Metals, Marchasites, Stones, Vegetable and Animal

Bodies of what kinde soever, and even Glass it self (first reduc'd to powder,) and in a word, all kinds of mixt Bodies in the World into their several similar Substances, without any Residence or *Caput mortuum*. And lastly, we may gather this further from his Informations, That the homogeneous Substances obtainable from compound Bodies by his piercing Liquor, were oftentimes different enough both as to Number and as to Nature, from those into which the same Bodies are wont to be divided by common Fire. Of which I shall need in this place to mention no other proof, then that whereas we know that in our common *Analysis* of a mixt Body, there remains a terrestrial and very fixt Substance, oftentimes associated with a Salt as fixt; Our Author tells us, that by his way he could Distill over all Concretes without any *Caput mortuum*, and consequently could make those parts of the Concrete volatile, which in the Vulgar *Analysis* would have been fixt. So that if our Chymists will not reject the solemn and repeated Testimony of a Person, who cannot but be acknowledg'd for one of the greatest Spagyrists that they can boast of, they must not deny that there is to be found in Nature another Agent able to Analyze compound Bodies less violently, and both more genuinely and more universally than the Fire. And for my own part, though I cannot but say on this Occasion what (you know) our Friend Mr. *Boyle* is wont to say, when he is askt his Opinion of any strange Experiment; *That He that hath seen it hath more Reason to beleeve it, than He that hath not*; yet I have found *Helmont* so faithful a Writer, even in divers of his improbable Experiments (I alwayes except that Extravagant Treatise *De Magnetica Vulnerum Curatione*, which some of his Friends affirm to have been first publish'd by his Enemies) that I think it somewhat harsh to give him the Lye, especially to what he delivers upon his own proper Tryal. And I have heard from very credible Eye-witnesses some things, and seen some others my self, which argue so strongly, that a circulated Salt, or a *Menstruum* (such as it may be) may by being abstracted from compound Bodies, whether Mineral, Animal, or Vegetable, leave them more unlockt than a wary Naturalist would easily beleeve, that I dare not confidently measure the Power of Nature and Art by that of the *Menstruums*, and other Instruments that eminent Chymists themselves are as yet wont to Empoly [Errata: employ] about the Analyzing of Bodies; nor Deny that a *Menstruum* may at least from this or that particular Concrete obtain some apparently similar Substance, differing from any obtainable from the same Body by any degree or manner of Application of the Fire. And I am the more backward to deny peremptorily, that there may be such Openers of compound Bodies, because among the Experiments that make me speak thus warily, there wanted not some in which it appear'd not, that one of the Substances not separable by common Fires and **Menstruums** could retain any thing of the Salt by which the separation was made.

And here, **Eleutherius**, (sayes **Carneades**) I should conclude as much of my Discourse as belongs to the first Consideration I propos'd, but that I foresee, that what I have delivered will appear liable to two such specious Objections, that I cannot safely proceed any further till I have examin'd them.

And first, one sort of Opposers will be forward to tell me, That they do not pretend by Fire alone to separate out of all compound Bodies their **Hypostatical** Principles; it being sufficient that the Fire divides them into such, though afterwards they employ other Bodies to collect the similar parts of the Compound; as 'tis known, that though they make use of water to collect the Saline parts of Ashes from the Terrestrial wherewith they are blended, yet it is the Fire only that Incinerates Bodies, and reduces the fix'd part of them into the Salt and Earth, whereof Ashes are made up. This Objection is not, I confess, inconsiderable, and I might in great part allow of it, without granting it to make against me, if I would content my self to answer, that it is not against those that make it that I have been disputing, but against those Vulgar Chymists, who themselves believe, and would fain make others do so, That the Fire is not only an universal, but an adaequate [Transcriber's Note: adequate] and sufficient Instrument to analyze mixt Bodies with. For as to their Practice of Extracting the fix'd Salt out of Ashes by the Affusion of Water, 'tis obvious to alleadge, that the Water does only assemble together the Salt the Fire had before divided from the Earth: as a Sieve does not further break the Corn, but only bring together into two distinct heaps the Flour and the Bran, whose Corpuscles before lay promiscuously blended together in the Meal. This I say I might alleadge, and thereby exempt my self from the need of taking any farther notice of the propos'd Objection. But not to lose the Rise it may afford me of Illustrating the matter under Consideration, I am content briefly to consider it, as far forth as my present Disquisition may be concern'd in it.

Not to repeat then what has been already answer'd, I say farther, that though I am so civil an Adversary, that I will allow the Chymists, after the Fire has done all its work, the use of fair Water to make their Extractions with, in such cases wherein the Water does not cooperate with the Fire to make the *Analysis*; yet since I Grant this but upon Supposition that the Water does only wash off the Saline Particles, which the Fire Alone has Before Extricated in the Analyz'd Body, it will not be Reasonable, that this Concession should Extend to other Liquors that may Add to what they Dissolve, nor so much as to other Cases than those Newly Mentioned: Which Limitation I Desire You would be Pleas'd to Bear in Mind till I shall Anon have Occasion to make Use of it. And This being thus Premis'd, I shall Proceed to Observe,

First, That Many of the Instances I Propos'd in the Preceding Discourse are Such, that the Objection we are Considering will not at all Reach Them. For Fire can no more with the Assistance of Water than without it Separate any of the Three Principles, either from Gold, Silver, Mercury, or some Others of the Concretes named Above.

Hence We may Inferre, That Fire is not an Universal Analyzer of all Mixt Bodies, since of Metals and Minerals, wherein Chymists have most Exercis'd Themselves, there Appear scarce Any which they are able to Analyze by Fire, Nay, from which they can Unquestionably Separate so much as any One of their Hypostatical Principles; Which may well Appear no small Disparagement as well to their *Hypothesis* as to their Pretensions.

It will also remain True, notwithstanding the Objection, That there may be Other Wayes than the wonted *Analysis* by Fire, to Separate from a Compound Body Substances as Homogeneneous [Transcriber's Note: Homogeneous] as those that Chymists Scruple not to Reckon among their *Tria Prima* (as some of them, for Brevity Sake, call their Three Principles.)

And it Appears, That by Convenient Additaments such Substances may be Separated by the Help of the Fire, as could not be so by the Fire alone: Witness the Sulphur of Antimony.

And Lastly, I must Represent, That since it appears too that the Fire is but One of the Instruments that must be Employ'd in the Resolution of Bodies, We may Reasonably Challenge the Liberty of doing Two Things. For when ever any *Menstruum* or other Additament is Employ'd, together with the Fire to Obtain a Sulphur or a Salt from a Body, We may well take the Freedom to Examine, whether or no That *Menstruum* do barely Help to Separate the Principle Obtain'd by It, or whether there Intervene not a Coalition of the Parts of the Body Wrought upon with Those of the *Menstruum*, whereby the Produc'd Concrete may be Judg'd to Result from the Union of Both. And it will be farther Allowable for Us to Consider, how far any Substance, Separated by the Help of such Additaments, Ought to pass for one of the *Tria Prima*; since by One Way of Handling the same Mixt Body it may according to the Nature of the Additaments, and the Method of Working upon it, be made to Afford differing Substances from those Obtainable from it by other Additaments, and another Method, nay and (as may appear by what I Formerly told You about Tartar) Differing from any of the Substances into which a Concrete is Divisible by the Fire without Additaments, though perhaps those Additaments do not, as Ingredients, enter the Composition of the Obtained Body, but only Diversify the Operation of the Fire upon the Concrete; and though that Concrete by the Fire alone may be Divided into a Number of Differing Substances, as Great as any of the Chymists that I have met with teach us that of the Elements to be. And having said thus much (sayes *Carneades*) to the Objection likely to be Propos'd by some Chymists, I am now to Examine that which I Foresee will be Confidently press'd by Divers Peripateticks, who, to Prove Fire to be the true Analyzer of Bodies, will Plead, That it is the very Definition of Heat given by *Aristotle*, and Generally Received, *Congregare Homogenea, & Heterogenea Segregare*, to Assemble Things of a Resembling, and Disjoyn those of a Differing Nature. To this I answer, That this Effect is far from being so Essential to Heat, as 'tis Generally Imagin'd; for it rather Seems, that the True and Genuine Property of Heat is, to set a Moving, and thereby to Dissociate the parts of Bodies, and Subdivide them into Minute Particles, without regard to their being Homogeneous or Heterogeneous, as is apparent in the Boyling of Water, the Distillation of Quicksilver, or the Exposing of Bodies to the action of the Fire, whose Parts either Are not (at least in that Degree of Heat Appear not) Dissimilar, where all that the Fire can do, is to Divide the Body into very Minute Parts which are of the same Nature with one another, and with their *Totum*, as their Reduction by Condensation Evinces. And even when the Fire seems most so *Congregare Homogenea, & Segregare Heterogenea*, it Produces that Effect but by Accident; For the Fire does but Dissolve the Cement, or rather Shatter the Frame, or [tructure [Errata: structure] that kept the Heterogeneous Parts of

Bodies together, under one Common Form; upon which Dissolution the Component Particles of the Mixt, being Freed and set at Liberty, do Naturally, and oftentimes without any Operation of the Fire, Associate themselves each with its Like, or rather do take those places which their Several Degrees of Gravity and Levity, Fixedness or Volatility (either Natural, or Adventitious from the Impression of the Fire) Assigne them. Thus in the Distillation (for Instance) of Man's Blood, the Fire do's First begin to Dissolve the *Nexus* or Cement of the Body; and then the Water, being the most Volatile, and Easy to be Extracted, is either by the Igneous Atomes, or the Agitation they are put into by the Fire, first carried up, till Forsaken by what carried it up, its Weight sinks it down into the Receiver: but all this while the other Principles of the Concrete Remain Unsever'd, and Require a stronger Degree of Heat to make a Separation of its more Fixt Elements; and therefore the Fire must be Increas'd which Carries over the Volatile Salt and the Spirit, they being, though Beleev'd to be Differing Principles, and though Really of Different Consistency, yet of an almost Equal Volatility. After them, as less Fugitive, comes over the Oyl, and leaves behinde the Earth and the *Alcali*, which being of an Equal Fixednesse, the Fire Severs them not, for all the Definition of the Schools. And if into a Red-hot Earthen or Iron Retort you cast the Matter to be Distill'd, You may Observe, as I have often done, that the Predominant Fire will Carry up all the Volatile Elements Confusedly in one Fume, which will afterwards take their Places in the Receiver, either according to the Degree of their Gravity, or according to the Exigency of their respective Textures; the Salt Adhering, for the most part, to the Sides and Top, and the Phlegme Fastening it self there too in great Drops, the Oyle and Spirit placing themselves Under, or Above one another, according as their Ponderousness makes them Swim or Sink. For 'tis Observable, that though Oyl or Liquid Sulphur be one of the Elements Separated by this Fiery *Analysis*, yet the Heat which Accidentally Unites the Particles of the other Volatile Principles, has not alwayes the same Operation on this, there being divers Bodies which Yield Two Oyls, whereof the One sinks to the Bottom of that Spirit on which the other Swims; as I can shew You in some Oyls of the same Deers Blood, which are yet by Me: Nay I can shew you Two Oyls carefully made of the same Parcel of Humane Blood, which not only Differ extreamly in Colour, but Swim upon one another without Mixture, and if by Agitation Confounded will of themselves Divorce again.

And that the Fire doth oftentimes divide Bodies, upon the account that some of their Parts are more Fixt, and some more Volatile, how far soever either of these Two may be from a pure Elementary Nature is Obvious enough, if Men would but heed it in the Burning of Wood, which the Fire Dissipates into Smoake and Ashes: For not only the latter of these is Confessedly made up of two such Differing Bodies as Earth and Salt; but the Former being condens'd into that Soot which adheres to our Chimneys, Discovers it self to Contain both Salt and Oyl, and Spirit and Earth, (and some Portion of Phlegme too) which being, all almost, Equally Volatile to that Degree of Fire which Forces them up, (the more Volatile Parts Helping perhaps, as well as the Urgency of the Fire, to carry up the more Fixt ones, as I have often Try'd in Dulcify'd **Colcothar**, Sublim'd by **Sal Armoniack** Blended with it) are carried Up together, but may afterwards be Separated by other Degrees of Fire, whose orderly Gradation allowes the Disparity of their Volatileness to Discover it self. Besides, if Differing Bodies United into one Mass be both sufficiently Fixt, the Fire finding no Parts Volatile enough to be Expell'd or carried up, makes no Separation at all; as may appear by a Mixture of Colliquated Silver and Gold, whose Component Metals may be easily Sever'd by **Aqua Fortis**, or **Aqua Regis** (according to the Predominancy of the Silver or the Gold) but in the Fire alone, though vehement, the Metals remain unsever'd, the Fire only dividing the Body into smaller Particles (whose Littlenesse may be argu'd from their Fluidity) in which either the little nimble Atoms of Fire, or its brisk and numberless strokes upon the Vessels, hinder Rest and Continuity, without any Sequestration of Elementary Principles. Moreover, the Fire sometimes does not Separate, so much as Unite, Bodies of a differing Nature; provided they be of an almost resembling Fixedness, and have in the Figure of their Parts an Aptnesse to Coalition, as we see in the making of many Plaisters, Oyntments, &c. And in such Metalline Mixtures as that made by Melting together two parts of clean Brass with one of pure Copper, of which some Ingenious Tradesmen cast such curious Patterns (for Gold and Silver Works) as I have sometimes taken great Pleasure to Look upon. Sometimes the Bodies mingled by the Fire are Differing enough as to Fixidity and Volatility, and yet are so combin'd by the first Operation of the Fire, that it self does scarce afterwards Separate them, but only Pulverize them; whereof an Instance is afforded us by the Common Preparation of **Mercurius Dulcis**, where the Saline Particles of the Vitriol, Sea Salt, and sometimes Nitre, Employ'd to make the Sublimate, do so unite themselves with the Mercurial Particles made use of, first to Make Sublimate, and then to Dulcifie it, that the Saline and Metalline Parts arise together in many successive Sublimations, as if they all made but one Body. And sometimes too the Fire does not only not Sever the Differing Elements of a Body, but Combine them so firmly, that Nature her self does very seldom, if ever, make Unions less Dissoluble. For the Fire meeting with some Bodies exceedingly and almost equally Fixt, instead of making a Separation, makes an Union so strict, that it self, alone, is unable to Dissolve it; As we see, when an Alcalizate Salt and the Terrestrial Residue of the Ashes are Incorporated with pure Sand, and by Vitrification made one permanent Body, (I mean the course or greenish sort of Glass) that mocks the greatest Violence of the Fire, which though able to Marry the Ingredients of it, yet is not able to Divorce them. I can shew you some pieces of Glass which I saw flow down from an Earthen Crucible purposely Expos'd for a good while, with Silver in it, to a very vehement Fire. And some that deal much in the Fusion of Metals Informe me, that the melting of a great part of a Crucible into Glass is no great Wonder in their Furnaces. I remember, I have Observ'd too in the Melting of great Quantities of Iron out of the Oar, by the Help of store of Charcoal (for they Affirm that Sea-Coal will not yield a Flame strong enough) that by the prodigious Vehemence of the Fire, Excited by vast Bellows (made to play by great Wheels turn'd about by Water) part of the Materials Expos'd to it was, instead of being Analyz'd, Colliquated, and turn'd into a Dark, Solid and very Ponderous Glass, and that in such Quantity, that in some places I have seen the very Highwayes, neer such Iron-works, mended with Heaps of such Lumps of Glasse, instead of Stones and Gravel. And I have also Observ'd, that some kind of Fire-stone it Self, having been employ'd in Furnaces wherein it was expos'd to very strong and lasting Fires, has had all its Fixt Parts so Wrought on by the Fire, as to be Perfectly Vitrifi'd, which I have try'd by Forcing from it Pretty large Pieces of Perfect and Transparent Glass. And lest You might think, *Eleutherius*, that the Question'd Definition of Heat may be Demonstrated, by the Definition which is wont to be given and Acquiesc'd in, of its contrary Quality, Cold, whose property is taught to be **tam Homogenea, quam Heterogenea congregare**; Give me leave to represent to You, that neither is this Definition unquestionable; for not to Mention the Exceptions, which a **Logician**, as such, may Take at it, I Consider that the Union of Heterogeneous Bodies which is Suppos'd to be the Genuine Production of Cold, is not Perform'd by every Degree of Cold. For we see for Instance that in the Urine of Healthy Men, when the Liquor has been Suffer'd a while to stand, the Cold makes a Separation of the Thinner Part from the Grosser, which Subsides to the Bottom, and Growes Opacous there; whereas if the Urinal be Warme, these Parts readily Mingle again, and the whole Liquor becomes Transparent as before. And when, by Glaciation, Wood, Straw, Dust, Water, &c. are Suppos'd to be United into one Lump of Ice, the Cold does not Cause any Real Union or Adunation, (if I may so Speak) of these Bodies, but only Hardening the Aqueous Parts of the Liquor into Ice, the other Bodies being Accidentally Present in that Liquor are frozen up in it, but not Really United. And accordingly if we Expose a Heap of Mony Consisting of Gold, Silver and Copper Coynes, or any other Bodies of Differing Natures, which are Destitute of Aqueous Moisture, Capable of Congelation, to never so intense a Cold, we find not that these Differing Bodies are at all thereby so much as Compacted, much less United together; and even in Liquors Themselves we find **Phaenomena** which Induce us to Question the Definition which we are examining. If **Paracelsus** his Authority were to be look't upon as a Sufficient Proof in matters of this Nature, I might here insist on that Process of his, whereby he Teaches that the Essence of Wine may be Sever'd from the Phlegme and Ignoble Part by the Assistance of Congelation: and because much Weight has been laid upon this Process, not only by **Paracelsians**, but other Writers, some of whom seem not to have perus'd it themselves, I shall give You the entire Passage in the Authors own Words, as I lately found them in the sixth Book of his **Archidoxis**, an Extract whereof I have yet about me; and it sounds thus. *De Vino sciendum est, faecem phlegmaque ejus esse Mineram, & Vini substantiam esse corpus in quo conservatur Essentia, prout auri in auro latet Essentia. Juxta quod Practicam nobis ad Memoriam ponimus, ut non obliviscamur, ad hunc modum: Recipe Vinum vetustissimum & optimum quod habere poteris, calore saporeque ad placitum, hoc in vas vitreum infundas ut tertiam ejus partem impleat, & sigillo Hermetis occlusum in equino ventre mensibus quatuor, & in continuato calore teneatur qui non deficiat. Quo peracto, Hyeme cum frigus & gelu maxime saeviunt, his per mensem exponatur ut congeletur. Ad hunc modum frigus vini spiritum una cum ejus* *substantia protrudit in vini centrum, ac separat a phlegmate: Congelatum abjice, quod vero congelatum non est, id Spiritum cum substantia esse judicato. Hunc in Pelicanum positum in arenae digestione non adeo calida per aliquod tempus manere finito; Postmodum eximito vini Magisterium, de quo locuti sumus.*

But I dare not *Eleu.* lay much Weight upon this Process, because I have found that if it were True, it would be but seldom Practicable in this Country upon the best Wine: for Though this present Winter hath been Extraordinary Cold, yet in very Keen Frosts accompanied with lasting Snowes, I have not been able in any Measure to Freeze a thin Vial full of Sack; and even with Snow and Salt I could Freeze little more then the Surface of it; and I suppose *Eleu.* that tis not every Degree of Cold that is Capable of Congealing Liquors, which is able to make such an *Analysis* (if I may so call it) of them by Separating their Aqueous and Spirituous Parts; for I have sometimes, though not often, frozen severally, Red-wine, Urine and Milk, but could not Observe the expected Separation. And the Dutch-Men that were forc'd to Winter in that Icie Region neer the Artick Circle, call'd *Nova Zembla*, although they relate, as we shall see below, that there was a Separation of Parts made in their frozen Beer about the middle of *November*, yet of the Freezing of their Back [Errata: Sack] in *December* following they give but this Account: *Yea and our Sack, which is so hot, was Frozen very hard, so that when we were every Man to have his part, we were forc'd to melt it in the Fire; which we shar'd every second Day, about half a Pinte for a Man, wherewith we were forc'd to sustain our selves.* In which words they imply not, that their Back [Errata: Sack] was divided by the Frost into differing Substances, after such manner as their Beer had been. All which notwithstanding, *Eleu.* suppose that it may be made to appear, that even Cold sometimes may *Congregare Homogenea, & Heterogenea Segregare*: and to Manifest this I may tell you, that I did once, purposely cause to be Decocted in fair Water a Plant abounding with Sulphureous and Spirituous Parts, and having expos'd the Decoction to a keen North-Wind in a very Frosty Night, I observ'd, that the more Aqueous Parts of it were turn'd by the next Morning into Ice, towards the innermost part of which, the more Agile and Spirituous parts, as I then conjectur'd, having Retreated, to shun as much as might be their Environing Enemy, they had there preserv'd themselves unfrozen in the Form of a high colour'd Liquor, the Aqueous and Spirituous parts having been so sleightly (Blended rather than) United in the Decoction, that they were easily Separable by such a Degree of Cold as would not have been able to have Divorc'd the Parts of Urine or Wine, which by Fermentation or Digestion are wont, as Tryal has inform'd me, to be more intimately associated each with other. But I have already intimated, *Eleutherius*, that I shall not Insist on this Experiment, not only because, having made it but once I may possibly have been mistaken in it; but also (and that principally) because of that much more full and eminent Experiment of the Separative Virtue of extream Cold, that was made, against their Wills, by the foremention'd Dutch men that Winter'd in *Nova Zembla*; the Relation of whose Voyage being a very scarce Book, it will not be amiss to give you that Memorable part of it which concerns our present Theme, as I caus'd the Passage to be extracted out of the Englished Voyage it self.

"*Gerard de Veer*, *John Cornelyson* and Others, sent out of *Amsterdam*, *Anno Dom.* 1596. being forc'd by unseasonable Weather to Winter in *Nova Zembla*, neer Ice-Haven; on the thirteenth of *October*, Three of us (sayes the Relation) went aboard the Ship, and laded a Sled with Beer; but when we had laden it, thinking to go to our House with it, suddenly there arose such a Winde, and so great a Storm and Cold, that we were forc'd to go into the Ship again, because we were not able to stay without; and we could not get the Beer into the Ship again, but were forc'd to let it stand without upon the Sled: the Fourteenth, as we came out of the Ship, we found the Barrel of Beer standing upon the Sled, but it was fast frozen at the Heads; yet by reason of the great Cold, the Beer that purg'd out froze as hard upon the Side of the Barrel, as if it had been glu'd thereon: and in that sort we drew it to our House, and set the Barrel an end, and drank it up; but first we were forc'd to melt the Beer, for there was scarce any unfrozen Beer in the barrel; but in that thick Yiest that was unfrozen lay the Strength of the Beer, so that it was too strong to drink alone, and that which was frozen tasted like Water; and being melted we Mix'd one with the other, and so drank it; but it had neither Strength nor Taste."

And on this Occasion I remember, that having the last very Sharp Winter purposely try'd to Freeze, among other Liquors, some Beer moderately strong, in Glass Vessels, with Snow and Salt, I observ'd, that there came out of the Neck a certain thick Substance, which, it seems, was much better able then the rest of the Liquor (that I found turn'd into Ice) to resist a Frost, and which, by its Colour and consistence seem'd mafestly [Transcriber's Note: manifestly] enough to be Yiest, whereat, I confess, I somewhat marvail'd, because I did not either discerne by the Taste, or find by Enquiry, that the Beer was at all too New to be very fit to be Drank. I might confirm the Dutchmens Relation, by what happen'd a while since to a neere Friend of mine, who complained to me, that having Brew'd some Beer or Ale for his own drinking in **Holland** (where he then dwelt) the Keenness of the late bitter Winter froze the Drink so as to reduce it into Ice, and a small Proportion of a very Strong and Spirituous Liquor. But I must not entertain you any longer concerning Cold, not onely because you may think I have but lost my way into a Theme which does not directly belong to my present Undertaking; but because I have already enlarg'd my self too much upon the first Consideration I propos'd, though it appears so much a Paradox, that it seem'd to Require that I should say much to keep it from being thought a meere Extravagance; yet since I Undertook but to make the common Assumption of our Chymists and **Aristotelians** appear Questionable, I hope I have so Perform'd that Task, that I may now Proceed to my Following Considerations, and Insist lesse on them than I have done on the First.

The Second Part.

The Second Consideration I Desire to have Notice Taken of, is This, That it is not so Sure, as Both Chymists and *Aristotelians* are wont to Think it, that every Seemingly Similar or Distinct Substance that is Separated from a Body by the Help of the Fire, was Pre existent in it as a Principle or Element of it.

That I may not make this Paradox a Greater then I needs must, I will First Briefly Explain what the Proposition means, before I proceed to Argue for it.

And I suppose You will easily Believe That I do not mean that any thing is separable from a Body by Fire, that was not Materially pre-existent in it; for it Far Exceeds the power of Meerly Naturall Agents, and Consequently of the Fire, to produce anew, so Much as one Atome of Matter, which they can but Modifie and Alter, not Create; which is so Obvious a Truth, that almost all Sects of Philosophers have Deny'd the Power of producing Matter to Second Causes; and the *Epicureans* and some Others have Done the Like, in Reference to their Gods themselves.

Nor does the Proposition peremptorily Deny but that some Things Obtain'd by the Fire from a Mixt Body, may have been more then barely Materially pre-existent in it, since there are Concretes, which before they be Expos'd to the Fire afford us several Documents of their abounding, some with Salt, and Others with Sulphur. For it will serve the present Turn, if it appear that diverse things Obtain'd from a Mixt Body expos'd to the Fire, were not its Ingredients Before: for if this be made to appear it, will [Errata: appear, it will] be Rationall enough to suspect that Chymists may Decieve themselves, and Others, in concluding Resolutely and Universally, those Substances to be the Elementary Ingredients of Bodies barely separated by the Fire, of which it yet may be Doubted Whether there be such or No; at least till some other Argument then that drawn from the *Analysis* be Brought to resolve the

Doubt.

That then which I Mean by the Proposition I am Explaining, is, That it may without Absurdity be Doubted whether or no the Differing Substances Obtainable from a Concrete Dissipated by the Fire were so Exsistent in it in that Forme (at least as to their minute Parts) wherein we find them when the *Analysis* is over, that the Fire did only Dis-joyne and Extricate the Corpuscles of one Principle from those of the other wherewith before they were Blended.

Having thus Explain'd my Proposition, I shall endeavour to do two things, to prove it; The first of which is to shew that such Substances as Chymists call Principles May be produc'd *De novo* (as they speak.) And the other is to make it probable that by the Fire we may Actually obtain from some Mixt Bodies such Substances as were not in the Newly Expounded sence, pre-existent in them.

To begin then with the First of these, I Consider that if it be as true as 'tis probable, that Compounded Bodies Differ from One Another but in the Various Textures Resulting from the Bigness, Shape, Motion, and contrivance of their smal parts, It will not be Irrationall to conceive that one and the same parcel of the Universal Matter may by Various Alterations and Contextures be brought to Deserve the Name, somtimes of a Sulphureous, and sometimes of a Terrene, or Aqueous Body. And this I could more largely Explicate, but that our Friend Mr. *Boyle* has promis'd us something about Qualities, wherein the Theme I now willingly Resign him, Will I Question not be Studiously Enquired into. Wherefore what I shall now advance in favour of what I have lately Deliver'd shall be Deduc'd from Experiments made Divers Years since. The first of which would have been much more considerable, but that by some intervening Accidents I was Necessitated to lose the best time of the year, for a trial of the Nature of that I design'd; it being about he [Transcriber's Note: the] middle of *May* before I was able to begin an Experiment which should have then been two moneths old; but such as it was, it will not perhaps be impertinent to Give You this Narrative of it. At the time newly Mention'd, I caus'd My Gardiner (being by Urgent Occasions Hinder'd from being present myself) to dig out a convenient quantity of good Earth, and dry it well in an Oven, to weigh it, to put it in an Earthen pot almost level with the Surface of the ground, and to set in it a selected seed he had before received from me, for that purpose, of Squash, which is an Indian kind of Pompion, that Growes apace; this seed I Ordered Him to Water only with Rain or Spring Water. I did not (when my Occasions permitted me to visit it) without delight behold how fast it Grew, though unseasonably sown; but the Hastning Winter Hinder'd it from attaining any thing neer its due and Wonted magnitude; (for I found the same Autumn, in my Garden, some of those plants, by Measure, as big about as my Middle) and made me order the having it taken Up; Which about the Middle of *October* was carefully Done by the same Gardiner, who a while after sent me this account of it; *I have Weighed the Pompion with the Stalk and Leaves, all which Weighed three pound wanting a quarter; Then I took the Earth, baked it as formerly, and found it just as much as I did at First, which made me think I had not dry'd it Sufficiently: then I put it into the Oven twice More, after the Bread was Drawn, and Weighed it the Second time, but found it Shrink little or nothing.*

But to deal Candidly with You, *Eleutherius*, I must not conceal from You the Event of another Experiment of this Kind made this present Summer, wherein the Earth seems to have been much more Wasted; as may appear by the following account, Lately sent me by the same Gardiner, in these Words. To give You an Account of your Cucumbers, I have Gain'd two Indifferent Fair Ones, the Weight of them is ten Pound and a Halfe, the Branches with the Roots Weighed four Pounds wanting two Ounces; and when I had weighed them I took the Earth, and bak'd it in several small Earthen Dishes in an Oven; and when I had so done, I found the Earth wanted a Pound and a halfe of what it was formerly; yet I was not satisfi'd, doubting the Earth was not dry: I put it into an Oven the Second Time, (after the Bread was drawn) and after I had taken it out and weighed it, I found it to be the Same Weight: So I Suppose there was no Moisture left in the Earth. Neither do I think that the Pound and Halfe that was wanting was Drawn away by the Cucumber but a great Part of it in the Ordering was in Dust (and the like) wasted: (the Cucumbers are kept by themselves, lest You should send for them.) *But yet in this Tryal,* Eleutherius, it appears that though some of the Earth, or rather the dissoluble Salt harbour'd in it, were wasted, the main Body of the Plant consisted of Transmuted Water. And I might add, that a year after I caus'd the formerly mentioned Experiment, touching large Pompions, to be reiterated, with so good success, that if my memory does not much mis-inform me, it did not only much surpass any that I made before, but seem'd strangely to conclude what I am pleading for; though (by reason I have un-happily lost the particular Account my Gardiner writ me up of the Circumstances) I dare not insist upon them. The like Experiment may be as conveniently try'd with the seeds of any Plant, whose growth is hasty, and its size Bulky. If Tobacco will in These Cold Climates Grow well in Earth undung'd, it would not be amiss to make a Tryal with it; for 'tis an annual Plant, that arises where it prospers, sometimes as high as a Tall Man; and I have had leaves of it in my Garden neer a Foot and a Halfe broad. But the next time I Try this Experiment, it shall be with several seeds of the same sort, in the same pot of Earth, that so the event may be the more Conspicuous. But because every Body has not Conveniency of time and place for this Experiment neither, I made in my Chamber, some shorter and more Expeditions [Transcriber's Note: Expeditious] Tryals. I took a Top of Spearmint, about an Inch Long, and put it into a good Vial full of Spring water, so as the upper part of the Mint was above the neck of the Glass, and the lower part Immers'd in the Water; within a few Dayes this Mint began to shoot forth Roots into the Water, and to display its Leaves, and aspire upwards; and in a short time it had numerous Roots and Leaves, and these very strong and fragrant of the Odour of the Mint: but the Heat of my Chamber, as I suppose, kill'd the Plant when it was grown to have a pretty thick Stalk, which with the various and ramified Roots, which it shot into the Water as if it had been Earth, presented in its Transparent Flower-pot a Spectacle not unpleasant to be-hold. The like I try'd with sweet Marjoram, and I found the Experiment succeed also, though somewhat more slowly, with Balme and Peniroyal, to name now no other Plants. And one of these Vegetables, cherish'd only by Water, having obtain'd a competent Growth, I did, for Tryals sake, cause to be Distill'd in a small Retort, and thereby obtain'd some Phlegme, a little Empyreumaticall Spirit, a small Quan-tity of adust Oyl, and a ***Caput mortuum***; which appearing to be a Coal concluded it to consist of Salt and Earth: but the Quantity of it was so small that I forbore to Calcine it. The Water I us'd to nourish this Plant was not shifted nor renewed; and I chose Spring-water rather than Rain-water, because the latter is more discern-ably a kinde of [Greek: panspermia], which, though it be granted to be freed from grosser Mixtures, seems yet to Contain in it, besides the Steams of several Bodies wandering in the Air, which may be suppos'd to impregnate it, a certain Spirituous Substance, which may be Extracted out of it, and is by some mistaken for the Spirit of the World Corporify'd, upon what Grounds, and with what Probability, I may elsewhere perchance, but must not now, Discourse to you.

But perhaps I might have sav'd a great part of my Labour. For I finde that *Helmont* (an Author more considerable for his Experiments than many Learned men are pleas'd to think him) having had an Opportunity to prosecute an Experiment much of the same nature with those I have been now speaking of, for five Years together, obtain'd at the end of that time so notable a Quantity of Transmuted Water, that I should scarce Think it fit to have his Experiment, and Mine Mention'd together, were it not that the Length of Time Requisite to this may deterr the Curiosity of some, and exceed the leasure of Others; and partly, that so Paradoxical a Truth as that which these Experiments seem to hold forth, needs to be Confirm'd by more Witnesses then one, especially since the Extravagancies and Untruths to be met with in *Helmonts* Treatise of the Magnetick Cure of Wounds, have made his Testimonies suspected in his other Writings, though as to some of the Unlikely matters of Fact he delivers in them, I might safely undertake to be his Compurgator. But that Experiment of his which I was mentioning to You, he sayes, was this. He took 200 pound of Earth dry'd in an Oven, and having put it into an Earthen Vessel and moisten'd it with Raine water he planted in it the Trunk of a Willow tree of five pound Weight; this he Water'd, as need required, with Rain or with Distill'd Water; and to keep the Neighbouring Earth from getting into the Vessell, he employ'd a plate of Iron tinn'd over and perforated with many holes. Five years being efflux'd, he took out the Tree and weighed it, and (with computing the leaves that fell during four Autumnes) he found it to weigh 169 pound, and about three Ounces. And Having again Dry'd the Earth it grew in, he found it want of its Former Weight of 200 Pound, about a couple only of Ounces; so that 164 pound of the Roots, Wood, and Bark, which Constituted the Tree, seem to have Sprung from the Water. And though it appears not that *Helmont* had the Curiosity to make any *Analysis* of this Plant, yet what I lately told You I did to One of the Vegetables I nourish'd with Water only, will I suppose keep You from Doubting that if he had Distill'd this Tree, it would have afforded him the like Distinct Substances as another Vegetable of the same kind. I need not Subjoyne that I had it also in my thoughts to try how Experiments to the same purpose with those I related to You would succeed in other Bodies then Vegetables, because importunate Avocations having hitherto hinder'd me from putting my Design in Practise, I can yet speak but Confecturally [Transcriber's Note: Conjecturally] of the Success: but the best is, that the Experiments already made and mention'd to you need not the Assistance of new Ones, to Verifie as much as my present task makes it concern me to prove by Experiments of this Nature.

One would suspect (sayes *Eleutherius* after his long silence) by what You have been discoursing, that You are not far from *Helmonts* Opinion about the Origination of Compound Bodies, and perhaps too dislike not the Arguments which he imploes to prove it.

What *Helmontian* Opinion, and what Arguments do you mean (askes *Carneades*.)

What You have been Newly Discoursing (replies *Eleutherius*) tells us, that You cannot but know that this bold and Acute Spagyrist scruples not to Assert that all mixt Bodies spring from one Element; and that Vegetables, Animals, Marchasites, Stones, Metalls, &c. are Materially but simple Water disguis'd into these Various Formes, by the plastick or Formative Virtue of their seeds. And as for his Reasons you may find divers of them scatter'd up and down his writings; the considerabl'st of which seem to be these three; The Ultimate Reduction of mixt Bodies into Insipid Water, the Vicissitude of the supposed Elements, and the production of perfectly mixt Bodies out of simple Water. And first he affirmes that the *Sal circulatus Paracelsi*, or his Liquor *Alkahest*, does adequately resolve Plants, Animals, and Mineralls into one Liquor or more, according to their several internall Disparities of Parts (without *Caput Mortuum*, or the Destruction of their seminal Virtues;) and that the *Alkahest* being abstracted from these Liquors in the same weight and Virtue wherewith it Dissolv'd them, the Liquors may by frequent Cohobations from chalke or some other idoneous matter, be Totally depriv'd of their seminal Endowments, and return at last to their first matter, Insipid Water; some other wayes he proposes here and there, to divest some particular Bodies of their borrow'd shapes, and make them remigrate to their first Simplicity. The second Topick whence *Helmont* drawes his Arguments, to prove Water to be the Material cause of Mixt Bodies, I told You was this, that the other suppos'd Elements may be transmuted into one another. But the Experiments by him here and there produc'd on this Occasion, are so uneasie to be made and to be judg'd of, that I shall not insist on them; not to mention, that if they were granted to be true, his Inference from them is somewhat disputable; and therefore I shall pass on to tell You, That as, in his First Argument, our Paradoxical Author endeavours to prove Water the Sole Element of Mixt Bodies, by their Ultimate Resolution, when by his ***Alkahest***, or some other conquering Agent, the Seeds have been Destroy'd, which Disguis'd them, or when by time those seeds are Weari'd or Exantlated or unable to Act their Parts upon the Stage of the Universe any Longer: So in His Third Argument he Endeavours to evince the same Conclusion, by the constitution of Bodies which he asserts to be nothing but Water Subdu'd by Seminal Virtues. Of this he gives here and there in his Writings several Instances, as to Plants and Animals; but divers of them being Difficult either to be try'd or to be Understood, and others of them being not altogether Unobnoxious to Exceptions, I think you have singl'd out the Principal and less Questionable Experiment when you lately mention'd that of the Willow Tree. And having thus, Continues ***Eleutherius***, to Answer your Question, given you a Summary Account of what I am Confident You know better then I do, I shall be very glad to receive Your Sence of it, if the giving it me will not too much Divert You from the Prosecution of your Discourse.

That ***If*** (replies ***Carneades***) was not needlessly annex'd: for thorowly to examine such an Hypothesis and such Arguments would require so many Considerations, and Consequently so much time, that I should not now have the Liesure [Errata: leasure] to perfect such a Digression, and much less to finish my Principle [Errata: principal] Discourse. Yet thus much I shall tell You at present, that you need not fear my rejecting this Opinion for its Novelty; since, however the ***Helmontians*** may in complement to their Master pretend it to be a new Discovery, Yet though the Arguments be for the most part his, the Opinion it self is very Antient: For ***Diogenes Laertius*** and divers other Authors speak of ***Thales***, as the first among the ***Graecians*** that made disquisitions upon nature. And of this ***Thales***, I Remember, ***Tully***[5] informes us, that he taught all things were at first made of Water. And it seems by ***Plutarch*** and ***Justin Martyr***, that the Opinion was Ancienter then he: For they tell us that he us'd to defend his Tenet by the Testimony of ***Homer***. And a Greek Author, (the ***Scholiast*** of ***Apollonius***) upon these Words

[Greek: Ex iliou [Transcriber's Note: iluos] eblastese chthon aute],[6]

The Earth of Slime was made,

Affirms (out of *Zeno*) that the *Chaos*, whereof all things were made, was, according to *Hesiod*, Water; which, settling first, became Slime, and then condens'd into solid Earth. And the same Opinion about the Generation of Slime seems to have been entertain'd by *Orpheus*, out of whom one of the Antients[7] cites this Testimony,

[Greek: Ek tou hydatos ilui katiste.]

Of Water Slime was made.

[5: De Natura Deorum.]
[6: Argonaut. 4.]
[7: Athenagoras.]

It seems also by what is delivered in *Strabo*[8] out of another Author, concerning the *Indians*, That they likewise held that all things had differing Beginnings, but that of which the World was made, was Water. And the like Opinion has been by some of the Antients ascrib'd to the *Phoenicians*, from whom *Thales* himself is conceiv'd to have borrow'd it; as probably the Greeks did much of their Theologie, and, as I am apt to think, of their Philosophy too; since the Devising of the Atomical *Hypothesis* commonly ascrib'd to *Lucippus* and his Disciple *Democritus*, is by Learned Men attributed to one *Moschus* a *Phoenician*. And possibly the Opinion is yet antienter than so; For 'tis known that the *Phoenicians* borrow'd most of their Learning from the *Hebrews*. And among those that acknowledge the Books of *Moses*, many have been inclin'd to think Water to have been the Primitive and Universal Matter, by perusing the Beginning of *Genesis*, where the Waters seem to be mention'd as the Material Cause, not only of Sublunary Compounded Bodies, but of all those that make up the Universe; whose Component Parts did orderly, as it were, emerge out of that vast Abysse, by the Operation of the Spirit of God, who is said to have been moving Himself as hatching Females do (as the Original [Hebrew: merachephet], **Meracephet**[9] is said to Import, and as it seems to signifie in one of the two other places, wherein alone I have met with it in the Hebrew Bible)[10] upon the Face of the Waters; which being, as may be suppos'd, Divinely Impregnated with the seeds of all things, were by that productive Incubation qualify'd to produce them. But you, I presume, Expect that I should Discourse of this Matter like a Naturalist, not a Philologer. Wherefore I shall add, to Countenance **Helmont's** Opinion, That whereas he gives not, that I remember, any Instance of any Mineral Body, nor scarce of any Animal, generated of Water, a French Chymist, **Monsieur de Rochas**, has presented his Readers an Experiment, which if it were punctually such as he has deliver'd it, is very Notable. He then, Discoursing of the Generation of things according to certain Chymical and Metaphorical Notions (which I confess are not to me Intelligible) sets down, among divers Speculations not pertinent to our Subject, the following Narrative, which I shall repeat to you the sence of in English, with as little variation from the Literal sence of the French words, as my memory will enable me. **Having** (says he) **discern'd such great Wonders by the Natural Operation of Water, I would know what may be done with it by Art Imitating Nature. Wherefore I took Water which I well knew not to be compounded, nor to be mix'd with any other thing than that Spirit of Life** (whereof he had spoken before;) **and with a Heat Artificial, Continual and Proportionate, I prepar'd and dispos'd it by the above mention'd Graduations of Coagulation, Congelation, and Fixation, untill it was turn'd into Earth, which Earth produc'd Animals, Vegetables and Minerals. I tell not what Animals, Vegetables and Minerals, for that is reserv'd for another Occasion: but the Animals did Move of themselves, Eat, &c.--and by the true Anatomie I made of them, I found that they were compos'd of much Sulphur, little Mercury, and less Salt.--The Minerals began to grow and encrease by converting into their own Nature one part of the Earth thereunto dispos'd; they were solid and heavy. And by this truly Demonstrative Science, namely Chymistry, I found that they were compos'd of much Salt, little Sulphur, and less Mercury.**

[8: Universarum rerum primordia diverta esse, faciendi autem mundi initium aquam. Strabo. Geograp. lib. 15. circa medium.]

[9: Deuter. 32. 11.]

[10: Jerem. 23. 9.]

But (sayes *Carneades*) I have some Suspitions concerning this strange Relation, which make me unwilling to Declare an Opinion of it, unless I were satisfied concerning divers Material Circumstances that our Author has left unmentioned; though as for the Generation of Living Creatures, both Vegetable and Sensitive, it needs not seem Incredible, since we finde that our common water (which indeed is often Impregnated with Variety of Seminal Principles and Rudiments) being long kept in a quiet place will putrifie and stink, and then perhaps too produce Moss and little Worms, or other Insects, according to the nature of the Seeds that were lurking in it. I must likewise desire you to take Notice, that as *Helmont* gives us no Instance of the Production of Minerals out of Water, so the main Argument that he employ's to prove that they and other Bodies may be resolv'd into water, is drawn from the Operations of his *Alkahest*, and consequently cannot be satisfactorily Examin'd by You and Me.

Yet certainly (sayes *Eleutherius*) You cannot but have somewhat wonder'd as well as I, to observe how great a share of Water goes to the making up of Divers Bodies, whose Disguises promise nothing neere so much. The Distillation of Eeles, though it yielded me some Oyle, and Spirit, and Volatile Salt, besides the *Caput mortuum*, yet were all these so disproportionate to the Phlegm that came from them (and in which at first they boyl'd as in a Pot of Water) that they seem'd to have bin nothing but coagulated Phlegm, which does likewise strangely abound in Vipers, though they are esteem'd very hot in Operation, and will in a Convenient Aire survive some dayes the loss of their Heads and Hearts, so vigorous is their Vivacity. Mans Bloud it self as Spirituous, and as Elaborate a Liquor as 'tis reputed, does so abound in Phlegm, that, the other Day, Distilling some of it on purpose to try the Experiment (as I had formerly done in Deers Bloud) out of about seven Ounces and a half of pure Bloud we drew neere six Ounces of Phlegm, before any of the more operative Principles began to arise, and Invite us to change the Receiver. And to satisfie my self that some of these Animall Phlegms were void enough of Spirit to deserve that Name, I would not content my self to taste them only, but fruitlesly pour'd on them acid Liquors, to try if they contain'd any Volatile Salt or Spirit, which (had there been any there) would probably have discover'd it self by making an Ebullition with the affused Liquor. And now I mention Corrosive Spirits, I am minded to Informe you, That though they seem to be nothing else but Fluid Salts, yet they abound in Water, as you may Observe, if either you Entangle, and so Fix their Saline Part, by making them Corrode some idoneous Body, or else if you mortifie it with a contrary Salt; as I have very manifestly Observ'd in the making a Medecine somewhat like *Helmont's Balsamus Samech*, with Distill'd Vinager instead of Spirit of Wine, wherewith he prepares it: For you would scarce Beleeve (what I have lately Observ'd) that of that acid Spirit, the Salt of Tartar, from which it is Distill'd, will by mortifying and retaining the acid Salt turn into worthless Phlegm neere twenty times its weight, before it be so fully Impregnated as to rob no more Distill'd Vinager of its Salt. And though Spirit of Wine Exquisitely rectify'd seem of all Liquors to be the most free from Water, it being so Igneous that it will Flame all away without leaving the least Drop behinde it, yet even this Fiery Liquor is by *Helmont* not improbably affirm'd, in case what he relates be True, to be Materially Water, under a Sulphureous Disguise: For, according to him, in the making that excellent Medecine, *Paracelsus* his *Balsamus Samech*, (which is nothing but *Sal Tartari* dulcify'd by Distilling from it Spirit of Wine till the Salt be sufficiently glutted with its Sulphur, and suffer [Errata: and till it suffer] the Liquor to be drawn off, as strong as it was pour'd on) when the Salt of Tartar from which it is Distill'd hath retain'd, or depriv'd it of the Sulphureous parts of the Spirit of Wine, the rest, which is incomparably the greater part of the Liquor, will remigrate into Phlegm. I added that Clause [*In case what he Relates be True*] because I have not as yet sufficiently try'd it my self. But not only something of Experiment keeps me from thinking it, as many Chymists do, absurd, (though I have, as well as they, in vain try'd it with ordinary Salt of Tartar;) but besides that *Helmont* often Relates it, and draws Consequences from it; A Person noted for his Sobernesse and Skill in Spagyrical Preparations, having been askt by me, Whether the Experiment might not be made to succeed, if the Salt and Spirit were prepar'd according to a way suitable to my Principles, he affirm'd to me, that he had that way I propos'd made *Helmont's* Experiment succeed very well, without adding any thing to the Salt and Spirit. But our way is neither short nor Easie.

I have indeed (sayes *Carneades*) sometimes wonder'd to see how much Phlegme may be obtain'd from Bodies by the Fire. But concerning that Phlegme I may anon have Occasion to note something, which I therefore shall not now anticipate. But to return to the Opinion of *Thales*, and of *Helmont*, I consider, that supposing the *Alkahest* could reduce all Bodies into water, yet whether that water, because insipid, must be Elementary, may not groundlesly be doubted; For I remember the Candid and Eloquent *Petrus Laurembergius* in his Notes upon *Sala's* Aphorismes affirmes, that he saw an insipid *Menstruum* that was a powerfull Dissolvent, and (if my Memory do not much mis-informe me) could dissolve Gold. And the water which may be Drawn from Quicksilver without Addition, though it be almost Tastless, You will I believe think of a differing Nature from simple Water, especially if you Digest in it Appropriated Mineralls. To which I shall add but this, that this Consideration may be further extended. For I see no Necessity to conceive that the Water mention'd in the Beginning of *Genesis*, as the Universal Matter, was simple and Elementary Water; since though we should Suppose it to have been an Agitated Congeries or Heap consisting of a great Variety of Seminal Principles and Rudiments, and of other Corpuscles fit to be subdu'd and Fashion'd by them, it might yet be a Body Fluid like Water, in case the Corpuscles it was made up of, were by their Creator made small enough, and put into such an actuall Motion as might make them Glide along one another. And as we now say, the Sea consists of Water, notwithstanding [Errata: (notwithstanding] the Saline, Terrestrial, and other Bodies mingl'd with it,) such a Liquor may well enough be called Water, because that was the greatest of the known Bodies whereunto it was like; Though, that a Body may be Fluid enough to appear a Liquor, and yet contain Corpuscles of a very differing Nature, You will easily believe, if You but expose a good Quantity of Vitriol in a strong Vessel to a Competent Fire. For although it contains both Aqueous, Earthy, Saline, Sulphureous, and Metalline Corpuscles, yet the whole Mass will at first be Fluid like water, and boyle like a seething pot.

I might easily (Continues *Carneades*) enlarge my self on such Considerations, if I were Now Oblig'd to give You my Judgment of the *Thalesian*, and *Helmontian*, *Hypothesis*. But Whether or no we conclude that all things were at first Generated of Water, I may Deduce from what I have try'd Concerning the Growth of Vegetables, nourish'd with water, all that I now propos'd to my Self or need at present to prove, namely that Salt, Spirit, Earth, and ev'n Oyl (though that be thought of all Bodies the most opposite to Water) may be produc'd out of Water;

and consequently that a Chymical Principle as well as a Peripatetick Element, may (in some cases) be Generated anew, or obtain'd from such a parcel of Matter as was not endow'd with the form of such a principle or Element before.

And having thus, **Eleutherius**, Evinc'd that 'tis possible that such Substances as those that Chymists are wont to call their **Tria Prima**, may be Generated, anew: I must next Endeavour to make it Probable, that the Operation of the Fire does Actually (sometimes) not only divide Compounded Bodies into smal Parts, but Compound those Parts after a new Manner; whence Consequently, for ought we Know, there may Emerge as well Saline and Sulphureous Substances, as Bodies of other Textures. And perhaps it will assist us in our Enquiry after the Effects of the Operations of the Fire upon other Bodies, to Consider a little, what it does to those Mixtures which being Productions of the Art of Man, We best know the Composition of. You may then be pleas'd to take Notice that though Sope is made up by the Sope-Boylers of Oyle or Grease, and Salt, and Water Diligently Incorporated together, yet if You expose the Mass they Constitute to a Graduall Fire in a Retort, You shall then indeed make a Separation, but not of the same Substances that were United into Sope, but of others of a Distant and yet not an Elementary Nature, and especially of an Oyle very sharp and Faetid, and of a very Differing Quality from that which was Employ'd to make the Sope: fo [Errata: so] if you Mingle in a due Proportion, **Sal Armoniack** with Quick-Lime, and Distill them by Degrees of Fire, You shall not Divide the **Sal Armoniack** from the Quick-Lime, though the one be a Volatile, and the other a Fix'd Substance, but that which will ascend will be a Spirit much more Fugitive, Penetrant, and stinking, then **Sal Armoniack**; and there will remain with the Quick-Lime all or very near all the Sea Salt that concurr'd to make up the **Sal Armoniack**; concerning which Sea Salt I shall, to satisfie You how well it was United to the Lime, informe You, that I have by making the Fire at length very Vehement, caus'd both the Ingredients to melt in the Retort it self into one Mass and such Masses are apt to Relent in the Moist Air. If it be here Objected, that these Instances are taken from factitious Concretes which are more Compounded then those which Nature produces; I shall reply, that besides that I have Mention'd them as much to Illustrate what I propos'd, as to prove it, it will be Difficult to Evince that Nature her self does not make Decompound Bodies, I mean mingle together such mixt Bodies as are already Compounded of Elementary, or rather of more simple ones. For Vitriol (for Instance) though I have sometimes taken it out of Minerall Earths, where Nature had without any assistance of Art prepar'd it to my Hand, is really, though Chymists are pleas'd to reckon it among Salts, a De-compounded Body Consisting (as I shall have occasion to declare anon) of a Terrestriall Substance, of a Metal, and also of at least one Saline Body, of a peculiar and not Elementary Nature. And we see also in Animals, that their blood may be compos'd of Divers very Differing Mixt Bodies, since we find it observ'd that divers Sea-Fowle tast rank of the Fish on which they ordinarily feed; and *Hipocrates* himself Observes, that a Child may be purg'd by the Milke of the Nurse, if she have taken *Elaterium*; which argues that the purging Corpuscles of the Medicament Concurr to make up the Milke of the Nurse; and that white Liquor is generally by Physitians suppos'd to be but blanch'd and alter'd Blood. And I remember I have observ'd, not farr from the *Alps*, that at a certain time of the Year the Butter of that Country was very Offensive to strangers, by reason of the rank tast of a certain Herb, whereon the Cows were then wont plentifully to feed. But (proceeds *Carneades*) to give you Instances of another kind, to shew that things may be obtain'd by the Fire from a Mixt Body that were not Pre-existent in it, let Me Remind You, that from many Vegetables there may without any Addition be Obtain'd Glass, a Body, which I presume You will not say was Pre-existent in it, but produc'd by the Fire. To which I shall add but this one Example more, namely that by a certain Artificial way of handling Quicksilver, You may without Addition separate from it at least a 5th. or 4th. part of a clear Liquor, which with an Ordinary Peripatetick would pass for Water, and which a Vulgar Chymist would not scruple to call Phlegme, and which, for ought I have yet seen or heard, is not reducible into Mercury again, and Consequently is more then a Disguise of it. Now besides that divers Chymists will not allow Mercury to have any or at least any Considerable Quantity of either of the Ignoble Ingredients, Earth and Water; Besides this, I say, the great Ponderousness of Quicksilver makes it very unlikely that it can have so much Water in it as may be thus obtain'd from it, since Mercury weighs 12 or 14 times as much as water of the same Bulk. Nay for a further Confirmation of this Argument, I will add this Strange Relation, that two Friends of mine, the one a Physitian, and the other a Mathematician, and both of them Persons of unsuspected Credit, have Solemnly assured me, that after many Tryals they made, to reduce Mercury into Water, in Order to a Philosophicall Work, upon

Gold (which yet, by the way, I know prov'd Unsuccesfull) they did once by divers Cohobations reduce a pound of Quicksilver into almost a pound of Water, and this without the Addition of any other Substance, but only by pressing the Mercury by a Skillfully Manag'd Fire in purposely contriv'd Vessels. But of these Experiments our Friend (sayes *Carneades*, pointing at the Register of this Dialogue) will perhaps give You a more Particular Account then it is necessary for me to do: Since what I have now said may sufficiently evince, that the Fire may sometimes as well alter Bodies as divide them, and by it we may obtain from a Mixt Body what was not Pre-existent in it. And how are we sure that in no other Body what we call Phlegme is barely separated, not Produc'd by the Action of the Fire: Since so many other Mixt Bodies are of a much less Constant, and more alterable Nature, then Mercury, by many Tricks it is wont to put upon Chymists, and by the Experiments I told You of, about an hour since, Appears to be. But because I shall ere long have Occasion to resume into Consideration the Power of the Fire to produce new Concretes, I shall no longer insist on this Argument at present; only I must mind You, that if You will not dis-believe *Helmonts* Relations, You must confess that the *Tria Prima* are neither ingenerable nor incorruptible Substances; since by his *Alkahest* some of them may be produc'd of Bodies that were before of another Denomination; and by the same powerfull *Menstruum* all of them may be reduc'd into insipid Water.

Here *Carneades* was about to pass on to his Third Consideration, when *Eleutherius* being desirous to hear what he could say to clear his second General Consideration from being repugnant to what he seem'd to think the true Theory of Mistion, prevented him by telling him, I somewhat wonder, *Carneades*, that You, who are in so many Points unsatisfied with the Peripatetick Opinion touching the Elements and Mixt Bodies, should also seem averse to that Notion touching the manner of Mistion, wherein the Chymists (though perhaps without knowing that they do so) agree with most of the Antient Philosophers that preceded *Aristotle*, and that for Reasons so considerable, that divers Modern Naturalists and Physitians, in other things unfavourable enough to the Spagyrists, do in this case side with them against the common Opinion of the Schools. If you should ask me (continues *Eleutherius*) what Reasons I mean? I should partly by the Writings of *Sennertus* and other learned Men, and partly by my own Thoughts, be supply'd with more, then 'twere at present proper for me to Insist largely on. And therefore I shall mention only, and that briefly, three or four. Of these, I shall take the First from the state of the Controversie itself, and the genuine Notion of Mistion, which though much intricated by the Schoolmen, I take in short to be this, **Aristotle**, at least as many of his Interpreters expound him, and as indeed he Teaches in some places, where he professedly Dissents from the Antients, declares Mistion to be such a mutual Penetration, and perfect Union of the mingl'd Elements, that there is no Portion of the mixt Body, how Minute soever, which does not contain All, and Every of the Four Elements, or in which, if you please, all the Elements are not. And I remember, that he reprehends the Mistion taught by the Ancients, as too sleight or gross, for this Reason, that Bodies mixt according to their **Hypothesis**, though they appear so to humane Eyes, would not appear such to the acute Eyes of a **Lynx**, whose perfecter Sight would discerne the Elements, if they were no otherwise mingled, than as his Predecessors would have it, to be but Blended, not United; whereas the Antients, though they did not all Agree about what kind of Bodies were Mixt, yet they did almost unanimously hold, that in a compounded Bodie, though the **Miscibilia**, whether Elements, Principles, or whatever they pleas'd to call them, were associated in such small Parts, and with so much Exactness, that there was no sensible Part of the Mass but seem'd to be of the same Nature with the rest, and with the whole; Yet as to the Atomes, or other Insensible Parcels of Matter, whereof each of the **Miscibilia** consisted, they retain'd each of them its own Nature, being but by Apposition or **Juxta**-Position united with the rest into one Bodie. So that although by virtue of this composition the mixt Body did perhaps obtain Divers new Qualities, yet still the Ingredients that Compounded it, retaining their own Nature, were by the Destruction of the **Compositum** separable from each other, the minute Parts disingag'd from those of a differing Nature, and associated with those of their own sort returning to be again, Fire, Earth, or Water, as they were before they chanc'd to be Ingredients of that **Compositum**. This may be explain'd (Continues **Eleutherius**,) by a piece of Cloath made of white and black threds interwoven, wherein though the whole piece appear neither white nor black, but of a resulting Colour, that is gray, yet each of the white and black threds that compose it, remains what it was before, as would appear if the threds were pull'd asunder, and sorted each

Colour by it self. This (pursues **Eleutherius**) being, as I understand it, the State of the Controversie, and the **Aristotelians** after their Master Commonly Defining, that Mistion is **Miscibilium alteratorum Unio**, that seems to comport much better with the Opinion of the Chymists, then with that of their Adversaries, since according to that as the newly mention'd Example declares, there is but a **Juxta**-position of separable Corpuscles, retaining each its own Nature, whereas according to the **Aristotelians**, when what they are pleas'd to call a mixt Body results from the Concourse of the Elements, the **Miscibilia** cannot so properly be said to be Alter'd, as Destroy'd, since there is no Part in the mixt Body, how small soever, that can be call'd either Fir [Transcriber's Note: Fire], or Air, or Water, or Earth.

Nor indeed can I well understand, how Bodies can be mingl'd other wayes then as I have declar'd, or at least how they can be mingl'd, as our Peripateticks would have it. For whereas **Aristotle** tells us, that if a Drop of Wine be put into ten thousand Measures of Water, the Wine being Overpower'd by so Vast a Quantity of Water will be turn'd into it, he speaks to my Apprehension, very improbably; For though One should add to that Quantity of Water as many Drops of Wine as would a Thousand times exceed it all, yet by his Rule the whole Liquor should not be a **Crama**, a Mixture of Wine and Water, wherein the Wine would be Predominant, but Water only; Since the Wine being added but by a Drop at a time would still Fall into nothing but Water, and Consequently would be turn'd into it. And if this would hold in Metals too, 'twere a rare secret for Goldsmiths, and Refiners; For by melting a Mass of Gold, or Silver, and by but casting into it Lead or Antimony, Grain after Grain, they might at pleasure, within a reasonable Compass of time, turn what Quantity they desire, of the Ignoble into the Noble Metalls. And indeed since a Pint of wine, and a pint of water, amount to about a Quart of Liquor, it seems manifest to sense, that these Bodies doe not Totally Penetrate one another, as one would have it; but that each retains its own Dimensions; and Consequently, that they are by being Mingl'd only divided into minute Bodies, that do but touch one another with their Surfaces, as do the Grains, of Wheat, Rye, Barley, &c. in a heap of severall sorts of Corn: And unless we say, that as when one measure of wheat, for Instance, is Blended with a hundred measures of Barley, there happens only a **Juxta**-position and Superficial Contact betwixt the Grains of wheat, and as many or thereabouts of the Grains of Barley. So when a Drop of wine is mingl'd with a great deal of water, there is but an Apposition of so many Vinous Corpuscles to a Correspondent Number of Aqueous ones; Unless I say this be said, I see not how that Absurdity will be avoyded, whereunto the Stoical Notion of mistion (namely by [Greek: synchysis] [Errata: [Greek: Synchysis]], or Confusion) was Liable, according to which the least Body may be co-extended with the greatest: Since in a mixt Body wherein before the Elements were Mingl'd there was, for Instance, but one pound of water to ten thousand of Earth, yet according to them there must not be the least part of that Compound, that Consisted not as well of Earth, as water. But I insist, Perhaps, too long (sayes *Eleutherius*) upon the proofs afforded me by the Nature of Mistion: Wherefore I will but name Two or Three other Arguments; whereof the first shall be, that according to *Aristotle* himself, the motion of a mixt Body followes the Nature of the Predominant Element, as those wherein the Earth prevails, tend towards the Centre of heavy Bodies. And since many things make it Evident, that in divers Mixt Bodies the Elementary Qualities are as well Active, though not altogether so much so as in the Elements themselves, it seems not reasonable to deny the actual Existence of the Elements in those Bodies wherein they Operate.

To which I shall add this Convincing Argument, that Experience manifests, and *Aristotle* Confesses it, that the *Miscibilia* may be again separated from a mixt Body, as is Obvious in the Chymical Resolutions of Plants and Animalls, which could not be unless they did actually retain their formes in it: For since, according to *Aristotle*, and I think according to truth, there is but one common Mass of all things, which he has been pleas'd to call *Materia Prima*; And since tis not therefore the Matter but the Forme that Constitutes and Discriminates Things, to say that the Elements remain not in a Mixt Body, according to their Formes, but according to their Matter, is not to say that they remain there at all; Since although those Portions of Matter were Earth and water, &c. before they concurr'd, yet the resulting Body being once Constituted, may as well be said to be simple as any of the Elements, the Matter being confessedly of the same Nature in all Bodies, and the Elementary Formes being according to this *Hypothesis* perish'd and abolish'd.

And lastly, and if we will Consult Chymical Experiments, we shall find the Advantages of the Chymical Doctrine above the Peripatetick Title little less then Palpable. For in that Operation that Refiners call Quartation, which they employ to purifie Gold, although three parts of Silver be so exquisitely mingl'd by Fusion with a fourth Part of Gold (whence the Operation is Denominated) that the resulting Mass acquires severall new Qualities, by virtue of the Composition, and that there is scarce any sensible part of it that is not Compos'd of both the metalls; Yet if You cast this mixture into *Aqua Fortis*, the Silver will be dissolv'd in the *Menstruum*, and the Gold like a dark or black Powder will fall to the Bottom of it, and either Body may be again reduc'd into such a Metal as it was before, which shews: that it retain'd its Nature, notwithstanding its being mixt *per Minima* with the other: We likewise see, that though one part of pure Silver be mingled with eight or ten Parts, or more, of Lead, yet the Fire will upon the Cuppel easily and perfectly separate them again. And that which I would have you peculiarly Consider on this Occasion is, that not only in Chymicall Anatomies there is a Separation made of the Elementary Ingredients, but that some Mixt Bodies afford a very much greater Quantity of this or that Element or Principle than of another; as we see, that Turpentine and Amber yield much more Oyl and Sulphur than they do Water, whereas Wine, which is confess'd to be a perfectly mixt Bodie, yields but a little Inflamable Spirit, or Sulphur, and not much more Earth; but affords a vast proportion of Phlegm or water: which could not be, if as the Peripateticks suppose, every, even of the minutest Particles, were of the same nature with the whole, and consequently did contain both Earth and Water, and Aire, and Fire; Wherefore as to what *Aristotle* principally, and almost only Objects, that unless his Opinion be admitted, there would be no true and perfect Mistion, but onely Aggregates or Heaps of contiguous Corpuscles, which, though the Eye of Man cannot discerne, yet the Eye of a *Lynx* might perceive not to be of the same Nature with one another and with their *Totum*, as the Nature of Mistion requires, if he do not beg the Question, and make Mistion to consist in what other Naturalists deny to be requisite to it, yet He at least objects That as a great Inconvenience which I cannot take for such, till he have brought as Considerable Arguments as I have propos'd to prove the contrary, to evince that Nature makes other Mistions than such as I have allowed, wherein the *Miscibilia* are reduc'd into minute Parts, and United as farr as sense can discerne: which if You will not grant to be sufficient for a true Mistion, he must have the same Quarrel with Nature her self, as with his Adversaries.

Wherefore (Continues *Eleutherius*) I cannot but somewhat marvail that *Car-*

neades should oppose the Doctrine of the Chymist in a Particular, wherein they do as well agree with his old Mistress, Nature, as dissent from his old Adversary, *Aristotle*.

I must not (replies *Carneades*) engage my self at present to examine thorowly the Controversies concerning Mistion: And if there were no third thing, but that I were reduc'd to embrace absolutely and unreservedly either the Opinion of *Aristotle*, or that of the Philosophers that went before him, I should look upon the latter, which the Chymists have adopted, as the more defensible Opinion: But because differing in the Opinions about the Elements from both Parties, I think I can take a middle Course, and Discourse to you of Mistion after a way that does neither perfectly agree, nor perfectly disagree with either, as I will not peremptorily define, whether there be not Cases wherein some *Phaenomena* of Mistion seem to favour the Opinion that the Chymists Patrons borrow'd of the Antients, I shall only endeavour to shew You that there are some cases which may keep the Doubt, which makes up my second General Consideration from being unreasonable.

I shall then freely acknowledge to You (says *Carneades*) that I am not over well satisfi'd with the Doctrine that is ascribed to *Aristotle*, concerning Mistion, especially since it teaches that the four Elements may again be separated from the mixt Body; whereas if they continu'd not in it, it would not be so much a Separation as a Production. And I think the Ancient Philosophers that Preceded *Aristotle*, and Chymists who have since receiv'd the same Opinion, do speak of this matter more intelligibly, if not more probably, then the Peripateticks: but though they speak Congruously enough, to their believing, that there are a certain Number of Primogeneal Bodies, by whose Concourse all those we call Mixts are Generated, and which in the Destruction of mixt Bodies do barely part company, and recede from one another, just such as they were when they came together; yet I, who meet with very few Opinions that I can entirely Acquiesce in, must confess to You that I am inclin'd to differ not only from the *Aristotelians*, but from the old Philosophers and the Chymists, about the Nature of Mistion: And if You will give me leave, I shall Briefly propose to you my present Notion of it, provided you will look upon it, not so much as an Assertion as an *Hypothesis*; in talking of which I do not now pretend to propose and debate the whole Doctrine of Mistion, but to shew that 'tis not Improbable, that sometimes mingl'd substances may be so strictly united, that it doth not by the usuall Operations of the Fire, by which Chymists are wont to suppose themselves to have made the *Analyses* of mixt Bodies, sufficiently appear, that in such Bodies the *Miscibilia* that concurr'd to make them up do each of them retain its own peculiar Nature: and by the *Spagyrists* Fires may be more easily extricated and Recover'd, than Alter'd, either by a Change of Texture in the Parts of the same Ingredient, or by an Association with some parts of another Ingredient more strict than was that of the parts of this or that *Miscibile* among themselves. At these words *Eleu.* having press'd him to do what he propos'd, and promis'd to do what he desir'd;

I consider then (resumes *Carneades*) that, not to mention those improper Kinds of mistion, wherein *Homogeneous* Bodies are Joyn'd, as when Water is mingl'd with water, or two Vessels full of the same kind of Wine with one another, the mistion I am now to Discourse of seems, Generally speaking, to be but an Union *per Minima* of any two or more Bodies of differing Denominations; as when Ashes and Sand are Colliquated into Glass or Antimony, and Iron into *Regulus Martis*, or Wine and Water are mingl'd, and Sugar is dissolv'd in the Mixture. Now in this general notion of Mistion it does not appear clearly comprehended, that the *Miscibilia* or Ingredients do in their small Parts so retain their Nature and remain distinct in the Compound, that they may thence by the Fire be again taken asunder: For though I deny not that in some Mistions of certain permanent Bodies this Recovery of the same Ingredients may be made, yet I am not convinc'd that it will hold in all or even in most, or that it is necessarily deducible from Chymicall Experiments, and the true Notion of Mistion. To explain this a little, I assume, that Bodies may be mingl'd, and that very durably, that are not Elementary or resolv'd [Errata: nor have been resolved] into Elements or Principles that they may be mingl'd; as is evident in the *Regulus* of Colliquated Antimony, and Iron newly mention'd; and in Gold Coyne, which lasts so many ages; wherein generally the Gold is alloy'd by the mixture of a quantity, greater or lesser, (in our Mints they use about a 12th. part) of either silver, or Copper, or both. Next, I consider, that there being but one Universal matter of things, as 'tis known that the *Aristotelians* themselves acknowledge, who call it *Materia Prima* (about which nevertheless I like not all their Opinions,) the Portions of this matter seem to differ from One Another, but in certain Qualities or Accidents, fewer or more; upon whose Account the Corporeal Substance they belong to receives its Denomination, and is referr'd to this or that particular sort of Bodies; so that if it come to lose, or be depriv'd of those Qualities, though it ceases not to be a body, yet it ceases from being that kind of Body as a Plant, or Animal; or Red, Green, Sweet, Sowre, or the like. I consider that it very often happens that the small parts of Bodies cohere together but by immediate Contact and Rest; and that however, there are few Bodies whose minute Parts stick so close together, to what cause soever their Combination be ascrib'd, but that it is possible to meet with some other Body, whose small Parts may get between them, and so dis-joyn them; or may be fitted to cohere more strongly with some of them, then those some do with the rest; or at least may be combin'd so closely with them, as that neither the Fire, nor the other usual Instruments of Chymical Anatomies will separate them. These things being promis'd, I will not peremptorily deny, but that there may be some Clusters of Particles, wherein the Particles are so minute, and the Coherence so strict, or both, that when Bodies of Differing Denominations, and consisting of such durable Clusters, happen to be mingl'd, though the Compound Body made up of them may be very Differing from either of the Ingredients, yet each of the little Masses or Clusters may so retain its own Nature, as to be again separable, such as it was before. As when Gold and Silver being melted together in a Due Proportion (for in every Proportion, the Refiners will tell You that the Experiment will not succeed) **Aqua Fortis** will dissolve the Silver, and leave the Gold untouch't; by which means, as you lately noted, both the Metalls may be recover'd from the mixed Mass. But (Continues **Carneades**) there are other Clusters wherein the Particles stick not so close together, but that they may meet with Corpuscles of another Denomination, which are dispos'd to be more closely United with some of them, then they were among themselves. And in such case, two thus combining Corpuscles losing that Shape, or Size, or Motion, or other Accident, upon whose Account they were endow'd with such a Determinate Quality or Nature, each of them really ceases to be a Corpuscle of the same Denomination it was before; and from the Coalition of these there may emerge a new Body, as really one, as either of the Corpuscles was before they were mingl'd, or, if you please, Confounded: Since this Concretion is really endow'd with its own Distinct qualities, and can no more by the Fire, or any other known way of *Analysis*, be divided again into the Corpuscles that at first concurr'd to make it, than either of them could by the same means be subdivided into other Particles. But (sayes *Eleutherius*) to make this more intelligible by particular examples; If you dissolve Copper in *Aqua Fortis*, or Spirit of Nitre, (for I remember not which I us'd, nor do I think it much Material) You may by Crystalizing the Solution Obtain a goodly Vitriol; which though by Virtue of the Composition it have manifestly diverse Qualities, not to be met with in either of the Ingredients, yet it seems that the Nitrous Spirits, or at least many of them, may in this Compounded Mass retain their former Nature; for having for tryal sake Distill'd this Vitrioll Spirit, there came over store of Red Fumes, which by that Colour, by their peculiar stinke, and by their Sourness, manifested themselves to be, Nitrous Spirits; and that the remaining Calx continu'd Copper, I suppose you'l easily beleeve. But if you dissolve *Minium*, which is but Lead Powder'd by the Fire, in good Spirit of Vinager, and Crystalize the Solution, you shall not only have a Saccharine Salt exceedingly differing from both its Ingredients; but the Union of some Parts of the *Menstruum* with some of those of the Metal is so strict, that the Spirit of Vinager seems to be, as such, destroy'd, since the Saline Corpuscles have quite lost that acidity, upon whose Account the Liquor was call'd Spirit of Vinager; nor can any such Acid Parts as were put to the *Minium* be Separated by any known way from the *Saccharum Saturni* resulting from them both; for not only there is no Sowrness at all, but an admirable Sweetness to be tasted in the Concretion; and not only I found not that Spirit of Wine, which otherwise will immediately hiss when mingl'd with strong Spirit of Vinager, would hiss being pour'd upon *Saccharum Saturni*, wherein yet the Acid Salt of Vinager, did it Survive, may seem to be concentrated; but upon the Distillation of *Saccharum Saturni* by its Self I found indeed a Liquor very Penetrant, but not at all Acid, and differing as well in smell and other Qualities, as in tast, from the Spirit of Vinager; which likewise seem'd to have left some of its Parts very firmly united to the *Caput Mortuum*, which though of a Leaden Nature was in smell, Colour, &c. differing from *Minium*; which brings into my mind, that though two Powders, the one Blew, and the other Yellow, may appear a Green mixture, without either of them losing its own Colour, as a good Microscope has sometimes inform'd me; yet having mingl'd *Minium* and *Sal*

Armoniack in a requisite Proportion, and expos'd them in a Glass Vessel to the Fire, the whole Mass became White, and the Red Corpuscles were destroy'd; for though the Calcin'd Lead was separable from the Salt, yet you'l easily beleeve it did not part from it in the Forme of a Red Powder, such as was the ***Minium***, when it was put to the ***Sal Armoniack***. I leave it also to be consider'd, whether in Blood, and divers other Bodies, it be probable, that each of the Corpuscles that concurr to make a Compound Body doth, though some of them in some Cases may, retain its own Nature in it, so that Chymsts [Transcriber's Note: Chymists] may Extricate each sort of them from all the others, wherewith it concurr'd to make a Body of one Denomination.

I know there may be a Distinction betwixt Matter ***Immanent***, when the material Parts remain and retain their own Nature in the things materiated, as some of the Schoolmen speak, (in which sence Wood, Stones and Lime are the matter of a House,) and ***Transient***, which in the materiated thing is so alter'd, as to receive a new Forme, without being capable of re-admitting again the Old. In which sence the Friends of this Distinction say, that ***Chyle*** is the matter of Blood, and Blood that of a Humane Body, of all whose Parts 'tis presum'd to be the Aliment. I know also that it may be said, that of material Principles, some are ***common*** to all mixt Bodies, as ***Aristotles*** four Elements, or the Chymists ***Tria Prima***; others ***Peculiar***, which belong to this or that sort of Bodies; as Butter and a kind of whey may be said to be the Proper Principles of Cream: and I deny not, but that these Distinctions may in some Cases be of Use; but partly by what I have said already, and partly by what I am to say, You may easily enough guess in what sence I admit them, and discerne that in such a sence they will either illustrate some of my Opinions, or at least will not overthrow any of them.

To prosecute then what I was saying before, I will add to this purpose, That since the Major part of Chymists Credit, what those they call Philosophers affirme of their Stone, I may represent to them, that though when Common Gold and Lead are mingled Together, the Lead may be sever'd almost un-alter'd from the Gold; yet if instead of Gold a ***Tantillum*** of the Red ***Elixir*** be mingled with the Saturn, their Union will be so indissoluble in the perfect Gold that will be produc'd by it, that there is no known, nor perhaps no possible way of separating the diffus'd ***Elixir*** from the fixed Lead, but they both Constitute a most permanent Body, wherein the Saturne seems to have quite lost its Properties that made it be call'd Lead, and to have been rather transmuted by the *Elixir*, then barely associated to it. So that it seems not alwayes necessary, that the Bodies that are put together *per minima*, should each retain its own Nature; So as when the Mass it Self is dissipated by the Fire, to be more dispos'd to re-appear in its Pristine Forme, then in any new one, which by a stricter association of its Parts with those of some of the other Ingredients of the *Compositum*, then with one another, it may have acquired.

And if it be objected, that unless the *Hypothesis* I oppose be admitted, in such Cases as I have proposed there would not be an Union but a Destruction of mingled Bodies, which seems all one as to say, that of such Bodies there is no mistion at all; I answer, that *though* the Substances that are mingl'd remain, only their Accidents are Destroy'd, and *though* we may with tollerable Congruity call them *Miscibilia*, because they are Distinct Bodies before they are put together, however afterwards they are so Confounded that I should rather call them Concretions, or Resulting Bodies, than mixt ones; and *though*, perhaps, some other and better Account may be propos'd, upon which the name of mistion may remain; yet if what I have said be thought Reason, I shall not wrangle about Words, though I think it fitter to alter a Terme of Art, then reject a new Truth, because it suits not with it. If it be also Objected that this Notion of mine, concerning mixtion, though it may be allow'd, when Bodies already Compounded are put to be mingl'd, yet it is not applicable to those mixtions that are immediately made of the Elements, or Principles themselves; I Answer in the first place, that I here Consider the Nature of mixtion somewhat more Generally, then the Chymists, who yet cannot deny that there are oftentimes Mixtures, and those very durable ones, made of Bodies that are not Elementary. And in the next place, that though it may be probably pretended that in those Mixtures that are made immediately of the Bodies that are call'd Principles or Elements, the mingl'd Ingredients may better retain their own Nature in the Compounded Mass, and be more easily separated from thence; yet, besides that it may be doubted, whether there be any such Primary Bodies, I see not why the reason I alleadg'd, of the destructibility of the Ingredients of Bodies in General, may not sometimes be Applicable to Salt Sulphur or Mercury; 'till it be shewn upon what account we are to believe them Priviledged. And however, (if you please but to re-call to mind, to what purpose I told you at First, I meant to speak of Mistion at this

Time) you will perhaps allow that what I have hitherto Discoursed about it may not only give some Light to the Nature of it in general (especially when I shall have an Opportunity to Declare to you my thoughts on that subject more fully) but may on some Occasions also be Serviceable to me in the Insuing Part of this Discourse.

But, to look back Now to that part of our Discourse, whence this Excursion concerning Mistion has so long diverted us, though we there Deduc'd, from the differing Substances obtained from a Plant nourished only with Water, and from some other things, that it was not necessary that nature should alwaies compound a Body at first of all such differing bodies as the fire could afterwards make it afford; yet this is not all that may be collected from those Experiments. For from them there seems also Deducible something that Subverts an other Foundation of the Chymical Doctrine. For since that (as we have seen) out of fair Water alone, not only Spirit, but Oyle, and Salt, and Earth may be Produced; It will follow that Salt and Sulphur are not Primogeneal Bodies, and principles, since they are every Day made out of plain Water by the Texture which the Seed or Seminal principle of plants puts it into. And this would not perhaps seem so strange, if through pride, or negligence, We were not Wont to Overlook the Obvious and Familiar Workings of Nature; For if We consider what slight Qualities they are that serve to denominate one of the *Tria Prima*, We shall find that Nature do's frequently enough work as great Alterations in divers parcells of matter: For to be readily dissoluble in water, is enough to make the body that is so, passe for a Salt. And yet I see not why from a new shufling and Disposition of the Component Particles of a body, it should be much harder for Nature to compose a body dissoluble in Water, of a portion of Water that was not so before, then of the Liquid substance of an Egg, which will easily mix with Water, to produce by the bare warmth of a hatching Hen, Membrans, Feathers, Tendons, and other parts, that are not dissoluble in Water as that Liquid Substance was: Nor is the Hardness and Brittleness of Salt more difficult for Nature to introduce into such a yielding body as Water, then it is for her to make the Bones of a Chick out of the tender Substance of the Liquors of an Egg. But instead of prosecuting this consideration, as I easily might, I will proceed, as soon as I have taken notice of an objection that lies in my Way. For I easily foresee it will be alledged, that the above mentioned Examples are all taken from Plants, and Animals, in whom the Matter is Fashioned by the Plastick power of the seed, or something analogous thereunto.

Whereas the Fire do's not act like any of the Seminal Principles, but destroyes them all, when they come within its Reach. But to this I shall need at present to make but this easy Answer, That whether it be a Seminal Principle, or any other which fashions that Matter after those various manners I have mentioned to You, yet 'tis Evident, that either by the Plastick principle Alone, or that and Heat Together, or by some Other cause capable to contex the matter, it is yet possible that the matter may be Anew contriv'd into such Bodies. And 'tis only for the Possibility of this that I am now contending.

The Third Part.

What I have hitherto Discours'd, **Eleutherius**, (sayes his Friend to Him) has, I presume, shew'n You, that a Considering Man may very well question the Truth of those very Suppositions which Chymists as well as Peripateticks, without proving, take for granted; and upon which Depends the Validity of the Inferences they draw from their Experiments. Wherefore having dispach't that, which though a Chymist Perhaps will not, yet I do, look upon as the most Important, as well as Difficult, part of my Task, it will now be Seasonable for me to proceed to the Consideration of the Experiments themselves, wherein they are wont so much to Triumph and Glory. And these will the rather deserve a serious Examination, because those that Alledge them are wont to do it with so much Confidence and Ostentation, that they have hitherto impos'd upon almost all Persons, without excepting Philosophers and Physitians themselves, who have read their Books, or heard them talk. For some learned Men have been content rather to beleeve what they so boldly Affirm, then be at the trouble and charge, to try whether or no it be True. Others again, who have Curiosity enough to Examine the Truth of what is Averr'd, want Skill and Opportunity to do what they Desire. And the Generality even of Learned Men, seeing the Chymists (not contenting themselves with the Schools to amuse the World with empty words) Actually Perform'd divers strange things, and, among those Resolve Compound Bodies into several Substances not known by former Philosophers to be contain'd in them: Men I say, seeing these Things, and Hearing with what Confidence Chymists Averr the Substances Obtain'd from Compound Bodies by the Fire to be the True Elements, or, (as they speak) Hypostaticall Principles of them, are forward to think it but Just as well as Modest, that according to the **Logicians** Rule, the Skilfull **Artists** should be Credited in their own Art; Especially when those things whose Nature they so

Confidently take upon them to teach others are not only Productions of their own Skill, but such as others Know not else what to make of.

But though (Continues *Carneades*) the Chymists have been able upon some or other of the mention'd Acounts, not only to Delight but Amaze, and almost to bewitch even Learned Men; yet such as You and I, who are not unpractis'd in the Trade, must not suffer our Selves to be impos'd upon by hard Names, or bold Assertions; nor to be dazl'd by that Light which should but assist us to discern things the more clearly. It is one thing to be able to help Nature to produce things, and another thing to Understand well the Nature of the things produc'd. As we see, that many Persons that can beget Children, are for all that as Ignorant of the Number and Nature of the parts, especially the internal ones, that Constitute a Childs Body, as they that never were Parents. Nor do I Doubt, but you'l excuse me, if as I thank the Chymists for the things their *Analysis* shews me, so I take the Liberty to consider how many, and what they are, without being astonish'd at them; as if, whosoever hath Skill enough to shew men some new thing of his own making, had the Right to make them believe whatsoever he pleases to tell them concerning it.

Wherefore I will now proceed to my Third General Consideration, which is, That it does not appear, that *Three* is precisely and Universally the Number of the Distinct Substances or Elements, whereinto mixt Bodies are resoluble by the Fire; I mean that 'tis not prov'd by Chymists, that all the Compound Bodies, which are granted to be perfectly mixt, are upon their Chymical *Analysis* divisible each of them into just Three Distinct Substances, neither more nor less, which are wont to be lookt upon as Elementary, or may as well be reputed so as those that are so reputed. Which last Clause I subjoyne, to prevent your Objecting, that some of the Substances I may have occasion to mention by and by, are not perfectly Homogeneous, nor Consequently worthy of the name of Principles. For that which I am now to consider, is, into how many Differing Substances, that may plausibly pass for the Elementary Ingredients of a mix'd Body, it may be Analyz'd by the Fire; but whether each of these be un-compounded, I reserve to examine, when I shall come to the next General Consideration; where I hope to evince, that the Substances which the Chymists not only allow, but assert to be the Component Principles of the Body resolv'd into them, are not wont to be uncompounded.

Now there are two Kind of Arguments (pursues *Carneades*) which may be brought to make my Third Proposition seem probable; one sort of them being of a more Speculative Nature, and the other drawn from Experience. To begin then with the first of these.

But as **Carneades** was going to do as he had said, **Eleutherius** interrupted him, by saying with a somewhat smiling countenance;

If you have no mind I should think, that the Proverb, **That Good Wits have bad Memories**, is Rational and Applicable to You, You must not Forget now you are upon the Speculative Considerations, that may relate to the Number of the Elements; that your Self did not long since Deliver and Concede some Propositions in Favour of the Chymical Doctrine, which I may without disparagement to you think it uneasie, even for **Carneades** to answer.

I have not, replies he, Forgot the Concessions you mean; but I hope too, that you have not forgot neither with what Cautions they were made, when I had not yet assumed the Person I am now sustaining. But however, I shall to content You, so discourse of my Third general consideration, as to let You see, That I am not Unmindful of the things you would have me remember.

To talk then again according to such principles as I then made use of, I shall represent, that if it be granted rational to suppose, as I then did, that the Elements consisted at first of certain small and primary Coalitions of the minute Particles of matter into Corpuscles very numerous, and very like each other, It will not be absurd to conceive, that such primary Clusters may be of far more sorts then three or five; and consequently, that we need not suppose, that in each of the compound Bodies we are treating of there should be found just three sorts of such primitive Coalitions, as we are speaking of.

And if according to this Notion we allow a considerable number of differing Elements, I may add, that it seems very possible, that to the constitution of one sort of mixt Bodies two kinds of Elementary ones may suffice (as I lately Exemplify'd to you, in that most durable Concrete, Glass,) another sort of Mixts may be compos'd of three Elements, another of four, another of five, and another perhaps of many more. So that according to this Notion, there can be no determinate number assign'd, as that of the Elements; of all sorts of compound Bodies whatsoever, it being very probable that some Concretes consist of fewer, some of more Elements. Nay, it does not seem Impossible, according to these Principles, but that there may be two sorts of Mixts, whereof the one may not have any of all the same Elements as the other consists of; as we oftentimes see two words, whereof the one has not any one of the Letters to be met with in the other; or as we often meet with diverse Electuaries, in which no Ingredient (except Sugar) is common to any two of them. I will not here debate whether there may not be a multitude of these Corpuscles, which by reason of their being primary and simple, might be called Elementary, if several sorts of them should convene to compose any Body, which are as yet free, and neither as yet contex'd and entangl'd with primary Corpuscles of other kinds, but remains liable to be subdu'd and fashion'd by Seminal Principles, or the like powerful and Transmuting Agent, by whom they may be so connected among themselves, or with the parts of one of the bodies, as to make the compound Bodies, whose Ingredients they are, resoluble into more, or other Elements then those that Chymists have hitherto taken notice of.

To all which I may add, that since it appears, by what I observ'd to you of the permanency of Gold and Silver, that even Corpuscles that are not of an Elementary but compounded Nature, may be of so durable a Texture, as to remain indissoluble in the ordinary *Analysis* that Chymists make of Bodies by the Fire; 'Tis not impossible but that, though there were but three Elements, yet there may be a greater number of Bodies, which the wonted wayes of Anatomy will not discover to be no Elementary Bodies.

But, sayes *Carneades*, having thus far, in compliance to you, talk't conjecturally of the number of the Elements, 'tis now time to consider, not of how many Elements it is possible that Nature may compound mix'd Bodies, but (at least as farr as the ordinary Experiments of Chymists will informe us) of how many she doth make them up.

I say then, that it does not by these sufficiently appear to me, that there is any one determinate number of Elements to be uniformly met with in all the several sorts of Bodies allow'd to be perfectly mixt.

And for the more distinct proof of this Proposition, I shall in the first place Represent, That there are divers Bodies, which I could never see by fire divided into so many as three Elementary substances. I would fain (as I said lately to *Philoponus*) see that fixt and noble Metal we call Gold separated into Salt, Sulphur and Mercury: and if any man will submit to a competent forfeiture in case of failing, I shall willingly in case of prosperous successe pay both for the Materials and the charges of such an Experiment. 'Tis not, that after what I have try'd my self I dare peremptorily deny, that there may out of Gold be extracted a certain substance, which I cannot hinder Chymists from calling its Tincture or Sulphur; and which leaves the remaining Body depriv'd of its wonted colour. Nor am I sure, that there cannot be drawn out of the same Metal a real quick and running Mercury. But for the Salt of Gold, I never could either see it, or be satisfied that there was ever such a thing separated, ***in rerum natura***, by the relation of any credible eye witnesse. And for the several Processes that Promise that effect, the materials that must be wrought upon are somewhat too pretious and costly to be wasted upon so groundlesse adventures, of which not only the successe is doubtful, but the very possibility is not yet demonstrated. Yet that which most deterres me from such tryalls, is not their chargeablenesse, but their unsatisfactorinesse, though they should succeed. For the Extraction of this golden Salt being in Chymists Processes prescribed to be effected by corrosive ***Menstruums***, or the Intervention of other Saline Bodies, it will remain doubtful to a wary person, whether the Emergent Salt be that of the Gold it self; or of the Saline Bodies or Spirits employ'd to prepare it; For that such disguises of Metals do often impose upon Artists, I am sure ***Eleutherius*** is not so much a stranger to Chymistry as to ignore. I would likewise willingly see the three principles separated from the pure sort of Virgin-Sand, from ***Osteocolla***, from refined Silver, from Quicksilver, freed from its adventitious Sulphur, from ***Venetian*** Talk [Transcriber's Note: Talck], which by long detention in an extreme ***Reverberium***, I could but divide into smaller Particles, (not the constituent principles,) Nay, which, when I caused it to be kept, I know not how long, in a Glasse-house fire, came out in the Figure it's Lumps had when put in, though alter'd to an almost ***Amethystine*** colour; and from divers other Bodies, which it were now unnecessary to enumerate. For though I dare not absolutely affirme it to be impossible to Analyze these Bodies into their ***Tria Prima***; yet because, neither my own Experiments, nor any competent Testimony hath hitherto either taught me how such an ***Analysis*** may be made, or satisfy'd me, that it hath been so, I must take the Liberty to refrain from believing it, till the Chymists prove it, or give us intelligible and practicable Processes to performe what they pretend. For whilst they affect that ***AEnigmatical*** obscurity with which they are wont to puzzle the Readers of their divulg'd Processes concerning the Analyticall Preparation of Gold or Mercury, they leave wary persons much unsatisfyed whether or no the differing Substances, they promise to produce, be truly the Hypostatical Principles, or only some intermixtures of the divided Bodies with those employ'd to work upon them, as is Evident in the seeming Crystalls of Silver, and those of Mercury; which though by some inconsiderately supposed to be the Salts of those Metalls, are plainly but mixtures of the Metalline Bodies, with the Saline parts of *Aqua fortis* or other corrosive Liquors; as is evident by their being reducible into Silver or Quicksilver, as they were before.

I cannot but Confesse (saith *Eleutherius*) that though Chymists may upon probable grounds affirm themselves Able to obtain their *Tria Prima*, from Animals and Vegetables, yet I have often wondred that they should so confidently pretend also to resolve all Metalline and other Mineral bodies into Salt, Sulphur, and Mercury. For 'tis a saying almost Proverbial, among those Chymists themselves that are accounted Philosophers; and our famous Countryman *Roger Bacon* has particularly adopted it; that *Facilius est aurum facere quam destruere*. And I fear, with You, that Gold is not the only Mineral from which Chymists are wont fruitlessly to attempt the separating of their three Principles. I know indeed (continues *Eleutherius*) that the Learned *Sennertus*, even in that book where he takes not upon him to play the Advocate for the Chymists, but the Umpier betwixt them and the Peripateticks, expresses himself roundly, thus;[11] Salem omnibus inesse (mixtis scilicet) & ex iis fieri posse omnibus in resolutionibus Chymicis versatis notissimum est. *And in the next Page,* Quod de sale dixi*, saies he,* Idem de Sulphure dici potest*: but by his favour I must see very good proofs, before I believe such general Assertions, how boldly soever made; and he that would convince me of their truth, must first teach me some true and practicable way of separating Salt and Sulphur from Gold, Silver, and those many different sort of Stones, that a violent Fire does not bring to Lime, but to Fusion; and not only I, for my own part, never saw any of those newly nam'd Bodies so resolved; but* Helmont*, who was much better vers'd in the Chymical Anatomizing of Bodies then either* Sennertus *or* I, has somewhere this resolute passage;[12] *Scio* (saies he) *ex arena, silicibus & saxis, non Calcariis, nunquam Sulphur aut Mercurium trahi posse*; Nay *Quer-*

cetanus himself, though the grand stickler for the **Tria Prima**, has this Confession of the Irrolubleness of Diamonds;[13] **Adamas** (saith he) **omnium factus Lapidum solidissimus ac durissimus ex arctissima videlicet trium principiorum unione ac Cohaerentia, quae nulla arte separationis in solutionem principiorum suorum spiritualium disjungi potest.** And indeed, pursues **Eleutherius**, I was not only glad, but somewhat surprized to find you inclined to Admit that there may be a Sulphur and a running Mercury drawn from Gold; for unlesse you do (as your expression seem'd to intimate) take the word Sulphur in a very loose sence, I must doubt whether our Chymists can separate a Sulphur from Gold: For when I saw you make the experiment that I suppose invited you to speak as you did, I did not judge the golden Tincture to be the true principle of Sulphur extracted from the body, but an aggregate of some such highly colour'd parts of the Gold, as a Chymist would have called a **Sulphur incombustible**, which in plain English seems to be little better than to call it a Sulphur and no Sulphur. And as for Metalline Mercuries, I had not **wondred** at it, though you had expressed much more severity in speaking of them: For I remember that having once met an old and famous Artist, who had long been (and still is) Chymist to a great Monarch, the repute he had of a very honest man invited me to desire him to tell me ingenuously whether or no, among his many labours, he had ever really extracted a true and running Mercury out of Metalls; to which question he freely replyed, that he had never separated a true Mercury from any Metal; nor had ever seen it really done by any man else. And though Gold is, of all Metalls, That, whose Mercury Chymists have most endeavoured to extract, and which they do the most brag they have extracted; yet the Experienced **Angelus Sala**, in his **Spagyrical** account of the seven **Terrestrial** Planets (that is the seven metals) affords us this memorable Testimony, to, our present purpose; **Quanquam** (saies he) &c. experientia tamen (quam stultorum Magistrum [Errata: Magistram] vocamus) certe Comprobavit, Mercurium auri adeo fixum, maturum, & arcte cum reliquis ejusdem corporis substantiis conjungi, ut nullo modo retrogredi possit. **To which he sub-joynes, that he himself had seen much Labour spent upon that Design, but could never see any such Mercury produc'd thereby. And I easily beleeve what he annexes;** that he had often seen Detected many tricks and Impostures of Cheating **Alchymists. For, the most part of those that are fond** *of such* Charlatans*, being unskilfull or Credulous, or both, 'tis very easie for such as have some Skill, much craft, more boldness, and no Conscience, to impose upon them; and therefore, though many profess'd* Alchymists, and divers Persons of Quality have told me that they have made or seen the Mercury of Gold, or of this or that other Metal; yet I have been still apt to fear that either these persons have had a Design to deceive others; or have not had Skill and circumspection enough to keep themselves from being deceived.

[11: Sennert. lib. de cons. & dissens. pag. 147.]

[12: Helmon. pag. 409.]

[13: Quercet. apud Billich. in Thessalo redivivo. pag. 99.]

You recall to my mind (sayes **Carneades**) a certain Experiment I once devis'd, innocently to deceive some persons, and let them and others see how little is to be built upon the affirmation of those that are either unskillfull or unwary, when they tell us they have seen **Alchymists** make the Mercury of this or that Metal; and to make this the more evident, I made my Experiment much more Slight, Short and Simple, than the Chymists usuall processes to Extract Metalline Mercuries; which Operations being commonly more Elaborate and Intricate, and requiring a much more longer time, give the **Alchymists** a greater opportunity to Cozen, and Consequently are more Obnoxious to the Spectators suspicion. And that wherein I endeavour'd to make my Experiment look the more like a True **Analysis**, was, that I not only pretended as well as others to extract a Mercury from the Metal I wrought upon, but likewise to separate a large proportion of manifest and inflamable Sulphur. I take then, of the filings of Copper, about a Drachme or two, of common sublimate, powder'd, the like Weight, and **Sal Armoniack** near about as much as of Sublimate; these three being well mingl'd together I put into a small Vial with a long neck, or, which I find better, into a Glass Urinall, which (having first stopped it with Cotton) to avoid the Noxious Fumes, I approach by degrees to a competent Fire of well kindled coals, or (which looks better, but more endangers the Glass) to the Flame of a candle; and after a while the bottom of the Glass being held Just upon the Kindled Coals, or in the flame, You may in about a quarter of an Hour, or perchance in halfe that time, perceive in the Bottom of the Glass some running Mercury; and if then You take away the Glass and break it, You shall find a Parcel of Quicksilver, Perhaps altogether, and perhaps part of it in the pores of the Solid

Mass; You shall find too, that the remaining Lump being held to the Flame of the Candle will readily burn with a greenish Flame, and after a little while (perchance presently) will in the Air Acquire a Greenish Blew, which being the Colour that is ascrib'd to Copper, when its Body is unlocked, 'Tis easie to perswade Men that this is the True Sulphur of *Venus*, especially since not only the Salts may be Suppos'd partly to be Flown away, and partly to be Sublim'd to the upper part of the Glass, whose inside (will Commonly appear Whitened by them) but the Metal seems to be quite Destroy'd, the Copper no longer appearing in a Metalline Forme, but almost in that of a Resinous Lump; whereas indeed the Case is only this, That the Saline parts of the Sublimate, together with the ***Sal Armoniack***, being excited and actuated by the Vehement heat, fall upon the Copper, (which is a Metal they can more easily corrode, than silver) whereby the small parts of the Mercury being freed from the Salts that kept them asunder, and being by the heat tumbled up and down after many Occursions, they Convene into a Conspicuous Mass of Liquor; and as for the Salts, some of the more Volatile of them Subliming to the upper part of the Glass, the others Corrode the Copper, and uniting themselves with it do strangely alter and Disguise its Metallick Form, and compose with it a new kind of Concrete inflamable like Sulphur; concerning which I shall not now say any thing, since I can Referr You to the Diligent Observations which I remember Mr. ***Boyle*** has made concerning this Odde kind of Verdigrease. But Continues ***Carneades*** smiling, you know I was not cut out for a Mountebank, and therefore I will hasten to resume the person of a Sceptick, and take up my discourse where You diverted me from prosecuting it.

In the next place, then, I consider, that, as there are some Bodies which yield not so many as the three Principles; so there are many others, that in their Resolution Exhibite more principles than three; and that therefore the Ternary Number is not that of the Universal and Adequate Principles of Bodies. If you allow of the Discourse I ately [Errata: lately] made You, touching the primary Associations of the small Particles of matter, You will scarce think it improbable, that of such Elementary Corpuscles there may be more sorts then either three, or four, or five. And if you will grant, what will scarce be deny'd, that Corpuscles of a compounded Nature may in all the wonted Examples of Chymists pass for Elementary, I see not, why you should think it impossible, that as ***Aqua Fortis***, or ***Aqua Regis*** will make a Separation of colliquated Silver and Gold, though the Fire cannot; so there may be some Agent found out so subtile and so powerfull, at least in respect of those particular compounded Corpuscles, as to be able to resolve them into those more simple ones, whereof they consist, and consequently encrease the number of the Distinct Substances, whereinto the mixt Body has been hitherto thought resoluble. And if that be true, which I recited to you a while ago out of **Helmont** concerning the Operations of the **Alkahest**, which divides Bodies into other Distinct Substances, both as to number and Nature, then the Fire does; it will not a little countenance my Conjecture. But confining our selves to such wayes of Analyzing mix'd Bodies, as are already not unknown to Chymists, it may without Absurdity be Question'd, whether besides those grosser Elements of Bodies, which they call Salt Sulphur and Mercury, there may not be Ingredients of a more Subtile Nature, which being extreamly little, and not being in themselves Visible, may escape unheeded at the Junctures of the Destillatory Vessels, though never so carefully Luted. For let me observe to you one thing, which though not taken notice of by Chymists, may be a notion of good Use in divers Cases to a Naturalist, that we may well suspect, that there may be severall Sorts of Bodies, which are not Immediate Objects of any one of our senses; since we See, that not only those little Corpuscles that issue out of the Loadstone, and perform the Wonders for which it is justly admired; But the **Effluviums** of Amber, Jet, and other Electricall Concretes, though by their effects upon the particular Bodies dispos'd to receive their Action, they seem to fall under the Cognizance of our Sight, yet do they not as Electrical immediately Affect any of our senses, as do the bodies, whether minute or greater, that we See, Feel, Taste, &c. But, continues **Carneades**, because you may expect I should, as the Chymists do, consider only the sensible Ingredients of Mixt Bodies, let us now see, what Experience will, even as to these, suggest to us.

It seems then questionable enough, whether from Grapes variously order'd there may not be drawn more distinct Substances by the help of the Fire, then from most other mixt Bodies. For the Grapes themselves being dryed into Raysins and distill'd, will (besides **Alcali**, Phlegm, and Earth) yield a considerable quantity of an Empyreumatical Oyle, and a Spirit of a very different nature from that of Wine. Also the unfermented Juice of Grapes affords other distil'd Liquors then Wine doth. The Juice of Grapes after fermentation will yield a **Spiritus Ardens**;

which if competently rectifyed will all burn away without leaving any thing remaining. The same fermented Juice degenerating into Vinager, yields an acid and corroding Spirit. The same Juice turn'd [Errata: tunned] up, armes it self with Tartar; out of which may be separated, as out of other Bodies, Phlegme, Spirit, Oyle, Salt and Earth: not to mention what Substances may be drawn from the Vine it self, probably differing from those which are separated from Tartar, which is a body by it self, that has few resemblers in the World. And I will further consider that what force soever you will allow this instance, to evince that there are some Bodies that yield more Elements then others, it can scarce be deny'd but that the Major part of bodies that are divisible into Elements, yield more then three. For, besides those which the Chymists are pleased to name Hypostatical, most bodies contain two others, Phlegme and Earth, which concurring as well as the rest to the constitution of Mixts, and being as generally, if not more, found in their *Analysis*, I see no sufficient cause why they should be excluded from the number of Elements. Nor will it suffice to object, as the *Paracelsians* are wont to do, that the *Tria prima* are the most useful Elements, and the Earth and Water but worthlesse and unactive; for Elements being call'd so in relation to the constituting of mixt Bodies, it should be upon the account of its Ingrediency, not of its use, that any thing should be affirmed or denyed to be an Element: and as for the pretended uselessness of Earth and Water, it would be consider'd that usefulnesse, or the want of it, denotes only a Respect or Relation to us; and therefore the presence, or absence of it, alters not the Intrinsick nature of the thing. The hurtful Teeth of Vipers are for ought I know useless to us, and yet are not to be deny'd to be parts of their Bodies; and it were hard to shew of what greater Use to Us, then Phlegme and Earth, are those Undiscern'd Stars, which our New *Telescopes* discover to Us, in many Blanched places of the Sky; and yet we cannot but acknowledge them Constituent and Considerably great parts of the Universe. Besides that whether or no the Phlegme and Earth be immediately Useful, but necessary to constitute the Body whence they are separated; and consequently, if the mixt Body be not Useless to us, those constituent parts, without which it could not have been That mixt Body, may be said not to be Unuseful to Us: and though the Earth and Water be not so conspicuously Operative (after separation) as the other three more active Principles, yet in this case it will not be amiss to remember the lucky Fable of *Menemius Aggrippa*, of the dangerous Sedition of the Hands and Legs, and other more busie parts of the Body, against the seemingly unactive Stomack. And to this case also we may not unfitly apply that Reasoning of an Apostle, to another purpose; *If the Ear shall say, because I Am not the Eye, I am not of the Body; Is it therefore not of the Body? If the whole Body were Eye, where were the Hearing? If the whole were for hearing, where the smelling?* In a word, since Earth and water appear, as clearly and as generally as the other Principles upon the resolution of Bodies, to be the Ingredients whereof they are made up; and since they are useful, if not immediately to us, or rather to Physitians, to the Bodies they constitute, and so though in somewhat a remoter way, are serviceable to us; to exclude them out of the number of Elements, is not to imitate Nature.

[Transcriber's Note: See the printer's note (beginning "The Authors constant Absence") at the end of the book for material that the printer inadvertently omitted from this page.]

But, pursues *Carneades*, though I think it Evident, that Earth and Phlegme are to be reckon'd among the Elements of most Animal and Vegetable Bodies, yet 'tis not upon that Account alone, that I think divers Bodies resoluble into more Substances then three. For there are two Experiments, that I have sometimes made to shew, that at least some Mixts are divisible into more Distinct Substances then five. The one of these Experiments, though 'twill be more seasonable for me to mention it fully anon, yet in the mean time, I shall tell you thus much of it, That out of two Distill'd Liquors, which pass for Elements of the Bodies whence they are drawn, I can without Addition make a true Yellow and Inflamable Sulphur, notwithstanding that the two Liquors remain afterwards Distinct. Of the other Experiment, which perhaps will not be altogether unworthy your Notice, I must now give you this particular Account. I had long observ'd, that by the Destillation of divers Woods, both in Ordinary, and some unusuall sorts of Vessels, the Copious Spirit that came over, had besides a strong tast, to be met with in the Empyreumaticall Spirits of many other Bodies, an Acidity almost like that of Vinager: Wherefore I suspected, that though the sowrish Liquor Distill'd, for Instance, from Box-Wood, be lookt upon by Chymists as barely the Spirit of it, and therefore as one single Element or Principle; yet it does really consist of two Differing Substances, and may be divisible into them; and consequently, that such Woods and other Mixts as abound with such a Vinager, may be said to consist of one Element or Principle, more then the Chymists as yet are Aware of; Wherefore bethinking my self, how the separation of these two Spirits might be made, I Quickly found, that there were several wayes of Compassing it. But that of them which I shall at present mention, was this, Having Destill'd a Quantity of Box-Wood *per se*, and slowly rectify'd the sowrish Spirit, the better to free it both from Oyle and Phlegme, I cast into this Rectify'd Liquor a convenient Quantity of Powder'd Coral, expecting that the Acid part of the Liquor would Corrode the Coral, and being associated with it would be so retain'd by it, that the other part of the Liquor, which was not of an acid Nature, nor fit to fasten upon the Corals, would be permitted to ascend alone. Nor was I deceiv'd in my Expectation; For having gently abstracted the Liquor from the Coralls, there came over a Spirit of a Strong smell, and of a tast very piercing, but without any sourness; and which was in diverse qualities manifestly different, not only from a Spirit of Vinager, but from some Spirit of the same Wood, that I purposely kept by me without depriving it of its acid Ingredient. And to satisfy you, that these two Substances were of a very differing Nature, I might informe you of several Tryals that I made, but must not name some of them, because I cannot do so without making some unseasonable discoveries. Yet this I shall tell you at present, that the sowre Spirit of **Box**, not only would, as I just now related, dissolve Corals, which the other would not fasten on, but being pour'd upon Salt of Tartar would immediately boile and hiss, whereas the other would lye quietly upon it. The acid Spirit pour'd upon **Minium** made a Sugar of Lead, which I did not find the other to do; some drops of this penetrant spirit being mingl'd with some drops of the blew Syrup of Violets seem'd rather to dilute then otherwise alter the colour; whereas the Acid Spirit turn'd the syrup of a reddish colour, and would probably have made it of as pure a red as Acid Salts are wont to do, had not its operation been hindered by the mixture of the other Spirit. A few drops of the compound Spirit being Shaken into a pretty quantity of the infusion of **Lignum Nephriticum**, presently destroyed all the blewish colour, whereas the other Spirit would not take it away. To all which it might be added, that having for tryals sake pour'd fair water upon the Corals that remained in the bottom of the glass wherein I had rectifyed the double spirit (if I may so call it) that was first drawn from the Box, I found according to my expectation that the Acid Spirit had really dissolved the Corals, and had coagulated with them. For by the affusion of fair Water, I Obtain'd a Solution, which (to note that singularity upon the bye) was red, whence the Water being evaporated, there remained a soluble Substance much like the Ordinary Salt of Coral, as Chymists are pleas'd to call that Magistery of Corals, which they make by dissolving them in common spirit of Vinager, and abstracting the ***Menstruum ad Siccitatem***. I know not whether I should subjoine, on this occasion, that the simple spirit of Box, if Chymists will have it therefore Saline because it has a strong tast, will furnish us with a new kind of Saline Bodies, differing from those hitherto taken notice of. For whereas of the three chief sorts of Salts, the Acid, the Alcalizate, and the Sulphureous, there is none that seems to be friends with both the other two, as I may, e're it be long, have occasion to shew; I did not find but that the simple spirit of Box did agree very well (at least as farr as I had occasion to try it) both with the Acid and the other Salts. For though it would lye very quiet with salt of Tartar, Spirit of Urine, or other bodies, whose Salts were either of an Alcalizate or fugitive Nature; yet did not the mingling of Oyle of Vitriol it self produce any hissing or Effervescence, which you know is wont to ensue upon the Affusion of that highly Acid Liquor upon either of the Bodies newly mentioned.

I think my self, sayes ***Eleutherius***, beholden to you, for this Experiment; not only because I forsee you will make it helpful to you in the Enquiry you are now upon, but because it teaches us a Method, whereby we may prepare a numerous sort of new spirits, which though more simple then any that are thought Elementary, are manifestly endow'd with peculiar and powerfull qualities, some of which may probably be of considerable use in Physick, as well alone, as associated with other things; as one may hopefully guess by the redness of that Solution your sour Spirit made of Corals, and by some other circumstances of your Narrative. And suppose (pursues ***Eleutherius***) that you are not so confin'd, for the separation of the Acid parts of these compound Spirits from the other, to employ Corals; but that you may as well make use of any Alcalizate Salt, or of Pearls, or Crabs eyes, or any other Body, upon which common Spirit of Vinager will easily work, and, to speak in an ***Helmontian*** Phrase, Exantlate it self.

I have not yet tryed, sayes ***Carneades***, of what use the mention'd liquors may be in Physick, either as Medicines or as ***Menstruums***: But I could mention now (and may another time) divers of the tryals that I made to satisfy my self of the difference of these two Liquors. But that, as I allow your thinking what you newly told me about Corals, I presume you will allow me, from what I have said already, to deduce this Corollary; That there are divers compound bodies, which may be resolv'd into four such differing Substances, as may as well merit the name of Principles, as those to which the Chymists freely give it. For since they scruple not to reckon that which I call the compound Spirit of Box, for the spirit, or as others would have it, the Mercury of that Wood, I see not, why the Acid liquor, and the other, should not each of them, especially that last named, be lookt upon as more worthy to be called an Elementary Principle; since it must needs be of a more simple nature then the Liquor, which was found to be divisible into that, and the Acid Spirit. And this further use (continues **Carneades**) may be made of our experiment to my present purpose, that it may give us a rise to suspect, that since a Liquor reputed by the Chymists to be, without dispute, Homogeneous, is by so slight a way divisible into two distinct and more simple Ingredients, some more skilful or happier Experimenter then I may find a way either further to divide one of these Spirits, or to resolve some or other, if not all, of those other Ingredients of mixt Bodies, that have hitherto pass'd among Chymists for their Elements or Principles.

The Fourth Part.

A nd thus much (sayes ***Carneades***) may suffice to be said of the ***Number*** of the Distinct substances separable from mixt Bodies by the Fire: Wherefore I now proceed to consider the ***nature*** of them, and shew you, That though they seem ***Homogeneous*** Bodies, yet have they not the purity and simplicity that is requisite to Elements. And I should immediately proceed to the proof of my Assertion, but that the Confidence wherewith Chymists are wont to call each of the Substances we speak of by the name of Sulphur or Mercury, or the other of the Hypostaticall Principles, and the intollerabln [Errata: intolerable] Ambiguity they allow themselves ie [Errata: in] their Writings and Expressions, makes it necessary for me in Order to the Keeping you either from mistaking me, or thinking I mistake the Controversie, to take Notice to you and complain of the unreasonable Liberty they give themselves of playing with Names at pleasure. And indeed if I were oblig'd in this Dispute, to have such regard to the Phraseology of each particular Chymist, as not to Write any thing which this or that Author may not pretend, not to contradict this or that sence, which he may give as Occasion serves to his Ambiguous Expressions, I should scarce know how to dispute, nor which way to turn myself. For I find that even Eminent Writers, (such as ***Raymund Lully***, ***Paracelsus*** and others) do so abuse the termes they employ, that as they will now and then give divers things, one name; so they will oftentimes give one thing, many Names; and some of them (perhaps) such, as do much more properly signifie some Distinct Body of another kind; nay even in Technical Words or Termes of Art, they refrain not from this Confounding Liberty; but will, as I have Observ'd, call the same Substance, sometimes the Sulphur, and Sometimes the Mercury of a Body. And now I speak of Mercury, I cannot but take Notice, that the Descriptions they give us of that Principle or Ingredient of mixt Bodies, are so intricate, that even those that have Endeavour'd to Pollish and Illustrate the Notions of the Chymists, are fain to confess that they know not what to make of it, either by Ingenuous Acknowledgments, or Descriptions that are not Intelligible.

I must confess (sayes *Eleutherius*) I have, in the reading of *Paracelsus* and other Chymical Authors, been troubled to find, that such hard Words and Equivocal Expressions, as You justly complain of, do even when they treat of Principles, seem to be studiously affected by those Writers; whether to make themselves to be admir'd by their Readers, and their Art appear more Venerable and Mysterious, or, (as they would have us think) to conceal from them a Knowledge themselves judge inestimable.

But whatever (sayes *Carneades*) these Men may promise themselves from a Canting way of delivering the Principles of Nature, they will find the Major part of Knowing Men so vain, as when they understand not what they read, to conclude, that it is rather the Writers fault then their own. And those that are so ambitious to be admir'd by the Vulgar, that rather then go without the Admiration of the Ignorant they will expose themselves to the contempt of the Learned, those shall, by my consent, freely enjoy their Option. As for the Mystical Writers scrupling to Communicate their Knowledge, they might less to their own Disparagement, and to the trouble of their Readers, have conceal'd it by writing no Books, then by Writing bad ones. If *Themistius* were here, he would not stick to say, that Chymists write thus darkly, not because they think their Notions too precious to be explain'd, but because they fear that if they were explain'd, men would discern, that they are farr from being precious. And indeed, I fear that the chief Reason why Chymists have written so obscurely of their three Principles, may be, That not having Clear and Distinct Notions of them themselves, they cannot write otherwise then Confusedly of what they but Confusedly Apprehend: Not to say that divers of them, being Conscious to the Invalidity of their Doctrine, might well enough discerne that they could scarce keep themselves from being confuted, but by keeping themselves from being clearly understood. But though much may be said to Excuse the Chymists when they write Darkly, and AEnigmatically, about the Preparation of their *Elixir*, and Some few other grand *Arcana*, the divulging of which they may upon Grounds Plausible enough esteem unfit; yet when they pretend to teach the General Principles of Natural Philosophers, this Equivocall Way of Writing is not to be endur'd.

For in such Speculative Enquiries, where the naked Knowledge of the Truth is the thing Principally aim'd at, what does he teach me worth thanks that does not, if he can, make his Notion intelligible to me, but by Mystical Termes, and Ambiguous Phrases darkens what he should clear up; and makes me add the Trouble of guessing at the sence of what he Equivocally expresses, to that of examining the Truth of what he seems to deliver. And if the matter of the Philosophers Stone, and the manner of preparing it, be such Mysteries as they would have the World believe them, they may Write Intelligibly and Clearly of the Principles of mixt Bodies in General, without Discovering what they call the Great Work. But for my part (Continues *Carneades*) what my Indignation at this Un-philosophical way of teaching Principles has now extorted from me, is meant chiefly to excuse my self, if I shall hereafter oppose any Particular Opinion or assertion, that some Follower of *Paracelsus* or any Eminent Artist may pretend not to be his Masters. For, as I told you long since, I am not Oblig'd to examine private mens writings, (which were a Labour as endless as unprofitable) being only engag'd to examine those Opinions about the *Tria Prima*, which I find those Chymists I have met with to agree in most: And I Doubt not but my Arguments against their Doctrine will be in great part easily enough applicable ev'n to those private Opinions, which they do not so directly and expresly oppose. And indeed, that which I am now entering upon being the Consideration of the things themselves whereinto *Spagyrists* resolve mixt Bodies by the Fire, If I can shew that these are not of an Elementary Nature, it will be no great matter what names these or those Chymists have been pleased to give them. And I question not that to a Wise man, and consequently to *Eleutherius*, it will be lesse considerable to know, what Men Have thought of Things, then what they Should have thought.

In the fourth and last place, then, I consider, that as generally as Chymists are wont to appeal to Experience, and as confidently as they use to instance the several substances separated by the Fire from a Mixt Body, as a sufficient proof of their being its component Elements: Yet those differing Substances are many of them farr enough from Elementary simplicity, and may be yet look'd upon as mixt Bodies, most of them also retaining, somewhat at least, if not very much, of the Nature of those Concretes whence they were forc'd.

I am glad (sayes *Eleutherius*) to see the Vanity or Envy of the canting Chymists thus discover'd and chastis'd; and I could wish, that Learned Men would conspire together to make these deluding Writers sensible, that they must no longe [Transcriber's Note: longer] hope with Impunity to abuse the World. For whilst such Men are quietly permitted to publish Books with promising Titles, and therein to Assert what they please, and contradict others, and ev'n themselves as they please, with as little danger of being confuted as of being understood, they are encourag'd to get themselves a name, at the cost of the Readers, by finding that intelligent Men are wont for the reason newly mention'd, to let their Books and Them alone: And the ignorant and credulous (of which the number is still much greater then that of the other) are forward to admire most what they least understand. But if Judicious men skill'd in Chymical affaires shall once agree to write clearly and plainly of them, and thereby keep men from being stunn'd, as it were, or imposd upon by dark or empty Words; 'tis to be hop'd that these men finding that they can no longer write impertinently and absurdly, without being laugh'd at for doing so, will be reduc'd either to write nothing, or Books that may teach us something, and not rob men, as formerly, of invaluable Time; and so ceasing to trouble the World with Riddles or Impertinencies, we shall either by their Books receive an Advantage, or by their silence escape an Inconvenience.

But after all this is said (continues ***Eleutherius***) it may be represented in favour of the Chymists, that, in one regard the Liberty they take in using names, if it be excusable at any time, may be more so when they speak of the substances whereinto their ***Analysis*** resolves mixt Bodies: Since as Parents have the Right to name their own Children, it has ever been allow'd to the Authors of new Inventions, to Impose Names upon them. And therefore the subjects we speak of being so the Productions of the Chymist's Art, as not to be otherwise, but by it, obtainable; it seems but equitable to give the Artists leave to name them as they please: considering also that none are so fit and likely to teach us what those Bodies are, as they to whom we ow'd them.

I told You already (sayes ***Carneades***) that there is great Difference betwixt the being able to make Experiments, and the being able to give a Philosophical Account of them. And I will not now add, that many a Mine-digger may meet, whilst he follows his work, with a Gemm or a Mineral which he knowes not what to make of, till he shews it a Jeweller or a Mineralist to be inform'd what it is. But that which

I would rather have here observ'd, is, That the Chymists I am now in debate with have given up the Liberty You challeng'd for them, of using Names at Pleasure, and confin'd Themselves by their Descriptions, though but such as they are, of their Principles; so that although they might freely have call'd any thing their *Analysis* presents them with, either Sulphur, or Mercury, or Gas, or Blas, or what they pleas'd; yet when they have told me that Sulphur (for instance) is a Primogeneal and simple Body, Inflamable, Odorous, &c. they must give me leave to dis-believe them, if they tell me that a Body that is either compounded or uninflamable is such a Sulphur; and to think they play with words, when they teach that Gold and some other Minerals abound with an Incombustible Sulphur, which is as proper an Expression, as a Sun-shine Night, or Fluid Ice.

But before I descend to the Mention of Particulars belonging to my Fourth Consideration, I think it convenient to premise a few Generals; some of which I shall the less need to insist on at present, because I have Touched on them already.

And first I must invite you to take notice of a certain passage in *Helmont*;[14] which though I have not Found much heeded by his Readers, He Himself *mentions* as a notable thing, and I take to be a very considerable one; for whereas the Distill'd oyle of *oyle-olive*, though drawn *per se* is (as I have try'd) of a very sharp and fretting Quality, and of an odious tast, He tells us that Simple oyle being only digested with *Paracelsus's sal circulatum*, is reduc'd into dissimilar parts, and yields a sweet Oyle, very differing from the oyle distill'd, from [Errata: distill'd from] sallet oyle; as also that by the same way there may be separated from Wine a very sweet and gentle Spirit, partaking of a far other and nobler quality then that which is immediately drawn by distillation and call'd *Dephlegm'd Aqua vitae*, from whose Acrimony this other spirit is exceedingly remote, although the *sal circulatum* that makes these *Anatomies* be separated from the Analyz'd Bodies, in the same weight and with the same qualities it had before; which Affirmation of *Helmont* if we admit to be true, we must acknowledge that there may be a very great disparity betwixt bodies of the same denomination (as several oyles, or several spirits) separable from compound Bodies: For, besides the differences I shall anon take notice of, betwixt those distill'd Oyles that are commonly known to Chymists, it appears by this, that by means of the *Sal Circulatum*, There may be quite another sort of Oyles obtain'd from the same Body; and who knowes but that there may be yet other Agents found in Nature, by whose help there may, whether by Transmutation or otherwise, be obtain'd from the Bodies Vulgarly call'd Mixt, Oyles or other substances, Differing from those of the same Denomination, known either to Vulgar Chymists, or even to *Helmont* Himself: but for fear You should tell me, that this is but a conjecture grounded upon another Man's Relation, whose Truth we have not the means to Experiment, I will not Insist upon it; but leaving You to Consider of it at leasure, I shall proceed to what is next.

[14: Illud notabile, in vino esse Spiritum quendam mitiorem ulterioris & nobilioris qualitatis participem qu[=a] qui immediate per distillationem elicitur diciturque aqua vitae dephlegmata, quod facilius in simplici Olivarum oleo ad oculum spectatur. Quippe distillatum oleum absque laterum aut tigularum [Errata: tegularum] additamento, quodque oleum Philosophorum dicitur, multum dissert ab ejus oleitate; quae elicitur prius reducto oleo simplici in partes dissimilares sola digestione & Salis circulati Paracelsici appositione; siquidem sal circulatum idem in pondere & quantitatibus pristinis ab oleo segregatur postquam oleum olivarum in sui heterogeneitates est dispositum. Dulce enim tunc Oleum Olivarum ex oleo, prout & suavissimus vini spiritus a vino hoc pacto separantur, longeque ab aquae vitae acrimonia distinctus.--Helmont. Aura vitalis, pag. 725.]

Secondly, Then if that be True which was the Opinion of *Lucippus*, *Democritus*, and other prime *Anatomists* of old, and is in our dayes reviv'd by no mean Philosophers; namely, That our Culinary Fire, such as Chymists use, consists of swarmes of little Bodies swiftly moving, which by their smallness and motion are able to permeate the sollidest and Compactest Bodies, and even Glass it Self; If this (I say) be True, since we see that In flints and other Concretes, the Fiery part is Incorporated with the Grosser, it will not be Irrationall to conjecture, that multitudes of these Fiery Corpuscles, getting in at the Pores of the Glass, may associate themselves with the parts of the mixt Body whereon they work, and with them Constitute new Kinds of Compound Bodies, according as the Shape, Size, and other Affections of the Parts of the Dissipated Body happen to dispose them, in Reference to such Combinations; of which also there may be the greater Number; if it be likewise granted that the Corpuscles of the Fire, though all exceeding minute, and very swiftly moved, are not all of the same bigness, nor Figure. And if I had not

Weightier Considerations to Discourse to you of, I could name to you, to Countenance what I have newly said, some particular Experiments by which I have been Deduc'd to think, that the Particles of an open Fire working upon some Bodies may really Associate themselves therewith, and add to the Quantity. But because I am not so sure, that when the Fire works upon Bodies included in Glasses, it does it by a reall Trajection of the Fiery Corpuscles themselves, through the Substance of the Glass, I will proceed to what is next to be mention'd.

I could (sayes *Eleutherius*) help you to some Proofes, whereby I think it may be made very probable, that when the Fire acts immediately upon a Body, some of its Corpuscles may stick to those of the burnt Body, as they seem to do in Quicklime, but in greater numbers, and more permanently. But for fear of retarding Your Progress, I shall desire you to deferr this Enquiry till another time, and proceed as you intended.

You may then in the next place (sayes *Carneades*) observe with me, that not only there are some Bodies, as Gold, and Silver, which do not by the usual Examens, made by Fire, Discover themselves to be mixt; but if (as You may Remember I formerly told You) it be a De-compound Body that is Dissipable into several Substances, by being expos'd to the Fire it may be resolv'd into such as are neither Elementary, nor such as it was upon its last mixture Compounded of; but into new Kinds of mixts. Of this I have already given You some Examples in Sope, Sugar of Lead, and Vitrioll. Now if we shall Consider that there are some Bodies, as well Natural, (as that I last nam'd) as Factitious, manifestly De-compounded; That in the Bowells of the Earth Nature may, as we see she sometimes does, make strange Mixtures; That Animals are nourish'd with other Animals and Plants; And, that these themselves have almost all of them their Nutriment and Growth, *either* from a certain Nitrous Juice Harbour'd in the Pores of the Earth, *or* from the Excrements of Animalls, *or* from the putrify'd Bodies, either of living Creatures or Vegetables, *or* from other Substances of a Compounded Nature; If, I say, we consider this, it may seem probable, that there may be among the Works of Nature (not to mention those of Art) a greater Number of De-compound Bodies, then men take Notice of; And indeed, as I have formerly also observ'd, it does not at all appear, that all Mixtures must be of Elementary Bodies; but it seems farr more probable, that there are divers sorts of compound Bodies, even in regard of all or some of their Ingredients, consider'd Antecedently to their Mixture. For though some seem to be made up by the immediate Coalitions of the Elements, or Principles themselves, and therefore may be call'd **Prima Mista**, or **Mista Primaria**; yet it seems that many other Bodies are mingl'd (if I may so speak) at the second hand, their immediate Ingredients being not Elementary, but these primary Mixts newly spoken of; And from divers of these Secondary sort of Mixts may result, by a further Composition, a Third sort, and so onwards. Nor is it improbable, that some Bodies are made up of Mixt Bodies, not all of the same Order, but of several; as (for Instance) a Concrete may consist of Ingredients, whereof the one may have been a primary, the other a Secondary Mixt Body; (as I have in Native Cinnaber, by my way of Resolving it, found both that Courser the [Errata: delete "the"] part that seems more properly to be Oar, and a Combustible Sulphur, and a Running Mercury:) or perhaps without any Ingredient of this latter sort, it may be compos'd of Mixt Bodies, some of them of the first, and some of the third Kind; And this may perhaps be somewhat Illustrated by reflecting upon what happens in some Chymical Preparations of those Medicines which they call their **Bezoardicum's**. For first, they take Antimony and Iron, which may be look'd upon as **Prima Mista**; of these they compound a Starry **Regulus**, and to this they add according to their Intention, either Gold, or Silver, which makes with it a new and further Composition. To this they add Sublimate, which is it self a De-compound body, (consisting of common Quicksilver, and divers Salts United by Sublimation into a Crystalline Substance) and from this Sublimate, and the other Metalline Mixtures, they draw a Liquor, which may be allow'd to be of a yet more Compounded Nature. If it be true, as Chymists affirm it, that by this Art some of the Gold or Silver mingl'd with the **Regulus** may be carry'd over the Helme with it by the Sublimate; as indeed a Skilfull and Candid person complain'd to me a while since, That an experienc'd Friend of His and mine, having by such a way brought over a great Deal of Gold, in hope to do something further with it, which might be gainfull to him, has not only miss'd of his Aim, but is unable to recover his Volatiliz'd Gold out of the Antimonial butter, wherewith it is strictly united.

Now (Continues **Carneades**) if a Compound body consist of Ingredients that are not meerly Elementary; it is not hard to conceive, that the Substances into which the Fire Dissolves it, though seemingly Homogeneous enough, may be of a Compounded Nature, those parts of each body that are most of Kin associating themselves into a Compound of a new Kind. As when (for example sake) I have caus'd Vitrioll and *Sal Armoniack*, and Salt Petre to be mingl'd and Destill'd together, the Liquor that came over manifested it self not to be either Spirit of Nitre, or of *Sal Armoniack*, or of Vitrioll. For none of these would dissolve crude gold, which yet my Liquor was able readily to do; and thereby manifested it self to be a new Compound, consisting at least of Spirit of Nitre, and *Sal Armoniack*, (for the latter dissolv'd in the former, will Work on Gold) which nevertheless are not by any known way separable, and consequently would not pass for a Mixt Body, if we our selves did not, to obtain it, put and Distill together divers Concretes, whose Distinct Operations were known before hand. And, to add on this Occasion the Experiment I lately promis'd You, because it is Applicable to our present purpose, I shall Acquaint You, that suspecting the Common Oyle of Vitrioll not to be altogether such a simple Liquor as Chymists presume it, I mingl'd it with an equal or a Double Quantity (for I try'd the Experiment more then once) of common Oyle of Turpentine, such as together with the other Liquor I bought at the Drugsters. And having carefully (for the Experiment is Nice, and somewhat dangerous) Distill'd the Mixture in a small Glass Retort, I obtain'd according to my Desire, (besides the two Liquors I had put in) a pretty Quantity of a certain substance, which sticking all about the Neck of the Retort Discover'd it self to be Sulphur, not only by a very strong Sulphureous smell, and by the colour of Brimstone; but also by this, That being put upon a coal, it was immediately kindl'd, and burn'd like common Sulphur. And of this Substance I have yet by me some little Parcells, which You may command and examine when you please. So that from this Experiment I may deduce either one, or both of these Propositions, That a real Sulphur may be made by the Conjunction of two such Substances as Chymists take for Elementary, And which did not either of them apart appear to have any such body in it; or that Oyle of Vitrioll though a Distill'd Liquor, and taken for part of the Saline Principle of the Concrete that yields it, may yet be so Compounded a body as to contain, besides its Saline part, a Sulphur like common brimstone, which would hardly be it self a simple or un-compounded body.

I might (pursues *Carneades*) remind You, that I formerly represented it, as possible, That as there may be more Elements then five, or six; so the Elements of one body may be Different from those of another; whence it would follow, that from the Resolution of De-compound body [Errata: bodies], there may result Mixts of an altogether new kind, by the Coalition of Elements that never perhaps conven'd before. I might, I say, mind You of this, and add divers things to this second Consideration; but for fear of wanting time I willingly pretermit them, to pass on to the third, which is this, That the Fire does not always barely resolve or take asunder, but may also after a new manner mingle and compound together the parts (whether Elementary or not) of the Body Dissipated by it.

This is so evident, sayes **Carneades**, in some obvious Examples, that I cannot but wonder at their Supiness that have not taken notice of it. For when Wood being burnt in a Chimney is dissipated by the Fire into Smoke and Ashes, that smoke composes soot, which is so far from being any one of the principles of the Wood, that (as I noted above) you may by a further *Analysis* separate five or six distinct substances from it. And as for the remaining Ashes, the Chymists themselves teach us, that by a further degree of fire they may be indissolubly united into glass. 'Tis true, that the *Analysis* which the Chymists principally build upon is made, not in the open air, but in close Vessels; but however, the Examples lately produc'd may invite you shrewdly to suspect, That heat may as well compound as dissipate the Parts of mixt Bodies: and not to tell you, that I have known a Vitrification made even in close vessels, I must remind you that the Flowers of Antimony, and those of Sulphur, are very mix'd Bodies, though they ascend in close vessells: And that 'twas in stopt glasses that I brought up the whole Body of Camphire. And whereas it may be objected, that all these Examples are of Bodies forc'd up in a dry, not a Fluid forme, as are the Liquors wont to be obtain'd by distillation; I answer, That besides that 'tis possible, that a Body may be chang'd from Consistent to Fluid, or from Fluid to Consistent, without being otherwise much altered, as may appear by the Easiness wherewith in Winter, without any Addition or Separation of Visible Ingredients, the same substance may be quickly harden'd into brittle Ice, and thaw'd again into Fluid Water; Besides this, I say it would be consider'd, that common Quick-silver it self, which the Eminentest Chymists confess to be a mixt Body, may be Driven over the Helme in its Pristine forme of Quicksilver, and consequently, in that of a Liquor. And certainly 'tis possible that very compounded Bodies may concur to Constitute Liquors; Since, not to mention that I have found it possible, by the help of a certain *Menstruum*, to distill Gold it self through a Retort, even with a Moderate Fire: Let us but consider what happens in Butter of Antimony. For if that be carefully rectify'd, it may be reduc'd into a very clear Liquor; and yet if You cast a quantity of fair water upon it, there will quickly precipitate a Ponderous and Vomitive Calx, which made before a considerable part of the Liquor, and yet is indeed (though some eminent Chymists would have it Mercurial) an Antimonial Body carryed over and kept dissolv'd by the Salts of the Sublimate, and consequently a compounded one; as You may find if You will have the Curiosity to Examine this White powder by a skilful Reduction. And that You may not think that Bodies as compounded as flowers of Brimstone cannot be brought to Concurr to Constitute Distill'd Liquors; And also That You may not imagine with Divers Learned Men that pretend no small skill in Chymistry, that at least no mixt Body can be brought over the Helme, but by corrosive Salts, I am ready to shew You, when You please, among other wayes of bringing over Flowers of Brimstone (perhaps I might add even Mineral Sulphurs) some, wherein I employ none but Oleaginous bodies to make Volatile Liquors, in which not only the colour, but (which is a much surer mark) the smell and some Operations manifest that there is brought over a Sulphur that makes part of the Liquor.

One thing more there is, *Eleutherius*, sayes *Carneades*, which is so pertinent to my present purpose, that though I have touch'd upon it before, I cannot but on this occasion take notice of it. And it is this, That the Qualities or Accidents, upon whose account Chymists are wont to call a portion of Matter by the name of Mercury or some other of their Principles, are not such but that 'tis possible as Great (and therefore why not the like?) may be produc'd by such changes of Texture, and other Alterations, as the Fire may make in the small Parts of a Body. I have already prov'd, when I discours'd of the second General Consideration, by what happens to plants nourish'd only with fair water, and Eggs hatch'd into Chickens, that by changing the disposition of the component parts of a Body, Nature is able to effect as great Changes in a parcell of Matter reputed similar, as those requisite to Denominate one of the *Tria Prima*. And though *Helmont* do somewhere wittily call the Fire the Destructor and the Artificial Death of Things; And although another Eminent Chymist and Physitian be pleas'd to build upon this, That Fire can never generate any thing but Fire; Yet You will, I doubt not, be of another mind, If You consider how many new sorts of mixt Bodies Chymists themselves have produc'd by means of the Fire: And particularly, if You consider how that Noble and Permanent Body, Glass, is not only manifestly produc'd by the violent action of the Fire, but has never, for ought we know, been produc'd any other way. And indeed it seems but an inconsiderate Assertion of some *Helmontians*, that every sort of Body of a Peculiar Denomination must be produc'd by some Seminal power; as I think I could evince, if I thought it so necessary, as it is for me to hasten to what I have further to discourse. Nor need it much move us, that there are some who look upon whatsoever the Fire is employ'd to produce, not as upon Natural but Artificial Bodies. For there is not alwaies such a difference as many imagine betwixt the one and the other: Nor is it so easy as they think, clearly to assigne that which Properly, Constantly, and Sufficiently, Discriminates them. But not to engage my self in so nice a Disquisition, it may now suffice to observe, that a thing is commonly termed Artificial, when a parcel of matter is by the Artificers hand, or Tools, or both, brought to such a shape or Form, as he Design'd before-hand in his Mind: Whereas in many of the Chymical Productions the effect would be produc'd whether the Artificer intended it or no; and is oftentimes very much other then he Intended or Look't for; and the Instruments employ'd, are not Tools Artificially fashion'd and shaped, like those of Tradesmen, for this or that particular Work; but, for the most part, Agents of Nature's own providing, and whose chief Powers of Operation they receive from their own Nature or Texture, not the Artificer. And indeed, the Fire is as well a Natural Agent as Seed: And the Chymist that imploies it, does but apply Natural Agents and Patients, who being thus brought together, and acting according to their respective Natures, performe the worke themselves; as Apples, Plums, or other fruit, are natural Productions, though the Gardiner bring and fasten together the Sciens of the Stock, and both Water, and do perhaps divers other wayes Contribute to its bearing fruit. But, to proceed to what I was going to say, You may observe with me, *Eleutherius*, that, as I told You once before, Qualities sleight enough may serve to Denominate a Chymical Principle. For, when they anatomize a compound Body by the Fire, if they get a Substance inflamable, and that will not mingle with Water, that they presently call Sulphur; what is sapid and Dissoluble in Water, that must pass for Salt; Whatsoever is fix'd and indissoluble in Water, that they name Earth. And I was going to add, that, whatsoever Volatile substance they know not what to make of, not to say, whatsoever they please, that they call Mercury. But that these Qualities may either be produc'd, otherwise then by such as they call Seminal Agents, or may belong to bodies of a compounded Nature, may be shewn, among other Instances, in Glass made of ashes, where the exceeding strongly-tasted *Alcalizate* Salt joyning with the Earth becomes insipid, and with it constitutes a Body, which though also dry, fixt, and indissoluble in Water, is yet manifestly a mixt Body; and made so by the Fire itself.

And I remmember to our present purpose, that *Helmont*,[15] amongst other Medicines that he commends, has a short processe, wherein, though the Directions for Practice are but obscurely intimated; yet I have some reason not to Dis-believe the Process, without affirming or denying any thing about the vertues of the remedy to be made by it. *Quando* (sayes he) *oleum cinnamomi &c. suo sali alkali miscetur absque omni aqua, trium mensium artificiosa occultaque circulatione, totum in salem volatilem commutatum est, vere essentiam sui simplicis in nobis exprimit, & usque in prima nostri constitutivasese ingerit.* A not unlike Processe he delivers in another place; from whence, if we suppose him to say true, I may argue, that since by the Fire there may be produc'd a substance that is as well Saline and volatile as the Salt of Harts-horn, blood, &c. which pass for Elementary; and since that this Volatile Salt is really compounded of a Chymical Oyle and a fixt Salt, the one made Volatile by the other, and both associated by the fire, it may well be suspected that other Substances, emerging upon the Dissipation of Bodies by the Fire, may be new sorts of Mixts, and consist of Substances of differing natures; and particularly, I have sometimes suspected, that since the Volatile Salts of Blood, Harts-horn, &c. are figitive [Errata: fugitive] and endow'd with an exceeding strong smell, either that Chymists do Erroneously ascribe all odours to sulphurs, or that such Salts consist of some oyly parts well incorporated with the Saline ones. And the like conjecture I have also made concerning Spirit of Vinager, which, though the Chymists think one of the Principles of that Body, and though being an Acid Spirit it seems to be much less of kin then Volatile Salts to sulphurs; yet, not to mention its piercing smell; which I know not with what congruity the Chymist will deduce from Salt, I wonder they have not taken notice of what their own *Tyrocinium Chymicum* teach us concerning the Destillation of *Saccharum Saturni*; out of which *Beguinus*[16] assures Us, that he distill'd, besides a very fine spirit, no lesse then two Oyles, the one blood-red and ponderous, but the other swimming upon the top of the Spirit, and of a yellow colour; of which he sayes that he kept then some by him, to verify what he delivers. And though I remember not that I have had two distinct Oyles from Sugar of Lead, yet that it will though distill'd without addition yield some Oyle, disagrees not with my Experience. I know the Chymists will be apt to pretend, that these Oyls are but the volatiliz'd sulphur of the lead; and will perhaps argue it from what *Beguinus* relates, that when the Distillation is ended, you'l find a *Caput Mortuum* extreamly black, and (as he speaks) *nullius momenti*, as if the Body, or at least the chief part of the Metal it self were by the distillation carried over the Helme. But since you know as well as I that *Saccharum Saturni* is a kind of Magistery, made only by calcining of Lead *per se*, dissolving it in distill'd Vinager, and crystalizing the solution; if I had leasure to tell You how Differing a thing I did upon examination find the *Caput Mortuum*, so sleighted by *Beguinus*, to be from what he represents it, I believe you would think the conjecture propos'd less probable then one or other of these three; either that this Oyle did formerly concur to constitute the Spirit of Vinager, and so that what passes for a Chymical Principle may yet be further resoluble into distinct substances; or that some parts of the Spirit together with some parts of the Lead may constitute a Chymical Oyle, which therefore though it pass for Homogeneous, may be a very compounded Body: or at least that by the action of the Distill'd Vinager and the Saturnine Calx one upon another, part of the Liquor may be so alter'd as to be transmuted from an Acid Spirit into an Oyle. And though the truth of either of the two former conjectures would make the example I have reflected on more pertinent to my present argument; yet you'l easily discern, the Third and last Conjecture cannot be unserviceable to confirm some other passages of my discourse.

[15: Helmont pag. 412.]

[16: Tyroc. Chym. L. 1. C. 4.]

To return then to what I was saying just before I mention'd *Helmont's* Experiment, I shall subjoyne, That Chymists must confess also that in the perfectly Dephlegm'd spirit of Wine, or other Fermented Liquors, that which they call the Sulphur of the Concrete loses, by the Fermentation, the Property of Oyle, (which the Chymists likewise take to be the true Sulphur of the Mixt) of being unminglable with the Water. And if You will credit *Helmont*,[17] all [Errata: a pound] of the purest Spirit of Wine may barely by the help of pure Salt of Tartar (which is but the fixed Salt of Wine) be resolv'd or Transmuted into scarce half an ounce of Salt, and as much Elementary Water as amounts to the remaining part of the mention'd weight. And it may (as I think I formerly also noted) be doubted, whether that Fixt and Alcalizate Salt, which is so unanimously agreed on to be the Saline Principle of incinerated Bodies, be not, as 'tis Alcalizate, a Production of the Fire? For though the tast of Tartar, for Example, seem to argue that it contains a Salt before it be burn'd, yet that Salt being very Acid is of a quite Differing Tast from the Lixiviate Salt of Calcin'd Tartar. And though it be not truly Objected against the Chymists, that they obtain all Salts they make, by reducing the Body they work on into Ashes with Violent Fires, (since Hartshorn, Amber, Blood, and divers other Mixts yield a copious Salt before they be burn'd to Ashes) yet this Volatile Salt Differs much, as we shall see anon, from the Fixt Alcalizate Salt I speak of; which for ought I remember is not producible by any known Way, without Incineration. 'Tis not unknown to Chymists, that Quicksilver may be Precipitated, without Addition, into a dry Powder, that remains so in Water. And some eminent *Spagyrists*, and even ***Raimund Lully*** himself, teach, that meerly by the Fire Quicksilver may in convenient Vessels be reduc'd (at least in great part) into a thin Liquor like Water, and minglable with it. So that by the bare Action of the Fire, 'tis possible, that the parts of a mixt Body should be so dispos'd after new and differing manners, that it may be sometimes of one consistence, sometimes of another; And may in one State be dispos'd to be mingl'd with Water, and in another not. I could also shew you, that Bodies from which apart Chymists cannot obtain any thing that is Combustible, may by being associated together, and by the help of the Fire, afford an inflamable Substance. And that on the other side, 'tis possible for a Body to be inflamable, from which it would very much puzzle any ordinary Chymist; and perhaps any other, to separate an inflamable Principle or Ingredient. Wherefore, since the Principles of Chymists may receive their Denominations from Qualities, which it often exceeds not the power of Art, nor always that of the Fire to produce; And since such Qualities may be found in Bodies that differ so much in other Qualities from one another, that they need not be allow'd to agree in that pure and simple Nature, which Principles, to be so indeed, must have; it may justly be suspected, that many Productions of the Fire that are shew'd us by Chymists, as the Principles of the Concrete that afforded them, may be but a new kind of Mixts. And to annex, on this Occasion, to these arguments taken from the Nature of the thing, one of those which **Logicians** call **ad Hominem**, I shall desire You to take Notice, that though **Paracelsus** Himself, and some that are so mistaken as to think he could not be so, have ventur'd to teach, that not only the bodies here below, but the Elements themselves, and all the other Parts of the Universe, are compos'd of Salt, Sulphur and Mercury; yet the learned **Sennertus**, and all the more wary Chymists, have rejected that conceit, and do many of them confess, that the **Tria Prima** are each of them made up of the four Elements; and others of them make Earth and Water concur with Salt, Sulphur and Mercury, to the Constitution of Mixt bodies. So that one sort of these **Spagyrists**, notwithstanding the specious Titles they give to the productions of the Fire, do in effect grant what I contend for. And, of the other sort I may well demand, to what Kind of Bodies the Phlegme and dead Earth, to be met with in Chymical Resolutions, are to be referr'd? For either they must say, with **Paracelsus**, but against their own Concessions as well as against Experience, that these are also compos'd of the **Tria Prima**, whereof they cannot separate any one from either of them; or else they must confess that two of the vastest Bodies here below, Earth, and Water, are neither of them compos'd of the **Tria Prima**; and that consequently those three are not the Universal, and Adequate Ingredients, neither of all Sublunary Bodies, nor even of all mixt Bodies.

[17: *Ostendi alias, quomodo lib. una aquae vitae combibita in sale Tartari siccato, vix fiat semuncia salis, caeterum totum corpus fiat aqua Elementalis. Helmont. in Aura vitali.*]

I know that the chief of these Chymists represent, that though the Distinct Substances into which they divide mixt bodies by the Fire, are not pure and Homogeneous; yet since the four Elements into which the **Aristotelians** pretend to resolve the like bodies by the same Agent, are not simple neither, as themselves acknowledge, 'tis as allowable for the Chymists to call the one Principles, as for the Peripateticks to call the other Elements; since in both cases the Imposition of the name is grounded only upon the Predominancy of that Element whose name is ascrib'd to it. Nor shall I deny, that this Argument of the Chymists is no ill one against the **Aristotelians**. But what Answer can it prove to me, who you know am disputing against the **Aristotelian** Elements, as the Chymicall Principles, and must not look upon any body as a true Principle or Element, but as yet compounded, which is not perfectly Homogeneous, but is further Resoluble into any number of Distinct Substances how small soever. And as for the Chymists calling a body Salt, or Sulphur, or Mercury, upon pretence that the Principle of the same name is predominant in it, That it self is an Acknowledgment of what I contend for; namely that these productions of the Fire, are yet compounded bodies. And yet whilst this is granted, it is affirm'd, but not prov'd, that the reputed Salt, or Sulphur, or Mercury, consists mainly of one body that deserves the name of a principle of the same Denomination. For how do Chymists make it appear that there are any such primitive and simple bodies in those we are speaking of; since 'tis upon the matter confess'd by the answer lately made, that these are not such? And if they pretend by Reason to evince what they affirm, what becomes of their confident boasts, that the Chymists [Errata: Chymist] (whom they therefore, after *Beguinus*, call a *Philosophus* or *Opifex Sensatus*) can convince our Eyes, by manifestly shewing in any mixt body those simple substances he teaches them to be compos'd of? And indeed, for the Chymists to have recourse in this case to other proofs then Experiments, as it is to wave the grand Argument that has all this while been given out for a Demonstrative One; so it releases me from the obligation to prosecute a Dispute wherein I am not engag'd to Examine any but Experimentall proofs. I know it may plausibly Enough be Represented, in favour of the Chymists, that it being evident that much the greater part of any thing they call Salt, or Sulphur, or Mercury, is really such; it would be very rigid to deny those Substances the names ascribed them, only because of some sleight mixture of another Body; since not only the Peripateticks call particular parcels of matter Elementary, though they acknowledge that Elements are not to be anywhere found pure, at least here below; And since especially there is a manifest Analogie and Resemblance betwixt the bodies obtainable by Chymical Anatomies and the principles whose names are given them; I have, I say, consider'd that these things may be represented: But as for what is drawn from the Custome of the Peripateticks, I have already told You, that though it may be employ'd against Them, Yet it is not available against me who allow nothing to be an Element that is not perfectly Homogeneous. And whereas it is alledg'd, that the Predominant Principle ought to give a name to the substance wherein it abounds; I answer, that that might much more reasonably be said, if either we or the Chymists had seen Nature take pure Salt, pure Sulphur, and pure Mercury, and compound of them every sort of Mixt Bodies. But, since 'tis to experience that they appeal, we must not take it for granted, that the Distill'd Oyle (for instance) of a plant is mainly compos'd of the pure principle call'd Sulphur, till they have given us an ocular proof, that there is in that sort of Plants such an Homogeneous Sulphur. For as for the specious argument, which is drawn from the Resemblance betwixt the Productions of the Fire, and the Respective, either ***Aristotelian*** Elements, or ***Chymical*** Principles, by whose names they are call'd; it will appear more plausible then cogent, if You will but recall to mind the state of the controversie; which is not, whether or no there be obtain'd from mixt Bodies certain substances that agree in outward appearance, or in some Qualities with Quicksilver or Brimstone, or some such obvious or copious Body; But whether or no all Bodies confess'd to be perfectly mixt were compos'd of, and are resoluble into a determinate number of primary unmixt Bodies. For, if you keep the state of the question in your Eye, you'l easily discerne that there is much of what should be Demonstrated, left unprov'd by those Chymical Experiments we are Examining. But (not to repeat what I have already discover'd more at large) I shall now take notice, that it will not presently follow, that because a Production of the Fire has some affinity with some of the greater Masses of matter here below, that therefore they are both of the same Nature, and deserve the same Name; for the Chymists are not content, that flame should be look't upon as a parcel of the Element of Fire, though it be hot, dry, and active, because it wants some other Qualities belonging to the nature of Elementary fire. Nor will they let the Peripateticks call Ashes, or Quicklime, Earth, notwithstanding the many likenesses between them; because they are not tastlesse, as Elementary Earth ought to be: But if you should ask me, what then it is, that all the Chymical Anatomies of Bodies do prove, if they prove not that they consist of the three Principles into which the fire resolves them? I answer, that their Dissections may be granted to prove, that some mixt bodies (for in many it will not hold) are by the fire, when they are included in close Vessels, (for that Condition also is often requisite) dissolube [Transcriber's Note: dissoluble] into several Substances differing in some Qualities, but principally in Consistence. So that out of most of them may be obtain'd a fixt substance partly saline, and partly insipid, an unctuous Liquor, and another Liquor or more that without being unctuous have a manifest taste. Now if Chymists will agree to call the dry and sapid substance salt, the Unctous liquor Sulphur, and the other Mercury, I shall not much quarrel with them for so doing: But if they will tell me that Salt, Sulphur, and Mercury, are simple and primary bodies whereof each mixt body was actually compounded, and which was really in it antecedently to the operation of the fire, they must give me leave to doubt whether (whatever their other arguments may do) their Experiments prove all this. And if they will also tell me that the Substances their Anatomies are wont to afford them, are pure and similar, as Principles ought to be, they must give me leave to believe my own senses; and their own confessions, before their bare Assertions. And that you may not (*Eleutherius*) think I deal so rigidly with them, because I scruple to Take these Productions of the Fire for such as the Chymists would have them pass for, upon the account of their having some affinity with them; consider a little with me, that in regard an Element or Principle ought to be perfectly Similar and Homogeneous, there is no just cause why I should rather give the body propos'd the Name of this or that Element or Principle, because it has a resemblance to it in some obvious Quality, rather then deny it that name upon the account of divers other Qualities, wherein the propos'd Bodies are unlike; and if you do but consider what sleight and easily producible qualities they are that suffice, as I have already more then once observ'd, to Denominate a Chymical Principle or an Element, you'l not, I hope, think my wariness to be destitute either of Example, or else of Reason. For we see that the Chymists will not allow the *Aristotelians* that the Salt in Ashes ought to be called Earth, though the Saline and Terrestrial part symbolize in weight, in dryness, in fixness and fusibility, only because the one is sapid and dissoluble in Water, and the other not: Besides, we see that sapidness and volatility are wont to denominate the Chymists Mercury or Spirit; and yet how many Bodies, think you, may agree in those Qualities which may yet be of very differing natures, and disagree in qualities either more numerous, or more considerable, or both. For not only Spirit of Nitre, Aqua Fortis, Spirit of Salt, Spirit of Oyle of Vitriol, Spirit of Allome, Spirit of Vinager, and all Saline Liquors Distill'd from Animal Bodies, but all the Acetous Spirits of Woods freed from their Vinager; All these, I say, and many others must belong to the Chymists Mercury, though it appear not why some of them should more be comprehended under one denomination then the Chymists Sulphur, or Oyle should likewise be; for their Distill'd Oyles are also Fluid, Volatile, and Tastable, as well as their Mercury; Nor is it Necessary, that their Sulphur should be Unctuous or Dissoluble in Water, since they generally referr Spirit of Wine to Sulphurs, although that Spirit be not Unctuous, and will freely mingle with Water. So that bare Inflamability must constitute the Essence of the Chymists Sulphur; as uninflamablenesse joyned with any taste is enough to intitle a Distill'd Liquor to be their Mercury. Now since I can further observe to You, that Spirit of Nitre and Spirit of Hartshorne being pour'd together will boile and hisse and tosse up one another into the air, which the Chymists make signes of great Antipathy in the Natures of Bodies (as indeed these Spirits differ much both in Taste, Smell, and Operations;) Since I elsewhere tell you of my having made two sorts of Oyle out of the same mans blood, that would not mingle with one another; And since I might tell You Divers Examples I have met with, of the Contrariety of Bodies which according to the Chymists must be huddl'd up together under one Denomination; I leave you to Judge whether such a multitude of Substances as may agree in these sleight Qualities, and yet Disagree in Others more Considerable, are more worthy to be call'd by the Name of a Principle (which ought to be pure and homogeneous,) than to have appellations given them that may make them differ, in name too, from the bodies from which they so wildly differ in Nature. And hence also, by the bye, you may perceive that 'tis not unreasonable to distrust the Chymists way of Argumentation, when being unable to shew us that such a Liquor is (for Example) purely saline, they prove, that at least salt is much the predominant principle, because that the propos'd substance is strongly tasted, and all Tast proceeds from salt; whereas those Spirits, such as spirit of Tartar, spirit of Harts-horn, and the like, which are reckoned to be the Mercuries of the Bodies that afford them, have manifestly a strong and piercing tast, and so has (according to what I formerly noted) the spirit of Box &c. even after the acid Liquor that concurr'd to compose it has been separated from it. And indeed, if sapidness belong not to the spirit or Mercurial Principle of Vegitables and Animals: I scarce know how it will be discriminated from their phlegm, since by the absence of Inflamability it must be distinguish'd from their sulphur, which affords me another Example, to prove how unacurate the Chymical Doctrine is in our present Case; since not only the spirits of Vegitables and Animals, but their Oyles are very strongly tasted, as he that shall but wet his tongue with Chymical Oyle of Cinnamon, or of Cloves, or even of Turpentine, may quickly find, to his smart. And not only I never try'd any Chymical Oyles whose tast was not very manifest and strong; but a skilful and inquisitive person who made it his business by elaborate operations to depurate Chymical Oyles, and reduce them to an Elementary simplicity, Informes us, that he never was able to make them at all Tastless; whence I might inferr, that the proof Chymists confidently give us of a bodies being saline, is so far from demonstrating the Predominancy, that it does not clearly Evince so much as the presence of the saline Principle in it. But I will not (pursues *Carneades*) remind you, that the Volatile salt of Harts-horn, Amber, Blood, &c. are exceeding strongly scented, notwithstanding that most Chymists deduce Odours from Sulphur, and from them argue the Predominancy of that Principle in the Odorous body, because I must not so much as add any new Examples of the incompetency of this sort of Chymical arguments; since having already detain'd You but too long in those generals that appertain to my fourth consideration, 'tis time that I proceed to the particulars themselves, to which I thought fit they should be previous:

These Generals (continues *Carneades*) being thus premis'd, we might the better survey the Unlikeness that an attentive and unprepossess'd observer may take notice of in each sort of Bodies which the Chymists are wont to call the salts or sulphurs or Mercuries of the Concretes that yield Them, as if they had all a simplicity, and Identity of Nature: whereas salts if they were all Elementary would as little differ as do the Drops of pure and simple Water. 'Tis known that both Chymists and Physitians ascribe to the fixt salts of calcin'd Bodies the vertues of their concretes; and consequently very differing Operations. So we find the *Alkali* of Wormwood much commended in distempers of the stomach; that of Eyebright for those that have a weak sight; and that of *Guaiacum* (of which a great Quantity yields but a very little salt) is not only much commended in Venereal Diseases, but is believed to have a peculiar purgative vertue, which yet I have not had occasion to try. And though, I confess, I have long thought, that these *Alkalizate* salts are, for the most part, very neer of kin, and retain very little of the properties of the Concretes whence they were separated; Yet being minded to Observe watchfully whether I could meet with any Exceptions to this General Observation, I observ'd at the Glasse-house, that sometimes the Metal (as the Workmen call it) or Masse of colliquated Ingredients, which by Blowing they fashion into Vessels of divers shapes, did sometimes prove of a very differing colour, and a somewhat differing Texture,

from what was usuall. And having enquired whether the cause of such Accidents
might not be derived from the peculiar Nature of the fixt salt employ'd to bring the
sand to fusion, I found that the knowingst Workmen imputed these Mis-adventures
to the Ashes, of [Errata: Ashes off] some certain kind of Wood, as having observ'd
the ignobler kind of Glass I lately mention'd to be frequently produc'd when they
had employ'd such sorts of Ashes which therefore they scruple to make use of, if
they took notice of them beforehand. I remember also, that an Industrious Man of
my acquaintance having bought a vast quantity of Tobacco stalks to make a fixt Salt
with, I had the Curiosity to go see whether that Exotick Plant, which so much
abounds in volatile salt, would afford a peculiar kind of *Alcali*; and I was pleas'd to
find that in the *Lixivium* of it, it was not necessary, as is usual, to evaporate all the
Liquor, that there might be obtain'd a Saline Calx, consisting like lime quench'd in
the Air of a heap of little Corpuscles of unregarded shapes; but the fixt salt shot into
figur'd Crystal, almost as Nitre or *Sal-armoniack* and other uncalcin'd salts are
wont to do; And I further remember that I have observ'd in the fixt Salt of Urine,
brought by depuration to be very white, a tast not so unlike to that of common salt,
and very differing from the wonted caustick Lixiviate tast of other salts made by
Incineration. But because the Instances I have alledg'd of the Difference of *Alcalizate* salt are but few, and therefore I am still inclin'd to think, that most Chymists
and many Physitians do, inconsiderately enough and without Warrant from Experience, ascribe the Vertues of the Concretes expos'd to Calcination, to the salts
obtain'd by it; I shall rather, to shew the Disparity of salts, mention in the first Place
the apparent Difference betwixt the Vegetable fixt salts and the Animal Volatile
ones: As (for Example) betwixt salt of Tartar, and salt of Harts-horn; whereof the
former is so fixt that 'twill indure the brunt of a violent Fire, and stand in fusion like
a Metal; whereas the other (besides that it has a differing tast and a very differing
smell) is so far from being fixt, that it will fly away in a gentle heat as easily as
Spirit of Wine it self. And to this I shall add, in the next place, That even among the
Volatile salts themselves, there is a considerable Difference, as appears by the distinct Properties of (for Instance) salt of Amber, salt of Urine, salt of Mans Skull, (so
much extoll'd against the falling Sicknesse) and divers others which cannot escape
an ordinary Observer. And this Diversity of Volatile salts I have observ'd to be somtimes Discernable even to the Eye, in their Figures. For the salt of Harts-horn I have

observ'd to adhere to the Receiver in the forme almost of a *Parallelipipedon*; and of the Volatile salt of humane blood (long digested before distillation, with spirit of Wine) I can shew you store of graines of that Figure which *Geometricians* call a *Rhombus*; though I dare not undertake that the Figures of these or other Saline Crystals (if I may so call Them) will be alwaies the same, whatever degree of Fire have been employ'd to force them up, or how hastily soever they have been made to convene in the spirits or liquors, in the lower part of which I have usually observ'd them after a while to shoot. And although, as I lately told You, I seldom found any Difference, as to Medical Vertues, in the fixt Salts of Divers Vegetables; and accordingly I have suspected that most of these volatile Salts, having so great a Resemblance in smell, in tast, and fugitiveness, differ but little, if at all, in their Medicinal properties: As indeed I have found them generally to agree in divers of them (as in their being somewhat Diaphoretick and very Deopilative; [Errata: Deopilative)] Yet I remember *Helmont*[18] somewhere informes us, that there is this Difference betwixt the saline spirit of Urine and that of Mans blood, that the former will not cure the Epilepsy, but the Latter will. Of the Efficacy also of the Salt of Common Amber against the same Disease in Children, (for in Grown Persons it is not a specifick) I may elsewhere have an Occasion to Entertain You. And when I consider that to the obtaining of these Volatile Salts (especially that of Urine) there is not requisite such a Destructive Violence of the Fire, as there is to get those Salts that must be made by Incineration, I am the more invited to conclude, that they may differ from one another, and consequently recede from an Elementary Simplicity. And, if I could here shew You what Mr. *Boyle* has Observ'd, touching the Various Chymicall Distinctions of Salts; You would quickly discern, not only that Chymists do give themselves a strange Liberty to call Concretes Salts, that are according to their own Rules to be look'd upon as very Compounded Bodies; but that among those very Salts that seem Elementary, because produc'd upon the Anatomy of the Bodies that yield them, there is not only a visible Disparity, but, to speak in the common Language, a manifest Antipathy or Contrariety: As is evident in the Ebullition and hissing that is wont to ensue, when the Acid Spirit of Vitrioll, for Instance, is pour'd upon pot ashes, or Salt of Tartar. And I shall beg leave of this Gentleman, says *Carneades*, casting his Eyes on me, to let me observe to You out of some of his papers, particularly those wherein he treats of some Preparations of Urine, that not only one and the same body may have two Salts of a contrary Nature, as he exemplifies in the Spirit and *Alkali* of Nitre; but that from the same body there may without addition be obtain'd three differing and Visible Salts. For He Relates, that he observ'd in Urine, not only a Volatile and Crystalline Salt, and a fixt Salt, but likewise a kind of *Sal Armoniack*, or such a Salt as would sublime in the form of a salt, and therefore was not fixt, and yet was far from being so fugitive as the Volatile salt; from which it seem'd also otherwise to differ. I have indeed suspected that this may be a *Sal Armoniack* properly enough so call'd, as Compounded of the Volatile salt of Urine, and the fixt of the same Liquor, which, as I noted, is not unlike sea-salt; but that it self argues a manifest Difference betwixt the salts, since such a Volatile salt is not wont to Unite thus with an ordinary *Alcali*, but to fly away from it in the Heat. And on this occasion I remember that, to give some of my Friends an Ocular proof of the difference betwixt the fixt and Volatile salt (of the same Concrete) Wood, I devis'd the following Experiment. I took common Venetian sublimate, and dissolv'd as much of it as I well could in fair Water: then I took Wood Ashes, and pouring on them Warme Water, Dissolv'd their salt; and filtrating the Water, as soon as I found the *Lixivium* sufficiently sharp upon the tongue, I reserv'd it for use: Then on part of the former solution of sublimate dropping a little of this Dissolv'd Fixt salt of Wood, the Liquors presently turn'd of an Orange Colour; but upon the other part of the clear solution of sublimate putting some of the Volatile salt of Wood (which abounds in the spirit of soot) the Liquor immediately turn'd white, almost like Milke, and after a while let fall a white sediment, as the other Liquor did a Yellow one. To all this that I have said concerning the Difference of salts, I might add what I Formerly told you, concerning the simple spirit of Box, and such like Woods, which differ much from the other salts hitherto mention'd, and yet would belong to the saline Principle, if Chymists did truly teach that all Tasts proceed from it. And I might also annex, what I noted to you out of *Helmont*[19] concerning Bodies, which, though they consist in great part of Chymical Oyles, do yet appear but Volatile salts; But to insist on these things, were to repeat; and therefore I shall proceed.

[18: *Error vero per distillationem nobis monstrat etiam Spiritum salinum plane volatilem odore nequicquam ut nec gustu distinguibilem a spiritu Urinae; In eo tamen essentialiter diversum, quod spiritus talis cruoris curat Epilepsiam, non autem Spiritus salis lotii.* Helmont. Aura Vitalis.]

[19: *Aliquando oleum Cinnamomi, &c. suo sali Alcali miscetur absque omni aqua, trium mensium Artificiosa occultaque circulatione, totum in salem volatilem commutatum est. Helmont. Tria Prima Chymicorum, &c. pag. 412.*]

This Disparity is also highly eminent in the separated sulphurs or Chymical Oyles of things. For they contain so much of the scent, and tast, and vertues, of the Bodies whence they were drawn, that they seem to be but the Material *Crasis* (if I may so speak) of their Concretes. Thus the Oyles of Cinnamon, Cloves, Nutmegs and other spices, seem to be but the United Aromatick parts that did ennoble those Bodies. And 'tis a known thing, that Oyl of Cinnamon, and oyle of Cloves, (which I have likewise observ'd in the Oyles of several Woods) will sink to the Bottom of Water: whereas those of Nutmegs and divers other Vegetables will swim upon it. The Oyle (abusively call'd spirit) of Roses swims at the Top of the Water in the forme of a white butter, which I remember not to have observ'd in any other Oyle drawn in any Limbeck; yet there is a way (not here to be declar'd) by which I have seen it come over in the forme of other Aromatick Oyles, to the Delight and Wonder of those that beheld it. In Oyle of Anniseeds, which I drew both with, and without Fermentation, I observ'd the whole Body of the Oyle in a coole place to thicken into the Consistence and Appearance of white Butter, which with the least heat resum'd its Former Liquidness. In the Oyl of Olive drawn over in a Retort, I have likewise more then once seen a spontaneous Coagulation in the Receiver: And I have of it by me thus Congeal'd; which is of such a strangely Penetrating scent, as if 'twould Perforate the Noses that approach it. The like pungent Odour I also observ'd in the Distill'd Liquor of common sope, which forc'd over from *Minium*, lately afforded an oyle of a most admirable Penetrancy; And he must be a great stranger, both to the Writings and preparations of Chymists, that sees not in the Oyles they distill from Vegetables and Animals, a considerable and obvious Difference. Nay I shall venture to add, *Eleutherius*, (what perhaps you will think of kin to a Paradox) that divers times out of the same Animal or Vegetable, there may be extracted Oyles of Natures obviously differing. To which purpose I shall not insist on the swimming and sinking Oyles, which I have sometimes observ'd to float on, and subside under the spirit of *Guajacum*, and that of divers other Vegetables Distill'd with a strong and lasting Fire; Nor shall I insist on the observation elsewhere mention'd, of the divers and unminglable oyles afforded us by Humane Blood long fermented and Digested with spirit of Wine, because these kind of oyles may seem chiefly to differ in Consistence and Weight, being all of them high colour'd and adust. But the Experiment which I devis'd to make out this Difference of the oyles of the same Vegetable, *ad Oculum*, (as they speak) was this that followes. I took a pound of Annisseeds, and having grosly beaten them, caused them to be put into a very large glass Retort almost filled with fair Water; and placing this Retort in a sand Furnace, I caus'd a very Gentle heat to be administer'd during the first day, and a great part of the second, till the Water was for the most part drawn off, and had brought over with it at least most of the Volatile and Aromatick Oyle of the seeds. And then encreasing the Fire, and changing the Receiver, I obtain'd besides an Empyreumatical Spirit, a quantity of adust oyle; whereof a little floated upon the Spirit, and the rest was more heavy, and not easily separable from it. And whereas these oyles were very dark, and smell'd (as Chymists speak) so strongly of the Fire, that their Odour did not betray from what Vegetables they had been forc'd; the other *Aromatick* Oyle was enrich'd with the genuine smell and tast of the Concrete; and spontaneously coagulating it self into white butter did manifest self [Errata: it self] to be the true Oyle of Annisseeds; which Concrete I therefore chose to employ about this Experiment, that the Difference of these Oyles might be more conspicuous then it would have been, had I instead of it destill'd another Vegetable.

I had almost forgot to take notice, that there is another sort of Bodies, which though not obtain'd from Concretes by Distillation, many Chymists are wont to call their Sulphur; not only because such substances are, for the most part, high colour'd (whence they are also, and that more properly, called Tinctures) as dissolv'd Sulphurs are wont to be; but especially because they are, for the most part, abstracted and separated from the rest of the Masse by Spirit of Wine: which Liquor those men supposing to be Sulphureous, they conclude, that what it works upon, and abstracts, must be a Sulphur also. And upon this account they presume, that they can sequester the sulphur even of Minerals and Metalls; from which 'tis known that they cannot by Fire alone separate it. To all This I shall answer; That if these sequestred substances where indeed the sulphurs of the Bodies whence they are drawn, there would as well be a great Disparity betwixt Chymical Sulphurs obtain'd by Spirit of Wine, as I have already shewn there is betwixt those obtain'd by Distillation in the forme of Oyles: which will be evident from hence, that not to urge that themselves ascribe distinct vertues to Mineral Tinctures, extolling the Tincture of Gold against such and such Diseases; the Tincture of Antimony, or of its Glass, against others; and the Tincture of Emerauld against others; 'tis plain, that in Tinctures drawn from Vegetables, if the superfluous spirit of Wine be distill'd off, it leaves at the bottom that thicker substance which Chymists use to call the Extract of the Vegetable. And that these Extracts are endow'd with very differing Qualities according to the Nature of the Particular Bodies that afforded them (though I fear seldom with so much of the specifick vertues as is wont to be imagin'd) is freely confess'd both by Physitians and Chymists. But, *Eleutherius*, (sayes *Carneades*) we may here take Notice that the Chymists do as well in this case, as in many others, allow themselves a License to abuse Words: For not again to argue from the differing properties of Tinctures, that they are not exactly pure and Elementary Sulphurs; they would easily appear not to be so much as Sulphur's, although we should allow Chymical Oyles to deserve that Name. For however in some Mineral Tinctures the Natural fixtness of the extracted Body does not always suffer it to be easily further resoluble into differing substances; Yet in very many extracts drawn from Vegetables, it may very easily be manifested that the spirit of Wine has not sequestred the sulphureous Ingredient from the saline and Mercurial ones; but has dissolv'd (for I take it to be a Solution) the finer Parts of the Concrete (without making any nice distinction of their being perfectly Sulphureous or not) and united it self with them into a kind of Magistery; which consequently must contain Ingredients or Parts of several sorts. For we see that the stones that are rich in vitriol, being often drench'd with rain-Water, the Liquor will then extract a fine and transparent substance coagulable into Vitriol; and yet though this Vitriol be readily dissoluble in Water, it is not a true Elementary Salt, but, as You know, a body resoluble into very differing Parts, whereof one (as I shall have occasion to tell You anon) is yet of a Metalline, and consequently not of an Elementary Nature. You may consider also, that common Sulphur is readily dissoluble in Oyle of Turpentine, though notwithstanding its Name it abounds as well, if not as much, in Salt as in true Sulphur; witness the great quantity of saline Liquor it affords being set to flame away under a glasse Bell. Nay I have, which perhaps You will think strange, with the same Oyle of Turpentine alone easily enough dissolv'd crude Antimony finely powder'd into a Blood-red Balsam, wherewith perhaps considerable things may be perform'd in Surgery. And if it were now Requisite, I could tell You of some other Bodies (such as Perhaps You would not suspect) that I have been able to work upon with certain Chymical Oyles. But instead of digressing further I shall make this use of the Example I have nam'd. That 'tis not unlikely, but that Spirit of Wine which by its pungent tast, and by some other Qualities that argue it better (especially its Reduciblenesse, according to **Helmont**, into **Alcali**, and Water,) seems to be as well of a Saline as of a Sulphureous Nature, may well be suppos'd Capable of Dissolving Substances That are not meerly Elementary sulphurs, though perhaps they may abound with Parts that are of kin thereunto. For I find that Spirit of Wine will dissolve **Gumm Lacca**, **Benzoine**, and the **Resinous** Parts of **Jallap**, and even of **Guaiacum**; whence we may well suspect that it may from Spices, Herbs, and other lesse compacted Vegetables, extract substances that are not perfect Sulphurs but mixt Bodies. And to put it past Dispute, there is many a Vulgar Extract drawn with Spirit of Wine, which committed to Distillation will afford such differing substances as will Loudly proclaim it to have been a very compounded Body. So that we may justly suspect, that even in Mineral Tinctures it will not alwaies follow, that because a red substance is drawn from the Concrete by spirit of Wine, that Substance is its true and Elementary Sulphur. And though some of these Extracts may perhaps be inflamable; Yet besides that others are not, and besides that their being reduc'd to such Minuteness of Parts may much facilitate their taking Fire; besides this, I say, We see that common Sulphur, common Oyle, Gumm Lac, and many Unctuous and Resinous Bodies, will flame well enough, though they be of very compounded natures: Nay Travellers of Unsuspected Credit assure Us, as a known thing, that in some Northern Countries where Firr trees and Pines abound, the poorer sort of Inhabitants use Long splinters of those Resinous Woods to burne instead of Candles. And as for the rednesse wont to be met with in such solutions, I could easily shew, that 'tis not necessary it should proceed from the Sulphur of the Concrete, Dissolv'd by the Spirit of Wine; if I had leasure to manifest how much Chymists are wont to delude themselves and others by the Ignorance of those other causes upon whose account spirit of Wine and other **Menstruums** may acquire a red or some other high colour. But to returne to our Chymical Oyles, supposing that they were exactly pure; Yet I hope they would be, as the best spirit of Wine is, but the more inflamable and deflagrable. And therefore since an Oyle can be by the Fire alone immediately turn'd into flame, which is something of a very differing Nature from it: I shall Demand how this Oyle can be a Primogeneal and Incorruptible Body, as most Chymists would have their Principles; Since it is further resoluble into flame, which whether or no it be a portion of the Element of Fire, as an **Aristotelian** would conclude, is certainly something of a very differing Nature from a Chymical Oyle, since it burnes, and shines, and mounts swiftly upwards; none of which a Chymical Oyle does, whilst it continues such. And if it should be Objected, that the Dissipated Parts of this flaming Oyle may be caught and collected again into Oyl or Sulphur; I shall demand, what Chymist appears to have ever done it; and without Examining whether it may not hence be as well said that sulphur is but compacted Fire, as that Fire is but diffus'd Sulphur, I shall leave you to consider whether it may not hence be argu'd, that neither Fire nor Sulphur are primitive and indestructible Bodies; and I shall further observe that, at least it will hence appear that a portion of matter may without being Compounded with new Ingredients, by having the Texture and Motion of its small parts chang'd, be easily, by the means of the Fire, endow'd with new Qualities, more differing from them it had before, then are those which suffice to discriminate the Chymists Principles from one another.

We are next to Consider, whether in the Anatomy of mixt Bodies, that which Chymists call the Mercurial part of them be un-compounded, or no. But to tell You True, though Chymists do Unanimously affirm that their Resolutions discover a Principle, which they call Mercury, yet I find them to give of it Descriptions so Differing, and so AEnigmaticall, that I, who am not asham'd to confess that I cannot understand what is not sence, must acknowledge to you that I know not what to make of them. **Paracelsus** himself, and therefore, as you will easily believe, many of his Followers, does somewhere call that Mercury which ascends upon the burning of Wood, as the Peripateticks are wont to take the same smoke for Air; and so seems to define Mercury by Volatility, or (if I may coyne such a Word) Effumability. But since, in this Example, both Volatile Salt and Sulphur make part of the smoke, which does indeed consist also both of Phlegmatick and Terrene Corpuscles, this Notion is not to be admitted; And I find that the more sober Chymists themselves disavow it. Yet to shew you how little of clearness we are to expect in the accounts even of latter **Spagyrists**, be pleas'd to take notice, that **Beguinus**, even in his *Tyrocinium Chymicum*,[20] written for the Instruction of Novices, when he comes to tell us what are meant by the *Tria Prima*, which for their being Principles ought to be defin'd the more accurately and plainly, gives us this Description of Mercury; *Mercurius* (says he) *est liquor ille acidus, permeabilis, penetrabilis, aethereus, ac purissimus, a quo omnis Nutricatio, Sensus, Motus, Vires, Colores, Senectutisque Praeproperae retardatio.* Which words are not so much a Definition of it, as an *Encomium*: and yet *Quercetanus* in his Description of the same Principle adds to these, divers other *Epithets*. But both of them, to skip very many other faults that may be found with their Metaphoricall Descriptions, speak incongruously to the Chymists own Principles. For if Mercury be an Acid Liquor, either Hermetical Philosophy must err in ascribing all Tasts to Salt, or else Mercury must not be a Principle, but Compounded of a Saline Ingredient and somewhat else. *Libavius*, though he find great fault with the obscurity of what the Chymists write concerning their Mercurial Principle, does yet but give us such a Negative Description of it, as *Sennertus*, how favourable soever to the *Tria Prima*, is not satisfi'd with. And this *Sennertus* Himself, though the Learnedst Champion for the Hypostatical Principles, does almost as frequently as justly complain of the unsatisfactoriness of what the Chymists teach concerning their Mercury; and yet he himself (but with his wonted modesty) Substitutes instead of the Description of *Libavius*, another, which many Readers, especially if they be not Peripateticks, will not know what to make of. For scarce telling us any more, then that in all bodies that which is found besides Salt and Sulphur, and the Elements, or, as they call them, Phlegm and Dead Earth, is that Spirit which in *Aristotles* Language may be call'd [Greek: ousian analogon [Errata: ousia analogos] to ton astron stoichaio [Errata: astron stoicheio]]. He sayes that which I confess is not at all satisfactory to me, who do not love to seem to acquiesce in any mans Mystical Doctrines, that I may be thought to understand them.

[20: *Chm. Tyrocin. lib. 1. Cap. 2.*]

If (sayes *Eleutherius*) I durst presume that the same thing would be thought clear by me, and those that are fond of such cloudy Expressions as You justly Tax the Chymists for, I should venture to offer to Consideration, whether or no, since the Mercurial Principle that arises from Distillation is unanimously asserted to be distinct from the salt and Sulphur of the same Concrete, that may not be call'd the Mercury of a Body, which though it ascend in Distillation, as do the Phlegme and Sulphur, is neither insipid like the former, nor inflamable like the latter. And therefore I would substitute to the too much abused Name of Mercury, the more clear and Familiar Appellation of Spirit, which is also now very much made use of even by the Chymists themselves, of our times, though they have not given us so Distinct an Explication, as were fit, of what may be call'd the Spirit of a mixt Body.

I should not perhaps (sayes **Carneades**) much quarrel with your Notion of Mercury. But as for the Chymists, what they can mean, with congruity to their own Principles, by the Mercury of Animals and Vegetables, 'twill not be so easie to find out; for they ascribe Tasts only to the Saline Principle, and consequently would be much put to it to shew what Liquor it is, in the Resolution of Bodies, that not being insipid, for that they call Phlegme, neither is inflamable as Oyle or Sulphur, nor has any Tast; which according to them must proceed from a Mixture, at least, of Salt. And if we should take Spirit in the sence of the Word receiv'd among Modern Chymists and Physitians, for any Distill'd Liquor that is neither Phlegme nor oyle, the Appellation would yet appear Ambiguous enough. For, plainly, that which first ascends in the Distillation of Wine and Fermented Liquors, is generally as well by Chymists as others reputed a Spirit. And yet pure Spirit of Wine being wholly inflamable ought according to them to be reckon'd to the Sulphureous, not the Mercurial Principle. And among the other Liquors that go under the name of Spirits, there are divers which seem to belong to the family of Salts, such as are the Spirits of Nitre, Vitriol, Sea-Salt and others, and even the Spirit of Harts-horn, being, as I have try'd, in great part, if not totally reducible into Salt and Phlegme, may be suspected to be but a Volatile Salt disguis'd by the Phlegme mingl'd with it into the forme of a Liquor. However if this be a Spirit, it manifestly differs very much from that of Vinager, the Tast of the one being Acid, and the other Salt, and their Mixture in case they be very pure, sometimes occasioning an Effervescence like that of those Liquors the Chymists count most contrary to one another. And even among those Liquors that seem to have a better title then those hitherto mention'd, to the name of Spirits, there appears a sensible Diversity; For spirit of Oak, for instance, differs from that of Tartar, and this from that of Box, or of **Guaiacum**. And in short, even these spirits as well as other Distill'd Liquors manifest a great Disparity betwixt themselves, either in their Actions on our senses, or in their other operations.

And (continues *Carneades*) besides this Disparity that is to be met with among those Liquors that the Modernes call spirits, & take for similar bodies, what I have formerly told you concerning the Spirit of Box-wood may let you see that some of those Liquors not only have qualities very differing from others, but may be further resolved into substances differing from one another.

And since many moderne Chymists and other Naturalists are pleased to take the Mercurial spirit of Bodies for the same Principle, under differing names, I must invite you to observe, with me, the great difference that is conspicuous betwixt all the Vegetable and Animal spirits I have mention'd and running Mercury. I speak not of that which is commonly sold in shops that many of themselves will confesse to be a mixt Body; but of that which is separated from Metals, which by some Chymists that seem more Philosophers then the rest, and especially by the above mentioned *Claveus*, is (for distinction sake) called *Mercurius Corporum*. Now this Metalline Liquor being one of those three Principles of which Mineral Bodies are by *Spagyrists* affirmed to be compos'd and to be resoluble into them, the many notorious Differences betwixt them and the Mercuries, as They call Them, of Vegetables and Animals will allow me to inferr, either that Minerals and the other two sorts of Mixt Bodies consist not of the same Elements, or that those Principles whereinto Minerals are immediately resolved, which Chymists with great ostentation shew us as the true principles, of them, are but Secundary Principles, or Mixts of a peculiar sort, which must be themselves reduc'd to a very differing forme, to be of the same kind with Vegetable and Animal Liquors.

But this is not all; for although I formerly told You how Little Credit there is to be given to the Chymical Processes commonly to be met with, of Extracting the Mercuries of Metals, Yet I will now add, that supposing that the more Judicious of Them do not untruly affirme that they have really drawn true and running Mercury from several Metals (which I wish they had cleerly taught Us how to do also,) yet it may be still doubted whether such extracted Mercuries do not as well differ from common Quicksilver, and from one another, as from the Mercuries of Vegetables and Animalls. *Claveus*,[21] in his Apology, speaking of some *experiments* whereby Metalline Mercuries may be fixt into the nobler metals, adds, that he spake of the Mercuries drawn from metals; because common Quicksilver by reason of its excessive coldnesse and moisture is unfit for that particular kind of operation; for which though a few lines before he prescribes in general the Mercuries of Metalline Bodies, yet he chiefly commends that drawn by art from silver. And elsewhere, in the same Book, he tells us, that he himself tryed, that by bare coction the quicksilver of Tin or Pewter (*argentum vivum ex stanno prolicitum*) may by an efficient cause, as he speaks, be turn'd into pure Gold. And the Experienc'd **Alexander van Suchten**, somewhere tells us, that by a way he intimates may be made a Mercury of Copper, not of the Silver colour of other Mercuries, but green; to which I shall add, that an eminent person, whose name his travells and learned writings have made famous, lately assur'd me that he had more then once seen the Mercury of Lead (which whatever Authors promise, you will find it very difficult to make, at least in any considerable quantity) fixt into perfect Gold. And being by me demanded whether or no any other Mercury would not as well have been changed by the same Operations, he assured me of the Negative.

[21: ***Dixi autem de argento vivo a metallis prolicito, quod vulgare ob nimiam frigiditatem & humiditatem nimium concoctioni est contumax, nec ab auro solum alterato coerceri potest.*** Gast. Clave. in Apoll.]

And since I am fallen upon the mention of the Mercuries of metals, you will perhaps expect (**Eleutherius**!) that I should say something of their two other principles; but must freely confess to you, that what Disparity there may be between the salts and sulphurs of Metals and other Menerals [Transcriber's Note: Minerals], I am not my self experienced enough in the separations and examens of them, to venture to determine: (for as for the salts of Metals, I formerly represented it as a thing much to be question'd, whether they have any at all:) And for the processes of separation I find in Authors, if they were (what many of them are not) successfully practicable, as I noted above, yet they are to be performed by the assistance of other bodies, so hardly, if upon any termes at all, separable from them, that it is very difficult to give the separated principles all their due, and no more. But the Sulphur of Antimony which is vehemently vomitive, and the strongly scented Anodyne Sulphur of Vitriol inclines me to think that not only Mineral Sulphurs differ from Vegetable ones, but also from one another, retaining much of the nature of their Concretes. The salts of metals, and of some sort of minerals, You will easily guesse by [Errata: (by] the Doubts I formerly express'd, whether metals have any salt at all [Errata: all)], that I have not been so happy as yet to see, perhaps not for want of curiosity. But if *Paracelsus* did alwaies write so consentaneously to himself that his opinion were **confidently** to be collected from every place of his writings where he seems to expresse it, I might safely take upon me to tell you, that he both countenances in general what I have delivered in my Fourth main consideration, and in particular warrants me to suspect that there may be a difference in metalline and mineral Salts, as well as we find it in those of other bodies. For, *Sulphur* (sayes he)[22] *aliud in auro, aliud in argento, aliud in ferro, aliud in plumbo, stanno, &c. sic aliud in Saphiro, aliud in Smaragdo, aliud in rubino, chrysolito, amethisto, magnete, &c. Item aliud in lapidibus, silice, salibus, fontibus, &c. nec vero tot sulphura tantum, sed & totidem salia; sal aliud in metallis, aliud in gemmis, aliud in lapidibus, aliud in salibus, aliud in vitriolo, aliud in alumine: similis etiam Mercurii est ratio. Alius in Metallis, alius in Gemmis, &c. Ita ut unicuique speciei suus peculiaris Mercurius sit. Et tamen res saltem tres sunt; una essentia est sulphur; una est sal; una est Mercurius. Addo quod & specialius adhuc singula dividantur; aurum enim non unum, sed multiplex, ut et non unum pyrum, pomum, sed idem multiplex; totidem etiam sulphura auri, salia auri, mercurii auri; idem competit etiam metallis & gemmis; ut quot saphyri praestantiores, laevioris, &c. tot etiam saphyrica sulphura, saphyrica salia, saphyrici Mercurii, &c. Idem verum etiam est de turconibus & gemmis aliis universis.* From which passage (*Eleutherius*) I suppose you will think I might without rashness conclude, either that my opinion is favoured by that of *Paracelsus*, or that *Paracelsus* his opinion was not alwaies the same. But because in divers other places of his writings he seems to talk at a differing rate of the three Principles and the four Elements, I shall content my self to inferr from the alledg'd passage, that if his doctrine be not consistent with that Part of mine which it is brought to countenance, it is very difficult to know what his opinion concerning salt, sulphur and mercury, was; and that consequently we had reason about the beginning of our conferences, to decline taking upon us, either to examine or oppose it.

[22: Paracel. de Mineral. Tract. 1. pag. 141.]

I know not whether I should on this occasion add, that those very bodies the Chymists call Phlegme and Earth do yet recede from an Elementary simplicity. That common Earth and Water frequently do so, notwithstanding the received contrary opinion, is not deny'd by the more wary of the moderne Peripateticks themselves: and certainly, most Earths are much lesse simple bodies then is commonly imagined even by Chymists, who do not so considerately to prescribe and employ Earths Promiscuously in those distillations that require the mixture of some *caput mortuum*, to hinder the flowing together of the matter, and to retain its grosser parts. For I have found some Earths to yield by distillation a Liquor very far from being inodorous or insipid; and 'tis a known observation, that most kinds of fat Earth kept cover'd from the rain, and hindred from spending themselves in the production of vegetables, will in time become impregnated with Salt-Petre.

But I must remember that the Water and Earths I ought here to speak of, are such as are separated from mixt Bodies by the fire; and therefore to restrain my Discourse to such, I shall tell you, That we see the Phlegme of Vitriol (for instance) is a very effectual remedie against burnes; and I know a very Famous and experienc'd *Physitian*, whose unsuspected secret (himself confess'd to me) it is, for the discussing of hard and Obstinate Tumours. The Phlegme of Vinager, though drawn exceeding leasurly in a digesting Furnace, I have purposely made tryall of; and sometimes found it able to draw, though slowly, a saccharine sweetness out of Lead; and as I remember by long Digestion, I dissolv'd Corpals [Errata: Corals] in it. The Phlegme of the sugar of Saturne is said to have very peculiar properties. Divers Eminent Chymists teach, that it will dissolve Pearls, which being precipitated by the spirit of the same concrete are thereby (as they say) rendred volatile; which has been confirmed to me, upon his own observation, by a person of great veracity. The Phlegme of Wine, and indeed divers other Liquors that are indiscriminately condemnd to be cast away as phlegm, are endow'd with qualities that make them differ both from meer water, and from each other; and whereas the Chymists are pleas'd to call the *caput mortuum* of what they have distill'd (after they have by affusion of water drawn away its salt) *terra damnata*, or Earth, it may be doubted whether or no those earths are all of them perfectly alike: and it is scarce to be doubted, but that there are some of them which remain yet unreduc'd to an Elementary nature. The ashes of wood depriv'd of all the salt, and bone-Ashes, or calcin'd Harts-horn, which Refiners choose to make Tests of, as freest from Salt, seem unlike: and he that shall compare either of these insipid ashes to Lime, and much more to the *calx* of Talk [Transcriber's Note: Talck] (though by the affusion of water they be exquisitely dulcify'd) will perhaps see cause to think them things of a somewhat differing nature. And it is evident in Colcothar that the exactest calcination, follow'd by an exquisite dulcification, does not alwaies reduce the remaining body into elementary earth; for after the salt or Vitriol (if the Calcination have been too faint) is drawn out of the Colcothar, the residue is not earth, but a mixt body, rich in Medical vertues (as experience has inform'd me) and which ***Angelus Sala*** affirmes to be partly reducible into malleable Copper; which I judge very probable: for though when I was making Experiments upon Colcothar, I was destitute of a Furnace capable of giving a heat intense Enough to bring such a Calx to Fusion; yet having conjectur'd that if Colcothar abounded with that Metal, Aqua Fortis would find it out there, I put some dulcifi'd Colcothar into that ***Menstruum***, and found the Liquor, according to my Expectation, presently Colour'd as Highly as if it had been an Ordinary Solution of Copper.

The Fifth Part.

Here *Carneades* making a pause, I must not deny (sayes his Friend to him) that I think You have sufficiently prov'd that these distinct Substances which Chymists are wont to obtain from Mixt Bodies, by their Vulgar Destillation, are not pure and simple enough to deserve, in Rigour of speaking, the Name of Elements, or Principles. But I suppose You have heard, that there are some Modern *Spagyrists*, who give out that they can by further and more Skilfull Purifications, so reduce the separated Ingredients of Mixt Bodies to an Elementary simplicity, That the Oyles (for Instance) extracted from all Mixts shall as perfectly resemble one another, as the Drops of Water do.

If you remember (replies *Carneades*) that at the Beginning of our Conference with *Philoponus*, I declar'd to him before the rest of the Company, that I would not *engage* my self at present to do any more then examine the usual proofs alledg'd by Chymists, for the Vulgar doctrine of their three Hypostatical Principles; You will easily perceive that I am not oblig'd to make answer to what you newly propos'd; and that it rather grants, then disproves what I have been contending for: Since by pretending to make so great a change in the reputed Principles that Destillation affords the common *Spagyrists*, 'tis plainly enough presuppos'd, that before such Artificial Depurations be made, the Substances to be made more simple were not yet simple enough to be look'd upon as Elementary; Wherefore in case the *Artists* you speak of could perform what they give out they can, yet I should not need to be asham'd of having question'd the Vulgar Opinion touching the *tria Prima*. And as to the thing it self, I shall freely acknowledge to you, that I love not to be forward in determining things to be impossible, till I know and have consider'd the means by which they are propos'd to be effected. And therefore I shall not peremptorily deny

either the possibility of what these *Artists* promise, or my Assent to any just Inference; however destructive to my Conjectures, that may be drawn from their perfor-
mances. But give me leave to tell you withall, that because such promises are wont
(as Experience has more then once inform'd me) to be much more easily made, then
made good by Chymists, I must withhold my Beliefe from their assertions, till their
Experiments exact it; and must not be so easie as to expect before hand, an unlikely
thing upon no stronger Inducements then are yet given me: Besides that I have not
yet found by what I have heard of these Artists, that though they pretend to bring
the several Substances into which the Fire has divided the Concrete, to an exquisite
simplicity, They pretend also to be able by the Fire to divide all Concretes, Minerals, and others, into the same number of Distinct Substances. And in the mean time
I must think it improbable, that they can either truly separate as many differing
Bodies from Gold (for Instance) or *Osteocolla*, as we can do from Wine, or Vitriol;
or that the Mercury (for Example) of Gold or Saturn would be perfectly of the same
Nature with that of Harts-horn; and that the sulphur of Antimony would be but
Numerically different from the Distill'd butter or oyle of Roses.

But suppose (sayes *Eleutherius*) that you should meet with Chymists, who
would allow you to take in Earth and Water into the number of the principles of
Mixt Bodies; and being also content to change the Ambiguous Name of Mercury
for that more intelligible one of spirit, should consequently make the principles of
Compound Bodies to be Five; would you not think it something hard to reject so
plausible an Opinion, only because the Five substances into which the Fire divides
mixt Bodies are not exactly pure, and Homogeneous? For my part (Continues *Carneades*) I cannot but think it somewhat strange, in case this Opinion be not true,
that it should fall out so luckily, that so great a Variety of Bodies should be Analyz'd
by the Fire into just five Distinct substances; which so little differing from the Bodies that bear those names, may so Plausibly be call'd Oyle, Spirit, Salt, Water, and
Earth.

The Opinion You now propose (answers *Carneades*) being another then that I
was engag'd to examine, it is not requisite for me to Debate it at present; nor should
I have leisure to do it thorowly. Wherefore I shall only tell you in General, that
though I think this Opinion in some respects more defensible then that of the Vulgar Chymists; yet you may easily enough learn from the past Discourse what may be

thought of it: Since many of the Objections made against the Vulgar Doctrine of the Chymists seem, without much alteration, employable against this **Hypothesis** also. For, besides that this Doctrine does as well as the other take it for granted, (what is not easie to be prov'd) that the Fire is the true and Adequate Analyzer of Bodies, and that all the Distinct substances obtainable from a mixt Body by the Fire, were so pre-existent in it, that they were but extricated from each other by the **Analysis**; Besides that this Opinion, too, ascribe [Errata: ascribes] to the Productions of the Fire an Elementary simplicity, which I have shewn not to belong to them; and besides that this Doctrine is lyable to some of the other Difficulties, wherewith That of the **Tria Prima** is incumber'd; Besides all this, I say, this quinary number of Elements, (if you pardon the Expression) ought at least to have been restrain'd to the Generality of Animal and Vegetable Bodies, since not only among these there are some Bodies (as I formerly argu'd) which, for ought has yet been made to appear, do consist, either of fewer or more similar substances then precisely Five. But in the Mineral Kingdom, there is scarce one Concrete that has been evinc'd to be adequatly divisible into such five Principles or Elements, and neither more nor less, as this Opinion would have every mixt Body to consist of.

And this very thing (continues **Carneades**) may serve to take away or lessen your Wonder, that just so many Bodies as five should be found upon the Resolution of Concretes. For since we find not that the fire can make any such **Analysis** (into five Elements) of Metals and other Mineral Bodies, whose Texture is more strong and permanent, it remains that the Five Substances under consideration be Obtain'd from Vegetable and Animal Bodies, which (probably by reason of their looser Contexture) are capable of being Distill'd. And as to such Bodies, 'tis natural enough, that, whether we suppose that there are, or are not, precisely five Elements, there should ordinarily occurr in the Dissipated parts a five Fold Diversity of Scheme (if I may so speak.) For if the Parts do not remain all fix'd, as in Gold, Calcin'd Talck, &c. nor all ascend, as in the Sublimation of Brimstone, Camphire, &c. but after their Dissipation do associate themselves into new Schemes of Matter; it is very likely, that they will by the Fire be divided into fix'd and Volatile (I mean, in Reference to that degree of heat by which they are destill'd) and those Volatile parts will, for the most part, ascend either in a dry forme, which Chymists are pleas'd to call, if they be Tastless, Flowers; if Sapid, Volatile Salt; or in a Liquid Forme. And this Liquor must be either inflamable, and so pass for oyl, or not inflamable, and yet subtile and pungent, which may be call'd Spirit; or else strengthless or insipid, which may be nam'd Phlegme, or Water. And as for the fixt part, or **Caput Mortuum**, it will most commonly consist of Corpuscles, partly Soluble in Water, or Sapid, (especially if the Saline parts were not so Volatile, as to fly away before) which make up its fixt salt; and partly insoluble and insipid, which therefore seems to challenge the name of Earth. But although upon this ground one might easily enough have foretold, that the differing substances obtain'd from a perfectly mixt Body by the Fire would for the most part be reducible to the five newly mentioned States of Matter; yet it will not presently follow, that these five Distinct substances were simple and primogeneal bodies, so pre-existent in the Concrete that the fire does but take them asunder. Besides that it does not appear, that all Mixt Bodies, (witness, Gold, Silver, Mercury, &c.) Nay nor perhaps all Vegetables, which may appear by what we said above of **Camphire**, **Benzoin**, &c. are resoluble by Fire into just such differing Schemes of Matter. Nor will the Experiments formerly alledg'd permit us to look upon these separated Substances as Elementary, or uncompounded. Neither will it be a sufficient Argument of their being Bodies that deserve the Names which Chymists are pleas'd to give them, that they have an Analogy in point of Consistence, or either Volatility or Fixtness, or else some other obvious Quality, with the suppos'd Principles, whose names are ascrib'd to them. For, as I told you above, notwithstanding this Resemblance in some one Quality, there may be such a Disparity in others, as may be more fit to give them Differing Appellations, then the Resemblance is to give them one and the same. And indeed it seems but somewhat a gross Way of judging of the Nature of Bodies, to conclude without Scruple, that those must be of the same Nature that agree in some such General Quality, as Fluidity, Dryness, Volatility, and the like: since each of those Qualities, or States of Matter, may Comprehend a great Variety of Bodies, otherwise of a very differing Nature; as we may see in the Calxes of Gold, of Vitriol, and of Venetian Talck, compar'd with common Ashes, which yet are very dry, and fix'd by the vehemence of the Fire, as well as they. And as we may likewise gather from what I have formerly Observ'd, touching the Spirit of Box-Wood, which though a Volatile, Sapid, and not inflamable Liquor, as well as the Spirits of Harts-horn, of Blood and others, (and therefore has been hitherto call'd, the Spirit, and esteem'd for one of the Principles of the Wood that affords it;) may yet, as I told You, be subdivided into two Liquors, differing from one another, and one of them at least, from the Generality of other Chymical Spirits.

But you may your self, if you please, (pursues **Carneades**) accommodate to the **Hypothesis** you propos'd what other particulars you shall think applicable to it, in the foregoing Discourse. For I think it unseasonable for me to meddle now any further with a Controversie, which since it does not now belong to me, Leaves me at Liberty to Take my Own time to Declare my Self about it.

Eleutherius perceiving that **Carneades** was somewhat unwilling to spend any more time upon the debate of this Opinion, and having perhaps some thoughts of taking hence a Rise to make him Discourse it more fully another time, thought not fit as then to make any further mention to him of the propos'd opinion, but told him;

I presume I need not mind you, **Carneades**, That both the Patrons of the ternary number of Principles, and those that would have five Elements, endeavour to back their experiments with a specious Reason or two; and especially some of those Embracers of the Opinion last nam'd (whom I have convers'd with, and found them Learned men) assigne this Reason of the necessity of five distinct Elements; that otherwise mixt Bodies could not be so compounded and temper'd as to obtain a due consistence and competent Duration. For Salt (say they) is the **Basis** of Solidity; and Permanency in Compound Bodies, without which the other four Elements might indeed be variously and loosly blended together, but would remain incompacted; but that Salt might be dissolv'd into minute Parts, and convey'd to the other Substances to be compacted by it, and with it, there is a Necessity of Water. And that the mixture may not be too hard and brittle, a Sulphureous or Oyly Principle must intervene to make the mass more tenacious; to this a Mercurial spirit must be superadded; which by its activity may for a while premeate [Transcriber's Note: permeate], and as it were leaven the whole Mass, and thereby promote the more exquisite mixture and incorporation of the Ingredients. To all which (lastly) a portion of Earth must be added, which by its drinesse and poracity [Errata: porosity] may soak up part of that water wherein the Salt was dissolv'd, and eminently concurr with the other ingredients to give the whole body the requisite consistence.

I perceive (sayes **Carneades** smiling) that if it be true, as 'twas lately rooted

[Errata: noted] from the Proverb, *That good Wits have bad Memories*, You have that Title, as well as a better, to a place among the good Wits. For you have already more then once forgot, that I declar'd to you that I would at this Conference Examine only the Experiments of my Adversaries, not their Speculative Reasons. Yet 'tis not (Subjoynes *Carneades*) for fear of medling with the Argument you have propos'd, that I decline the examining it at present. For if when we are more at leasure, you shall have a mind that we may Solemnly consider of it together; I am confident we shall scarce find it insoluble. And in the mean time we may observe, that such a way of Arguing may, it seems, be speciously accommodated to differing *Hypotheses*. For I find that *Beguinus*, and other Assertors of the *Tria Prima*, pretend to make out by such a way, the requisiteness of their Salt, Sulphur and Mercury, to constitute mixt Bodies, without taking notice of any necessity of an Addition of Water and Earth.

And indeed neither sort of Chymists seem to have duly consider'd how great Variety there is in the Textures and Consistences of Compound Bodie; sand [Errata: Bodies; and] how little the consistence and Duration of many of them seem to accommodate and be explicable by the propos'd Notion. And not to mention those almost incorruptible Substances obtainable by the Fire, which I have prov'd to be somewhat compounded, and which the Chymists will readily grant not to be perfectly mixt Bodies: (Not to mention these, I say) If you will but recall to mind some of those Experiments, whereby I shew'd You that out of common Water only mixt Bodies (and even living ones) of very differing consistences, and resoluble by Fire into as many Principles as other bodies acknowledg'd to be perfectly mixt; if you do this, I say, you will not, I suppose, be averse from beleeving, that Nature by a convenient disposition of the minute parts of a portion of matter may contrive bodies durable enough, and of this, or that, or the other Consistence, without being oblig'd to make use of all, much less of any Determinate quantity of each of the five Elements, or of the three Principles to compound such bodies of. And I have (pursues *Carneades*) something wonder'd, Chymists should not consider, that there is scarce any body in Nature so permanent and indissoluble as Glass; which yet themselves teach us may be made of bare Ashes, brought to fusion by the meer Violence of the Fire; so that, since Ashes are granted to consist but of pure Salt and simple Earth, sequestred from all the other Principles or Elements, they must acknowledge, That even Art it self can of two Elements only, or, if you please, one Principle and one Element, compound a Body more durable then almost any in the World. Which being undeniable, how will they prove that Nature cannot compound Mixt Bodies, and even durable Ones, under all the five Elements or material Principles.

But to insist any longer on this Occasional Disquisition, Touching their Opinion that would Establish five Elements, were to remember as little as You did before, that the Debate of this matter is no part of my first undertaking; and consequently, that I have already spent time enough in what I look back upon but as a digression, or at best an Excursion.

And thus, *Eleutherius*, (sayes *Carneades*) having at length gone through the four Considerations I propos'd to Discourse unto you, I hold it not unfit, for fear my having insisted so long on each of them may have made you forget their *Series*, briefly to repeat them by telling you, that

Since, in the first place, it may justly be doubted whether or no the Fire be, as Chymists suppose it, the genuine and Universal Resolver of mixt Bodies;

Since we may doubt, in the next place, whether or no all the Distinct Substances that may be obtain'd from a mixt body by the Fire were pre-existent there in the formes in which they were separated from it;

Since also, though we should grant the Substances separable from mixt Bodies by the fire to have been their component Ingredients, yet the Number of such substances does not appear the same in all mixt Bodies; some of them being Resoluble into more differing substances than three, and Others not being Resoluble into so many as three.

And Since, Lastly, those very substances that are thus separated are not for the most part pure and Elementary bodies, but new kinds of mixts;

Since, I say, these things are so, I hope you will allow me to inferr, that the Vulgar Experiments (I might perchance have Added, the Arguments too) wont to be Alledg'd by Chymists to prove, that their three Hypostatical Principles do adequately compose all mixt Bodies, are not so demonstrative as to reduce a wary Person to acquiesce in their Doctrine, which, till they Explain and prove it better, will by its perplexing darkness be more apt to puzzle then satisfy considering men, and will to them appear incumbred with no small Difficulties.

And from what has been hitherto deduc'd (continues *Carneades*) we may

Learn, what to Judge of the common Practice of those Chymists, who because they have found that Diverse compound Bodies (for it will not hold in All) can be resolv'd into, or rather can be brought to afford two or three differing Substances more then the Soot and Ashes, whereinto the naked fire commonly divides them in our Chymnies, cry up their own Sect for the Invention of a New Philosophy, some of them, as *Helmont, &c.* styling themselves Philosophers by the Fire; and the most part not only ascribing, but as far as in them lies, engrossing to those of their Sect the Title of PHILOSOPHERS.

But alas, how narrow is this Philosophy, that reaches but to some of those compound Bodies, which we find but upon, or in the crust or outside of our terrestrial Globe, which is it self but a point in comparison of the vast extended Universe, of whose other and greater parts the Doctrine of the *Tria Prima* does not give us an Account! For what does it teach us, either of the Nature of the Sun, which Astronomers affirme to be eight-score and odd times bigger then the whole Earth? or of that of those numerous fixt Starrs, which, for ought we know, would very few, if any of them, appear inferiour in bulke and brightness to the Sun, if they were as neer us as He? What does the knowing that Salt, sulphur and Mercury, are the Principles of Mixt Bodies, informe us of the Nature of that vast, fluid, and AEtherial Substance, that seemes to make up the interstellar, and consequently much the greatest part of the World? for as for the opinion commonly ascrib'd to *Paracelsus*, as if he would have not only the four Peripatetick Elements, but even the Celestial parts of the Universe to consist of his three Principles, since the modern Chymists themselves have not thought so groundless a conceit worth their owning, I shall not think it Worth my confuting.

But I should perchance forgive the Hypothesis I have been all this while examining, if, though it reaches but to a very little part of the World, it did at least give us a satisfactory account of those things to which 'tis said to reach. But I find not, that it gives us any other then a very imperfect information even about mixt Bodies themselves: For how will the knowledge of the *Tria Prima* discover to us the Reason, why the Loadstone drawes a Needle and disposes it to respect the Poles, and yet seldom precisely points at them? how will this Hypothesis teach Us how a Chick is formed in the Egge, or how the Seminal Principles of Mint, Pompions, and other Vegitables, that I mention'd to You above, can fashion Water into Various

Plants, each of them endow'd with its peculiar and determinate shape, and with divers specifick and discriminating Qualities? How does this Hypothesis shew us, how much Salt, how much Sulphur, and how much Mercury must be taken to make a Chick or a Pompion? and if We know that, what Principle is it, that manages these Ingredients, and contrives (for instance) such Liquors as the White and Yelk of an Egge into such a variety of Textures as is requisite to fashion the Bones, Veines, Arteries, Nerves, Tendons, Feathers, Blood, and other parts of a Chick; and not only to fashion each Limbe, but to connect them altogether, after that manner that is most congruous to the perfection of the Animal which is to Consist of Them? For to say, that some more fine and subtile part of either or all the Hypostatical Principles is the Director in all this business, and the Architect of all this Elaborate structure, is to give one occasion to demand again, what proportion and way of mixture of the *Tria Prima* afforded this *Architectonick* Spirit, and what Agent made so skilful and happy a mixture? And the Answer to this Question, if the Chymists will keep themselves within their three Principles, will be lyable to the same Inconvenience, that the Answer to the former was. And if it were not to intrench upon the Theame of a Friend of ours here present, I could easily prosecute the Imperfections of the Vulgar Chymists Philosophy, and shew you, that by going about to explicate by their three Principles, I say not, all the abstruse Properties of mixt Bodies, but even such Obvious and more familiar *Phaenomena* as *Fluidity* and *Firmness*, The Colours and Figures of Stones, Minerals, and other compound Bodies, The Nutrition of either Plants or Animals, the Gravity of Gold or Quicksilver compar'd with Wine or Spirit of Wine; By attempting, I say, to render a reason of these (to omit a thousand others as difficult to account for) from any proportion of the three simple Ingredients, Chymists will be much more likely to discredit themselves and their *Hypothesis*, then satisfy an intelligent Inquirer after Truth.

But (interposes *Eleutherus*) [Transcriber's Note: Eleutherius] This Objection seems no more then may be made against the four Peripatetick Elements. And indeed almost against any other *Hypothesis*, that pretends by any Determinate Number of Material Ingredients to render a reason of the *Phaenomena* of Nature. And as for the use of the Chymical Doctrine of the three Principles, I suppose you need not be told by me, that The great Champion of it, The Learned *Sennertus*,[23] assignes this noble use of the *Tria Prima*, That from Them, as the neerest and most

Proper Principles, may be Deduc'd and Demonstrated the Properties which are in Mixt Bodies, and which cannot be Proximately (as They speak) deduc'd from the Elements. And This, sayes he, is chiefly Apparent, when we Inquire into the Properties and Faculties of Medecines. And I know (continues *Eleutherius*) That the Person You have assum'd, of an Opponent of the **Hermetick Doctrine**, will not so far prevaile against your Native and wonted Equity, as To keep You from acknowledging that Philosophy is much beholden to the Notions and Discoveries of Chymists.

[23: ***Senn. de Cons. & Dissen. p. 165.***]

If the Chymists You speak of (Replyes **Carneades**) had been so modest, or so Discreet, as to propose their Opinion of the **Tria Prima**, but as a Notion useful among Others, to increase Humane knowledge, they had deserv'd more of our thanks; and less of our Opposition; but since the Thing that they pretend is not so much to contribute a Notion toward the Improvement of Philosophy, as to make this Notion attended [Errata: (attended] by a few lesse considerable ones) pass for a New Philosophy itself. Nay, since they boast so much of this phancie of theirs, that the famous **Quercetanus** scruples not to write, that if his most certain Doctrine of the three Principles were sufficiently Learned, Examin'd, and Cultivated, it would easily Dispel all the Darkness that benights our minds, and bring in a Clear Light, that would remove all Difficulties. This School affording Theorems and Axiomes irrefragable, and to be admitted without Dispute by impartial Judges; and so useful withal, as to exempt us from the necessity of having recourse, for want of the knowledg of causes, to that Sanctuary of the igorant [Transcriber's Note: ignorant], Occult Qualities; since, I say, this Domestick Notion of the Chymists is so much overvalued by them, I cannot think it unfit, they should be made sensible of their mistake; and be admonish'd to take in more fruitful and comprehensive Principles, if they mean to give us an account of the **Phaenomena** of Nature; and not confine themselves and (as far as they can) others to such narrow Principles, as I fear will scarce inable them to give an account (I mean an intelligible one) of the tenth part (I say not) of all the **Phaenomena** of Nature; but even of all such as by the **Leucippian** or some of the other sorts of Principles may be plausibly enough explicated. And though I be not unwilling to grant, that the incompetency I impute to the Chymical *Hypothesis* is but the same which may be Objected against that of the four Elements, and divers other Doctrines that have been maintain'd by Learned men; yet since 'tis the Chymical *Hypothesis* only which I am now examining, I see not why, if what I impute to it be a real inconvenience, either it should cease to be so, or I should scruple to object it, because either Theories are lyable thereunto, as well as the Hermetical. For I know not why a Truth should be thought lesse a Truth for the being fit to overthrow variety of Errors.

I am oblig'd to You (continues *Carneades*, a little smiling) for the favourable Opinion You are pleas'd to express of my Equity, if there be no design in it. But I need not be tempted by an Artifice, or invited by a Complement, to acknowledge the great service that the Labours of Chymists have done the Lovers of useful Learning; nor even on this occasion shall their Arrogance hinder my Gratitude. But since we are as well examining to [Errata: delete "to"] the truth of their Doctrine as the merit of their industry, I must in order to the investigation of the first, continue a reply, to talk at the rate of the part I have assum'd; And tell you, that when I acknowledg the usefulness of the Labours of *Spagyrists* to Natural Philosophy, I do it upon the score of their experiments, not upon that of Their Speculations; for it seems to me, that their Writings, as their Furnaces, afford as well smoke as light; and do little lesse obscure some subjects, then they illustrate others. And though I am unwilling to deny, that 'tis difficult for a man to be an Accomplisht Naturalist, that is a stranger to Chymistry, yet I look upon the common Operations and practices of Chymists, almost as I do on the Letters of the Alphabet, without whose knowledge 'tis very hard for a man to become a Philosopher; and yet that knowledge is very far from being sufficient to make him One.

But (sayes *Carneades*, resuming a more serious Look) to consider a little more particularly what you alledg in favour of the Chymical Doctrine of the *Tria Prima*, though I shall readily acknowledge it not to be unuseful, and that the Divisers [Errata: devisers] and Embracers of it have done the Common-Wealth of Learning some service, by helping to destroy that excessive esteem, or rather veneration, wherewith the Doctrine of the four Elements was almost as generally as undeservedly entertain'd; yet what has been alledg'd concerning the usefulness of the *Tria Prima*, seems to me liable to no contemptible Difficulties.

And first, as for the very way of Probation, which the more Learned and more

Sober Champions of the Chymical cause employ to evince the Chymical Principles in Mixt Bodies, it seems to me to be farr enough from being convincing. This grand and leading Argument, your **Sennertus** Himself, who layes Great weight upon it, and tells us, that the most Learned Philosophers employ this way of Reasoning to prove the most important things, proposes thus: *Ubicunque* (sayes he) *pluribus eaedem affectiones & qualitates insunt, per commune quoddam Principium insint necesse est, sicut omnia sunt Gravia propter terram, calida propter Ignem. At Colores, Odores, Sapores, esse* [Greek: phlogiston] *& similia alia, mineralibus, Metallis, Gemmis, Lapidibus, Plantis, Animalibus insunt. Ergo per commune aliquod principium, & subiectum, insunt. At tale principium non sunt Elementa. Nullam enim habent ad tales qualitates producendas potentiam. Ergo alia principia, unde fluant, inquirenda sunt.*

In the Recital of this Argument, (sayes **Carneades**) I therefore thought fit to retain the Language wherein the Author proposes it, that I might also retain the propriety of some Latine Termes, to which I do not readily remember any that fully answer in English. But as for the Argumentation it self, 'tis built upon a precarious supposition, that seems to me neither Demonstrable nor true; for, how does it appear, that where the same Quality is to be met with in many Bodies, it must belong to them upon the Account of some one Body whereof they all partake? (For that the Major of our Authors Argument is to be Understood of the Material Ingredients of bodies, appears by the Instances of Earth and Fire he annexes to explain it.) For to begin with that very Example which he is pleas'd to alledge for himself; how can he prove, that the Gravity of all Bodies proceeds from what they participate of the Element of Earth? Since we see, that not only common Water, but the more pure Distill'd Rain Water is heavy; and Quicksilver is much heavier than Earth it self; though none of my Adversaries has yet prov'd, that it contains any of that Element. And I the Rather make use of this Example of Quicksilver, because I see not how the Assertors of the Elements will give any better Account of it then the Chymists. For if it be demanded how it comes to be Fluid, they will answer, that it participates much of the Nature of Water. And indeed, according to them, Water may be the Predominant Element in it, since we see, that several Bodies which by Distillation afford Liquors that weigh more then their **Caput Mortuum** do not yet consist of

Liquor enough to be Fluid. Yet if it be demanded how Quicksilver comes to be so heavy, then 'tis reply'd, that 'tis by reason of the Earth that abounds in it; but since, according to them, it must consist also of air, and partly of Fire, which they affirm to be light Elements, how comes it that it should be so much heavier then Earth of the same bulk, though to fill up the porosities and other Cavities it be made up into a mass or paste with Water, which it self they allow to be a heavy Element. But to returne to our *Spagyrists*, we see that Chymical Oyles and fixt Salts, though never so exquisitely purify'd and freed from terrestrial parts, do yet remain ponderous enough. And Experience has inform'd me, that a pound, for instance, of some of the heaviest Woods, as *Guajacum* that will sink in Water, being burnt to Ashes will yield a much less weight of them (whereof I found but a small part to be Alcalyzate) then much lighter Vegetables: As also that the black Charcoal of it will not sink as did the wood, but swim; which argues that the Differing Gravity of Bodies proceeds chiefly from their particular Texture, as is manifest in Gold, the closest and Compactest of Bodies, which is many times heavier then we can possibly make any parcell of Earth of the same Bulk. I will not examine, what may be argu'd touching the Gravity or Quality Analagous thereunto, of even Celestial bodies, from the motion of the spots about the Sun, d [Errata: and] from the appearing equality of the suppos'd Seas in the Moon; nor consider how little those *Phaemonea* [Transcriber's Note: Phaenomena] would agree with what *Sennertus* presumes concerning Gravity. But further to invalidate his supposition, I shall demand, upon what Chymical Principle Fluidity depends? And yet Fluidity is, two or three perhaps excepted, the most diffused quality of the universe, and far more General then almost any other of those that are to be met with in any of the Chymicall Principles, or *Aristotelian* Elements; since not only the Air, but that vast expansion we call Heaven, in comparison of which our Terrestrial Globe (supposing it were all Solid) is but a point; and perhaps to [Errata: too] the Sun and the fixt Stars are fluid bodies. I demand also, from which of the Chymical Principles Motion flowes; which yet is an affection of matter much more General then any that can be deduc'd from any of the three Chymical Principles. I might ask the like Question concerning Light, which is not only to be found in the Kindl'd Sulphur of mixt Bodis [Transcriber's Note: Bodies], but (not to mention those sorts of rotten Woods, and rotten Fish that shine in the Dark) in the tails of living Glow-wormes, and in the Vast bodies of the Sun and Stars. I would gladly also know, in which of the three Principles the Quality, we call Sound, resides as in its proper Subject; since either Oyl falling upon Oyle, or Spirit upon Spirit, or Salt upon Salt, in a great quantity, and from a considerable height, will make a noise, or if you please, create a sound, and (that the objection may reach the *Aristotelians*) so will also water upon water, and Earth upon Earth. And I could name other qualities to be met within divers bodies, of which I suppose my Adversaries will not in haste assign any Subject, upon whose Account it must needs be, that the quality belongs to all the other several bodies.

And, before I proceed any further, I must here invite you to compare the supposition we are examining, with some other of the Chymical Tenents. For, first they do in effect teach that more then one quality may belong to, and be deduc'd from, one Principle. For, they ascribe to Salt Tasts, and the power of Coagulation; to sulphur, as well Odours as inflamableness; And some of them ascribe to Mercury, Colours; as all of them do effumability, as they speak. And on the other side, it is evident that Volatility belongs in common to all the three Principles, and to Water too. For 'tis manifest, that Chymical Oyles are Volatile; That also divers Salts Emerging, upon the Analysis of many Concretes, are very Volatile, is plain from the figitiveness [Errata: fugitivenesse] of Salt, of Harts-horne, flesh, &c. ascending in the Distillation of those bodies. How easily water may be made to ascend in Vapours, there is scarce any body that has not observ'd. And as for what they call the Mercuriall Principle of bodies, that is so apt to be rais'd in the form of Steam, that *Paracelsus* and others define it by that aptness to fly up; so that (to draw that inference by the way) it seems not that Chymists have been accurate in their Doctrine of qualities, and their respective Principles, since they both derive several qualities from the same Principle, and must ascribe the same quality to almost all their Principles and other bodies besides. And thus much for the first thing taken for granted, without sufficient proof, by your *Sennertus*: And to add that upon the Bye (continues *Carneades*) we may hence learn what to judge of the way of Argumentation, which that fierce Champion of the *Aristotelians* against the Chymists, *Anthonius Guntherus Billichius*[24] employes, where he pretends to prove against *Beguinus*, that not only the four Elements do immediately concur to Constitute every mixt body, and are both present in it, and obtainable from it upon its Dissolution; but that in the *Tria Prima* themselves, whereinto Chymists are wont to resolve mixt Bodies, each of them clearly discovers it self to consist of four Elements. The Ratiocination it self (pursues *Carneades*) being somewhat unusual, I did the other Day Transcribe it, and (sayes He, pulling a Paper out of his Pocket) it is this. *Ordiamur, cum Beguino, a ligno viridi, quod si concremetur, videbis in sudore Aquam, in fumo Aerem, in flamma & Prunis Ignem, Terram in cineribus: Quod si Beguino placuerit ex eo colligere humidum aquosum, cohibere humidum oleaginosum, extrahere ex cineribus salem; Ego ipsi in unoquoque horum seorsim quatuor Elementa ad oculum demonstrabo, eodem artificio quo in ligno viridi ea demonstravi. Humorem aquosum admovebo Igni. Ipse Aquam Ebullire videbit, in Vapore Aerem conspiciet, Ignem sentiet in aestu, plus minus Terrae in sedimento apparebit. Humor porro Oleaginosus aquam humiditate & fluiditate per se, accensus vero Ignem flamma prodit, fumo Aerem, fuligine, nidore & amurca terram. Salem denique ipse Beguinus siccum vocat & Terrestrem, qui tamen nec fusus Aquam, nec caustica vi ignem celare potest; ignis vero Violentia in halitus versus nec ab Aere se alienum esse demonstrat; Idem de Lacte, de Ovis, de semine Lini, de Garyophyllis, de Nitro, de sale Marino, denique de Antimonio, quod fuit de Ligno viridi Judicium; eadem de illorum partibus, quas* Beguinus *adducit, sententia, quae de viridis ligni humore aquoso, quae de liquore ejusdem oleoso, quae de sale fuit.*

[24: *In Thessalo redivivo. Cap. 10. pag. 73. & 74.*]

This bold Discourse (resumes *Carneades*, putting up again his Paper,) I think it were not very difficult to confute, if his Arguments were as considerable as our time will probably prove short for the remaining and more necessary Part of my Discourse; wherefore referring You for an Answer to what was said concerning the Dissipated Parts of a burnt piece of green Wood, to what I told *Themistius* on the like occasion, I might easily shew You, how sleightly and superficially our *Guntherus* talks of the dividing the flame of Green Wood into his four Elements; **When** he makes that vapour to be air, which being caught in Glasses and condens'd, presently discovers it self to have been but an Aggregate of innumerable very minute drops of Liquor; and **When** he would prove the Phlegmes being compos'd of Fire by that Heat which is adventitious to the Liquor, and ceases upon the absence of what produc'd it (whether that be an Agitation proceeding from the motion of the External Fire, or the presence of a Multitude of igneous Atomes pervading the pores of the Vessel, and nimbly permeating the whole Body of the Water) I might, I say, urge these and divers other Weaknesses of His Discourse. But I will rather take Notice of what is more pertinent to the Occasion of this Digression, namely, that Taking it for Granted, that Fluidity (with which he unwarily seems to confound Humidity) must proceed from the Element of Water, he makes a Chymical Oyle to Consist of that Elementary Liquor; and yet in the very next Words proves, that it consists also of Fire, by its Inflamability; not remembring that exquisitely pure Spirit of Wine is both more Fluid then Water it self, and yet will Flame all away without leaving the Least Aqueous Moisture behind it; and without such an ***Amurca*** and Soot as he would Deduce the presence of Earth from. So that the same Liquor may according to his Doctrine be concluded by its great Fluidity to be almost all Water; and by its burning all away to be all disguised Fire. And by the like way of Probation our Author would shew that the fixt salt of Wood is compounded of the four Elements. For (sayes he) being turn'd by the violence of the Fire into steames, it shews it self to be of kin to Air; whereas I doubt whether he ever saw a true fixt Salt (which to become so, must have already endur'd the violence of an Incinerating Fire) brought by the Fire alone to ascend in the Forme of Exhalations; but I do not doubt that if he did, and had caught those Exhalations in convenient Vessels, he would have found them as well as the Steames of common Salt, &c. of a Saline and not an Aereal Nature. And whereas our Authour takes it also for Granted, that the Fusibility of Salt must be Deduc'd from Water, it is indeed so much the Effect of heat variously agitating the Minute Parts of a Body, without regard to Water, that Gold (which by its being the heavyest and fixtest of Bodies, should be the most Earthy) will be brought to Fusion by a strong Fire; which sure is more likely to drive away then increase its Aqueous Ingredient, if it have any; and on the other side, for want of a sufficient agitation of its minute parts, Ice is not Fluid, but Solid; though he presumes also that the Mordicant Quality of Bodies must proceed from a fiery ingredient; whereas, not to urge that the Light and inflamable parts, which are the most likely to belong to the Element of Fire, must probably be driven away by that time the violence of the Fire has reduc'd the Body to ashes; Not to urge this, I I [Transcriber's Note: extra "I" in original] say, nor that Oyle of Vitriol which quenches Fire, burnes the Tongue and flesh of those that Unwarily tast or apply it, as a caustick doth, it is precarious to prove the Presence of Fire in fixt salts from their Caustick power, unlesse it were first shewn, that all the Qualities ascribed to salts must be deduc'd from those of the Elements; which, had I Time, I could easily manifest to be no easy talk. And not to mention that our Authour makes a Body as Homogeneous as any he can produce for Elementary, belong both to Water and Fire, Though it be neither Fluid nor Insipid, like Water; nor light and Volatile, like Fire; he seems to omit in this Anatomy the Element of Earth, save That he intimates, That the salt may pass for that; But since a few lines before, he takes Ashes for Earth, I see not how he will avoid an Inconsistency either betwixt the Parts of his Discourse or betwixt some of them and his Doctrine. For since There is a manifest Difference betwixt the Saline and the insipid Parts of Ashes, I see not how substances That Disagree in such Notable Qualities can be both said to be Portions of an Element, whose Nature requires that it be Homogeneous, especially in this case where an *Analysis* by the Fire is suppos'd to have separated it from the admixture of other Elements, which are confess'd by most *Aristotelians* to be Generally found in common Earth, and to render it impure. And sure if when we have consider'd for how little a Disparities sake the Peripateticks make these Symbolizing Bodies Aire and Fire to be two Distinct Elements, we shall also consider that the Saline part of Ashes is very strongly Tasted, and easily soluble in Water; whereas the other part of the same Ashes is insipid and indissoluble in the same Liquor: Not to add, that the one substance is Opacous, and the other somewhat Diaphanous, nor that they differ in Divers other Particulars; If we consider those things, I say, we shall hardly think that both these Substances are Elementary Earth; And as to what is sometimes objected, that their Saline Tast is only an Effect of Incineration and Adustion, it has been elsewhere fully reply'd to, when propos'd by *Themistius*, and where it has been prov'd against him, that however insipid Earth may perhaps by Additaments be turn'd into Salt, yet 'tis not like it should be so by the Fire alone: For we see that when we refine Gold and Silver, the violentest Fires We can Employ on them give them not the least Rellish of Saltness. And I think *Philoponus* has rightly observ'd, that the Ashes of some Concretes contain very little salt if any at all; For Refiners suppose that bone-ashes are free from it, and therefore make use of them for Tests and Cuppels, which ought to be Destitute of Salt, lest the Violence of the Fire should bring them to Vitrification;

And having purposely and heedfully tasted a Cuppel made of only bone-ashes and fair water, which I had caus'd to be expos'd to a Very Violent Fire, acuated by the Blast of a large pair of Double Bellows, I could not perceive that the force of the Fire had imparted to it the least Saltness, or so much as made it less Insipid.

But (sayes **Carneades**) since neither You nor I love Repetitions, I shall not now make any of what else was urg'd against **Themistius** but rather invite You to take notice with me that when our Authour, though a Learned Man, and one that pretends skill enough in Chymistry to reforme the whole Art, comes to make good his confident Undertaking, to give us an occular Demonstration of the immediate Presence of the four Elements in the resolution of Green Wood, He is fain to say things that agree very little with one another. For about the beginning of that passage of His lately recited to you, he makes the sweat as he calls it of the green Wood to be Water, the smoke Aire, the shining Matter Fire, and the Ashes Earth; whereas a few lines after, he will in each of these, nay (as I just now noted) in one Distinct Part of the Ashes, shew the four Elements. So that either the former *Analysis* must be incompetent to prove that Number of Elements, since by it the burnt Concrete is not reduc'd into Elementary Bodies, but into such as are yet each of them compounded of the four Elements; or else these Qualities from which he endeavours to deduce the presence of all the Elements, in the fixt salt, and each of the other separated substances, will be but a precarious way of probation: especially if you consider, that the extracted *Alcali* of Wood, being for ought appears at least as similar a Body as any that the Peripateticks can shew us, if its differing Qualities must argue the presence of Distinct Elements, it will scarce be possible for them by any way they know of employing the fire upon a Body, to shew that any Body is a Portion of a true Element: And this recals to my mind, that I am now but in an occasional excussion, which aiming only to shew that the Peripateticks as well as the Chymists take in our present Controversie something for granted which they ought to prove, I shall returne to my exceptions, where I ended the first of them, and further tell you, that neither is that the only precarious thing that I take notice of in **Sennertus** his Argumentation; for when he inferrs, that because the Qualities he Mentions as Colours, Smels, and the like, belong not to the Elements; they therefore must to the Chymical Principles, he takes that for granted, which will not in haste be prov'd; as I might here manifest, but that I may by and by have a fitter opportunity to take notice of it. And thus much at present may suffice to have Discours'd against the Supposition, that almost every Quality must have some [Greek: dektikon proton], as they speak, some Native receptacle, wherein as in its proper Subject of inhesion it peculiarly resides, and on whose account that quality belongs to the other Bodies, Wherein it is to be met with. Now this Fundamental supposition being once Destroy'd, whatsoever is built upon it, must fall to ruine of it self.

But I consider further, that Chymists are (for ought I have found) far from being able to explicate by any of the *Tria Prima*, those qualities which they pretend to belong primarily unto it, and in mixt Bodies to Deduce from it. Tis true indeed, that such qualities are not explicable by the four Elements; but it will not therefore follow, that they are so by the three hermetical Principles; and this is it that seems to have deceiv'd the Chymists, and is indeed a very common mistake amongst most Disputants, who argue as if there could be but two Opinions concerning the Difficulty about which they contend; and consequently they inferr, that if their Adversaries Opinion be Erroneous, Their's must needs be the Truth; whereas many questions, and especially in matters Physiological, may admit of so many Differing *Hypotheses*, that 'twill be very inconsiderate and fallacious to conclude (except where the Opinions are precisely Contradictory) the Truth of one from the falsity of another. And in our particular case 'tis no way necessary, that the Properties of mixt Bodies must be explicable either by the Hermetical, or the *Aristotelian Hypothesis*, there being divers other and more plausible wayes of explaining them, and especially that, which deduces qualities from the motion, figure, and contrivance of the small parts of Bodies; as I think might be shewn, if the attempt were as seasonable, as I fear it would be Tedious.

I will allow then, that the Chymists do not causelessly accuse the Doctrine of the four elements of incompetency to explain the Properties of Compound bodies. And for this Rejection of a Vulgar Error, they ought not to be deny'd what praise men may deserve for exploding a Doctrine whose Imperfections are so conspicuous, that men needed but not to shut their Eyes, to discover them. But I am mistaken, if our Hermetical Philosophers Themselves need not, as well as the Peripateticks, have Recourse to more Fruitfull and Comprehensive Principles then the *tria Prima*, to make out the Properties of the Bodies they converse with. Not to accumulate Examples to this purpose, (because I hope for a fitter opportunity to prosecute this

Subject) let us at present only point at Colour, that you may guess by what they say of so obvious and familiar a Quality, how little Instruction we are to expect from the *Tria Prima* in those more abstruse ones, which they with the *Aristotelians* stile Occult. For about Colours, neither do they at all agree among themselves, nor have I met with any one, of which of the three Perswasions soever, that does intelligibly explicate Them. The Vulgar Chymists are wont to ascribe Colours to Mercury; *Paracelsus* in divers places attributes them to Salt; and *Sennertus*,[25] having recited their differing Opinions, Dissents from both, and referrs Colours rather unto Sulphur. But how Colours do, nay, how they may, arise from either of these Principles, I think you will scarce say that any has yet intelligibly explicated. And if Mr. *Boyle* will allow me to shew you the Experiments which he has collected about Colours, you will, I doubt not, confess that bodies exhibit colours, not upon the Account of the Predominancy of this or that Principle in them, but upon that of their Texture, and especially the Disposition of their superficial parts, whereby the Light rebounding thence to the Eye is so modifi'd, as by differing Impressions variously to affect the Organs of Sight. I might here take notice of the pleasing variety of Colours exhibited by the Triangular glass, (as 'tis wont to be call'd) and demand, what addition or decrement of either Salt, Sulphur, or Mercury, befalls the Body of the Glass by being Prismatically figur'd; and yet 'tis known, that without that shape it would not affor'd those colours as it does. But because it may be objected, that these are not real, but apparent Colours; that I may not lose time in examing the Distinction, I will alledge against the Chymists, a couple of examples of Real and Permanent Colours Drawn from Metalline Bodies, and represent, that without the addition of any extraneous body, Quicksilver may by the Fire alone, and that in glass Vessels, be depriv'd of its silver-like Colour, and be turn'd into a Red Body; and from this Red Body without Addition likewise may be obtain'd a Mercury Bright and Specular as it was before; So that I have here a lasting Colour Generated and Destroy'd (as I have seen) at pleasure, without adding or taking away either Mercury, Salt, or Sulphur; and if you take a clean and slender piece of harden'd steel, and apply to it the flame of a candle at some little distance short of the point, You shall not have held the Steel long in the flame, but You shall perceive divers Colours, as Yellow, Red and Blew, to appear upon the Surface of the metal, and as it were run along in chase of one another towards the point; So that the same body, and that in one and the same part, may not only have a new colour produc'd in it, but exhibite successively divers Colours within a minute of an hour, or thereabouts, and any of these Colours may by Removing the Steel from the Fire, become Permanent, and last many years. And this Production and Variety of Colours cannot reasonably be suppos'd to proceed from the Accession of any of the three Principles, to which of them soever Chymists will be pleas'd to ascribe Colours; especially considering, that if you but suddenly Refrigerate that Iron, First made Red hot, it will be harden'd and Colourless again; and not only by the Flame of a Candle, but by any other equivalent heat Conveniently appli'd, the like Colours will again be made to appear and succeed one another, as at the First. But I must not any further prosecute an Occasional Discourse, though that were not so Difficult for me to do, as I fear it would be for the Chymists to give a better Account of the other Qualities, by their Principles, then they have done of Colours. And your *Sennertus* Himself (though an Author I much value) would I fear have been exceedingly puzl'd to resolve, by the *Tria Prima*, halfe that Catalogue of Problems, which he challenges the Vulgar Peripateticks to explicate by their four Elements.[26] And supposing it were true, that Salt or Sulphur were the Principle to which this or that Quality may be peculiarly referr'd, yet though he that teaches us this teaches us something concerning That quality, yet he Teaches us but something. For indeed he does not Teach us That which can in any Tollerable measure satisfie an inquisitive Searcher after Truth. For what is it to me to know, that such a quality resides in such a Principle or Element, whilst I remain altogether ignorant of the Cause of that quality, and the manner of its production and Operation? How little do I know more then any Ordinary Man of Gravity, if I know but that the Heaviness of mixt bodies proceeds from that of the Earth they are compos'd of, if I know not the reason why the Earth is Heavy? And how little does the Chymist teach the Philosopher of the Nature of Purgatition, if he only tells him that the Purgative Vertue of Medicines resides in their Salt? For, besides that this must not be conceded without Limitation, since the purging parts of many Vegetables Extracted by the Water wherein they are infus'd, are at most but such compounded Salts, (I mean mingl'd with Oyle, and Spirit, and Earth, as Tartar and divers other Subjects of the Vegetable Kingdom afford;) And since too that Quicksilver precipitated either with Gold, or without Addition, into a powder, is wont to be strongly enough Cathartical, though the Chymists have not yet prov'd, that either Gold or Mercury have any Salt at all, much less any that is Purgative; Besides this, I say, how little is it to me, to know That 'tis the Salt of the Rhubarb (for Instance) that purges, if I find That it does not purge as Salt; since scarce any Elementary Salt is in small quantity cathartical. And if I know not how Purgation in general is effected in a Humane Body? In a word, as 'tis one thing to know a mans Lodging, and another, to be acquainted with him; so it may be one thing to know the subject wherein a Quality principally resides, and another thing to have a right notion and knowledg of the quality its self. Now that which I take to be the reason of this Chymical Deficiency, is the same upon whose account I think the *Aristotelian* and divers other Theories incompetent to explicate the Origen [Errata: origine] of Qualities. For I am apt to think, that men will never be able to explain the *Phaenomena* of Nature, while they endeavour to deduce them only from the Presence and Proportion of such or such material Ingredients, and consider such ingredients or Elements as Bodies in a state of rest; whereas indeed the greatest part of the affections of matter, and consequently of the *Phaenomena* of nature, seems to depend upon the motion and the continuance [Errata: contrivance] of the small parts of Bodies. For 'tis by motion that one part of matter acts upon another; and 'tis, for the most part, the texture of the Body upon which the moving parts strike, that modifies to motion or Impression, and concurrs with it to the production of those Effects which make up the chief part of the Naturalists Theme.

[25: *De Cons. & dissen. cap. 11. pag. 186.*]

[26: Sennert. de Con. seus. [Transcriber's Note: Consens.] & Dissens. pag. 165. 166.]

But (sayes *Eleutherius*) me thinks for all this, you have left some part of what I alledg'd in behalf of the three principles, unanswer'd. For all that you have said will not keep this from being a useful Discovery, that since in the Salt of one Concrete, in the Sulphur of another and the Mercury of a third, the Medicinal vertue of it resides, that Principle ought to be separated from the rest, and there the desired faculty must be sought for.

I never denyed (Replyes *Carneades*) that the Notion of the *Tria Prima* may be of some use, but (continues he laughing) by what you now alledg for it, it will but appear That it is useful to Apothecaries, rather than to Philosophers, The being able to make things Operative being sufficient to those, whereas the Knowledge of Causes is the Thing looked after by These. And let me Tell You, **Eleutherius**, even this it self will need to be entertained with some caution.

For first, it will not presently follow, That if the Purgative or other vertue of a simple may be easily extracted by Water or Spirit of Wine, it Resides in the Salt or Sulphur of the Concrete; Since unlesse the Body have before been resolved by the Fire, or some Other Powerful Agent, it will, for the most part, afford in the Liquors I have named, rather the finer compounded parts of it self, Than the Elementary ones. As I noted before, That Water will dissolve not only pure Salts, but Crystals of Tartar, Gumme Arabick, Myrr'h, and Other Compound Bodies. As also Spirit of Wine will Dissolve not only the pure Sulphur of Concretes, but likewise the whole Substance of divers Resinous Bodies, as Benzoin, the Gummous parts of Jallap, Gumme Lacca, and Other bodies that are counted perfectly Mixt. And we see that the Extracts made either with Water or Spirit of Wine are not of a simple and Elementary Nature, but Masses consisting of the looser Corpuscles, and finer parts of the Concretes whence they are Drawn; since by Distillation they may be Divided into more Elementary substances.

Next, we may consider That even when there intervenes a Chymical resolution by he [Transcriber's Note: the] Fire, 'tis seldom in the Saline or Sulphureous principle, as such, that the desir'd Faculty of the Concrete Resides; But, as that Titular Salt or Sulphur is yet a mixt body, though the Saline or Sulphureous Nature be predominant in it. For, if in Chymical Resolutions the separated Substances were pure and simple Bodies, and of a perfect Elementary Nature; no one would be indued with more Specifick Vertues, than another; and their qualities would Differ as Little as do those of Water. And let me add this upon the bye, That even Eminent Chymists have suffer'd themselves to be reprehended by me for their over great Diligence in purifying some of the things they obtain by Fire from mixt Bodies. For though such compleatly purifyed Ingredients of Bodies might perhaps be more satisfactory to our Understanding; yet others are often more useful to our Lives, the efficacy of such Chymical Productions depending most upon what they retain of the Bodies whence they are separated, or gain by the new associations of the Dissipated among themselves; whereas if they were meerly Elementary, their uses would be comparatively very small; and the vertues of Sulphurs, Salts, or Other such Substances of one denomination, would be the very same.

And by the Way (*Eleutherius*) I am inclin'd upon this ground to Think, That the artificial resolution of compound bodies by Fire does not so much enrich mankind, as it divides them into their supposed Principles; as upon the score of its making new compounds by now [Transcriber's Note: new] combinations of the dissipated parts of the resolv'd Body. For by this means the Number of mixt Bodies is considerably increased. And many of those new productions are indow'd with useful qualities, divers of which they owe not to the body from which they were obtein'd, but to Their newly Acquired Texture.

But thirdly, that which is principally to be Noted is this, that as there are divers Concretes whose Faculties reside in some one or other of those differing Substances that Chymists call their Sulphurs, Salts, and Mercuries, and consequently may be best obtain'd, by analyzing the Concrete whereby the desired Principles may be had sever'd or freed from the rest; So there are other wherein the noblest properties lodge not in the Salt, or Sulphur, or Mercury, but depend immediately upon the form (or if you will) result from the determinate structure of the Whole Concrete; and consequently they that go about to extract the Vertues of such bodies, by exposing them to the Violence of the Fire, do exceedingly mistake, and take the way to Destroy what they would obtain.

I remmember that *Helmont* himself somewhere confesses, That as the Fire betters some things and improves their Vertues, so it spoyles others and makes them degenerate. And elsewhere he judiciously affirmes, that there may be sometimes greater vertue in a simple, such as Nature has made it, than in any thing that can by the fire be separated from it. And lest you should doubt whether he means by the vertues of things those that are Medical; he has in one place[27] this ingenuous confession; *Credo* (sayes he) *simplicia in sua simplicitate esse sufficientia pro sanatione omnium morborum.* Nag. [Errata: Nay,] Barthias, even in a Comment upon *Beguinus*,[28] scruples not to make this acknowledgment; *Valde absurdum est* (sayes he) *ex omnibus rebus extracta facere, salia, quintas essentias; praesertim ex substantiis per se plane vel subtilibus vel homogeneis, quales sunt uniones, Corallia, Moscus, Ambra, &c.* Consonantly whereunto he also tells Us (and Vouches the famous *Platerus*, for having candidly given the same Advertisement to his Auditors,) that some things have greater vertues, and better suited to our humane nature, when unprepar'd, than when they have past the Chymists Fire; as we see, sayes my Author, in Pepper; of which some grains swallowed perform more towards the relief of a Distempered stomack, than a great quantity of the Oyle of the same spice.

[27: Helmont Pharm. & Dispens. Nov. p. 458.]

[28: Vide Jer. ad Begu. Lib. 1. Cap. 17.]

It has been (pursues **Carneades**) by our Friend here present observ'd concerning Salt-petre, that none of the substances into which the Fire is wont to divide it, retaines either the Tast, the cooling vertue, or some other of the properties of the Concrete; and that each of those Substances acquires new qualities, not to be found in the Salt-Petre it self. The shining property of the tayls of gloworms does survive but so short a time the little animal made conspicuous by it, that inquisitive men have not scrupled publickly to deride **Baptista Porta** and others; who deluded perhaps with some Chymical surmises have ventur'd to prescribe the distillation of a Water from the tayles of Glowormes, as a sure way to obtain a liquor shining in the Dark. To which I shall now add no other example than that afforded us by Amber; which, whilst it remains an intire body, is endow'd with an Electrical faculty of drawing to it self fethers, strawes, and such like Bodies; which I never could observe either in its Salt, its Spirit, its Oyle, or in the Body I remember I once made by the reunion of its divided Elements; none of these having such a Texture as the intire Concrete. And however Chymists boldly deduce such and such properties from this or that proportion of their component Principles; yet in Concretes that abound with this or that Ingredient, 'tis not alwayes so much by vertue of its presence, nor its plenty, that the Concrete is qualify'd to perform such and such Effects; as upon the account of the particular texture of that and the other Ingredients, associated after a determinate Manner into one Concrete (though possibly such a proportion of that ingredient may be more convenient than an other for the constituting of such a body.) Thus in a clock the hand is mov'd upon the dyal, the bell is struck, and the other actions belonging to the engine are perform'd, not because the Wheeles are of brass or iron, or part of one metal and part of another, or because the weights are of Lead, but by Vertue of the size, shape, bigness, and co-aptation of the several parts; which would performe the same things though the wheels were of Silver, or Lead, or Wood, and the Weights of Stone or Clay; provided the Fabrick or Contrivance of the engine were the same: though it be not to be deny'd, that Brasse and Steel are more convenient materials to make clock-wheels of than Lead, or Wood. And to let you see, ***Eleutherius***, that 'tis sometimes at least, upon the Texture of the small parts of a body, and not alwaies upon the presence, or recesse, or increase, or Decrement of any one of its Principle, that it may lose some such Qualities, and acquire some such others as are thought very strongly inherent to the bodies they Reside in. [Errata: in;] I will add to what may from my past discourse be refer'd to this purpose, this Notable Example, from my Own experience; That Lead may without any additament, and only by various applications of the Fire, lose its colour, and acquire sometimes a gray, sometimes a yellowish, sometimes a red, sometimes an ***amethihstine*** [Transcriber's Note: amethistine] colour; and after having past through these, and perhaps divers others, again recover its leaden colour, and be made a bright body. That also this Lead, which is so flexible a metal, may be made as brittle as Glasse, and presently be brought to be again flexible and Malleable as before. And besides, that the same lead, which I find by ***Microscopes*** to be one of the most opacous bodies in the World, may be reduced to a fine transparent glasse; whence yet it may returne to an opacous Nature again; and all this, as I said, without the addition of any extraneous body, and meerly by the manner and Method of exposing it to the Fire.

But (sayes ***Carneades***) after having already put you to so prolix a trouble, it is time for me to relieve you with a promise of putting speedily a period to it; And to make good that promise, I shall from all that I have hitherto discoursed with you, deduce but this one proposition by way of Corollary. [***That it may as yet be doubted, whether or no there be any determinate Number of Elements; Or, if you please, whether or no all compound bodies, do consist of the same number of Elementary ingredients or material Principles.***]

This being but an inference from the foregoing Discourse, it will not be requisite to insist at large on the proofs of it; But only to point at the chief of Them, and Referr You for Particulars to what has been already Delivered.

In the First place then, from what has been so largely discours'd, it may appear, that the Experiments wont to be brought, whether by the common Peripateticks, or by the vulgar Chymists, to demonstrate that all mixt bodies are made up precisely either of the four Elements, or the three Hypostatical Principles, do not evince what they are alledg'd to prove. And as for the other common arguments, pretended to be drawn from Reason in favour of **Aristotelian Hypothesis** (for the Chymists are wont to rely almost altogether upon Experiments) they are Commonly grounded upon such unreasonable or precarious Suppositions, that 'tis altogether as easie and as just for any man to reject them, as for those that take them for granted to assert them, being indeed all of them as indemonstrable as the conclusion to be inferr'd from them; and some of them so manifestly weak and prooflesse; that he must be a very courteous adversary, that can be willing to grant them; and as unskilful a one, that can be compelled to do so.

In the next place, it may be considered, if what those Patriarchs of the **Spagyrists**, **Paracelsus** and **Helmont**, do on divers occasions positively deliver, be true; namely that the **Alkahest** does Resolve all mixt Bodies into other Principles than the fire, it must be decided which of the two resolutions (that made by the **Alkahest**, or that made by the fire) shall determine the number of the Elements, before we can be certain how many there are.

And in the mean time, we may take notice in the last place, that as the distinct substances whereinto the **Alkahest** divides bodies, are affirm'd to be differing in nature from those whereunto they are wont to be reduc'd by fire, and to be obtain'd from some bodies more in Number than from some others; since he tells us, he could totally reduce all sorts of Stones into Salt only, whereas of a coal he had two distinct Liquors.[29] So, although we should acquiesce in that resolution which is made by fire, we find not that all mixt bodies are thereby divided into the same number of Elements and Principles; some Concretes affordding more of them than others do; Nay and sometimes this or that Body affording a greater number of Differing substances by one way of management, than the same yields by another. And they that out of Gold, or Mercury, or Muscovy-glasse, will draw me as many distinct substances as I can separate from Vitriol, or from the juice of Grapes variously orderd, may teach me that which I shall very Thankfully learn. Nor does it appear more congruous to that variety that so much conduceth to the perfection of the Universe, that all elemented bodies be compounded of the same number of Elements, then it would be for a language, that all its words should consist of the same number of Letters.

[29: **Novi saxum & lapides omnes in merum salem suo saxo aut lapidi**

& aequiponderantem reducere absque omni prorsus sulphure aut Mercurio.
Helmont. pag. 409.]

A Paradoxical Appendix to the Foregoing Treatise.
The Sixth Part.

Here *Carneades* Having Dispach't what he Thought Requisite to oppose against what the Chymists are wont to alledge for Proof of their three Principles, Paus'd awhile, and look'd about him, to discover whether it were Time for him and his Friend to Rejoyne the Rest of the Company. But *Eleutherius* perceiving nothing yet to forbid Them to Prosecute their Discourse a little further, said to his Friend, (who had likewise taken Notice of the same thing) I halfe expected, *Carneades*, that after you had so freely declar'd Your doubting, whether there be any Determinate Number of Elements, You would have proceeded to question whether there be any Elements at all. And I confess it will be a Trouble to me if You defeat me of my Expectation; especially since you see the leasure we have allow'd us may probably suffice to examine that Paradox; because you have so largly Deduc'd already many Things pertinent to it, that you need but intimate how you would have them Apply'd, and what you would inferr from them.

Carneades having in Vain represented that their leasure could be but very short, that he had already prated very long, that he was unprepared to maintain so great and so invidious a Paradox, was at length prevail'd with to tell his Friend; Since, *Eleutherius*, you will have me Discourse *Ex Tempore* of the Paradox you mention, I am content, (though more perhaps to express my Obedience, then my Opinion) to tell you that (supposing the Truth of *Helmonts* and *Paracelsus's* Alkahestical Experiments, if I may so call them) though it may seem extravagant, yet it is not absurd to doubt, whether, for ought has been prov'd, there be a necessity to admit any Elements, or Hypostatical Principles, at all.

And, as formerly, so now, to avoid the needless trouble of Disputing severally with the **Aristotelians** and the Chymists, I will address my self to oppose them I have last nam'd, Because their Doctrine about the Elements is more applauded by the Moderns, as pretending highly to be grounded upon Experience. And, to deal not only fairly but favourably with them, I will allow them to take in Earth and Water to their other Principles. Which I consent to, the rather that my Discourse may the better reach the Tenents of the Peripateticks; who cannot plead for any so probably as for those two Elements; that of fire above the Air being Generally by Judicious Men exploded as an Imaginary thing; And the Air not concurring to compose Mixt Bodies as one of their Elements, but only lodging in their pores, or Rather replenishing, by reason of its Weight and Fluidity, all those Cavities of bodies here below, whether compounded or not, that are big enough to admit it, and are not fill'd up with any grosser substance.

And, to prevent mistakes, I must advertize You, that I now mean by Elements, as those Chymists that speak plainest do by their Principles, certain Primitive and Simple, or perfectly unmingled bodies; which not being made of any other bodies, or of one another, are the Ingredients of which all those call'd perfectly mixt Bodies are immediately compounded, and into which they are ultimately resolved: now whether there be any one such body to be constantly met with in all, and each, of those that are said to be Elemented bodies, is the thing I now question.

By this State of the controversie you will, I suppose, Guess, that I need not be so absur'd [Errata: absurd] as to deny that there are such bodies as Earth, and Water, and Quicksilver, and Sulphur: But I look upon Earth and Water, as component parts of the Universe, or rather of the Terrestrial Globe, not of all mixt bodies. And though I will not peremptorily deny that there may sometimes either a running Mercury, or a Combustible Substance be obtain'd from a Mineral, or even a Metal; yet I need not Concede either of them to be an Element in the sence above declar'd; as I shall have occasion to shew you by and by.

To give you then a brief account of the grounds I intend to proceed upon, I must tell you, that in matters of Philosophy, this seems to me a sufficient reason to doubt of a known and important proposition, that the Truth of it is not yet by any competent proof made to appear. And congruously herunto, if I shew that the grounds upon which men are perswaded that there are Elements are unable to satisfie a considering man, I suppose my doubts will appear rational.

Now the Considerations that induce men to think that there are Elements, may be conveniently enough referr'd to two heads. Namely, the one, that it is necessary that Nature make use of Elements to constitute the bodies that are reputed Mixt. And the other, That the Resolution of such bodies manifests that nature had compounded them of Elementary ones.

In reference to the former of these Considerations, there are two or three things that I have to Represent.

And I will begin with reminding you of the Experiments I not long since related to you concerning the growth of pompions, mint, and other vegetables, out of fair water. For by those experiments its seems evident, that Water may be Transmuted into all the other Elements; from whence it may be inferr'd, both, That 'tis not every Thing Chymists will call Salt, Sulphur, or Spirit, that needs always be a Primordiate and Ingenerable body. And that Nature may contex a Plant (though that be a perfectly mixt Concrete) without having all the Elements previously presented to her to compound it of. And, if you will allow the relation I mention'd out of **Mounsieur De Rochas** to be True; then may not only plants, but Animals and Minerals too, be produced out of Water, And however there is little doubt to be made, but that the plants my tryals afforded me as they were like in so many other respects to the rest of the plants of the same Denomination; so they would, in case I had reduc'd them to putrefaction, have likewise produc'd Wormes or other insects, as well as the resembling Vegetables are wont to do; so that Water may, by Various Seminal Principles, be successively Transmuted into both plants and Animals. And if we consider that not only Men, but even sucking Children are, but too often, Tormented with Solid Stones, but that divers sorts of Beasts themselves, (whatever **Helmont** against Experience think to the contrary) may be Troubled with great and Heavy stones in their Kidneys and Bladders, though they Feed but upon Grass and other Vegetables, that are perhaps but Disguised Water, it will not seem improbable that even some Concretes of a mineral Nature, may Likewise be form'd of Water.

We may further Take notice, that as a Plant may be nourisht, and consequently may Consist of Common water; so may both plants and Animals, (perhaps even from their Seminal Rudiments) consist of compound Bodies, without having any thing meerly Elementary brought them by nature to be compounded by them: This is evident in divers men, who whilst they were Infants were fed only with Milk, afterwards Live altogether upon Flesh, Fish, wine, and other perfectly mixt Bodies. It may be seen also in sheep, who on some of our English Downs or Plains, grow very fat by feeding upon the grasse, without scarce drinking at all. And yet more manifestly in the magots that breed and grow up to their full bignesse within the pulps of Apples, Pears, or the like Fruit. We see also, that Dungs that abound with a mixt Salt give a much more speedy increment to corn and other Vegetables than Water alone would do: And it hath been assur'd me, by a man experienc'd in such matters, that sometimes when to bring up roots very early, the Mould they were planted in was made over-rich, the very substance of the Plant has tasted of the Dung. And let us also consider a Graft of one kind of Fruit upon the upper bough of a Tree of another kind. As for instance, the Ciens of a Pear upon a White-thorne; for there the ascending Liquor is already alter'd, either by the root, or in its ascent by the bark, or both wayes, and becomes a new mixt body: as may appear by the differing qualities to be met with in the saps of several trees; as particularly, the medicinal vertue of the Birch-Water (which I have sometimes drunk upon *Helmonts* great and not undeserved commendation) Now the graft, being fasten'd to the stock must necessarily nourish its self, and produce its Fruit, only out of this compound Juice prepared for it by the Stock, being unable to come at any other aliment. And if we consider, how much of the Vegetable he feeds upon may (as we noted above) remain in an Animal; we may easily suppose, That the blood of that Animal who Feeds upon this, though it be a Well constituted Liquor, and have all the differing Corpuscles that make it up kept in order by one praesiding form, may be a strangely Decompounded Body, many of its parts being themselves decompounded. So little is it Necessary that even in the mixtures which nature her self makes in Animal and Vegetable Bodies, she should have pure Elements at hand to make her compositions of.

Having said thus much touching the constitution of Plants and Animals, I might perhaps be able to say as much touching that of Minerals, and even Metalls, if it were as easy for us to make experiment in Order to the production of these, as of those. But the growth or increment of Minerals being usually a work of excessively long time, and for the most part perform'd in the bowels of the Earth, where we cannot see it, I must instead of Experiments make use, on this occasion, of Observations.

That stones were not all made at once, but that are some of them now adayes generated, may (though it be deny'd by some) be fully prov'd by several examples, of which I shall now scarce alledg any other, then that famous place in *France* known by the name of **Les Caves Gentieres** [Errata: Goutieres], where the Water falling from the upper Parts of the cave to the ground does presently there condense into little stones, of such figures as the drops, falling either severally or upon one another, and coagulating presently into stone, chance to exhibit. Of these stones some Ingenuous Friends of ours, that went a while since to visit that place, did me the favour to present me with some that they brought thence. And I remember that both that sober Relator of his Voyages, **Van Linschoten**, and another good Author, inform us that in the Diamond Mines (as they call them) in the **East-Indies**, when having dig'd the Earth, though to no great depth, they find Diamonds and take them quite away; Yet in a very few years they find in the same place new Diamonds produc'd there since. From both which Relations, especially the first, it seems probable that Nature does not always stay for divers Elementary Bodies, when she is to produce stones. And as for Metals themselves, Authors of good note assure us, that even they were not in the beginning produc'd at once altogether, but have been observ'd to grow; so that what was not a Mineral or Metal before became one afterwards. Of this it were easie to alledg many testimonies of professed Chymists. But that they may have the greater authority, I shall rather present you with a few borrowed from more unsuspected writers. **Sulphuris Mineram** (as the inquisitive **P. Fallopius** notes) quae nutrix est caloris subterranei fabri seu Archaei fontium & mineralium, Infra terram citissime renasci testantur Historiae Metallicae. Sunt enim loca e quibus si hoc anno sulphur effossum fuerit; intermissa fossione per quadriennium redeunt fossores & omnia sulphure, ut autea [Errata: antea], rursus inveniunt plena. Pliny **Relates,** In Italiae Insula Ilva, gigni ferri metallum. **Strabo** multo expressius; effossum ibi metallum semper regenerari. Nam si effossio spatio centum annorum intermittebatur, & iterum illuc revertebantur, fossores reperisse maximam copiam ferri regeneratam. ***Which history not only is countenanced by*** Fallopius, *from the Incom which the Iron of that Island yielded the **Duke of** Florence in his time; but is mention'd more expressely to our purpose, by* *the Learned* Cesalpinus. Vena (says he) *ferri copiosissima est in Italia; ob eam nobilitata Ilva Tirrheni maris Insula incredibili copia, etiam nostris temporibus eam gignens: Nam terra quae eruitur dum vena effoditur tota, procedente tempore in venam convertitur.* Which last clause is therefore very notable, because from thence we may deduce, that earth, by a Metalline plastick principle latent in it, may be in processe of time chang'd into a metal. And even *Agricola* himself, though the Chymists complain of him as their adversary, acknowledges thus much and more; by telling us that at a Town called *Saga* in *Germany*,[30] they dig up Iron in the Fields, by sinking ditches two foot deep; And adding, that within the space of ten years the Ditches are digged again for Iron since produced, As the same Metal is wont to be obtain'd in *Elva*. Also concerning Lead, not to mention what even *Galen* notes, that it will increase both in bulk and Weight if it be long kept in Vaults or Sellars, where the Air is gross and thick, as he collects from the smelling of those pieces of Lead that were imploy'd to fasten together the parts of old Statues. Not to mention this, I say, *Boccacius Certaldus*, as I find him Quoted by a Diligent Writer, has this Passage touching the Growth of Lead. *Fessularum mons* (sayes he) *in Hetruria, Florentiae civitati imminens, lapides plumbarios habet; qui si excidantur, brevi temporis spatio, novis incrementis instaurantur; ut* (annexes my Author) tradit Boccacius Certaldus, qui id compotissimum [Errata: compertissimum] esse scribit. Nihil hoc novi est; sed de eadem Plinius, lib. 34. Hist. Natur. cap. 17. dudum prodidit, Inquiens, mirum in his solis plumbi metallis, quod derelicta fertilius reviviscunt. In plumbariis secundo Lapide ab Amberga dictis ad Asylum recrementa congesta in cumulos, exposita solibus pluviisque paucis annis, redunt suum metallum cum fenore. *I might Add to these, continues* Carneades, *many things that I have met with concerning the Generation of Gold and Silver. But, for fear of wanting time, I shall mention but two or three Narratives. The First you may find Recorded by* Gerhardus *the Physick Professor, in these Words.* In valle (sayes he) Joachimaca [Errata: Joachimica] argentum gramini [Errata: graminis] modo & more e Lapidibus minerae velut e radice excrevisse digiti Longitudine, testis est Dr. Schreterus, qui ejusmodi venas aspectu jucundas & admirabiles Domi sua aliis saepe monstravit & Donavit. Item Aqua caerulea Inventa est Annebergae, ubi argentum erat adhuc in primo ente, quae coagulata redacta est in calcem fixi &

boni argenti.

[30: ***In Lygiis, ad Sagam opidum; in pratis eruitur ferrum, fossis ad altitudinem bipedaneam actis. Id decennio renatum denuo foditur non aliter ac Ilvae ferrum.***]

The other two Relations I have not met with in Latine Authours, and yet they are both very memorable in themselves, and as pertinent to our present purpose.

The first I meet with in the Commentary of ***Johannes Valebius*** upon the ***Kleine Baur***, In which that Industrious Chymist Relates, with many circumstances, that at a Mine-Town (If I may so English the German ***Bergstat***) eight miles or Leagues distant from ***Strasburg*** call'd ***Mariakirch***, a Workman came to the Overseer, and desired employment; but he telling him that there was not any of the best sort at present for him, added that till he could be preferr'd to some such, he might in the mean time, to avoid idleness, work in a Grove or Mine-pit thereabouts, which at that time was little esteem'd. This Workman after some weeks Labour, had by a Crack appearing in the Stone upon a Stroak given near the wall, an Invitation Given him to Work his Way through, which as soon as he had done, his Eyes were saluted by a mighty stone or Lump which stood in the middle of the Cleft (that had a hollow place behind it) upright, and in shew like an armed-man; but consisted of pure fine Silver having no Vein or Ore by it, or any other Additament, but stood there free, having only underfoot something like a burnt matter; and yet this one Lump held in Weight above a 1000 marks, which, according to the Dutch, Account [Errata: Dutch account] makes 500 pound weight of fine silver. From which and other Circumstances my Author gathers; That by the warmth of the place, the Noble Metalline Spirits, (Sulphureous and Mercurial) were carri'd from the neighbouring Galleries or Vaults, through other smaller Cracks and Clefts, into that Cavity, and there collected as in a close Chamber or Cellar; whereinto when they were gotten, they did in process of time settle into the forementioned precious mass of Metal.

The other Germane Relation is of That great Traveller and Laborious Chymist ***Johannes*** (not ***Georgus***) ***Agricola***; who in his notes upon what ***Poppius*** has written of Antimony, Relates, that when he was among the ***Hungarian*** Mines in the deep Groves, he observ'd that there would often arise in them a warm Steam (not of that malignant sort which the Germains call ***Shwadt***, which (sayes he) is a meer poyson, and often suffocates the Diggers [Errata: diggers)], which fasten'd it self to the Walls; and that coming again to review it after a couple of dayes, he discern'd that it was all very fast, and glistering; whereupon having collected it and Distill'd it *per Retortam*, he obtain'd from it a fine Spirit, adding, that the Mine-Men inform'd him, that this Steam or Damp of the English Mine [Errata: damp as the Englishmen also call it] (retaining the dutch Term) would at last have become a Metal, as Gold or Silver.

I referr (sayes *Carneades*) to another Occasion, the Use that may be made of these Narratives towards the explicating the Nature of Metalls; and that of Fixtness, Malleableness, and some other Qualities conspicuous in them. And in the mean time, this I may at present deduce from these Observations, That 'tis not very probable, that, whensoever a Mineral, or even a Metall, is to be Generated in the Bowels of the Earth, Nature needs to have at hand both Salt, and Sulphur, and Mercury to Compound it of; for, not to urge that the two last Relations seem less to favour the Chymists than *Aristotle*, who would have Metals Generated of certain *Halitus* or steams, the foremention'd Observations together, make it seem more Likely that the mineral Earths or those Metalline steams (wherewith probably such Earths are plentifully imbu'd) do contain in them some seminal Rudiment, or some thing Equivalent thereunto; by whose plastick power the rest of the matter, though perhaps Terrestrial and heavy, is in Tract of time fashion'd into this or That metalline Ore; almost as I formerly noted, that fair water was by the seminal Principle of Mint, Pompions, and other Vegetables, contriv'd into Bodies answerable to such Seeds. And that such Alterations of Terrestrial matter are not impossible, seems evident from that notable Practice of the Boylers of Salt-Petre, who unanimously observe, as well here in *England* as in other Countries; That if an Earth pregnant with Nitre be depriv'd, by the affusion of water, of all its true and dissoluble Salt, yet the Earth will after some years yield them Salt-Petre again; For which reason some of the eminent and skillfullest of them keep it in heaps as a perpetual Mine of Salt Petre; whence it may appear, that the Seminal Principle of Nitre latent in the Earth does by degrees Transforme the neighbouring matter into a Nitrous Body; for though I deny that some Volatile Nitre may by such Earths be attracted (as they speak) out of the Air, yet that the innermost parts of such great heaps that lye so remote from the Air should borrow from it all the Nitre they abound with, is not probable, for other reasons besides the remoteness of the Air, though I have not the Leasure to mention them.

And I remember, that a person of Great Credit, and well acquainted with the wayes of making Vitriol, affirm'd to me, that he had observ'd, that a kind of mineral which abounds in that Salt, being kept within Doors and not expos'd (as is usual) to the free Air and Rains, did of it self in no very long time turn into Vitriol, not only in the outward or superficial, but even in the internal and most Central parts.

And I also remember, that I met with a certain kind of Merkasite that lay together in great Quantities under ground, which did, even in my chamber, in so few hours begin of it self to turne into Vitriol, that we need not distrust the newly recited narrative. But to return to what I was saying of Nitre; as Nature made this Salt-Petre out of the once almost and inodorous Earth it was bred in, and did not find a very stinking and corrosive Acid Liquor, and a sharp Alcalyzate Salt to compound it of, though these be the Bodies into which the Fire dissolves it; so it were not necessary that Nature should make up all Metals and other Minerals of Pre-existent Salt, and Sulphur, and Mercury, though such Bodies might by Fire be obtained from it. Which one consideration duly weigh'd is very considerable in the present controversy: And to this agree well the Relations of our two German Chymists; for besides that it cannot be convincingly prov'd, it is not so much as likely that so languid and moderate a heat as that within the Mines, should carry up to so great a heat [Errata: height], though in the forme of fumes, Salt, Sulphur and Mercury; since we find in our Distillations, that it requires a considerable Degree of Fire to raise so much as to the height of one foot not only Salt, but even Mercury it self, in close Vessels. And if it be objected, that it seems by the stink that is sometimes observ'd when Lightening falls down here below, that sulphureous steams may ascend very high without any extraordinary Degree of heat; It may be answer'd, among other things, that the Sulphur of Silver is by Chymists said to be a fixt Sulphur, though not altogether so well Digested as that of Gold.

But, proceeds **Carneades**, If it had not been to afford You some hints concerning the Origine of Metals, I need not have deduc'd any thing from these Observations; It not being necessary to the Validity of my Argument that my Deductions from them should be irrefragable, because my Adversaries the **Aristotelians** and Vulgar Chymists do not, I presume, know any better then I, *a priori*, of what ingredients Nature compounds Metals and Minerals. For their Argument to prove that those Bodies are made up of such Principles, is drawn *a posteriori*; I mean from this, that upon the ***Analysis*** of Mineral bodies they are resolv'd into those differing substances. That we may therefore examine this Argument, Let us proceed to consider what can be alledg'd in behalf of the Elements from the Resolutions of Bodies by the fire; which you remember was the second Tophick [Transcriber's Note: Topick] whence I told you the Arguments of my Adversaries were desum'd.

And that I may first dispatch what I have to say concerning Minerals, I will begin the remaining part of my discourse with considering how the fire divides them.

And first, I have partly noted above, that though Chymists pretend from some to draw salt, from others running Mercury, and from others a Sulphur; Yet they have not hitherto taught us by any way in us [Errata: use] among them to separate any one principle, whether Salt, Sulphur, or Mercury, from all sorts of Minerals without exception. And thence I may be allow'd to conclude that there is not any of the Elements that is an Ingredient of all Bodies, since there are some of which it is not so.

In the next place, supposing that either Sulphur or Mercury were obtainable from all sorts of Minerals. Yet still this Sulphur or Mercury would be but a compounded, not an Elementary body, as I told you already on another occasion. And certainly he that takes notice of the wonderful Operations of Quicksilver, whether it be common, or drawn from Mineral Bodies, can scarce be so inconsiderate as to think it of the very same nature with that immature and fugitive substance which in Vegetables and Animals Chymists have been pleas'd to call their Mercury. So that when Mercury is got by the help of the fire out of a metal or other Mineral Body, if we will not suppose that it was not pre-existent in it, but produc'd by the action of the fire upon the Concrete, we may at least suppose this Quicksilver to have been a perfect Body of its own kind (though perhaps lesse heterogeneous then more secundary mixts) which happen'd to be mingl'd ***per minima***, and coagulated with the other substances, whereof the Metal or Mineral consisted. As may be exemplyfied partly by Native Vermillion wherein the Quicksilver and Sulphur being exquisitely blended both with one another, and that other course Mineral stuff (what ever it be) that harbours them, make up a red body differing enough from both; and yet from which part of the Quicksilver, and of the Sulphur, may be easily

enough obtain'd; Partly by those Mines wherein nature has so curiously incorporated Silver with Lead, that 'tis extreamly difficult, and yet possible, to separate the
former out of the Latter. [Errata: latter;] And partly too by native Vitriol, wherein
the Metalline Corpuscles are by skill and industry separable from the saline ones,
though they be so con-coagulated with them, that the whole Concrete is reckon'd
among Salts.

And here I further observe, that I never could see any Earth or Water, properly so call'd, separated from either Gold or Silver (to name now no other Metalline
Bodies) and therefore to retort the argument upon my Adversaries, I may conclude,
that since there are some bodies in which, for ought appears, there is neither Earth
nor Water. [Errata: Water;] I may be allow'd to conclude that neither of those two
is an Universal Ingredient of all those Bodies that are counted perfectly mixt, which
I desire you would remember against Anon.

It may indeed be objected, that the reason why from Gold or Silver we cannot
separate any moisture, is, because that when it is melted out of the Oare, the vehement Fire requisite to its Fusion forc'd away all the aqueous and fugitive moisture;
and the like fire may do from the materials of Glass. To which I shall Answer, that
I Remember I read not long since in the Learned *Josephus Acosta*,[31] who relates
it upon his own observation; that in *America*, (where he long lived) there is a kind
of Silver which the *Indians* call *Papas*, and sometimes (sayes he) they find pieces
very fine and pure like to small round roots, the which is rare in that metal, but
usuall in Gold; Concerning which metal he tells us, that besides this they find some
which they call Gold in grains, which he tells us are small morsels of Gold that they
find whole without mixture of any other metal, which hath no need of melting or
Refining in the fire.

[31: *Acosta* Natural and Moral history of the Indies, L. 3. c. 5, p. 212.]

I remember that a very skilful and credible person affirmed to me, that being
in the *Hungarian* mines he had the good fortune to see a mineral that was there
digg'd up, wherein pieces of Gold of the length, and also almost of the bigness of a
humane Finger, grew in the Oar, as if they had been parts and Branches of Trees.

And I have my self seen a Lump of whitish Mineral, that was brought as a Rar-
ity to a Great and knowing Prince, wherein there grew here and there in the Stone,
which looked like a kind of sparr, divers little Lumps of fine Gold, (for such I was

assured that Tryal had manifested it to be) some of them Seeming to be about the Bigness of pease.

But that is nothing to what our *Acosta* subjoynes, which is indeed very memorable, namely, that of the morsels of Native and pure Gold, which we lately heard him mentioning he had now and then seen some that weighed many pounds;[32] to which I shall add, that I my self have seen a Lump of Oar not long since digged up, in whose stony part there grew, almost like Trees, divers parcels though not of Gold, yet of (what perhaps Mineralists will more wonder at) another Metal which seemed to be very pure or unmixt with any Heterogeneous Substances, and were some of them as big as my Finger, if not bigger. But upon Observations of this kind, though perhaps I could, yet I must not at present dwell any longer.

[32: See *Acosta* in the fore-cited Place, and the passage of *Pliny* quoted by him.]

To proceed Therefore now (sayes *Carneades*) to the Consideration of the *Analysis* of Vegetables, although my Tryals give me no cause to doubt but that out of most of them five differing Substances may be obtain'd by the fire, yet I think it will not be so easily Demonstrated that these deserve to be call'd Elements in the Notion above explain'd.

And before I descend to particulars, I shall repeat and premise this General Consideration, that these differing substances that are call'd Elements or Principles, differ not from each other as Metals, Plants and Animals, or as such Creatures as are immediately produc'd each by its peculiar Seed, and Constitutes a distinct propagable sort of Creatures in the Universe; but these are only Various Schemes of matter or Substances that differ from each other, but in consistence (as Running Mercury and the same Metal congeal'd by the Vapor of Lead) and some very few other accidents, as Tast, or Smel, or Inflamability, or the want of them. So that by a change of Texture not impossible to be wrought by the Fire and other Agents that have the Faculty not only to dissociate the smal parts of Bodies, but afterwards to connect them after a new manner, the same parcell of matter may acquire or lose such accidents as may suffice to Denominate it Salt, or Sulphur, or Earth. If I were fully to clear to you my apprehensions concerning this matter, I should perhaps be obliged to acquaint you with divers of the Conjectures (for I must yet call them no more) I have had Concerning the Principles of things purely Corporeal: For though because

I seem not satisfi'd with the Vulgar Doctrines, either of the Peripatetick or Paracelsian Schools, many of those that know me, (and perhaps, among Them, *Eleutherius* himself) have thought me wedded to the Epicurean *Hypotheses*, (as others have mistaken me for an *Helmontian*;) yet if you knew how little Conversant I have been with *Epicurean* Authors, and how great a part of *Lucretius* himself I never yet had the Curiosity to read, you would perchance be of another mind; especially if I were to entertain you at large, I say not, of my present Notions; but of my former thoughts concerning the Principles of things. But, as I said above, fully to clear my Apprehensions would require a Longer Discourse than we can now have.

For, I should tell you that I have sometimes thought it not unfit, that to the Principles which may be assign'd to things, as the World is now Constituted, we should, if we consider the Great Mass of matter as it was whilst the Universe was in making, add another, which may Conveniently enough be call'd an Architectonick Principle or power; by which I mean those Various Determinations, and that Skilfull Guidance of the motions of the small parts of the Universal matter by the most wise Author of things, which were necessary at the beginning to turn that confus'd *Chaos* into this Orderly and beautifull World; and Especially, to contrive the Bodies of Animals and Plants, and the Seeds of those things whose kinds were to be propagated. For I confess I cannot well Conceive, how from matter, Barely put into Motion, and then left to it self, there could Emerge such Curious Fabricks as the Bodies of men and perfect Animals, and such yet more admirably Contriv'd parcels of matter, as the seeds of living Creatures.

I should likewise tell you upon what grounds, and in what sence, I suspected the Principles of the World, as it now is, to be Three, *Matter*, *Motion* and *Rest*. I say, *as the World now is*, because the present Fabrick of the Universe, and especially the seeds of things, together with the establisht Course of Nature, is a Requisite or Condition, upon whose account divers things may be made out by our three Principles, which otherwise would be very hard, if possible, to explicate.

I should moreover declare in general (for I pretend not to be able to do it otherwise) not only why I Conceive that Colours, Odors, Tasts, Fluidness and Solidity, and those other qualities that Diversifie and Denominate Bodies may Intelligibly be Deduced from these three; *but how two of the Three* Epicurean Principles (which, I need not tell, you [Transcriber's Note: tell you,] are Magnitude, Figure and Weight) are Themselves Deducible from Matter and Motion; since the Latter of these Variously Agitating, and, as it were, Distracting the Former, must needs disjoyne its parts; which being Actually separated must Each of them necessarily both be of some Size, and obtain some shape or other. Nor did I add to our Principles the *Aristotelean Privation*, partly for other Reasons, which I must not now stay to insist on; and partly because it seems to be rather an Antecedent, or a *Terminus a quo*, then a True Principle, as the starting-Post is none of the Horses Legs or Limbs.

I should also explain why and how I made rest [Errata: Rest] to be, though not so considerable a Principle of things, as Motion, yet a Principle of them; partly because it is (for ought we know [Errata: know)] as Ancient at least as it, and depends not upon Motion, nor any other quality of matter; and partly, because it may enable the Body in which it happens to be, both to continue in a State of Rest till some external force put it out of that state, and to concur to the production of divers Changes in the bodies that hit against it, by either quite stopping or lessning their Motion (whilst the body formerly at Rest Receives all or part of it into it self) or else by giving a new Byass, or some other Modification, to Motion, that is, To the Grand and Primary instrument whereby Nature produces all the Changes and other Qualities that are to be met with in the World.

I should likewise, after all this, explain to you how, although Matter, Motion and Rest, seem'd to me to be the Catholick Principles of the Universe, I thought the Principles of Particular bodies might be Commodiously enough reduc'd to two, namely *Matter*, and (what Comprehends the two other, and their effects) the result or Aggregate [Errata: Aggregate or complex] of those Accidents, which are the Motion or Rest, (for in some Bodies both are not to be found) the Bigness, Figure, Texture) [Errata: delete)] and the thence resulting Qualities of the small parts) [Errata: delete)] which are necessary to intitle the Body whereto they belong to this or that Peculiar Denomination; and discriminating it from others to appropriate it to a Determinate Kind of Things, as [Errata: (as] Yellowness, Fixtness, such a Degree of Weight, and of Ductility, do make the Portion of matter wherein they Concur, to be reckon'd among perfect metals, and obtain the name of Gold.) Which [Errata: This] Aggregate or result of Accidents you may, if You please, call either *Structure* or Texture.

[Errata: no paragraph break] Though [Errata: (Though] indeed, that do not so properly Comprehend the motion of the constituent parts especially in case some of them be Fluid [Errata: Fluid)], or what other appellation shall appear most Expressive. Or if, retaining the Vulgar Terme, You will call it the **Forme** of the thing it denominates, I shall not much oppose it; Provided the word be interpreted to mean but what I have express'd, and not a Scholastick **Substantial Forme**, which so many intelligent men profess to be to them altogether Un-intelligible.

But, sayes **Carneades**, if you remember that 'tis a Sceptick speaks to you, and that 'tis not so much my present Talk to make assertions as to suggest doubts, I hope you will look upon what I have propos'd, rather as a Narrative of my former conjectures touching the principles of things, then as a Resolute Declaration of my present opinions of them; especially since although they cannot but appear Very much to their Disadvantage, If you Consider Them as they are propos'd without those Reasons and Explanations by which I could perhaps make them appear much lesse extravagant; yet I want time to offer you what may be alledg'd to clear and countenance these notions; my design in mentioning them unto you at present being, *partly*, to bring some Light and Confirmation to divers passages of my discourse to you; *partly* to shew you, that I do not (as you seem to have suspected) embrace all **Epicurus** his principles; but Dissent from him in some main things, as well as from **Aristotle** and the Chymists, in others; & *partly* also, or rather chiefly, to intimate to you the grounds upon which I likewise differ from **Helmont** in this, that whereas he ascribes almost all things, and even diseases themselves, to their determinate Seeds; I am of opinion, that besides the peculiar Fabricks of the Bodies of Plants and Animals (and perhaps also of some Metals and Minerals) which I take to be the Effects of seminal principles, there are many other bodies in nature which have and deserve distinct and Proper names, but yet do but result from such contextures of the matter they are made of, as may without determinate seeds be effected by heat, cold, artificial mixtures and compositions, and divers other causes which sometimes nature imployes of her own accord; and oftentimes man by his power and skill makes use of to fashion the matter according to his Intentions. This may be exemplified both in the productions of Nature, and in those of Art; of the first sort I might name multitudes; but to shew how sleight a variation of Textures without addition of new ingredients may procure a parcel of matter divers names, and make it be Lookt upon as Different Things;

I shall invite you to observe with me, That Clouds, Rain, Hail, Snow, Froth, and Ice, may be but water, having its parts varyed as to their size and distance in respect of each other, and as to motion and rest. And among Artificial Productions we may take notice (to skip the Crystals of Tartar) of Glass, Regulus, Martis-Stellatus [Errata: Regulus Martis Stellatus], and particularly of the Sugar of Lead, which though made of that insipid Metal and sour salt of Vinager, has in it a sweetnesse surpassing that of common Sugar, and divers other qualities, which being not to be found in either of its two ingredients, must be confess'd to belong to the Concrete it self, upon the account of its Texture.

This Consideration premis'd, it will be, I hope, the more easie to perswade you that the Fire may as well produce some new textures in a parcel of matter, as destroy the old.

Wherefore hoping that you have not forgot the Arguments formerly imploy'd against the Doctrine of the *Tria prima*; namely that the Salt, Sulphur and Mercury, into which the Fire seems to resolve Vegetable and Animal Bodies, are yet compounded, not simple and Elementary Substances; And that (as appeared by the Experiment of Pompions) the *Tria prima* may be made out of Water; hoping I say, that you remember These and the other Things that I formerly represented to the same purpose, I shall now add only, that if we doubt not the Truth of some of *Helmonts* Relation [Errata: Relations], We may well doubt whether any of these Heterogeneities be (I say not pre-existent, so as to convene together, when a plant or Animal is to be constituted but) so much as in-existent in the Concrete whence they are obtain'd, when the Chymists [Errata: Chymist] first goes about to resolve it; For not to insist upon the un-inflamable Spirit of such Concretes, because that may be pretended to be but a mixture of Phlegme and Salt; the Oyle or Sulphur of Vegetables or Animals is, according to him, reducible by the help of Lixiviate Salts into Sope; as that Sope is by the help of repeated Distillations from a *Caput Mortuum* of Chalk into insipid Water. And as for the saline substance that seems separable from mixt bodies; the same *Helmonts* tryals[33] give us cause to think, That it may be a production of the Fire, which by transporting and otherwise altering the particles of the matter, does bring it to a Saline nature.

[33: Omne autem Alcali addita pinguedine in aqueum liquorem, qui tandem mera & simplex aqua fit, reducitur, (ut videre est in Sapone, Lazurio lapide, &c.)

quoties per adjuncta fixa semen Pinguedinis deponit. Helmont.]

For I know (sayes he, in the place formerly alledg'd to another purpose) a way to reduce all stones into a meer Salt of equal weight with the stone whence it was produc'd, and that without any of the least either Sulphur or Mercury; which asseveration of my Author would perhaps seem less incredible to You, if I durst acquaint You with all I could say upon that subject. And hence by the way you may also conclude that the Sulphur and Mercury, as they call them, that Chymists are wont to obtain from compound Bodies by the Fire, may possibly in many Cases be the productions of it; since if the same bodies had been wrought upon by the Agents employ'd by *Helmont*, they would have yielded neither Sulphur nor Mercury; and those portions of them which the Fire would have presented Us in the forme of Sulphureous and Mercurial Bodies would have, by *Helmonts* method, been exhibited to us in the form of Salt.

But though (says *Eleutherius*) You have alledg'd very plausible Arguments against the *tria Prima*, yet I see not how it will be possible for you to avoid acknowledging that Earth and Water are Elementary Ingredients, though not of Mineral Concretes, yet of all Animal and Vegetable Bodies; Since if any of these of what sort soever be committed to Distillation, there is regularly and constantly separated from it a phlegme or aqueous part and a *Caput Mortuum* or Earth.

I readily acknowledged (answers *Carneades*) it is not so easy to reject Water and Earth (and especially the former) as 'tis to reject the *Tria Prima*, from being the Elements of mixt Bodies; but 'tis not every difficult thing that is impossible.

I consider then, as to Water, that the chief Qualities which make men give that name to any visible Substance, are, that it is Fluid or Liquid, and that it is insipid and inodorous. Now as for the tast of these qualities, I think you have never seen any of those separated substances that the Chymists call Phlegme which was perfectly devoyd both of Tast and Smell: and if you object, that yet it may be reasonably suppos'd, that since the whole Body is Liquid, the mass is nothing but Elementary Water faintly imbu'd with some of the Saline or Sulphureous parts of the same Concrete, which it retain'd with it upon its Separation from the Other Ingredients. To this I answer, That this Objection would not appear so stong [Transcriber's Note: strong] as it is plausible, if Chymists understood the Nature of Fluidity and Compactnesse; and that, as I formerly observ'd, to a Bodies being Fluid there is nothing necessary, but that it be divided into parts small enough; and that these parts be put into such a motion among themselves as to glide some this way and some that way, along each others Surfaces. So that, although a Concrete were never so dry, and had not any Water or other Liquor in-existent in it, yet such a Comminution of its parts may be made, by the fire or other Agents, as to turn a great portion of them into Liquor. Of this Truth I will give an instance, employ'd by our friend here present as one of the most conducive of his experiments to Illustrate the nature of Salts. If you Take, then, sea salt and melt it in the Fire to free it from the aqueous parts, and afterward distill it with a vehement Fire from burnt Clay, or any other, as dry a *Caput mortuum* as you please, you will, as Chymists confess, [Errata: confesse (delete comma)] by teaching it drive over a good part of the Salt in the form of a Liquor. And to satisfy some ingenious men, That a great part of this Liquor was still true sea salt brought by the Operation of the Fire into Corpuscles so small, and perhaps so advantageously shap'd, as to be capable of the forme of a Fluid Body, He did in my presence poure to such spiritual salts a due proportion of the spirit (or salt and Phlegme) of Urine, whereby having evaporated the superfluous moisture, he soon obtain'd such another Concrete, both as to tast and smell, and easie sublimableness as common Salt *Armoniack*, which you know is made up of grosse and undistill'd sea salt united with the salts of Urine and of Soot, which two are very neer of kin to each other. And further, to manifest that the Corpuscles of sea salt and the Saline ones of Urine retain their several Natures in this Concrete, He mixt it with a convenient quantity of Salt of Tartar, and committing it to Distillation soon regain'd his spirit of Urine in a liquid form by its self, the Sea salt staying behind with the Salt of Tartar. Wherefore it is very possible that dry Bodies may by the Fire be reduc'd to Liquors without any separation of Elements, but barely by a certain kind of Dissipation and Comminution of the matter, whereby its parts are brought into a new state. And if it be still objected, that the Phlegme of mixt Bodies must be reputed water, because so weak a tast needs but a very small proportion of Salt to impart it; It may be reply'd, that for ought appears, common Salt and divers other bodies, though they be distill'd never so dry, and in never so close Vessels, will yield each of them pretty store of a Liquor, wherein though (as I lately noted) Saline Corpuscles abound, Yet there is besides a large proportion of Phlegme, as may easily be discovered by coagulating the Saline Corpuscles with any convenient Body; as I lately told you, our Friend coagulated part of the Spirit of Salt with Spirit of Urine: and as I have divers times separated a salt from Oyle of Vitriol it self (though a very ponderous Liquor and drawn from a saline body) by boyling it with a just quantity of Mercury, and then washing the newly coagulated salt from the Precipitate with fair Water. Now to what can we more probably ascribe this plenty of aqueous Substance afforded us by the Distillation of such bodies, than unto this, That among the various operations of the Fire upon the matter of a Concrete, divers particles of that matter are reduc'd to such a shape and bignesse as is requisite to compose such a Liquor as Chymists are wont to call Phlegme or Water. How I conjecture this change may be effected, 'tis neither necessary for me to tell you, nor possible to do so without a much longer discourse then were now seasonable. But I desire you would with me reflect upon what I formerly told you concerning the change of Quicksilver into Water; For that Water having but a very faint tast, if any whit more than divers of those liquors that Chymists referr to Phlegme; By that experiment it seems evident, that even a metalline body, and therefore much more such as are but Vegetable or Animal, may by a simple operation of the Fire be turn'd in great part into Water. And since those I dispute with are not yet able out of Gold, or Silver, or divers other Concretes to separate any thing like Water; I hope I may be allow'd to conclude against Them, that water it self is not an Universal and pre-existent Ingredient of Mixt Bodies.

But as for those Chymists that, Supposing with me the Truth of what *Helmont* relates of the *Alkahest's* wonderful Effects, have a right to press me with his Authority concerning them, and to alledge that he could Transmute all reputedly mixt Bodies into insipid and meer Water; To those I shall represent, That though his Affirmations conclude strongly against the Vulgar Chymists (against whom I have not therefore scrupl'd to Employ Them) since they Evince that the Commonly reputed Principles or Ingredients of Things are not Permanent and indestructible, since they may be further reduc'd into Insipid Phlegme differing from them all; Yet till we can be allow'd to examine this Liquor, I think it not unreasonable to doubt whether it be not something else then meer Water. For I find not any other reason given by *Helmont* of his Pronouncing it so, then that it is insipid. Now Sapour being an Accident or an Affection of matter that relates to our Tongue, Palate, and other Organs of Tast, it may very possibly be, that the small Parts of a Body may be

of such a Size and Shape, as either by their extream Littleness, or by their slender-
ness, or by their Figure, to be unable to pierce into and make a perceptible Impression upon the Nerves or Membranous parts of the Organs of Tast, and what [Errata:
yet] may be fit to work otherwise upon divers other Bodies than meer Water can,
and consequently to Disclose it self to be of a Nature farr enough from Elementary.
In Silke dyed Red or of any other Colour, whilst many Contiguous Threads makes
up a skein, the Colour of the Silke is conspicuous; but if only a very few of them be
lookt upon, the Colour will appear much fainter then before. But if You take out
one simple Thread, you shall not easily be able to discern any Colour at all; So subtile an Object having not the Force to make upon the Optick Nerve an Impression
great enough to be taken Notice of. It is also observ'd, that the best sort of Oyl-Olive
is almost tastless, and yet I need not tell you how exceedingly distant in Nature
Oyle is from Water. The Liquor into which I told you, upon the Relation of *Lully*,
and [Errata: an] Eye-witness that Mercury might be Transmuted, has sometimes
but a very Languid, if any Tast, and yet its Operations even upon some Mineral
Bodies are very peculiar. Quicksilver it self also, though the Corpuscles it consists
of be so very small as to get into the Pores of that Closest and compactest of Bodies,
Gold, is yet (you know) altogether Tastless. And our *Helmont* several times tells us,
that fair Water wherein a little Quantity f [Errata: of] Quicksilver has lain for some
time, though it acquire no certain Tast or other sensible Quality from the Quicksilver; Yet it has a power to destroy wormes in humane Bodies; which he does much,
but not causelessly extoll. And I remember, a great Lady, that had been Eminent
for her Beauty in Divers Courts, confess'd to me, that this insipid Liquor was of all
innocent washes for the Face the best that she ever met with.

And here let me conclude my Discourse, concerning such waters or Liquors
as I have hitherto been examining, with these two Considerations. Whereof the
first is, That by reason of our being wont to drink nothing but Wine, Bear, Cyder,
or other strongly tasted Liquors, there may be in several of these Liquors, that are
wont to pass for insipid Phlegme, very peculiar and Distinct, Tasts [Errata: distinct
Tasts] though unheeded (and perhaps not to be perceiv'd) by Us. For to omit what
Naturalists affirm of Apes, (and which probably may be true of divers other Animals) that they have a more exquisite palate than Men: among Men themselves,
those that are wont to drink nothing but water may (as I have try'd in my self)

Discern very sensibly a great Difference of Tasts in several waters, which one un-accustomed to drink water would take to be all alike insipid. And this is the *first* of my two Considerations; the *Other* is, That it is not impossible that the Corpuscles into which a body is dissipated by the Fire may by the Operation of the same fire have their figures so altered, or may be by associations with one another brought into little Masses of such a Size and Shape, as not to be fit to make sensible Impressions on the Tongue. And that you may not think such alterations impossible, be pleased to consider with me, that not only the sharpest Spirit of Vinager having dissolved as much Corall as it can, will Coagulate with it into a Substance, which though soluble in water, like salt, is incomparably less strongly Tasted then the Vinager was before; but (what is more considerable) though the Acid salts that are carried up with Quicksilver in the preparation of common sublimate are so sharp, that being moistened with water it will Corrode some of the Metals themselves; yet this Corrosive Sublimate being twice or thrice re-sublim'd with a full proportion of insipid Quicksilver, Constitutes (as you know) that Factitious Concrete, which the Chymists call *Mercurius dulcis*; not because it is sweet, but because the sharpness of the Corrosive Salts is so taken away by their Combination with the Mercurial Corpuscles, that the whole mixture when it is prepar'd is judg'd to be insipid.

And thus (continues *Carneades*) having given you some Reasons why I refuse to admit Elementary water for a constant Ingredient of Mixt Bodies, It will be easie for me to give you an Account why I also reject Earth.

For first, it may well be suspected that many Substances pass among Chymists under the name of Earth, because, like it, they are Dry, and Heavy, and Fixt, which yet are very farr from an Elementary Nature. This you will not think improbable, If you recall to mind what I formerly told you concerning what Chymists call the Dead Earth of things, and especially touching the copper to be drawn from the *Caput Mortuum* of Vitriol; And if also you allow me to subjoyn a casual but memorable Experiment made by *Johannes Agricola* upon the *Terra Damnata* of Brimstone. Our Author then tells us (in his notes upon *Popius* [Transcriber's Note: Poppius],) that in the year 1621 he made an Oyle of Sulphur; the remaining *Faeces* he reverberated in a moderate Fire fourteen dayes; afterwards he put them well luted up in a Wind Oven, and gave them a strong Fire for six hours, purposing to calcine the *Faeces* to a perfect Whiteness, that he might make someting [Transcriber's Note: something] else out of them. But coming to break the pot, he found above but very little *Faeces*, and those Grey and not White; but beneath there lay a fine Red *Regulus* which he first marvell'd at and knew not what to make of, being well assured that not the least thing, besides the *Faeces* of the Sulphur, came into the pot; and that the Sulphur it self had only been dissolv'd in Linseed Oyle; this *Regulus* he found heavy and malleable almost as Lead; having caus'd a Goldsmith to draw him a Wire of it, he found it to be of the Fairest copper, and so rightly colour'd, that a Jew of *Prague* offer'd him a great price for it. And of this Metal he sayes he had 12 *loth* (or six ounces) out of one pound of Ashes or *Faeces*. And this Story may well incline us to suspect that since the *Caput Mortuum* of the Sulphur was kept so long in the fire before it was found to be any thing else then a *Terra damnata*, there may be divers other Residences of Bodies which are wont to pass only for the Terrestrial *Faeces* of things, and therefore to be thrown away as soon as the Distillation or Calcination of the Body that yielded them is ended; which yet if they were long and Skilfully examin'd by the fire would appear to be differing from Elementary Earth. And I have taken notice of the unwarrantable forwardness of common Chymists to pronounce things useless *Faeces*, by observing how often they reject the *Caput Mortuum* of Verdegrease; which is yet so farr from deserving that Name, that not only by strong fires and convenient Additaments it may in some hours be reduc'd into copper, but with a certain Flux Powder I sometimes make for Recreation, I have in two or three minutes obtain'd that Metal from it. To which I may add, that having for tryall sake kept Venetian Taclk [Errata: Talck] in no less a heat than that of a glass Furnace, I found after all the Brunt of the fire it had indur'd, the remaining Body though brittle and discolour'd, had not lost very much of its former Bulke, and seem'd still to be nearer of kin to Talck than to meer Earth. And I remember too, that a candid Mineralist, famous for his Skill in trying of Oars, requesting me one day to procure him a certain *American* Mineral Earth of a *Virtuoso*, who he thought would not refuse me; I enquir'd of him why he seem'd so greedy of it: he confess'd to me that this Gentleman having brought that Earth to the publick Say-Masters; and they upon their being unable by any means to bring it to fusion or make it fly away, he (the Relator) had procur'd a little of it; and having try'd it with a peculiar Flux separated from it neer a third part of pure Gold; so great mistakes may be committed in hastily concluding things to be Uselesse Earth.

Next, it may be suppos'd, That as in the Resolution of Bodies by the Fire some of the dissipated Parts may, by their various occursion occasion'd by the heat, be brought to stick together so closely as to constitute Corpuscles too heavy for the Fire to carry away; the aggregate of which Corpuscles is wont to be call'd Ashes or Earrh [Errata: Earth]; So other Agents may resolve the Concrete into Minute Parts, after so differing a manner as not to produce any *Caput mortuum*, or dry and heavy Body. As you may remember **Helmont** above inform'd us, that with his great Dissolvent he divided a Coal into two liquid and volatile Bodies, aequiponderant to the Coal, without any dry or fixt Residence at all.

And indeed, I see not why it should be necessary that all Agents that resolve Bodies into portions of differingly qualifi'd matter must work on them the same way, and divide them into just such parts, both for nature and Number, as the Fire dissipates them into. For since, as I noted before, the Bulk and shape of the small Parts of bodies, together with their Fitness and Unfitness to be easily put into Motion, may make the liquors or other substances such Corpuscles compose, as much to differ from each other as do some of the Chymical principles: Why may not something happen in this case, not unlike what is usuall in the grosser divisions of bodies by Mechanical Instruments? Where we see that some Tools reduce Wood, for Instance, into darts [Errata: parts] of several shapes, bignesse, and other qualities, as Hatchets and Wedges divide it into grosser parts; some more long and slender, as splinters; and some more thick and irregular, as chips; but all of considerable bulk; but Files and Saws makes a Comminution of it into Dust; which, as all the others, is of the more solid sort of parts; whereas others divide it into long and broad, but thin and flexible parts, as do *Planes*: And of this kind of parts it self there is also a variety according to the Difference of the Tools employ'd to work on the Wood; the shavings made by the *plane* being in some things differing from those shives or thin and flexible pieces of wood that are obtain'd by *Borers*, and these from some others obtainable by other Tools. Some Chymical Examples applicable to this purpose I have elsewhere given you. To which I may add, that whereas in a mixture of Sulphur and Salt of Tartar well melted and incorporated together, the action of pure spirit of wine digested on it is to separate the sulphureous from the Alcalizate Parts, by dissolving the former and leaving the latter, the action of Wine (probably upon the score of its copious Phlegme) upon the same mixture is to divide it into Corpuscles consisting of both Alcalizate and Sulphureous Parts united. And if it be objected, that this is but a Factitious Concrete; I answer, that however the instance may serve to illustrate what I propos'd, if not to prove it; and that Nature her self doth in the bowels of the Earth make Decompounded Bodies, as we see in Vitriol, Cinnaber, and even in Sulphur it self; I will not urge that the Fire divides new Milk into five differing Substances; but Runnet and Acid Liquors divide it into a Coagulated matter and a thin Whey: And on the other side churning divides it into Butter and Butter-milk, which may either of them be yet reduc'd to other substances differing from the former. I will not presse this, I say, nor other instances of this Nature, because I cannot in few words answer what may be objected, that these Concretes sequestred without the help of the Fire may by it be further divided into Hypostatical Principles. But I will rather represent, That whereas the same spirit of Wine will dissociare [Transcriber's Note: dissociate] the Parts of Camphire, and make them one Liquor with it self; *Aqua Fortis* will also disjoyn them, and put them into motion; but so as to keep them together, and yet alter their Texture into the form of an Oyle. I know also an uncompounded Liquor, that an extraordinary Chymist would not allow to be so much as Saline, which doth (as I have try'd) from Coral it self (as fixt as divers judicious writers assert that Concrete to be) not only obtain a noble Tincture, Without the Intervention of Nitre or other Salts; but will carry over the Tincture in Distillation. And if some reasons did not forbid me, I could now tell you of a *Menstruum* I make my self, that doth more odly dissociate the parts of Minerals very fixt in the fire. So that it seems not incredible, that there may be some Agent or way of Operation found, whereby this or that Concrete, if not all Firme Bodies, may be resolv'd into parts so very minute and so unapt to stick close to one another, that none of them may be fixt enough to stay behind in a strong Fire, and to be incapable of Distillation; nor consequently to be look'd upon as Earth. But to return to *Helmont*, the same Authour somewhere supply's me with another Argument against the Earth's being such an Element as my Adversaries would have it. For he somewhere affirms, that he can reduce all the Terrestrial parts of mixt bodies into insipid water; whence we may argue against the Earths being one of their Elements, even from that Notion of Elements which you may remember *Philoponus* recited out of *Aristotle* himself, when he lately disputed for his Chymists against *Themistius*. And here we may on this occasion consider, that since a Body from which the Fire hath driven away its looser parts is wont to be look'd upon as Earth, upon the Account of its being endow'd with both these qualities, Tastlessenesse and Fixtnesse, (for Salt of Tartar though Fixt passes not among the Chymists for Earth, because 'tis strongly Tasted) if it be in the power of Natural Agents to deprive the *Caput Mortuum* of a body of either of those two Qualities, or to give them both to a portion of matter that had them not both before, the Chymists will not easily define what part of a resolv'd Concrete is earth, and make out, that that Earth is a primary, simple, and indestructible Body. Now there are some cases wherein the more skilful of the Vulgar Chymists themselves pretend to be able, by repeated Cohobations and other fit Operations, to make the Distilled parts of a Concrete bring its own *Caput Mortuum* over the Helme, in the forme of a Liquor; in which state being both Fluid and Volatile, you will easily believe it would not be taken for Earth. And indeed by a skilful, but not Vulgar, way of managing some Concretes, there may be more effected in this kind, then you perhaps would easily think. And on the other side, that either Earth may be Generated, or at least Bodies that did not before appear to be neer Totally Earth, may be so alter'd as to pass for it, seems very possible, if *Helmont*[34] have done that by Art which he mentions in several places; especially where He sayes that he knowes wayes whereby Sulphur once dissolv'd is all of it fix'd into a Terrestrial Powder; and the whole Bodie of Salt-Petre may be turn'd into Earth: Which last he elsewhere sayes is Done by the Odour only of a certain Sulphureous Fire. And in another place He mentions one way of doing this, which I cannot give you an Account of; because the Materialls I had prepar'd for Trying it, were by a Servants mistake unhappily thrown away.

[34: Novi item modos quibus totum Salpetiae [Errata: sal-petrae] in terram convertitur, totumque Sulphur semel dissolutum fixetur in Pulvearem terreum. Helmont in Compl. atque Mist. Elementor. Sect. 24.]

And these Last Arguments may be confirm'd by the Experiment I have often had occasion to mention concerning the Mint I produc'd out of Water. And partly by an Observation of *Rondeletius* concerning the Growth of Animals also, Nourish'd but by Water, which I remember'd not to mention, when I discours'd to you about the Production of things out of Water. This Diligent Writer then in his instructive book of fishes,[35] affirmes That his Wife kept a fish in a Glass of water without any other Food for three years; in which space it was constantly augmented, till at last it could not come out of the Place at which it was put in, and at length was too big for the glass it self though that were of a large capacity. And because there is no just reason to doubt, that this Fish, if Distill'd, would have yielded the like differing substances with other Animals: And However, because the Mint which I had out of water afforded me upon Distillation a good quantity of Charcoal, I think I may from thence inferr, that Earth it self may be produc'd out of Water; or if you please, that water may be transmuted into Earth; and consequently, that though it could be prov'd that Earth is an Ingredient actually in-existent in the Vegetable and Animal Bodies whence it may be obtain'd by Fire: yet it would not necessarily follow, that Earth as a pre-existent Element Does with other Principles convene to make up those Bodies whence it seems to have been separated.

[35: *Lib. 1. cap. 2.*]

After all is said (sayes *Eleutherius*) I have yet something to Object, that I cannot but think considerable, since *Carneades* Himself alledg'd it as such; for, (continues *Eleutherius* smiling) I must make bold to try whether you can as luckily answer your own Arguments, as those of your Antagonists, I mean (pursues he) that part of your Concessions, wherein you cannot but remember that you supply'd your Adversaries with an Example to prove that there may be Elementary Bodies, by taking Notice that Gold may be an Ingredient in a multitude of differing Mixtures, and yet retain its Nature, notwithstanding all that the Chymists by their Fires and Corrosive Waters are able to do to Destroy it.

I sufficiently intimated to you at that time (replies *Carneades*) that I propos'd this Example, chiefly to shew you how Nature may be Conceived to have made Elements, not to prove that she actually has made any; And you know, that *a posse ad esse* the Inference will not hold. But (continues *Carneades*) to answer more directly to the Objection drawn from Gold, I must tell You, that though I know very well that divers of the more sober Chymists have complain'd of the Vulgar Chymists, as of Mountebanks or Cheats, for pretending so vainly, as hitherto they have done, to Destroy Gold; Yet I know a certain *Menstruum* (which our Friend has made, and intends shortly to communicate to the Ingenious) of so piercing and powerfull a Quality, That if notwithstanding much care, and some skill, I did not much deceive myself, I have with it really destroy'd even refin'd Gold, and brought it into a Metalline Body of another colour and Nature, as I found by Tryals purposely made. And if some just Considerations did not for the present Forbid it, I could Perchance here shew you by another Experiment or Two of my own Trying, that such **Menstruums** may be made as to entice away and retain divers parts, from Bodies, which even the more Judicious and Experienc'd **Spagyrists** have pronounc'd irresoluble by the Fire. Though (which I Desire you would mark) in neither of these Instances, the Gold or Precious Stones be Analys'd into any of the **Tria Prima**, but only Reduc'd to new Concretes. And indeed there is a great Disparity betwixt the Operations of the several Agents whereby the Parts of a Body come to be Dissipated. As if (for Instance) you dissolve the purer sort of Vitriol in common Water, the Liquor will swallow up the Mineral, and so Dissociate its Corpuscles, that they will seem to make up but one Liquor with those of the water; and yet each of these Corpuscles retains its Nature and Texture, and remains a Vitriolate and Compounded Body. But if the same Vitriol be exposed to a strong Fire, it will then be divided not only, as before, into smaller parts, but into Heterogeneous Substances, each of the Vitriolate Corpuscles that remain'd entire in the water, being it self upon the Destruction of its former Texture dissipated or divided into new Particles of differing Qualities. But Instances more fitly applicable to this purpose, I have already given you. Wherefore to return to what I told you about the Destruction of Gold, that Experiment Invites me to Represent to you, that Though there were either Saline, or Sulphureous, or Terrestrial Portions of Matter, whose parts were so small, so firmly united together, or of a figure so fit to make them cohere to one another, (as we see that in quicksilver broken into little Globes, the Parts brought to touch one another do immediately re-imbody) that neither the Fire, nor the usual Agents employ'd by Chymists, are pierceing enough to divide their Parts, so as to destroy the Texture of the single Corpuscles; yet it would not necessarily follow, That such Permanent Bodies were Elementary, since tis possible there may be Agents found in Nature, some of whose parts may be of such a Size and Figure as to take better Hold of some parts of these seemingly Elementary Corpuscles than these parts do of the rest, and Consequently may carry away such parts with them, and so dissolve the Texture of the Corpuscle by pulling its parts asunder. And if it be said, that at least we may this way discover the Elementary Ingredients of Things, by observing into what Substances these Corpuscles that were reputed pure are divided; I answer, that it is not necessary that such a Discovery should be practicable. For if the Particles of the Dissolvent do take such firme hold of those of the Dissolved Body, they must constitute together new Bodies, as well as Destroy the Old; and the strickt Union, which according to this **Hypothesis** may well be suppos'd betwixt the Parts of the Emergent Body, will make it as Little to be Expected that they should be pull'd asunder, but by little Parts of matter, that to Divide them Associate Themselves and stick extreamly close to those of them which they sever from their Former Adherents. Besides that it is not impossible, that a Corpuscle suppos'd to be Elementary may have its Nature changed, without suffering a Divorce of its parts, barely by a new Texture Effected by some powerfull Agent; as I formerly told you, the same portion of matter may easily by the Operation of the Fire be turn'd at pleasure into the form of a Brittle and Transparent, or an Opacous and Malleable Body.

And indeed, if you consider how farr the bare Change of Texture, whether made by Art or Nature (or rather by Nature with or without the assistance of man) can go in producing such New Qualities in the same parcel of matter, and how many inanimate Bodies (such as are all the Chymical productions of the Fire) we know are Denominated and Distinguish'd not so much by any Imaginary Substantial Form, as by the aggregate of these Qualities. If you consider these Things, I say, and that the varying of either the figure, or the Size, or the Motion, or the Situation, or Connexion of the Corpuscles whereof any of these Bodies is compos'd, may alter the Fabrick of it, you will possibly be invited to suspect, with me, that there is no great need that Nature should alwayes have Elements before hand, whereof to make such Bodies as we call mixts. And that it is not so easie as Chymists and others have hitherto Imagin'd, to discern, among the many differing Substances that may without any extraordinary skill be obtain'd from the same portion of matter, Which ought to be esteemed exclusively to all the rest, its in-existent Elementary Ingredients; much lesse to determine what Primogeneal and Simple Bodies convened together to compose it. To exemplify this, I shall add to what I have already on several occasions Represented, but this single instance.

You may remember (**Eleutherius**) that I formerly intimated to you, that besides Mint and Pompions, I produced divers other Vegetables of very differing Natures out of Water. Wherefore you will not, I presume, think it incongruous to suppose, that when a slender Vine-slip is set into the ground, and takes root, there it may likewise receive its Nutriment from the water attracted out of the earth by his roots, or impell'd by the warm'th of the sun, or pressure of the ambient air into the pores of them. And this you will the more easily believe, if you ever observ'd what a strange quantity of Water will Drop out of a wound given to the Vine, in a convenient place, at a seasonable time in the Spring; and how little of Tast or Smell this *Aqua Vitis*, as Physitians call it, is endow'd with, notwithstanding what concoction or alteration it may receive in its passage through the Vine, to discriminate it from common Water. Supposing then this Liquor, at its first entrance into the roots of the Vine, to be common Water; Let Us a little consider how many various Substances may be obtain'd from it; though to do so, I must repeat somewhat that I had a former occasion to touch upon. And first, this Liquor being Digested in the plant, and assimilated by the several parts of it, is turn'd into the Wood, Bark, Pith, Leaves, &c. of the Vine; The same Liquor may be further dry'd, and fashon'd into Vine-buds, and these a while after are advanced unto sour Grapes, which express'd yield Verjuice, a Liquor very differing in several qualities both from Wine and other Liquors obtainable from the Vine: These soure Grapes being by the heat of the Sun concocted and ripened, turne to well tasted Grapes; These if dry'd in the Sun and Distill'd, afford a faetid Oyle and a piercing *Empyreumatical* Spirit, but not a Vinous Spirit; These dry'd Grapes or Raisins boyl'd in a convenient proportion of Water make a sweet Liquor, which being betimes distill'd afford an Oyle and Spirit much like those of the Raisins themselves; If the juice of the Grapes be squeez'd out and put to Ferment, it first becomes a sweet and turbid Liquor, then grows lesse sweet and more clear, and then affords in common Distillations not an Oyle but a Spirit, which, though inflamable like Oyle, differs much from it, in that it is not fat, and that it will readily mingle with Water. I have likewise without Addition obtain'd in processe of time (and by an easie way which I am ready to teach you) from one of the noblest sorts of Wine, pretty store of pure and curiously figured Crystals of Salt, together with a great proportion of a Liquor as sweet almost as Hony; and these I obtained not from Must, but True and sprightly Wine; besides the Vinous Liquor, the fermented Juice of Grapes is partly turned into liquid Dregs or Leeze, and partly into that crust or dry feculancy that is commonly called Tartar; and this Tartar may by the Fire be easily divided into five differing substances; four of which are not Acid, and the other not so manifestly Acid as the Tartar it self; The same Vinous Juice after some time, especially if it be not carefully kept, Degenerates into that very sour Liquor called Vinegar; from which you may obtain by the Fire a Spirit and a Crystalline Salt differing enough from the Spirit and Lixiviate Salt of Tartar. And if you pour the Dephlegm'd Spirit of the Vinegar upon the Salt of Tartar, there will be produc'd such a Conflict or Ebullition as if there were scarce two more contrary Bodies in Nature; and oftentimes in this Vinager you may observe part of the matter to be turned into an innumerable company of swimming Animals, which our Friend having divers years ago observed, hath in one of his Papers taught us how to discover clearly without the help of a *Microscope*.

Into all these various Schemes of matter, or differingly Qualifyed Bodies, besides divers others that I purposely forbear to mention, may the Water that is imbib'd by the roots of the Vine be brought, partly by the formative power of the plant, and partly by supervenient Agents or Causes, without the visible concurrence of any extraneous Ingredient; but if we be allowed to add to the Productions of this transmuted Water a few other substances, we may much encrease the Variety of such Bodies; although in this second sort of Productions, the Vinous parts seem scarce to retain any thing of the much more fix'd Bodies wherewith they were mingl'd; but only to have by their Mixture with them acquir'd such a Disposition, that in their recess occasion'd by the Fire they came to be alter'd as to shape, or Bigness, or both, and associated after a New manner. Thus, as I formerly told you, I did by the Addition of a *Caput Mortuum* of Antimony, and some other Bodies unfit for Distillation, obtain from crude Tartar, store of a very Volatile and Crystalline Salt, differing very much in smell and other Qualities from the usuall salts of Tartar.

But (sayes *Eleutherius*, interrupting him at these Words) if you have no restraint upon you, I would very gladly before you go any further, be more particularly inform'd, how you make this Volatile Salt, because (you know) that such Multitudes of Chymists have by a scarce imaginable Variety of wayes, attempted in Vain the Volatilization of the Salt of Tartar, that divers learned *Spagyrists* speak as if it were impossible, to make any thing out of Tartar, that shall be Volatile in a Saline Forme, or as some of them express it, *in forma sicca*. I am very farr from thinking (answers *Carneades*) that the Salt I have mention'd is that which *Paracelsus* and *Helmont* mean when they speak of *Sal Tartari Volatile*, and ascribe such great things to it. For the Salt I speak of falls extreamly short of those Virtues, not seeming in its Tast, Smel, and other Obvious Qualities, to differ very much (though something it do differ) from Salt of Harts-horn, and other Volatile Salts drawn from the Distill'd Parts of Animals. Nor have I yet made Tryals enough to be sure, that it is a pure Salt of Tartar without participating any thing at all of the Nitre, or Antimony. But because it seems more likely to proceed from the Tartar, than from any of the other Ingredients, and because the Experiment is in it self not Ignoble, and Luciferous enough (as shewing a new way to produce a Volatile Salt contrary to Acid Salts from Bodies that otherwise are Observ'd to yield no such Liquor, but either only, or chiefly, Acid ones,) I shall, to satisfie you, acquaint you before any of my other Friends with the way I now use (for I have formerly us'd some others) to make it.

Take then of good Antimony, Salt-Petre and Tartar, of each an equal weight, and of Quicklime Halfe the Weight of any one of them; let these be powder'd and well mingl'd; this done, you must have in readiness a long neck or Retort of Earth, which must be plac'd in a Furnace for a naked Fire, and have at the top of it a hole of a convenient Bigness, at which you may cast in the Mixture, and presently stop it up again; this Vessel being fitted with a large Receiver must have Fire made under it, till the bottom of the sides be red hot, and then you must cast in the above prepar'd Mixture, by about halfe a spoonfull (more or less) at a time, at the hole made for that purpose; which being nimbly stopt, the Fumes will pass into the Receiver and con-dense there into a Liquor, that being rectifi'd will be of a pure golden Colour, and carry up that colour to a great height; this Spirit abounds in the Salt I told you of, part of which may easily enough be separated by the way I use in such cases, which is, to put the Liquor into a glass Egg, or bolthead with a long and narrow Neck. For if this be plac'd a little inclining in hot sand, there will sublime up a fine Salt, which, as I told you, I find to be much of kin to the Volatile Salts of Animals: For like them it has a Saltish, not an Acid Salt; it hisses upon the Affusion of Spirit of Nitre, or Oyle of Vitriol; it precipitates Corals Dissolv'd in Spirit of Vinager; it turnes the blew Syrup of Violets immediately green; it presently turnes the Solution of Sublimate into a Milkie whiteness; and in summ, has divers Operations like those that I have observ'd in that sort of Salts to which I have resembled it: and is so Volatile, that for Distinction sake, I call it ***Tartari Fugitivus*** [Errata: Sal Tartari Fugitivus]. What virtues it may have in Physick I have not yet had the opportunity to Try; but I am apt to think they will not be despicable. And besides that a very Ingenious Friend of mine tells me he hath done great matters against the stone, with a Preparation not very much Differing from ours, a very Experienc'd Germane Chymist finding that I was unacquainted with the wayes of making this salt, told me that in a great City in his Country, a noted Chymist prizes it so highly, that he had a while since procur'd a Priviledge from the Magistrates, that none but He, or by his Licence, should vent a Spirit made almost after the same Way with mine, save that he leaves out one of the Ingredients, namely the Quick-lime. But, continues *Carneades*, to resume my Former Discourse where your Curiosity interrupted it;

Tis also a common practice in *France* to bury thin Plates of Copper in the Marc (as the French call it) or Husks of Grapes, whence the Juice has been squeez'd out in the Wine-press, and by this means the more saline parts of those Husks working by little and little upon the Copper, Coagulate Themselves with it into that Blewish Green Substance we in English call Verdigrease. Of which I therefore take Notice, because having Distill'd it in a Naked Fire, I found as I expected, that by the Association of the Saline with the Metalline parts, the former were so alter'd, that the Distill'd Liquor, even without Rectification, seem'd by smell and Tast, strong almost like *Aqua Fortis*, and very much surpassed the purest and most Rectifi'd Spirit of Vinager that ever I made. And this Spirit I therefore ascribe to the salt of the Husks alter'd by their Co-Mixture with the copper (though the Fire afterwards Divorce and Transmute them) because I found this later in the bottom of the Retort in the Forme of a *Crocus* or redish powder: And because Copper is of too sluggish a Nature to be forc'd over in close Vessels by no stronger a heat. And that which is also somewhat Remarkable in the Destillation of good Verdigrease, (or at least of that sort that I us'd) is this, that I Never could observe that it yielded me any oyl, (unless a little black slime which was separated in Rectification may pass for Oyle) though both Tartar and Vinager, (especially the former) will by Destillation yield a Moderate proportion of it. If likewise you pour Spirit of Vinager upon Calcin'd Lead, the Acid Salt of the Liquor will by its Commixture with the Metalline parts, though Insipid, acquire in a few hours a more than Saccharine sweetness; and these Saline parts being by a strong Fire Destill'd from the Lead wherewith they were imbody'd, will, as I formerly also noted to a Different purpose, leave the Metal behind them alter'd in some qualities from what it was, and will themselves ascend, partly in the Forme of an unctuous Body or Oyle, partly in that of Phlegme; but for the greatest part in the Forme of a subtile Spirit, indow'd, besides divers new Qualities which I am not now willing to take notice of, with a strong smell very much other than that of Vinager, and a piercing tast quite differing both from the Sowerness of the Spirit of Vinager, and the Sweetness of the Sugar of Lead.

To be short, As the difference of Bodies may depend meerly upon that of the schemes whereinto their Common matter is put; So the seeds of Things, the Fire and the other Agents are able to alter the minute parts of a Body (either by breaking them into smaller ones of differing shapes, or by Uniting together these Fragments with the unbroken Corpuscles, or such Corpuscles among Themselves) and the same Agents partly by Altering the shape or bigness of the Constituent Corpuscles of a Body, partly by driving away some of them, partly by blending others with them, and partly by some new manner of connecting them, may give the whole portion of matter a new Texture of its minute parts; and thereby make it deserve a new and Distinct name. So that according as the small parts of matter recede from each other, or work upon each other, or are connected together after this or that determinate manner, a Body of this or that denomination is produced, as some other Body happens thereby to be alter'd or destroy'd.

Since then those things which Chymists produce by the help of the Fire are but inanimate Bodies; since such fruits of the Chymists skill differ from one another but in so few qualities that we see plainly that by fire and other Agents we can employ, we can easily enough work as great alterations upon matter, as those that are requisite to change one of these Chymical Productions into another; Since the same portion of matter may without being Compounded with any extraneous Body, or at least Element, be made to put on such a variety of formes, and consequently to be (successively) turn'd into so many differing Bodies. And since the matter cloath'd with so many differing formes was originally but water, and that in its passage thorow so many transformations, it was never reduc'd into any of those substances which are reputed to be the Principles or Elements of mixt Bodies, except by the violence of the fire, which it self divides not Bodies into perfectly simple or Elementary substances, but into new Compounds; Since, I say, these things are so, I see not why we must needs believe that there are any Primogeneal and simple

Bodies, of which as of Pre-exsistent Elements Nature is obliged to compound all others. Nor do I see why we may not conceive that she may produce the Bodies accounted mixt out of one another by Variously altering and contriving their minute parts, without resolving the matter into any such simple or Homogeneous substances as are pretended. Neither, to dispatch, do I see why it should be counted absur'd [Transcriber's Note: absurd] to think, that when a Body is resolv'd by the Fire into its suppos'd simple Ingredients, those substances are not true and proper Elements, but rather were, as it were, Accidentally produc'd by the fire, which by Dissipating a Body into minute Parts does, if those parts be shut up in Close Vessels, for the most part necessarily bring them to Associate Themselves after another manner than before, and so bring Them into Bodies of such Different Consistences as the Former Texture of the Body, and Concurrent Circumstances make such disbanded particles apt to Constitute; as experience shews us (and I have both noted it, and prov'd it already) that as there are some Concretes whose parts when dissipated by fire are fitted to be put into such Schemes of matter as we call Oyle, and Salt, and Spirit; So there are others, such as are especially the greatest part of Minerals, whose Corpuscles being of another Size or figure, or perhaps contriv'd another Way, will not in the Fire yield Bodies of the like Consistences, but rather others of differing Textures; Not to mention, that from Gold and some other Bodies, we see not that the Fire separates any Distinct Substances at all; nor That even those Similar Parts of Bodies which the Chymists Obtain by the Fire, are the Elements whose names they bear, but Compound Bodies, upon which, for their resemblance to them in consistence, or some other obvious Quality, Chymists have been pleas'd to bestow such Appellations.

THE CONCLUSION.

These last Words of **Carneades** being soon after follow'd by a noise which seem'd to come from the place where the rest of the Company was, he took it for a warning, that it was time for him to conclude or break off his Discourse; and told his Friend; By this time I hope you see, **Eleutherius**, that if **Helmonts** Experiments be true, it is no absurdity to question whether that Doctrine be one, that doth not assert Any Elements in the sence before explain'd. But because that, as divers of my Arguments suppose the marvellous power of the **Alkahest** in the Analyzing of Bodies, so the Effects ascrib'd to that power are so unparallell'd and stupendious, that though I am not sure but that there **may be** such an Agent, yet little less than [Greek: autopsia] seems requisite to make a man sure there **is**. And consequently I leave it to you to judge, how farre those of my Arguments that are built upon **Alkahestical** Operations are weakned by that Liquors being Matchless; and shall therefore desire you not to think that I propose this Paradox that rejects all Elements, as an Opinion equally probable with the former part of my discourse. For by that, I hope, you are satisfied, that the Arguments wont to be brought by Chymists, to prove That all Bodies consist of either Three Principles, or Five, are far from being so strong as those that I have employ'd to prove, that there is not any certain and Determinate number of such Principles or Elements to be met with Universally in all mixt Bodies. And I suppose I need not tell you, that these **Anti-Chymical** Paradoxes might have been manag'd more to their Advantage; but that having not confin'd my Curiosity to Chymical Experiments, I who am but a young Man, and younger Chymist, can yet be but slenderly furnished with them, in reference to so great and difficult a Task as you impos'd upon me; Besides that, to tell you the Truth, I durst not employ some even of the best Experiments I am acquainted with, because I must not yet disclose them; but however, I think I may presume that what I have hitherto Discoursed will induce you to think, that Chymists have been much more happy in finding Experiments than the Causes of them; or in assigning the Principles by which they may best be explain'd. And indeed, when in the writings of *Paracelsus* I meet with such Phantastick and Un-intelligible Discourses as that Writer often puzzels and tyres his Reader with, father'd upon such excellent Experiments, as though he seldom clearly teaches, I often find he knew; me thinks the Chymists, in their searches after truth, are not unlike the Navigators of *Solomons Tarshish* Fleet, who brought home from their long and tedious Voyages, not only Gold, and Silver, and Ivory, but Apes and Peacocks too; For so the Writings of several (for I say not, all) of your Hermetick Philosophers present us, together with divers Substantial and noble Experiments, Theories, which either like Peacocks feathers make a great shew, but are neither solid nor useful; or else like Apes, if they have some appearance of being rational, are blemish'd with some absurdity or other, that when they are *Attentively* consider'd, makes them appear Ridiculous.

Carneades having thus finish'd his Discourse against the received Doctrines of the *Elements*; *Eleutherius* judging he should not have time to say much to him before their separation, made some haste to tell him; I confess, *Carneades*, that you have said more in favour of your Paradoxes then I expected. For though divers of the Experiments you have mention'd are no secrets, and were not unknown to me, yet besides that you have added many of your own unto them, you have laid them together in such a way, and apply'd them to such purposes, and made such Deductions From them, as I have not Hitherto met with.

But though I be therefore inclin'd to think, that *Philoponus*, had he heard you, would scarce have been able in all points to defend the Chymical *Hypothesis* against the arguments wherewith you have oppos'd it; yet me thinks that however your Objections seem to evince a great part of what they pretend to, yet they evince it not all; and the numerous tryals of those you call the vulgar Chymists, may be allow'd to prove something too.

Wherefore, if it be granted you that you have made it probable,

First, that the differing substances into which mixt Bodies are wont to be resolved by the Fire are not of a pure and an Elementary nature, especially for this Reason, that they yet retain so much of the nature of the Concrete that afforded them, as to appear to be yet somewhat compounded, and oftentimes to differ in one Concrete from Principles of the same denomination in another:

Next, that as to the number of these differing substances, neither is it precisely three, because in most Vegetable and Animal bodies Earth and Phlegme are also to be found among their Ingredients; nor is there any one determinate number into which the Fire (as it is wont to be employ'd) does precisely and universally resolve all compound Bodies whatsoever, as well Minerals as others that are reputed perfectly mixt.

Lastly, that there are divers Qualities which cannot well be refer'd to any of these Substances, as if they primarily resided in it and belong'd to it; and some other qualities, which though they seem to have their chief and most ordinary residence in some one of these Principles or Elements of mixt Bodies, are not yet so deducible from it, but that also some more general Principles must be taken in to explicate them.

If, I say, the Chymists (continues *Eleutherius*) be so Liberall as to make you these three Concessions, I hope you will, on your part, be so civil and Equitable as to grant them these three other propositions, namely;

First, that divers Mineral Bodies, and therefore probably all the rest, may be resolv'd into a Saline, a Sulphureous, and a Mercurial part; And that almost all Vegetable and Animal Concretes may, if not by the Fire alone, yet, by a skilfull Artist Employing the Fire as his chief Instrument, be divided into five differing Substances, Salt, Spirit, Oyle, Phlegme and Earth; of which the three former by reason of their being so much more Operative than the Two Later, deserve to be Lookt upon as the Three active Principles, and by way of Eminence to be call'd the three principles of mixt bodies.

Next, that these Principles, Though they be not perfectly Devoid of all Mixture, yet may without inconvenience be stil'd the Elements of Compounded bodies, and bear the Names of those Substances which they most Resemble, and which are manifestly predominant in them; and that especially for this reason, that none of these Elements is Divisible by the Fire into Four or Five differing substances, like the Concrete whence it was separated.

Lastly, That Divers of the Qualities of a mixt Body, and especially the Medical Virtues, do for the most part lodge in some One or Other of its principles, and may

Therefore usefully be sought for in That Principle sever'd from the others.

And in this also (pursues *Eleutherius*) methinks both you and the Chymists may easily agree, that the surest way is to Learn by particular Experiments, what differing parts particular Bodies do consist of, and by what wayes (either Actual or potential fire) they may best and most Conveniently be Separated, as without relying too much upon the Fire alone, for the resolving of Bodies, so without fruitlessly contending to force them into more Elements than Nature made Them up of, or strip the sever'd Principles so naked, as by making Them Exquisitely Elementary to make them almost useless,

These things (subjoynes *Eleu.*) I propose, without despairing to see them granted by you; not only because I know that you so much preferr the Reputation of *Candor* before that of subtility, that your having once suppos'd a truth would not hinder you from imbracing it when clearly made out to you; but because, upon the present occasion, it will be no disparagement to you to recede from some of your Paradoxes, since the nature and occasion of your past Discourse did not oblige you to declare your own opinions, but only to personate an Antagonist of the Chymists. So that (concludes he, with a smile) you may now by granting what I propose, add the Reputation of Loving the truth sincerely to that of having been able to oppose it subtilly.

Carneades's haste forbidding him to answer this crafty piece of flattery; Till I shal (sayes he) have an opportunity to acquaint you with my own Opinions about the controversies I have been discoursing of, you will not, I hope, expect I should declare my own sence of the Arguments I have employ'd. Wherefore I shall only tell you thus much at present; that though not only an acute Naturalist, but even I my self could take plausible Exceptions at some of them; yet divers of them too are such as will not perhaps be readily answer'd, and will Reduce my Adversaries, at least, to alter and Reform their *Hypothesis*. I perceive I need not minde you that the Objections I made against the Quaternary of Elements and Ternary of Principles needed not to be oppos'd so much against the Doctrines Themselves (either of which, especially the latter, may be much more probably maintain'd than hitherto it seems to have been, by those Writers for it I have met with) as against the unaccurateness and the unconcludingness of the *Analytical* Experiments vulgarly Relyed On to Demonstrate them.

And therefore, if either of the two examin'd Opinions, or any other Theory of Elements, shall upon rational and Experimental grounds be clearly made out to me; 'Tis Obliging, but not irrational, in you to Expect, that I shall not be so farr in Love with my Disquieting Doubts, as not to be content to change them for undoubted truths. And (concludes *Carneades* smiling) it were no great disparagement for a Sceptick to confesse to you, that as unsatisfy'd as the past discourse may have made you think me with the Doctrines of the Peripateticks, and the Chymists, about the Elements and Principles, I can yet so little discover what to acquiesce in, that perchance the Enquiries of others have scarce been more unsatisfactory to me, than my own have been to my self.

The Codes Of Hammurabi And Moses
W. W. Davies

QTY

The discovery of the Hammurabi Code is one of the greatest achievements of archaeology, and is of paramount interest, not only to the student of the Bible, but also to all those interested in ancient history...

Religion   **ISBN:** *1-59462-338-4*   **Pages:132**
                                              MSRP $12.95

The Theory of Moral Sentiments
Adam Smith

QTY

This work from 1749. contains original theories of conscience amd moral judgment and it is the foundation for systemof morals.

Philosophy **ISBN:** *1-59462-777-0*   **Pages:536**
                                              MSRP $19.95

Jessica's First Prayer
Hesba Stretton

QTY

In a screened and secluded corner of one of the many railway-bridges which span the streets of London there could be seen a few years ago, from five o'clock every morning until half past eight, a tidily set-out coffee-stall, consisting of a trestle and board, upon which stood two large tin cans, with a small fire of charcoal burning under each so as to keep the coffee boiling during the early hours of the morning when the work-people were thronging into the city on their way to their daily toil...

Childrens   **ISBN:** *1-59462-373-2*   **Pages:84**
                                              MSRP $9.95

My Life and Work
Henry Ford

QTY

Henry Ford revolutionized the world with his implementation of mass production for the Model T automobile. Gain valuable business insight into his life and work with his own auto-biography... "We have only started on our development of our country we have not as yet, with all our talk of wonderful progress, done more than scratch the surface. The progress has been wonderful enough but..."

Biographies/ **ISBN:** *1-59462-198-5*   **Pages:300**
                                               MSRP $21.95

The Art of Cross-Examination
Francis Wellman

QTY

I presume it is the experience of every author, after his first book is published upon an important subject, to be almost overwhelmed with a wealth of ideas and illustrations which could readily have been included in his book, and which to his own mind, at least, seem to make a second edition inevitable. Such certainly was the case with me; and when the first edition had reached its sixth impression in five months, I rejoiced to learn that it seemed to my publishers that the book had met with a sufficiently favorable reception to justify a second and considerably enlarged edition. ..

Pages:412

Reference   ISBN: *1-59462-647-2*   *MSRP $19.95*

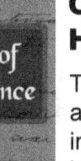

On the Duty of Civil Disobedience
Henry David Thoreau

QTY

Thoreau wrote his famous essay, On the Duty of Civil Disobedience, as a protest against an unjust but popular war and the immoral but popular institution of slave-owning. He did more than write—he declined to pay his taxes, and was hauled off to gaol in consequence. Who can say how much this refusal of his hastened the end of the war and of slavery ?

Law   ISBN: *1-59462-747-9*   **Pages:48**

MSRP $7.45

Dream Psychology Psychoanalysis for Beginners
Sigmund Freud

QTY

Sigmund Freud, born Sigismund Schlomo Freud (May 6, 1856 - September 23, 1939), was a Jewish-Austrian neurologist and psychiatrist who co-founded the psychoanalytic school of psychology. Freud is best known for his theories of the unconscious mind, especially involving the mechanism of repression; his redefinition of sexual desire as mobile and directed towards a wide variety of objects; and his therapeutic techniques, especially his understanding of transference in the therapeutic relationship and the presumed value of dreams as sources of insight into unconscious desires.

Pages:196

Psychology   ISBN: *1-59462-905-6*   *MSRP $15.45*

The Miracle of Right Thought
Orison Swett Marden

QTY

Believe with all of your heart that you will do what you were made to do. When the mind has once formed the habit of holding cheerful, happy, prosperous pictures, it will not be easy to form the opposite habit. It does not matter how improbable or how far away this realization may see, or how dark the prospects may be, if we visualize them as best we can, as vividly as possible, hold tenaciously to them and vigorously struggle to attain them, they will gradually become actualized, realized in the life. But a desire, a longing without endeavor, a yearning abandoned or held indifferently will vanish without realization.

Pages:360

Self Help   ISBN: *1-59462-644-8*   *MSRP $25.45*

The Rosicrucian Cosmo-Conception Mystic Christianity by *Max Heindel*   ISBN: *1-59462-188-8*   **$38.95**
The Rosicrucian Cosmo-conception is not dogmatic, neither does it appeal to any other authority than the reason of the student. It is: not controversial, but is: sent forth in the, hope that it may help to clear...   New Age/Religion Pages 646

Abandonment To Divine Providence by *Jean-Pierre de Caussade*   ISBN: *1-59462-228-0*   **$25.95**
"The Rev. Jean Pierre de Caussade was one of the most remarkable spiritual writers of the Society of Jesus in France in the 18th Century. His death took place at Toulouse in 1751. His works have gone through many editions and have been republished...   Inspirational/Religion Pages 400

Mental Chemistry by *Charles Haanel*   ISBN: *1-59462-192-6*   **$23.95**
Mental Chemistry allows the change of material conditions by combining and appropriately utilizing the power of the mind. Much like applied chemistry creates something new and unique out of careful combinations of chemicals the mastery of mental chemistry...   New Age Pages 354

The Letters of Robert Browning and Elizabeth Barret Barrett 1845-1846 vol II   ISBN: *1-59462-193-4*   **$35.95**
by *Robert Browning* and *Elizabeth Barrett*   Biographies Pages 596

Gleanings In Genesis (volume I) by *Arthur W. Pink*   ISBN: *1-59462-130-6*   **$27.45**
Appropriately has Genesis been termed "the seed plot of the Bible" for in it we have, in germ form, almost all of the great doctrines which are afterwards fully developed in the books of Scripture which follow...   Religion/Inspirational Pages 420

The Master Key by *L. W. de Laurence*   ISBN: *1-59462-001-6*   **$30.95**
In no branch of human knowledge has there been a more lively increase of the spirit of research during the past few years than in the study of Psychology, Concentration and Mental Discipline. The requests for authentic lessons in Thought Control, Mental Discipline and...   New Age/Business Pages 422

The Lesser Key Of Solomon Goetia by *L. W. de Laurence*   ISBN: *1-59462-092-X*   **$9.95**
This translation of the first book of the "Lernegton" which is now for the first time made accessible to students of Talismanic Magic was done, after careful collation and edition, from numerous Ancient Manuscripts in Hebrew, Latin, and French...   New Age/Occult Pages 92

Rubaiyat Of Omar Khayyam by *Edward Fitzgerald*   ISBN:*1-59462-332-5*   **$13.95**
Edward Fitzgerald, whom the world has already learned, in spite of his own efforts to remain within the shadow of anonymity, to look upon as one of the rarest poets of the century, was born at Bredfield, in Suffolk, on the 31st of March, 1809. He was the third son of John Purcell...   Music Pages 172

Ancient Law by *Henry Maine*   ISBN: *1-59462-128-4*   **$29.95**
The chief object of the following pages is to indicate some of the earliest ideas of mankind, as they are reflected in Ancient Law, and to point out the relation of those ideas to modern thought.   Religion/History Pages 452

Far-Away Stories by *William J. Locke*   ISBN: *1-59462-129-2*   **$19.45**
"Good wine needs no bush, but a collection of mixed vintages does. And this book is just such a collection. Some of the stories I do not want to remain buried for ever in the museum files of dead magazine-numbers an author's not unpardonable vanity..."   Fiction Pages 272

Life of David Crockett by *David Crockett*   ISBN: *1-59462-250-7*   **$27.45**
"Colonel David Crockett was one of the most remarkable men of the times in which he lived. Born in humble life, but gifted with a strong will, an indomitable courage, and unremitting perseverance...   Biographies/New Age Pages 424

Lip-Reading by *Edward Nitchie*   ISBN: *1-59462-206-X*   **$25.95**
Edward B. Nitchie, founder of the New York School for the Hard of Hearing, now the Nitchie School of Lip-Reading, Inc, wrote "LIP-READING Principles and Practice". The development and perfecting of this meritorious work on lip-reading was an undertaking...   How-to Pages 400

A Handbook of Suggestive Therapeutics, Applied Hypnotism, Psychic Science   ISBN: *1-59462-214-0*   **$24.95**
by *Henry Munro*   Health/New Age/Health/Self-help Pages 376

A Doll's House: and Two Other Plays by *Henrik Ibsen*   ISBN: *1-59462-112-8*   **$19.95**
Henrik Ibsen created this classic when in revolutionary 1848 Rome. Introducing some striking concepts in playwriting for the realist genre, this play has been studied the world over.   Fiction/Classics/Plays 308

The Light of Asia by *sir Edwin Arnold*   ISBN: *1-59462-204-3*   **$13.95**
In this poetic masterpiece, Edwin Arnold describes the life and teachings of Buddha. The man who was to become known as Buddha to the world was born as Prince Gautama of India but he rejected the worldly riches and abandoned the reigns of power when...   Religion/History/Biographies Pages 170

The Complete Works of Guy de Maupassant by *Guy de Maupassant*   ISBN: *1-59462-157-8*   **$16.95**
"For days and days, nights and nights, I had dreamed of that first kiss which was to consecrate our engagement, and I knew not on what spot I should put my lips..."   Fiction/Classics Pages 240

The Art of Cross-Examination by *Francis L. Wellman*   ISBN: *1-59462-309-0*   **$26.95**
Written by a renowned trial lawyer, Wellman imparts his experience and uses case studies to explain how to use psychology to extract desired information through questioning.   How-to/Science/Reference Pages 408

Answered or Unanswered? by *Louisa Vaughan*   ISBN: *1-59462-248-5*   **$10.95**
Miracles of Faith in China   Religion Pages 112

The Edinburgh Lectures on Mental Science (1909) by *Thomas*   ISBN: *1-59462-008-3*   **$11.95**
This book contains the substance of a course of lectures recently given by the writer in the Queen Street Hall, Edinburgh. Its purpose is to indicate the Natural Principles governing the relation between Mental Action and Material Conditions...   New Age/Psychology Pages 148

Ayesha by *H. Rider Haggard*   ISBN: *1-59462-301-5*   **$24.95**
Verily and indeed it is the unexpected that happens! Probably if there was one person upon the earth from whom the Editor of this, and of a certain previous history, did not expect to hear again...   Classics Pages 380

Ayala's Angel by *Anthony Trollope*   ISBN: *1-59462-352-X*   **$29.95**
The two girls were both pretty, but Lucy who was twenty-one who supposed to be simple and comparatively unattractive, whereas Ayala was credited, as her Bombwhat romantic name might show, with poetic charm and a taste for romance. Ayala when her father died was nineteen...   Fiction Pages 484

The American Commonwealth by *James Bryce*   ISBN: *1-59462-286-8*   **$34.45**
An interpretation of American democratic political theory. It examines political mechanics and society from the perspective of Scotsman James Bryce   Politics Pages 572

Stories of the Pilgrims by *Margaret P. Pumphrey*   ISBN: *1-59462-116-0*   **$17.95**
This book explores pilgrims religious oppression in England as well as their escape to Holland and eventual crossing to America on the Mayflower, and their early days in New England...   History Pages 268

www.bookjungle.com *email: sales@bookjungle.com fax: 630-214-0564 mail: Book Jungle PO Box 2226 Champaign, IL 61825*

QTY

The Fasting Cure *by Sinclair Upton*　　　　　　　　　　　ISBN: *1-59462-222-1*　**$13.95**
In the Cosmopolitan Magazine for May, 1910, and in the Contemporary Review (London) for April, 1910, I published an article dealing with my experiences in fasting. I have written a great many magazine articles, but never one which attracted so much attention... New Age/Self Help/Health Pages 164

Hebrew Astrology *by Sepharial*　　　　　　　　　　　ISBN: *1-59462-308-2*　**$13.45**
In these days of advanced thinking it is a matter of common observation that we have left many of the old landmarks behind and that we are now pressing forward to greater heights and to a wider horizon than that which represented the mind-content of our progenitors... Astrology Pages 144

Thought Vibration or The Law of Attraction in the Thought World　　　ISBN: *1-59462-127-6*　**$12.95**
by William Walker Atkinson　　　　　　　　　　　　　　Psychology/Religion Pages 144

Optimism *by Helen Keller*　　　　　　　　　　　ISBN: *1-59462-108-X*　**$15.95**
Helen Keller was blind, deaf, and mute since 19 months old, yet famously learned how to overcome these handicaps, communicate with the world, and spread her lectures promoting optimism. An inspiring read for everyone... Biographies/Inspirational Pages 84

Sara Crewe *by Frances Burnett*　　　　　　　　　　　ISBN: *1-59462-360-0*　**$9.45**
In the first place, Miss Minchin lived in London. Her home was a large, dull, tall one, in a large, dull square, where all the houses were alike, and all the sparrows were alike, and where all the door-knockers made the same heavy sound... Childrens/Classic Pages 88

The Autobiography of Benjamin Franklin *by Benjamin Franklin*　　　ISBN: *1-59462-135-7*　**$24.95**
The Autobiography of Benjamin Franklin has probably been more extensively read than any other American historical work, and no other book of its kind has had such ups and downs of fortune. Franklin lived for many years in England, where he was agent... Biographies/History Pages 332

Name	
Email	
Telephone	
Address	
City, State ZIP	

☐ **Credit Card**　　　　☐ **Check / Money Order**

Credit Card Number	
Expiration Date	
Signature	

Please Mail to:　Book Jungle
　　　　　　　　PO Box 2226
　　　　　　　　Champaign, IL 61825
or Fax to:　　　630-214-0564

ORDERING INFORMATION
web*: www.bookjungle.com*
email*: sales@bookjungle.com*
fax*: 630-214-0564*
mail*: Book Jungle PO Box 2226 Champaign, IL 61825*
or PayPal *to sales@bookjungle.com*

Please contact us for bulk discounts

DIRECT-ORDER TERMS

**20% Discount if You Order
Two or More Books**
Free Domestic Shipping!
Accepted: Master Card, Visa,
Discover, American Express